Chautona Havig

A BIRD DIED

Chautona Havig

Copyright © 2013 by Chautona Havig

First Edition

ISBN-13: 978-1492939641
ISBN-10: 1492939641

All rights reserved. No part of this book may be reproduced without the permission of Chautona Havig.

The scanning, uploading, and/or distribution of this book via the Internet or by any other means without the permission of the author and publisher is illegal and punishable by law. Please purchase only authorized electronic editions and avoid electronic piracy of copyrighted materials.

Your respect and support for the author's rights is appreciated. In other words, don't make me write you into another book as a villain!

Though this is a work of fiction, the events in this book did occur. People's names and sometimes genders were changed to fit the story and to provide privacy. No real person was ever painted in a negative light.

Edited by: Coyle Editing & Haug Editing

Interior fonts: Calibri and Letter Gothic Std.
Art fonts— BossHole (By Kevin and Amanda) and Alex Brush
Cover photos: MarkM73/istockphoto.com
ianmcdonnell/istockphoto.com
simoningate/istockphoto.com
James Steidl/shutterstock.com
Cover art by: Chautona Havig

Connect with Me Online:
Twitter: https://twitter.com/ - !/Chautona
Facebook:https://www.Facebook.com/pages/Chautona-Havig-Just-the-Write Escape/320828588943
My Blog: http://chautona.com/chautona/blog/
My Newsletter: (sign up for news of FREE Kindle promos)
http://chautona.com/chautona/newsletter

All Scripture references are from the NASB. NASB passages are taken from the NEW AMERICAN STANDARD BIBLE (registered), Copyright 1960, 1962, 1963, 1968, 1971, 1972, 1973, 1975, 1977, 1995 by The Lockman Foundation.

Fiction/Christian/Family

~Author's Note~

Nothing prepares you for a phone call so vague and rushed that you know something is horribly wrong, and nothing prepares you for learning that your grandson "should be dead."

When I decided to do this project, I knew that it would be difficult—in my head, I knew this. In reality, I had no idea. I imagined hard nights, writing about hydrotherapy and him trying to walk again. Once I got through those sections, I expected writing about the way the community came together to be so much easier. It wasn't. It was almost harder. Writing about the local heroes who gave of their time, their money, and their hearts to help pay my grandson's medical bills still chokes me with gratitude. I just want to take this moment to thank every single person again.

Separate from my personal journey, I need to acknowledge that I know this book is flawed. I know I did not do it justice. I never could. This book is fictionalized, but it faithfully renders almost every event that happened in spirit, if not in fact. I added very little, and what I did was speculative based upon things we know to be true.

Dearest extended Neipp family, I apologize right now for leaving so much of your family's contribution and support out of this story. I did not do it out of a lack of love and appreciation for you and all you did and do for Challice and David. Only time, space, and personal knowledge kept me from keeping the entire Neipp family as an integral part of this book.

Only one Author could do this book justice, and He is still writing Stephen's story. He'll do it justice, and that's all that truly matters.

~Chautona

~Acknowledgements~

Just the idea of trying to acknowledge every person involved in this project makes me want to curl into fetal position with my thumb in my mouth. I've always avoided it in my books. I didn't want to leave people out, so I dedicated each one to the right person for the right book, and I prayed that others who helped make it happen would understand.

However, an undertaking like this needs true acknowledgments so here goes. If I left you out, I am so sorry. Please forgive me.

First the Lord, God Almighty. All glory, praise, and honor to You. Your hand has carried me through the project and has held my family in its palm for the whole of our lives. We praise You.

My daughter, Challice, and her husband, David. You let me bare your story to the world. Challice shared her journal notes. David shared himself. I love both of you. Thank you.

The rest of my family—particularly those living within these four walls we call "home." Thank you for your patience with me when I was too tired to help proof a paper or answer a question. Thank you for your understanding when dinner didn't happen—again. Thank you for loving me despite my flaws, and I ask in advance that you forgive this flawed account of our family's journey. Kevin... you're just awesome. And brilliant. And handsome too. ;)

Lynn Riddick, I love you. The work Lynn did to make the Benefit Concert a success is phenomenal, definitely. But the work she did to help me tell this story is inexpressible. She contacted people to get permission for me to use their words, she typed up dozens of pages worth of information so I could faithfully account that amazing night, and she prayed me through every step.

My message board ladies, thank you for late night prayers, all day prayers, and for cheering me on when I really didn't think I could write another word.

My editor, Barbara, spent hours of every day reading the previous night's work, offering suggestions, and keeping up with me so that we could go straight from writing to finished product—not something I generally do. She was and is amazing.

Christy, my proofreader and promotional assistant, followed behind us, checking every word to help speed the process as well.

Thrivent Financial for Lutherans: Thank you for allowing me to use your name. I wanted to give you credit for all you did.

The Salvation Army: Thank you for allowing me to use your name as well. Your ongoing support for Challice and David blesses me constantly.

The Ridgecrest News Review: Thank you for allowing me to use your articles as a framework for the ones in the book.

The Bread of Life and Pat Ryan: I can't hope to articulate what you have done and what you continue to do. You bless many people. Many. Our town has a treasure in you—one I fear it doesn't appreciate.

Sam Celestine: Thank you for allowing me to use your Facebook message.

Trace Adkins, you were kind to my grandson. That makes you a hero in my book. Your episode of *Great American Heroes* in Bakersfield is a treasured DVD in our house.

The following songs were also referenced in this book. I thank the songwriters for penning them and the artists who sang them.

Paul Simon: Bridge over Troubled Waters
Bill Withers: Lean on Me
Craig Morris Reid/Charles Stobo Reid: My Life with You
John Newton: Amazing Grace
Bob Dylan: Make You Feel My Love
Alisha Brooks/Brian Keith Holland/William Irving Jr./Edward J. Holland/Lamont Herbert Dozier: Don't Go
Lee Hazelwood: These Boots Were Made for Walkin'
Dana Glover: Thinkin' Over
David Allan Stewart/Annie Lennox/David Hodges: Arms

To view the videos and pictures described in this book, visit:
www.facebook.com/HelpStephenandFamily

~Cast of Characters~

Jonathan Cox Family-

Jon- Husband/Father
Kelly- Wife/Mother
Aiden- Oldest Son
Nathan- Middle Son
Anna- Baby Daughter

Martin Cox Family-

Martin- Husband/Father
Mary- Wife/Mother
Naomi- Daughter
Pete- Son-in-law
Jonathan- Son (
Michael- Son (Husband of Rachel Delman-Cox)
Rachel Delman-Cox—Daughter-in-law

Keith Homstad Family-

Keith- Husband/Father
Dee- Wife/Mother
Kelly- Daughter (Wife of Jonathan Cox)
Lorena- Daughter
Breanne- Daughter
Lila- Daughter
Drew- Son
Jamie- Daughter
Unnamed Daughter
Unnamed Daughter
Logan - Son

James Rhodes Family-

James- Husband/Father
Claire- Wife/Mother
Joy- Daughter

Noelle- Daughter)

Hospital Personnel-

Allison- Nurse
Dr. Faulkner- Pediatrician
Dr. Smith- Surgeon
Nurse's Assistant- Heather

WEEK ONE

DAY ONE

June 5, 8:23 p.m.

The late, evening sky, streaked with a golden pink, darkened with each passing minute. Sprinklers sprayed lawns; the hum of leaf blowers and weed trimmers filled the air, racing against daylight to finish their Saturday evening chores. On the street, kids played or clustered in groups around streetlights as if waiting for them to glow in the coming twilight.

The amber lamps flickered on, glowing steady. Moths appeared almost as if breathed from the night air. Fireflies waltzed across lawns in weak but whimsical imitation of the nightlights of Fairbury.

The lights flickered. Dimmed. Blackness shrouded the neighborhood as screams pierced the night air.

8:19 p.m.

Linden Street. It lay at the edge of Fairbury—just three streets from the town limits. Four houses down, the Cox family worked in the back yard. Aiden fiddled with the chain on a bicycle he hadn't ridden in months and not because he'd gotten a ticket for riding sans helmet—not this time. Kelly Cox watched him as she nursed the baby. "What's wrong with it?"

"Just feels loose."

"You could give it a spin around the block..." Even as she spoke, Kelly knew he wouldn't do it. He hadn't ridden anything in longer than she could remember. When asked, he always said he didn't feel like it—whatever that was supposed to mean.

Her eyes roamed the yard in search of her other son. Nathan crouched next to his father in the alley, pulling out weeds while Jon dug out ant holes and filled them with boric acid. *Jon's got him. Good. Crazy kid could be halfway to China if I blink too long.* The baby let out a loud burp as Kelly rubbed her back. "Is that better, Anna? Still hungry, or are you good?" The child's eyes drifted closed in answer to the question.

Humidity made Kelly's clothes stick to her and her hair clung to her neck. The sunlight faded fast. Still, she laid the baby in the playpen and stretched. She could get the patio swept before nightfall. As she reached for the broom, Kelly glanced across the yard.

In that instant, her life changed.

The air sizzled and a transformer blew, sending sparks flying. The lights on Tanglewood Drive dimmed. Nathan, standing in the alley with his father, pointed to the ground. "Look, Daddy!"

A raven lay dead in the alley just two doors down. Smoke. Fire. The neighbor's weather beaten fence ignited and burst into flame. Jon, followed by Nathan, ran into the yard, calling for water. Kelly grabbed a towel from the garage and dunked it in the kiddie pool before shoving it in his hands. "Here."

Jon stared at it for a moment as if confused before rushing to help the neighbors as they fought to put out the fire. Nathan followed. As he turned into the alley, Kelly called out to her son. "Come back, Nathan!"

The three-year-old boy didn't hear—or maybe he didn't listen. Jon, several feet ahead, glanced over his shoulder and saw Nathan following him. He stopped, turned, and led Nathan back to the yard. Away from the fire. To safety.

Twilight arrived just as they reached the corner of their yard. The gate stood wide open. Inviting.

Screams pierced the night air. From across the yard, Kelly stared for a moment—shocked to see her little boy writhing in pain on the ground. Jon jerked him away from something. She ran. Did she drop the broom? She never knew. Kelly never saw that broom again.

Jon dropped to his knees, holding Nathan. The child screamed, convulsed, wailed, begged for help. Just as she started to ask what happened, they saw it. The power line lying in the shadow of the darkening alleyway. Her eyes widened. A neighbor cried out to them. "I called 9-1-1."

Mind numb, Kelly nodded. A chair appeared. The sickly, sweet stench of burnt flesh assaulted her. Even in the ever-darkening shadows, she saw the welts burned through the boy's pants.

As tears streamed down her son's face, instinct kicked in and took over for her. "Aloe. He needs aloe." She ran for the plant in the kitchen windowsill. Someone called her back.

"Wait for the paramedics."

The voice came from the crowd—who, she couldn't say. Kelly's mind tried to process the words but failed. The imperative, "Wait," gave her something to latch onto. She could wait—let someone else make that decision. It would be the first and last bit of relief—however tiny—she felt for what would seem like a lifetime.

Officer Joe Freidan arrived first, tearing through the side gate and racing across the backyard. "What happened?"

The power line sparked as if to answer.

Jon cradled his son in his arms, trying to soothe him. "It'll be all right, son."

Kelly, desperate to alleviate some of her son's pain, removed Nathan's pants and dropped them in the alley. The stench of burned flesh increased from unpleasant to overpowering.

"Can you do water on an electrical burn?" The voice came from somewhere in the crowd.

She didn't know.

Siren wails filled the air, blending with Nathan's cries. Lights flashed and glowed in the alley as a paramedic van crawled through the narrow passage to their house. People scattered, only to return again once the EMTs bolted from the vehicle.

A neighbor called out a warning. "Watch out—live power line!"

The man nodded to his partner, stepped over it, and rushed to Nathan's side. "What happened?"

"Tripped over the line—fell on it." Kelly stared at the man's nametag, trying to burn it into her consciousness. Simon Petrakis. "I—"

The crowd clustered closer. His partner pointed to the van. "Let's get him inside."

Simon lifted Nathan and carried him to the ambulance. "We're going to put this machine on you. Okay, Nathan? It'll tell us what's going on in your heart."

Nathan just wailed.

The woman reached into a pocket on the side of the van and pulled out a stuffed bear. "Here, Nathan. Hold onto him while we check you out, okay?"

"Isn't Candi sweet? Yep. That's her name. Candi. She gives bears to nice little boys like you. If that's not sweet, nothing is."

Nathan squirmed, trying to get away, but he clutched the bear and buried his face in the plush fur. "Noooo..."

His cries wrenched Kelly's heart. Words swirled in her mind as she listened to the paramedics talk about things like heart, ground, tissue, transport. Her heart wanted to cry out to the Lord—wanted to lean on Someone for strength. She glanced at Aiden standing at the end of the van and staring into its depths as Simon and Candi worked on his brother. Did he understand? *Forget that,* she thought to herself. *Do I?*

Candi glanced at her partner and then up at Kelly. "He should be dead."

"I was going to put some aloe—"

The EMT shook his head. "We've got to get him to the clinic."

"Is that necessary?" Jon stared at the burns, stunned.

The reply came instantly. "Yes."

Kelly's throat went dry. *Lord, we can't afford an ambulance ride—not now without insurance.*

Jon spoke up, his words soothing her rising panic as he said, "We'll take him then."

Kelly jumped up to grab the baby and her purse. As she ran to the back door she heard Candi tell Jon that he'd have to sign papers stating that they left against medical advice. Her purse lay next to the phone. As she fumbled for a diaper and container of wipes, she dialed home. Her mother answered and Kelly blurted, "Nathan's hurt. Going to the ER. No time to explain, just pray."

9:05 p.m.

"*He should be dead.*" The words echoed in Kelly's mind all the way to the clinic. What could they mean? It looked bad, sure, but dead?

The scent—that same sickly sweet scent of burned flesh filled the van. Her gag reflex went into overdrive. She covered her mouth and nose with the neckline of her shirt and tried to breathe slowly. Jon didn't seem to notice. He just drove without saying a word. Aiden noticed, however. The van didn't make it two doors down their street before he said, "What's that awful smell?"

"It's Nathan's legs."

"That's gross. Why didn't they give him something for it?" Aiden patted Nathan's shoulder before adding, "He's going to be okay, right?"

"They'll take care of him. They probably just have to clean up the wounds and show us how to keep ointment on it or something."

Nathan said nothing—didn't murmur, didn't cry. Kelly glanced back at him at the corner of their street, as they turned onto Elm, as they whizzed down Center at a speed that would earn them a ticket if anyone but Joe happened to be on patrol. *Is he alive? He's so quiet.* Her eyes slid across to Jon's face and caught him watching Nathan in the rearview mirror.

"He's so quiet now."

Jon nodded. "Maybe what they put on the gauze has a pain killer in it or maybe they overreacted. Maybe it's not that bad after all."

Her heart clung to those words. *"Maybe it's not that bad after all."*

At the clinic, Jon parked in the closest spot he could find and rushed from the van. He unbuckled Nathan from the car seat. Kelly waited for the cries of protest, but they didn't come. Aiden jumped from the van and followed Jon, while Kelly unbuckled Anna's car seat from the vehicle.

Inside, Kelly saw her siblings sitting on a nearby bench and relaxed just a little. She set Anna at Lila's feet and strode to the reception desk. The woman behind the counter started to push a sign-in sheet toward her, but Kelly said, "I think the paramedics called? My son is the one who got electrocuted by the power line."

The words acted almost like a magic wand. The woman grabbed a clip board and skirted around the desk. "Where's your son?"

"There—"

The moment Kelly pointed, the woman hurried across the room. "We'll take him back—just one of you for now. Who'll go—"

Kelly's eyes met Jon's. "I'll go." She lifted Nathan, wincing at the frozen, pained expression on her little boy's face.

A nurse arrived and led Kelly to the big door at the corner of the room. She lifted the phone and spoke to someone. The door buzzed and she led Kelly into the examination area. Events spun in slow, lazy circles that seemed to grow a little faster with each passing moment. The nurse, Rose, brought a gown and a Pull-Up. "Let's get him changed and then we'll work on an IV. Pulling off Nathan's shirt didn't require much effort, but swapping underwear for a Pull-Up took creative gymnastics.

With him changed and settled against the pillow once more, Rose tried to insert an IV. Nathan's silent shock vanished and cries of pain and protest took its place. As if a rallying cry for the rest of the clinic patients, the woman next to them began screaming obscenities as her gall bladder seized her with a fresh wave of pain.

Rose attached Nathan to a heart monitor and watched the readouts constantly. Between checks, on the monitor, the IV, and the blood pressure cuff, she asked questions. "What happened?"

At that moment, Kelly had one of those inconvenient epiphanies that only occurs with the realization of something unpleasant. She'd answer that question a thousand times before the ordeal ended. Tired and concerned for her son as he lay whimpering on the bed, she kept her answers short—clipped. "Bird flew into a power line. Blew the transformer. Line fell. Nathan tripped over it."

The woman nodded. "And is he current on all his shots?"

The question made her stomach churn with frustration. "No. Due to a family history of severe reactions, we don't risk vaccinations."

Rose scrawled something on the sheet—something short. Kelly suspected it read, "Not current."

"Has he complained of heart pain?"

She shook her head. "He's been silent since we left the house—until you put in the IV anyway." Kelly prayed that meant he wasn't as injured as the paramedics thought.

8:57 pm

The phone rang. Breanne glanced up from her laptop and saw the flash of irritation on her mother's face—irritation that always came when the phone rang. Another swipe across the touch pad, another click of the mouse, and the picture would be perfect.

"Wha—okay. Praying."

Breanne's eyes flew to her mother's face. "What is it?"

"Kelly—she just said 'Nathan's hurt. Going to the ER. No time to explain, just pray.'"

Her mother's fingers flew over the keyboard as she put a call out to her Internet friends across the world to pray for Nathan. Breanne's heart raced as she prayed for something she couldn't imagine. Her hands fingered her phone and she jumped up. "I'm going."

Drew and Lila burst through the door, laughing. Lila stared as Breanne grabbed her purse, digging for her keys. "Where are you going?"

"Nathan's hurt—at the ER."

Lila and Drew followed. From her corner of the couch, Mom called out, "Call me when you know something."

Heart pounding, Breanne raced to her car and jerked open the door, starting the engine almost before she seated herself. Lila and Drew climbed in after her. Drew slammed the door behind him and asked, "What happened?"

"I don't know."

Lila pressed for more information. "But *how* is he hurt?"

"I don't know, Lila! She just said they were going and that he's hurt."

"But—"

"Geez, Lila! I said I don't know!"

Tension sizzled between the girls as Breanne navigated the mile and a half drive through near-empty streets to the clinic. None of the local cops walked the beat around the square. Few pedestrians strolled along the sidewalks. As she pulled into a parking space near the emergency entrance, Breanne scanned the parking lot. "I don't see them."

"Maybe they went in from the ambulance side."

The girls nodded at Drew's suggestion and bolted from the car. They rushed through sliding doors and glanced around the waiting area. A few people waited their turn to see the doctor, but not many. Kelly and Jon weren't there. Lila spoke first. "Did they already go back?" Six eyes bored into the door leading to the examination area, but saw nothing.

"I don't know. It usually takes forever." Breanne bit her lip. "I wish Kelly hadn't canceled her cellphone."

"They can't afford it right now," Drew reminded her. "Either they aren't here yet or it's bad enough that he had to go right back."

"She did say she didn't have time to explain..." Dread filled another chamber of her heart.

"This is Kelly. She can be pretty dramatic about stuff."

Breanne shot Lila a disgusted look. "She's not five anymore!"

"I bet he broke an arm. That kid's a walking broken-bone time bomb," Drew joked.

"Or a leg. He's always climbing stuff—like up into Aiden's bed. We did let him watch part of that super hero movie the other day." Lila frowned. "I sure hope he didn't try to fly—sounds like something he'd do."

Drew and Breanne murmured reluctant agreement. "He's already lost a tooth and sliced open his finger," Breanne recalled. "It's just a matter of time before he cracked his head open."

Three pairs of eyes exchanged nervous glances. A head injury sounded exactly like the sort of thing Kelly might not have time to explain. Drew pointed to the doors. "There they are."

Jon carried a half-dressed Nathan with white gauze wrapped around his legs and clutching a stuffed bear. Kelly carried Anna in her car seat, and Aiden followed, his eyes rarely leaving Nathan's face. As Jon shifted him, the bear fell and Aiden picked it up. Nathan didn't notice—no one noticed but Breanne and her heart squeezed as Aiden tucked it under his arm, unwilling to let it go.

Breanne couldn't drag her eyes from Nathan once she allowed herself to really look at him. Pain had etched itself in Nathan's eyes, his mouth twisted in a grimace—frozen in shock. Jon tried to set the boy on the nearest bench, but no matter what he tried, he couldn't find a decent position for Nathan's legs. Instead, they twisted and contorted with every attempt to make him comfortable.

They all sat, staring at Nathan—shock slowly overtaking them as Kelly went to the reception desk. Breanne leaned forward, listening as Kelly explained why they were there. "I think the paramedics called? My son is the one who got electrocuted by the power line."

A nurse came out for Nathan and led Kelly back to the examining area. A receptionist thrust a clipboard into Jon's hands. With Nathan taken care of, the questions flowed.

Lila asked the question on everyone's mind. "What happened?"

9:21 pm

Kelly appeared through the door that had swallowed her and Nathan just minutes—or was it an hour—before while Jon disappeared behind it. As she dragged herself into the examination area, her eyes went straight to the car seat where Anna still slept. "She okay?"

"She's been sleeping since you got here." Lila adjusted the light blanket that kept the chill of the hospital's refrigerated air off the baby. "How's Nathan? What happened? Jon just said something about a transformer and a power line."

"We were in the backyard," Kelly explained as she sank into one of the uncomfortable chairs. Aiden leaned against her, and Kelly squirmed to try to get comfortable as she continued, "Jon and Nathan were trying to get the weeds and ants from around the fence. A raven flew into the power line and it blew the transformer. Caught the fence three doors down on fire, so we started to help—wet towels and buckets..."

"Right." Lila frowned. "Wait, water on electrical? Is that right?"

"Lila!" Breanne snapped. "Just let her tell us." Kelly continued with her story as if uninterrupted—as if she hadn't noticed the interruption at all. Breanne then realized that Kelly was too emotionally beaten to notice *or* care.

"—and Nathan followed." Tears filled Kelly's eyes. "I called him back, but he didn't come. Jon grabbed his hand and led him back, but he tripped or fell, or stepped—I don't know which—onto the power line."

"They didn't see it?"

Both sisters glared at Lila. Kelly shook her head. "It was getting dark, the shadows just hid it. He screamed—convulsed."

The two sisters exchanged pained glances before turning back to Kelly. Drew asked the question on all hearts. "Didn't Jon get electrocuted too?"

Confusion clouded Kelly's eyes. "I—I don't know. I didn't think about it." She frowned. "I don't even know if he knows." She squeezed Aiden, stood as she about the arrival of the paramedics, and peeked under Anna's blanket once more. "I've got to go back in. You sure you're okay with them out here?"

Breanne pointed to the door. "Just go. We've got this."

9:51 pm

Relief washed over Kelly as Jon stepped into the cubicle. "Breanne and the others have Aiden and Anna. How's he doing?"

"He was fine until they did the IV. He didn't like that much."

A doctor stepped into the cubicle and offered his hand. "I'm Dr. Singh. I'm here to take a look at his legs and get them wrapped for transport."

"Transport?" Kelly glanced from doctor to her husband and back to the doctor again. "Why?"

"We don't treat burns here—not serious burns. He'll be taken to the burn unit in Manchester."

"Not Rockland?" Jon's quiet voice seemed to echo in the tiny space.

"The Cunningham Burn Unit in Manchester is the best. Even Rockland sends some of its cases there."

Words flew at her—questions. They told the story again. Told what the paramedics had said—several times. More words. More questions. Panic welled in her heart as she heard words like "tissue damage" and "second-degree burns."

And as she tried to assimilate all the necessary information, Dr. Singh and Rose unwrapped the light gauze and began the tedious and painful process of rewrapping the legs properly. Nathan cried—wailed—begged them to stop. Unsure what else to do, she prayed aloud.

"Lord, help Nathan bear the pain. Help him feel better once the bandages are all done. Help him rest comfortably." She tried to think of more, but failed. "In Jesus' name, amen."

Nathan continued to cry. She glanced at Jon and then began singing softly, "*Jesus loves me; this I know, for the Bible...*"

The woman in the next cubicle sent out a stream of indignant and irritated profanity. At Kelly's involuntary wince, Rose mouthed, "Sorry."

9:53 p.m.

Once Kelly disappeared into the examination area again, Breanne stepped outside the hospital into the hot, muggy night. She slid her fingers over her phone and selected "Home." The phone picked up on the first ring. "Mom?"

"Yep. What's happening?" The words said little, but the tone—Dee Homstad's usual placid tones held an edge to them—an edge Breanne identified as concern.

"Well, they're saying it's second-degree burns. There was a power line..." Breanne felt that strange surreality that comes with telling a story for the first time and knowing it will be the first of many, many times. "—went back with her, so now we wait. We're going to bring Aiden over in a bit so he can get some sleep. Well, I think. I didn't ask Jon before he went back, so we have to wait for that."

"How is Aiden?"

"Concerned—quiet. I don't think he knows what to make of it."

"And Nathan?" Dee asked at last. "How does it look?"

"I couldn't see it." Tears flooded Breanne's eyes and voice. "But the smell—I was only next to him for a minute at most, but, Mom..."

"He'll be okay. God's got this."

"Okay... I'd better go. I'll call when I hear something new."

She stared at the blank screen, hesitating. Breanne wanted to ask for prayer, but with a particular abhorrence for drama, she wondered if it was too soon—too much. They couldn't give any information other than the basic facts and the paramedic's dire pronouncement. That thought made the decision for her. If the man—woman—whatever had been right, Nathan needed all the prayer he could get.

It took a moment to compose the text. How to convey all she wanted to with as few words as possible. Her fingers flew across the keyboard, punching each letter almost automatically.

```
MY NEPHEW NATHAN ELECTROCUTED AND BURNED. AT THE
HOSPITAL. PLEASE PRAY.
```

Before she could make it back to the ER doors, the first replies whizzed through the airwaves and sent her phone buzzing.

9:57 p.m.

Dee stared at the screen, her heart praying, her mind unable to find words that would make sense of the nightmare. That thought twisted her stomach. *My daughter is living a nightmare. Little Nathan is hurt—**our** Nathan.*

Again she stared at the screen. Her previous words stared back at her.

```
Please pray for Kelly and family. She called and
said "no time to explain, just pray."
```

An index finger slid up to the refresh icon and a thumb hit the left mouse button. *That's my finger.* The obvious and illogical thought snapped her out of the mental fog. A few new posts promising prayer filled in below the first ones. Dee scrolled up again, each movement much slower than she'd like it to be. *Just do it. It's not like putting it off changes anything. He needs their prayers. God gave you a hundred prayer warriors from all over the globe. **Someone** will be praying 'round the clock, but they need to know why.*

Dee clicked the "modify" button and waited for the screen to load. Above the previous post, she typed a response.

```
**UPDATE 1**
Ok, Breanne called and said that a bird hit the
power line at Kelly's house. That started a fire.
The line fell and hit Nathan (sounds like
particularly on the leg). He's badly burned, and I
couldn't understand what Breanne meant, but she
said, "He should be dead" whatever that means. So,
anyway, because of the fire, someone called 9-1-1.
An ambulance came, thank the Lord, and they checked
him out, wrapped the leg, and told Kelly and Jon
they could drive Nathan to the hospital themselves.
They just took Nathan back a second ago. That's all
we know at this point.
```

The arrow hovered over the submit button. Dee stared at it, wondering if it was too much information—too little? What if it wasn't accurate? Listening to Breanne had been a study in confusion. Things seemed to change by the second as more information filled in gaps that made previous information seem wrong rather than just incomplete. Would it be worse to perpetuate that? *I could just say,*

"Nathan was electrocuted and burned. They're at the hospital. All I know for sure is that it has to be serious because the paramedics said, 'He should be dead.' That's just all I know for sure right now. I'm hoping the paramedics were wrong."

The cursor highlighted her previous words and her finger slid across the keyboard, resting on delete. Before she could second guess herself again, Dee slid her thumb to the mouse button and clicked. *It is what it is. I'll rewrite until next week if I don't just get it done now.*

Dee's eyes slid up to the "Personal Message" link. She could ask Anne what to expect. Anne's husband had worked in a burn unit years ago. Still, maybe after they knew more. Anne would ask questions that she probably couldn't answer yet. *Help me be patient, Lord. I'm dying to **do** something.*

Across the room, Dee's husband, Keith, sat in his chair lost in thought. *He should be in bed by now, Lord. Should I do something? But what? What can I do?*

"Sounds like it could be a long night." Dee frowned as she heard herself state the obvious. "Why don't you try to get some sleep?"

"Yeah. I guess. Any news?"

"Just that he's burned; you heard that."

Keith nodded. "I heard." He stared at his hands. "Did someone call Lorena?"

"I think Breanne did—or texted. Whatever."

"Think she'll come home tomorrow?" Keith stood and carried his glass of water into the kitchen.

"Maybe. Unless she has a paper due or something. Probably depends on what the doctors say. Maybe next weekend."

A red bubble on Facebook signaled the arrival of a message. Dee clicked it as Keith came to kiss her goodnight. "I'll let you know if I hear anything that can't wait until morning."

"'Mkay. Night."

"Night..." Dee's eyes scanned the message.

```
If I can do anything, let me know. We're praying for
all of you. Jesus will carry this for you, Lily.
```

We have the best friends. Thank you, Lord. Dee began typing a reply. Just as she started to hit send, she realized it made no sense— none at all. Backspace did its job and she tried again. And again. In the end, she typed two words—two words that would become punctuation for nearly every sentence she spoke or wrote over the coming weeks.

Thank you.

9:28 p.m.

While Breanne called home, Drew stared at his phone. "Think we should call the Coxes?"
Lila shrugged. "Ask Mom."
"Breanne is talking to her."
"So ask her to ask Mom. I think you should call but…"
Drew stood. "Be right back."
"Can I come?" Aiden stared up at him, hope in the boy's eyes.
"Sure. C'mon."
At Breanne's "okay," Drew called Jon's parents' house. The phone rang. Twice. Three times. Again. Once more. Just as he started to end the call, the groggy voice of Martin Cox answered. "Hello?"
"Mr. Cox? This is Drew Homstad—Kelly's brother?"
"Yeess…"
"We're at the hospital with them. Nathan had an accident—got electrocuted. We just thought you might want to know."
"That's not funny, Drew."
Drew stared at his phone as if it would somehow explain how anyone could think he'd be crank calling about something like that. "I wasn't trying to joke, sir. Nathan really did step—or fall. I haven't gotten that straight yet—on a power line. They've been in the ER for the past half hour. We just thought we should tell you."
"I don't believe you."
With every effort to keep the exasperation from his tone, Drew tried again. "Well, it's not a joke or anything. We're just trying to let you know what happened."
"Have Jon call."
The line went dead. Dazed, Drew stared at his nephew. "Well, that wasn't helpful."
"That's just weird." Aiden glanced at the door. "Think Mom's back again?"

Choosing to consider that his cue, Drew led Aiden inside and dropped onto the bench. "Mr. Cox thought it was a crank call. Now what?"

"Mom? I could have Mom call him..." Breanne pulled out her phone. "Why would he think that? Jon might not be out for hours. You know how ERs are. Arrrgh!"

"I don't know. Maybe I woke him up and he thinks he's dreaming." Drew shrugged. "Or maybe he's not awake at all."

Breanne slid her finger through her contacts and selected home. Just as it rang, Jon stepped from the examination area. She slid her phone shut. "What do the doctors say?"

"They're transporting us to Manchester—a burn unit there."

"Why? They said—"

"Dr. Singh says because they don't do burns here at all."

"Oh." Breanne glanced at Drew, and he knew what she'd say next. "I'll go with you—help with Anna." Drew smiled inwardly. *Called it.*

He handed Jon his phone. "I tried calling your dad, but he wants you to call. I don't think he believed me." *That's an understatement.*

While Drew helped Jon with the phone, he heard Breanne tell Lila to go fill up Jon's van with gas.

"Got it." Lila flew out the door.

Drew turned away, giving Jon privacy on the phone, and tossed Breanne an exaggerated incredulous look. "You know she's going to terrify every person left on the road."

Breanne snickered. "Lila's plan to drive people to the feet of Jesus—salvation by road rage."

10:09 p.m.

The whoosh of the fans blowing out hot air as the clinic doors opened signaled the arrival of Martin and Mary Cox. Breanne jumped up and offered her seat. The Coxes preferred to stand. Jon stepped out into the waiting room. His mother wrapped her arms around him, lips quivering, and asked, "How's Nathan?"

"Better—but they're sending us to Manchester. Someone said something about these burns always looking better than they are."

"You mean worse?" Mary asked.

"No, it's just that they don't look bad—well they do, but not like you'd think—but it's actually worse somehow. I don't really understand it all yet. They're just giving bits and pieces of information as if they think someone else explained it all and we just need clarification. I'll just ask when we get to Manchester."

Aiden nudged Breanne. "Am I going too?"

"I don't think so. They might let Anna go since she's still nursing, but they don't usually let kids in hospitals unless they're the patient. We'll probably take you to our house."

"Is Logan still up?"

Breanne shook her head. "Probably not, but you guys can do stuff tomorrow. Maybe go swimming."

"Does Grandma have my suit still?" Aiden sounded as if he tried a little too hard not to sound eager—as if wanting to swim while Nathan couldn't was somehow wrong.

"I'm sure we've got one or can go get yours. It'll be good exercise too." Breanne nudged his shoulder. "They're gonna take good care of him, buddy. All you can do is try to have fun and be comfortable at our house so your mom doesn't have to worry about you."

"Yeah..." He pointed to his grandfather. "I guess Grandpa knows it's real now, huh?"

"I doubt he was really awake that first time. Probably didn't register who Drew was and just thought someone was being a jerk."

Aiden squeezed the bear he still held. "Think Nathan wants this now? I could—"

"Sorry, they're not going to let you go back—not now. But Grandma will take you to see him if we have to stay a couple of days."

The boy's eyes widened and he stared at Breanne shocked. "Stay? Like overnight?"

"It's possible. You know, to make sure it won't get infected or something." Breanne couldn't imagine it not taking a couple of days if it was bad enough to transfer him. "Second degree burns are pretty serious."

"What makes 'em degree?"

"Well," Breanne tried to explain, "it just means to what extent something happened. First is just like if you burn your tongue on hot chocolate or touch the stove really quick and it gets red. Second is when it blisters up—means it went down into the skin a bit."

"What's third? Is there a third?"

"Yeah, and a fourth, I think. Third's when it goes like all the way through the skin to the fat or muscle, but I think fourth is when it actually burns into those or goes to the bone, but Nathan's not that bad. They said second."

"So it just hurts a lot," Aiden asked. He seemed fixated on learning all he could.

"Well, yeah."

"So why can't they give him some drugs or something and let him come home? I get blisters all the time. Don't need the hospital for that."

"But stuff like this can get infected easily, so they probably want to clean it really well—just to be sure." *Oh, Lord. I hope I know what I'm talking about. I'd just tell him I don't know, but he seems so much calmer hearing what it's all about. Shut me up if I should stop talking.*

10:12 p.m.

Lila burst through the door. "They're going to Manchester so I've gotta gather up stuff for Breanne."

Jamie glanced up from her book and said, "Need help? Why Manchester?"

"Something about the burn unit there being the best." Lila spun in circles for a moment and started toward Drew and Logan's room. "Where does Drew keep his graduation money?"

"Top drawer." Jamie jumped up, tossing her book aside, and followed Lila into the boys' room. "Right..." The drawer slid open revealing a wad of cash. "Here. Why?"

"They need money and won't have time to go get cash, so it's faster than taking Mom's card. They'll be here any minute."

From her spot on the couch, Dee listened as the girls talked in the other room. Usually, their volume would have earned them a rebuke to quiet down so Keith could sleep, but she didn't want to miss anything. As Lila rushed through the living room, Dee stopped her. "Wha—"

"I'll explain in a minute. Breanne's coming with Jon. They're going to Manchester. Kelly said 'it burned him to the tissue.' Gotta pack her stuff." With that, she disappeared out the back door and into the girls' apartment over the garage.

Dee glanced at Jamie, silently waiting for more information. Jamie shrugged. "They just needed Drew's money. Oh, and Lila got gas for them if that makes a difference."

As if on auto-pilot, Dee clicked the link to the message board and hit the modify button again. So little information, but who knew when there'd be more? She hit a few hard returns on the keyboard and then began typing.

```
** UPDATE 2 **
It  "burned   him   to   the   tissue"   so   they're
transporting  him  to  Manchester  (about  100  miles
away).
```

"Feels inadequate," she said to an empty room.

10:32 p.m.

Time morphed from the linear event Kelly had always seen it as into a hurricane. They remained in the center as if time stood still and yet it swirled around them, faster and faster leaving a swath of destruction in its wake. All too soon, the ambulance arrived to drive them to Manchester; yet, it also seemed an age.

Discussion began in quick, hushed tones. Kelly panicked at the idea of trying to find her way alone through the convoluted Manchester streets. Jon nodded. "You go in the ambulance. I'll follow with Anna and Breanne."

"Breanne's coming?"

Jon nodded. "First thing she said when she heard we had to transfer. 'I'm coming.'"

Someone to hold Anna. Someone to run errands. Someone to cry with when Jon couldn't handle anything more. *That'll be a blessing.* "Good."

They followed the gurney to the ambulance and Jon's parents stood there. Choking back tears, Jon's father wrapped his arms around Kelly and hugged her. "We're praying. We love you."

Emotion welled up within her, choking her attempts to speak. After several seconds, she managed to blubber a few words of gratitude before climbing in the ambulance behind the attendant.

"Wave to Daddy, Nathan."

Nathan stared at them all with glassy, almost unseeing eyes. The door closed, and the ambulance pulled away from the bay and into the inky blackness of Fairbury on a late summer's evening. The small group huddled around the entrance as if unsure what to do next—where to go.

The Coxes glanced at Aiden and back at Jon. "Is he going home with them or would you like us to take him?" Mary Cox smiled at Aiden. "I know he has Logan there, so he might prefer it, but they're both welcome at our house if they want to come."

"Why don't we figure that out later, Mom?"

"That's fine. I just wanted to offer. I'll call Dee later and see if I can help with anything." Another hug, another whispered reminder of love and God's goodness, and the Coxes left, leaving Jon, Aidan, Breanne, and Drew.

"I guess we'd better get going…" Jon pulled out his keys, looking awkward and uncertain.

"I'll call and see if they've got my stuff," Breanne said. "Otherwise, we can grab yours first."

She dug her hands into her pockets but couldn't find the phone. "I bet I left it on the chair in there. Be right back."

Breanne dashed into the small waiting room but found no phone. She looked under chairs, asked the receptionist, and even asked a couple of waiting patients, but no one had seen one. Frustrated, she strode outdoors again and asked Drew, "Did I give it to you?"

"No…"

"Lila?"

"No… don't think so." Drew thought for a moment. "Is it in your car? The van? What—"

"Well, Lila has my car, so I doubt it's in there, and if it is, we can only look when we get home anyway. Let's check the van."

A first pass produced nothing, but Drew found it under a back seat. "No idea how it got there, but…"

Breanne stared at it, confused. "I wasn't even back there."

As he climbed into his seat, Jon said, "Maybe it slid back there when Lila went to get gas."

"I guess. At least I have it. We might need it." Breanne glanced back at Aiden. "Ready, buddy?"

"Yeah." He hesitated a moment, turmoil showing in every muscle of the boy's face. "Dad, can't I go—just for tonight?"

"Not until we know what they're doing with him. It's too far if they say you can't stay."

Aiden slid his eyes to the baby and back to Breanne. "But I'm less noisy than Anna—and I can help." He sat up, excited. "We could ask the hospital." Unhooking his buckle, he leaned forward to open the van door.

"They can't answer that question for another hospital. They'll say no. You'll just have to wait. I'm sorry. Now buckle up."

Discouraged, Aiden slumped against the seat. Breanne's heart constricted watching the emotions flit over his face. At one point, she could have sworn he whispered, "It should have been me," but chose not to go there now. They needed to get on the road as fast as possible. "I'm sorry." Breanne said, reaching back to squeeze his knee. "It'll be okay, though. It will."

10:40 p.m.

As the door shut behind her and the ambulance rolled out of the bay and along the dark, semi-empty streets of Fairbury, Kelly choked back overwhelmed tears. The ambulance attendant attempted a reassuring smile. "It's no real comfort, I know, but he's going to be okay. Manchester is the best."

Kelly, never taking her eyes from her son, nodded. "He's just so little."

"It's a mom thing. I get it. I've got a daughter a bit older. I can't imagine having to deal with this, but if I *did*, I'd want to be transferred to Manchester rather than Rockland. The RBU is good, it is, but it can't compare to Cunningham in Manchester. Fairbury is great about trying to get their serious patients in there first."

Justin, the driver, called out the window, "Hey, Chad. Almost off duty?"

"Yep!"

"Paintball at your place next weekend?" Officer Tesdall's response had to have been in the affirmative because Justin shouted back, "All right! I'll bring the hot dogs!"

Such normal conversation. Doesn't he realize that my world is spinning out of control? The moment she thought it, Kelly rebuked herself. *Because everyone has to ignore their own lives and focus on yours. Selfish.*

In an attempt to derail her various and unwelcome trains of thought, Kelly asked the obvious question. "So you think it's that serious?" She felt incredibly stupid for even asking, but aside from the sickening stench of her son's legs, the burns just didn't look *that* bad.

"Yeah. I mean, they send all burns out except for superficial ones, but they only send the worst to Cunningham. I mean, obviously," Debbie added as a cough up front suggested that perhaps the woman had said too much. Kelly started to reassure the woman that she understood, but Debbie rushed onward. "—worst is a broad term. It could be anything from burns like Nathan's to a guy black from a house fire."

"I can't even imagine that. The smell…"

Debbie nodded. "You never get used to it."

From his place on the gurney, Nathan lay, silent but in apparent fascination with their conversation. *Does he even understand?* It didn't seem possible—especially with the boy's pain levels. He whimpered, only when he shifted, but his eyes—something in his eyes screamed of the pain he didn't vocalize.

She knew the moment they hit the Rockland Loop. Cars whizzed past at rates of speed you'd expect more from an emergency vehicle, while she, in that vehicle, rolled along at the lower limit for trucks and trailers. *It's all surreal—as if we're playing an opposite game with the kids. Only these opposites—aren't. But they are. I don't even make sense. Do I sound like that when I talk?*

Her brain tripped over several thoughts until she fell flat on top of the obvious subject-changing idea. "So you have a daughter? Any other children?"

"Step-son. Teenager." The word sprayed an unexpected stench over the conversation.

Apparently she doesn't like teenagers or she doesn't like the step-son. Sad. "That's a cool age," Kelly mused. "Mom always says it's her favorite."

"She must not have had very many—or maybe it's boys. Nah, I've got friends with girls that are just as annoying as Brandon."

With her inner self screaming at her to stop before she alienated the woman helping them, Kelly shrugged. "Dunno. Mom's only had the one teen boy, but with six girls..."

"Your mom has seven kids?"

"Nine." The shocked horror—watching it emerge, creeping over people's faces or exploding all at once—it never got old. Kelly watched as Debbie tried to process the reality of life with nine children. *What would she look like if I mentioned the one bathroom and seven females? Nah, that'd just be cruel.*

"Well, then either I did something wrong, his dad did something wrong, or the ex did something wrong, because not even a mother of nine could make Brandon seem like anything but the walking cells of trouble that he is."

Kelly wanted to ask—wanted to remember what her mother would have wanted to know—what her father would have guessed. Did the kid just feel torn between two homes? Was it the way Debbie called his mother "the ex" instead of "his mother"? Were there drug temptations at school or maybe a few girls who made fun of him— perhaps one that he had thought he liked until she mocked him in front of the class?

The road narrowed. She couldn't see it in the darkness, but Kelly felt the ambulance slow, the curves taking them through the pass and over the hill into the Grouse River Valley. Kelly started when Justin called back, "We're about thirty minutes out."

Debbie leaned over, smiling at Nathan and said, "We'll be there soon. Won't be long now. There are some awfully cute nurses there."

And at three, do you really think he cares about cute nurses? Why do people do that with kids? "And Daddy and Aunt Breanne will be there soon. She's going to stay with us."

Nathan hardly acknowledged her words, prompting Kelly to ask, "Is he okay?"

"Just tired. It's probably way past his bed time."

The inky blackness with its occasional glow of amber headlights rushing toward the van verified the statement even without asking for the time. "I bet the baby's hungry. I hope Jon didn't take too long deciding what to do and where to go."

"The hospital gave them directions and everything. They'll be there in no time. Your job is just to be there for Nathan. Just let him know that Mommy's there and she loves him. We've got the rest covered."

Despite the comfort they brought, something about Debbie's

words also niggled at her—insisting it wasn't quite right. It would be weeks—a month or more—before the truth overshadowed the half-truth.

The last miles blended into the first steps of their new journey. Kelly found herself weaving through hospital corridors, up an elevator, and through heavy double doors that swung open at Justin's touch. "Transport from Fairbury," he said as the nurse looked up and jumped to help.

Name—they wanted Nathan's, not hers. Fingers clicked on a laptop. Date of birth—again, his not hers. Kelly racked her brain, searching for the simple numbers that she couldn't have forgotten the previous day. Fingers slid across a key pad. Parents' names. She started to say Dee and Keith Homstad when she realized the woman meant her.

Kelly looked at the nurse's name tag. Elizabeth. "I'm sorry. I keep getting confused. What did you ask?"

"Your name. Your husband's? They said your husband was coming too, is he here?"

"On his way. They're probably about twenty minutes behind us." Kelly watched, her stomach churning as a nurse carried a caddy with syringes and tubes to Nathan's side. "This isn't going to be easy."

"I'm used to it, sugah. Get my stick the first time every time, and little'ns don't like me, but they don't fear me. Don'cha worry yourself none."

Nathan watched—whether fascinated or too tired to protest, Kelly couldn't tell—as the nurse inserted the needle, withdrew the blood and capped the tube. "See there. That didn't hurt more than a love bite, did it?"

As the woman's drawl, the consistency of molasses, sweetened and slowed her words, even Kelly began to relax. Exhaustion crept closer, filling the air around her with sleeping potions until she didn't know that she'd stay awake long enough to feed Anna once Jon and she arrived.

Mistake—big one. The slow, familiar tingle began at her sides beneath her armpits and spread across the front. Kelly clutched her arms to her chest, trying to staunch the flow of milk before it soaked her shirt. *Oh, yuck. I don't have another one. If I leak, I'm going to stink.*

More questions—repeating the same things until it felt like an interrogation on the witness stand. *Do they think I'll give a different answer if they ask a different way? Why don't they read each other's notes before asking something? Wouldn't it be faster?*

The phone rang. Nurse Elizabeth snatched up the phone. "Patient name—oh, sure." She hit the door-opener. She winked at Nathan. "Daddy's here."

11:54 p.m.

The house remained quiet—still. Dee had often called them the "golden hours"—the wee hours of the night and morning when silence hovered over the busy, bustling Homstad house. From down the hall, she heard Keith's snores and then a book fell as someone, probably Jamie, rolled over in bed. The refrigerator pinged as it did every time the compressor kicked on.

But the sounds that she usually considered blissful silence became jabs—reminders that all of her children did not sleep snug in their beds. Her eldest daughter sped through the night in the back of an ambulance. Dear, goofy little Nathan wouldn't be running to greet her at church.

Dee stuffed down the rising emotions, and clicked open the post on the message board. She changed the title to "Update Three" and began typing.

```
** Update 3—story info **

Ok, now I know what she means by "should be dead."
Apparently the whole catching fire thing was the
fence. All neighbors were working to put it out.
Nathan ran over there as the wire fell and Jon
dragged him away. He fell just as Jon was dragging
him and landed on the wire. Had Jon not been right
there, Nathan would have died (electrocution I
suppose).
```

It seemed so inadequate—jumbled and disjointed. Even Breanne and Lila hadn't agreed on how Nathan had actually fallen. Had they noticed the wire before or after Nathan tripped? She didn't know—no one seemed to know, and Jon had better things to do than correct the timeline of an accident he'd rather forget.

Her finger shook as she slid it across the touchpad and clicked the Facebook icon. Time to post more than a "Please pray for our grandson, he had an accident" status. Family might want to know, and friends would pray. That knowledge—that people all over the country and even the world—prayed for her grandson kept her fingers marching across the keyboard. She chose each word with care, wanting to show that the injury sounded severe without falling into the easy trap of alarming folks with misinformation, no matter how innocent.

At last the words came, giving forthright, factual information with a minimum of the histrionics she felt welling up in her heart.

```
Kelly and Jon's Nathan was electrocuted by a downed
power line tonight and has been transferred to a
burn unit in Manchester for care. Please keep all of
them in your prayers. Thank you.
```

In a desperate move to escape the nightmare of her imagination, Dee shoved aside her laptop and stepped out onto the porch. The night air smothered her with its oppressive mugginess. *If it doesn't rain soon, we'll be cutting chunks out of the air to reach something more breathable.* Fireflies chased each other across the lawn in a dance too whimsical and carefree to be appropriate for such a heavy night. *Nathan would love this—would chase them and stuff them in a mason jar until morning. He's missing this, Lord.*

Crickets chirped, a night bird called out to his mate, and off in the distance, an ambulance siren wailed, signaling that someone else needed assistance. "Be with them, too," she whispered, turning back inside.

Cool air blasted her as Dee closed the door behind her. Her legs folded under her as she curled up in her favorite corner of the sectional and then sprang upright again. *Mint lemonade—gotta thank Willow for that one. I never remember to, but that stuff is an addiction that deserves some appreciation.*

Once more, Dee started to seat herself but dashed into the kitchen for cookies first. "Might as well," she muttered. *I won't sleep until Breanne calls or messages or something.*

In an irrational and ridiculous act of eternal optimism, Dee clicked the Facebook icon, just in case somehow Breanne's phone had morphed into a smartphone with a data plan and she'd zipped them an update on a situation she couldn't possibly have any new information about. As if to further torment her, a little red bubble with a one in it, hovered over messages. She clicked.

A friend's son—one of Kelly's childhood friends—had sent a message.

```
Heard about Nathan. I wondered if it would be okay
to make a Facebook page where people can get updates
and maybe a blog somewhere so we can have a PayPal
button for donations. Didn't want to do anything
without asking, but I thought it might help. And, of
course, we're praying for all of them.
```

"It would help," Dee whispered under her breath. "The bills are going to be staggering, and with Jon only working part time—probably fired if he missed more than a couple of days—they're going to need it for more than medical bills."

Before she could second-guess herself, Dee sent back a quick note.

```
We obviously can't do something like that. It would
be inappropriate for us to make such a request, but
if you'd like to, I'll take responsibility for
approving it. Thank you. It's hard to accept help
when I'd rather give, but we both know they're going
to need more than we can provide.
```

Tears crept from her heart and wormed their way into her throat, choking her.

Saturday, June 6th 1:10 a.m.

He's so quiet. Is he okay? He's probably blaming himself—not his fault, but he probably is. Should I say something or let it go? Probably shouldn't put thoughts in his head if he's too overwhelmed to think them himself. That'd be bad.

Breanne's hands shifted the papers in her lap. "This was nice of them—printing out the directions for us."

"Saved me having to go home. That's why I didn't. Figured I didn't need to since they'd given me those."

Stating the obvious. Classic Jon maneuver for trying to order his thoughts. *He is beating himself up. I knew it.*

The silence in the van nearly smothered her. She wanted to say it—ached to tell him he couldn't blame himself, but he hadn't yet. Not verbally anyway. Just as they emerged from the large tunnel on the near side of Manchester, Jon sighed. "I shouldn't have let him out of the yard."

"You didn't. He just followed. He did his own thing. No one could have predicted it."

"But it's my job—"

Interrupting, Breanne said, "To be God and know the mind of your child? That's just unreasonable. He doesn't expect it of us, why would you?"

"I know he's curious…"

"And you did what a good parent does." Breanne took a deep breath, trying to keep her tone calm and reasonable rather than the verbal shaking she ached to give him. "You saw your son start to do something dangerous and you removed him from the danger you saw. No one saw that power line. He'll be fine. They're going to take care of him."

The city loomed ahead. Breanne took the opportunity to change the subject. "So this says… we get off on Freeman Road."

"That says three exits ahead—one and a quarter miles. Then what?"

"Right turn onto Freeman itself. Go point three miles. Turn left on Telegraph and veer right almost immediately."

They followed instructions, despite the immediate veer looking like a one-way street to an industrial park. "Maybe," Jon said, slowing as the so-called road dead-ended. "It was the next 'almost' immediate right."

Retracing their steps took a three-point turn with sixteen actual points. Jon turned right and watched for an immediate veer. Not a single opportunity to turn right, veer right, or even stay in a right lane presented itself. Breanne reread the instructions. "It says to do that. I don't get it. That veer doesn't exist, or this hospital is in an abandoned warehouse."

After four more streets, Jon turned around once more and passed a strange yield triangle. "Well, that looks like it could be a left veer coming from the other way. Maybe…"

"Can't hurt to try. If it becomes Warner Park Road, then it's right."

"No, left."

Breanne glanced at Jon and laughed. "Got me. Good one." As they searched non-existent street signs for some idea of where they were, she nearly lost it. "This is just stupid. Of all the nights for them to give us messed up directions, this is just about the worst one possible."

"Look, there's a light. There should be decent signs there."

"There should be decent signs everywhere," Breanne protested. "This is a hospital. Where are the blue and white H signs telling us where to go so we don't die of a severed leg or heart attack?"

"You have a point…"

The light did have excellent signs. The intersection of Tele*phone* Road and 28th Street. Neither of which were mentioned anywhere in the pages of worthless directions. After passing several fast food restaurants, gas stations, and a Wal-Mart, Breanne remembered that for all his virtues, Jon was still a man.

"If you wanna pull over, I'll go in somewhere and ask. We have to be close."

She could see he didn't want to, but Jon pulled into a gas station, saying, "I'll go. Lock the doors."

The non-moving vehicle served as an alarm clock for Anna. The baby's soft cries soon increased into indignant wails as she demanded a late night snack. Breanne crawled to the backseat and rocked the carrier. "Soon, Anna. Soon. We're almost there. I bet Mommy wants you to come too. We're going to go see Nathan—get him some help."

The door jerked open and Jon stuck his head around the seat. "Everything all right?"

"Anna didn't like to find out we weren't really there after all."

"Well," he said, climbing into the vehicle, "We're actually on the right road. Does it say to turn left on Delgado anywhere?"

"Yeah, that's the next thing it says, but we never made it to Warner Park Road!"

"Apparently this is both 28th Street *and* Warner Park Road.

Delgado is two lights ahead."

Breanne glanced at the directions. "It says it's one block up the road on the right after we turn onto Delgado. That means we're almost there."

The strain in Jon's tone cut her as he echoed, "Yep. Almost there."

1:10 a.m.

Exhaustion demanded she rest, but Dee waited, refreshing her email, refreshing the pages upon pages of prayers for her grandson, and refreshing her spirit through the words of Scripture. The phone rang. "Hello?"

"Hey, Mom. So we're here. Just got in. Stupid directions. Anyway, I don't have much news but I thought you'd want to know everyone's here and Nathan is resting."

"He in a lot of pain?" The moment she asked, Dee wanted the words back. Of course he was in pain. Asking meant she'd now know how much. *Dumb move, girl.*

"He was, but they gave him something for it—morphine, I think. Oh, and they said it's much worse than it looks because electrical burns—" Breanne paused as she tried to remember what she'd been told. "Well, it's like they keep burning for a day or two. That's not quite it, but basically—damage continues anyway."

Dee closed her eyes as if doing so would black out all she didn't want to know. "Oh, yuck. Poor kid."

"How's Aiden?"

"Good. A bit of 'survivor's guilt' I think, but he'll be fine. He's already talking about riding with Logan to the deli tomorrow."

"Kelly told me last week that he still wasn't willing to ride anywhere on anything," Breanne mused. "Any idea why that is?"

"No, but I bet he'll tell Logan eventually."

"Okay, well, I'm going to go. I'm just so tired." Breanne yawned. "I'll call in the morning."

An email arrived as Breanne spoke. "Wait. Hold up. Just got an email from Bryan Little. He set up a Facebook page. It's called, 'Help Nathan Cox and Family.'" They've set up a blog too—for donations. You're an administrator."

"'Mkay. I'll check it out before I go to bed. Thanks, Mom."

"Love you."

Breanne's exhaustion dripped from her whispered, "Love you, too."

With one window open on Facebook, Dee pulled up another tab and typed in **www.home-bodies.com**. Nathan's updates had changed four times in six hours—or would have as soon as she added Breanne's latest news.

```
** Update 4 **
They said it is much worse than it looks because of
the electrical burn issue.
```

That done, she closed out, not expecting people on either coast to be up at that time of morning. She clicked the other link in the email. That link sent her to a blog with a single post.

```
Help Nathan Cox and Family—Nathan is 3 1/2 years old
and was seriously burned by a power line on June 5th.
They transported him to Manchester due to the
severity of the burns. His parents are Jonathan and
Kelly Cox of Fairbury, and they just had a new
little one. This is a fund-raiser to help with the
cost of the trip and any treatment that Nathan might
need. All the money will go directly to Jonathan and
Kelly. Funds are being collected by Nathan's
grandfather (via His PayPal account) and then given
directly to his parents to help with expenses.
Please click the "Donate" button below to help
Nathan & Family, and please pray for our dear
friends.

For updates on how he is doing please check his
Facebook HERE, and we will post updates when we can.
```

Would people donate? Dee stared at the button, curious. Friends would, but then they would have regardless of a page making it easy. Acquaintances might, but at what cost? Would they feel guilted into helping a semi-unemployed man and his family because of a page like that, or would they see it as the way to ease the burden on everyone?

Lord, this will make it so much easier. People won't have to ask. We won't have to respond to awkward money questions. Their bills already are probably more than Jon's made all year. Can people see that, or will they see it as a plea for a handout?

A new post appeared on the Facebook page as Dee mulled the ramifications of being proactive about the aid situation.

```
June 6 (2 minutes ago) From Aunt Breanne—Arrived at
the burn unit 30 minutes ago. Looks like he'll have
to stay here at least 2 days. They are worried
mainly because the electrical burns are hard to
predict and to identify everything that is wrong.
His foot/leg looks really bad... and smells bad...
but he seems to be doing okay so far.
```

With that, Dee closed the laptop, turned out the light, and crept through the darkened house to the master bedroom. Keith's enormous fan blasted air across the bed with enough force to flip the blanket back against itself—from the bottom. Dee tucked in her side, slid a granny-net over her head to keep the hair from irritating her face as she slept, and crawled between the sheets. Keith's arm slid around her waist and pulled her close. Seconds later, his snore managed to project over the noise of the fan and sink into her ear.

DAY TWO

Saturday, June 6, 7:11 a.m.

Beep! Beep! Beep! Breanne jumped up and raced for the nurse, hoping to keep Kelly and Jon from waking. They'd taken turns getting up all night, but as morning dawned, she heard it before they did. Despite her best efforts, the attempt failed. By the time she returned with Nurse Liz, Kelly stood over Nathan, trying to calm him. His moans and whimpers tore at her heart, and the exhaustion and pain etched in her sister's eyes rubbed salt into the wound.

It's hard to believe she used to drive me crazy, Breanne thought as she curled back on the makeshift bed and tried to fall asleep. *Stupid how important who's turn it is to sweep the room is when you don't know what real troubles are.*

8:22 am

As her tea steeped, Claire Rhodes flipped through the pages of the morning paper. Saturday papers—Fairbury's equivalent of a Sunday edition—often had interesting local tidbits. Concerts, achievements by locals, the rare police log that said something other than "Traffic stop—ticketed a minor for cycling without a helmet." Thursday had been uneventful. Thursdays usually were.

Her daughter stumbled into the kitchen and pulled milk from the fridge. "Morning, Joy. I thought you were gone."

Joy gave her a sleepy smile and reached for a bowl. "I'm going to be late. Overslept."

The phone interrupted Claire's response. "Good morning."

"Hey, Claire. It's Lily. I was wondering if you wanted to help with the prayer chain for Nathan."

"Nathan who?" Covering the phone, she mouthed to Joy, "Lily asking for prayer for Nathan."

Joy's eyes widened as she gave her mother a pointed look—one Claire assumed meant to ask, *"Well? Nathan who?"*

"Cox. Wait, didn't you hear? It's all over Facebook."

"Nathan? What happened?" As she listened, Claire mouthed, "Cox. Check Facebook."

Her eyes widened and her heart constricted as Lily Allen told of Nathan's electrocution. "Oh, no! Is he here—oh. I see. What can we do?" She nodded as Lily insisted prayer was their best option. "Right— of course. You just can't help but want to *do* something—physically, I mean. Okay then. Sure. I'll get right on that."

Joy's eyes rose from a laptop screen, her bowl of cereal abandoned and growing soggier by the minute. "Oh, Mom."

Claire snatched up the paper again, flipping page by page, she read the title of every article, no matter how short or tiny, but found nothing. "I guess they had already gone to press when it happened." She nodded at the screen. "What does it say on Facebook?"

"There's a whole page just for the family. They're taking donations and everything."

A fresh wave of dismay washed through her heart. "Oh. It must be serious if they did all that. Does it say how serious?"

"Third degree burns and two surgeries scheduled already." Joy continued reading. "It says, 'Hello family, friends, an—'" She slid the laptop across the counter. "It's too long. You read it."

As Joy dumped the soggy mess, otherwise known as her breakfast, in the trash and poured a fresh bowl, Claire began reading.

```
Hello family, friends, and new acquaintances. To do
a quick summary, a raven flew into the power lines
in our alley last night. It started a fire on one of
the wood fences. My husband went to go help put out
the fire and my 3 yr. old son followed him. Hubby
was bringing him back home, away from the
fire/danger, when Nathan tripped and fell onto a
broken wire in the road. Hubby managed to pull him
off of it quickly, but he suffered third degree
burns (originally told second degree but the burn
specialist said they're third degree).

We were transported here to the Manchester Burn
Center with some amazing compassionate doctors and
nurses. We just saw the burn doctor, who right now
said we need to just watch and wait. We are waiting
to see how extensive the tissue damage is which can
take up to two days to see. He is going to need
surgery to remove the dead skin and any other damage
that comes forth...
```

Claire gasped as her mind played out the upcoming surgeries in vivid detail. She glanced at the next section, unsure she wanted to continue. "Oh, Lord Jesus, help them," she murmured before she continued reading.

```
—and then another surgery later on to do a graft on
his leg. The doctor says the graft will be the
hardest because they will be taking some of his own
skin, removing it and placing it on the burns. It
will be like getting a burn all over again.
(Asphalt/rug burn type thing).
```

Again, Claire gasped, choking back emotion as she imagined the lively little Nathan going through such horrifying procedures. "But he's so little..."

Joy nodded. "I can't imagine." Her eyes widened as she glanced at her phone. "Oh, hey. I'm going to be late. Keep me updated if there's any news."

"Have a good day," Claire called absently as her eyes followed the rest of the message.

The doctor said that this will all take a number of years to fully heal right since Nathan is still growing and this hospital will "become like family."

Prayers for the upcoming days is much appreciated and welcomed. I have my two month old with me, and my nine-year-old is still home with grandparents. The days ahead will be different getting used to. God is good. The paramedics said something like, "He should have been dead" with the way the accident was described to them. The current did NOT pass through his heart.

8:54 a.m.

The pediatrician—Breanne didn't catch his name—stood at the foot of the bed, going over Nathan's medical history. She waited, dreading the question she knew would come next. There it was. "And is he current on his vaccinations?"

Kelly shook her head. "Due to a family history of severe reactions, we do not vaccinate."

The doctor launched into a discussion of the types of reactions, asking if they'd been documented. "Is he—"

Jon stepped out of the bathroom, drying his hands on a paper towel. He punched the hand sanitizer dispenser and stepped forward. "Hi, I'm Jon."

"Dr. Faulkner."

"Nice to meet you."

"We were just discussing Nathan's vaccination history," Dr.

Faulkner said. "I was about to tell Mrs. Cox that I would like to see him with at least a tetanus shot, considering the severity of his burns."

Kelly started to speak, but Jon preempted her. "We'll need to discuss it with the surgeon and do a little research before we get back to you on that."

The doctor nodded, looking as if he thought he'd fired the first "shot" in the battle for vaccinations and won. *You don't know them very well,* Breanne mused. She tried to get Nathan to eat a bit more, but the boy refused. "Are you full?"

"Mmm hmm."

9:03 a.m.

Bleary-eyed, Dee crawled from bed, ignoring the fuzz on the teeth she'd forgotten to brush just hours earlier. Her laptop booted slower than it ever had, and the moment it came online, the phone rang. Aiden glanced up from his place at the breakfast bar and jumped down, bringing the phone to her. "Here, Grandma."

"Thanks. You sleep okay?" she murmured as she answered. "Hello?"

Aiden nodded. "Yeah. Is that Mom?"

Breanne's voice prompted her to shake her head. "Sorry, bud. Aunt Breanne. I'll let you know what's up in a bit. Just finish your breakfast." Dee smiled and tapped the handset. "Thanks again."

"Is he doing okay?" Breanne asked.

"Looks like it. I just woke up to go to the bathroom and decided to see if there was any news." Even as she spoke, Dee saw the latest Facebook update. Her heart sank. "Third degree?"

"Yeah, the surgeon says it's going to be a long road." Breanne's next words were muffled.

"What?"

"Sorry, I wanted to step out of the room so Nathan didn't hear."

"Probably smart," Dee agreed.

"Well, they've got two surgeries scheduled—one on Monday and another on Wednesday." A yawn punctuated that unwelcome news.

"Did you get *any* sleep?"

"Some—not much. There just aren't beds here. We shoved a couple of chairs together, but still. The machine went off every few minutes. All he has to do is move and that machine starts screeching about something." Breanne yawned again. "And we got to bed so late as it is. They had to take pictures and do blood work and all kinds of stuff."

The mom side of Dee kicked in as her daughter spoke. "Okay, I know you're there to help, but make sure you get some sleep or you won't be any use to anyone."

"Yeah, I'll probably try to get a nap in a bit."

"Is Kelly around? I think Aiden would like to talk." Dee listened as Breanne spoke to Kelly and Jon, the words little more than a muffled jumble of sounds.

"We're going to Skype later, okay? There are more people coming in—some social worker, the nurses, it's kind of chaotic, so we'll get online when things settle down."

Dee sent her love to all and disconnected the call. Keith came in from the back yard, dripping pool water as he shuffled toward the bathroom. "I'm going to go back to bed for a bit if you've got things covered here."

He nodded. "We'll be fine. I think the boys wanted to take a walk around the lake, so we might drive over that way."

As she waited for her husband to vacate the bathroom, Dee pulled up the prayer thread and posted the latest update.

```
** UPDATE 7 **
Just woke up and found this:

Quick update (Kelly will probably be on to give a
better update later): The burns are not 2nd degree
burns as they first thought, they are 3rd degree
burns. The plastic surgeon came in today, and to sum
it up, he said "we'll be family for a long time."

Nathan has two surgeries so far scheduled, one
Monday and another on Wednesday. :/
```

By the time she crawled back beneath the covers, Dee had made a mental "to-do" list longer than the hours in which she had to do it. *Okay, Lord. Sleep first, list second. Going to beg for a loaves and fishes clock today. I'm going to need it. Oh, and while I'm in begging mode, please keep the papers from sensationalizing this thing. That's the last thing they need to deal with.*

The last thought that flitted through her mind before slumber overtook her sent her heart racing as she woke up several hours later. *Is this Sunday? Did we space church?*

9:17 a.m.

Music blared from her cellphone. Lila fumbled for it with one hand, while the other sought her glasses on the nightstand. Her sister's name flashed on the screen. "Hey, Breanne. What's up? How's Nathan?"

"Did I wake you up?"

"Yeah, but it's okay." Lila blinked away double vision and stumbled across her room to the bathroom. *Cool water. Must. Have. Cool. Water.*

"Look, sorry to call so early, but my boss is coming through here on her way to visit some friends. She offered to bring stuff, and since we're going to be here for a few days—"

"You are? Aw, man."

"Yeah, talk to Mom about it. I don't want to have to go through it all again. It's on the Facebook page too. Anyway, I've got a list of things Jon needs from the house. Can you go over there and get them?"

"Sure. Let me pee and find a notebook. I'll call you back in a minute."

"Ever so tactful, Lila."

"Whatever." Lila slid her phone shut. Minutes later, she called Breanne back. "Okay, got a pen. What do I need to get?" Lila blinked. "Wait, did you say Facebook page?"

"You really were out, weren't you?"

"Yeah, well—okay, give it to me." Lila sat, pen poised, ready to scribble a list. After the dozen or so items Jon and Kelly requested, she found herself scribbling down a couple of requests. "Make sure the water is off, take out the trash so it doesn't stink, and bring in the mail. Got it."

"Kelly says to call Mrs. Cox before you go over and she'll meet you there. She has the key and knows where stuff is," Breanne said before adding, "Oh, and don't forget the GPS. We're gonna need it. Okay, looks like the nurse is going to do something. Gotta go."

Lila stared at the dead phone in her hand before grabbing a brush and running it through her hair. As she brushed, she flipped open her laptop and searched through Breanne's Facebook wall until she found the link to the page. The picture of Nathan choked her. "Oh, Jesus! Why does he have to go through this?"

With her purse slung over one shoulder, she clattered down the garage stairs and hurried out to her car. Her favorite radio station blasted a song that she barely tolerated on the best of days. With an irritated sniff, she shoved a CD in the player and relaxed, albeit just the merest bit, as instrumental piano music filled the car.

On the other side of Fairbury, just past Tanglewood Drive, Lila turned onto Linden Street—and remembered that she was supposed to have called Mrs. Cox first. "Geez Lois!"

It took a call home to get the number for Mrs. Cox, and two calls to the Coxes before Mrs. Cox answered. "Oh, we just got in from working on the garden. I'll clean up and meet you there in just a little bit." Lila didn't bother to mention that she'd already arrived "there" and agreed.

Morbid curiosity propelled her through the side yard to the back. A broom lay in the middle of the yard and the back gate stood wide open. Lila picked her way through the yard, absently picking up the broom as she went, and out to the alley. Her eyes rose to the power lines ahead. *Fixed them already?* Music blaring in a house two doors down told her the neighborhood had power. *I suppose they had to fix it fast. Weird.* Several steps away, a bird lay dead, flies buzzing around it. She started to turn, revolted at the sight, but a group of kids, tearing through the alley on their bikes, gave her pause. *They wouldn't mess with it—would they?* Her hand gripped the broom tighter. *I could flip it into the weeds so they can't see...*

Lila shuddered as the kids whizzed past and the flies swirled before settling again. She found a stick and used it to flip the bird onto the broom bristles. Using the stick to hold it in place, she half-ran, dropping the bird twice, through the back yard to the garbage cans on the side of the house and dumped it in. "I am *so* glad Monday is trash day. Ugh."

With that task accomplished, she stared at the broom and shuddered once more. A nearby hose called to her, but she couldn't do it. She flipped the lid to the other trash can, shoved the broom as far down as she could, and tried to close the lid. It wouldn't quite close, but Lila deemed it good enough.

She started to go back out front to wait for Mrs. Cox when the morning breeze caught the gate just enough to coax a squeak out of the hinges. Once more, Lila crossed the yard, this time to latch the gate. As she neared, two people wearing safety hats stepped out of a Rockland Gas & Electric truck. The man immediately crossed the alley and met her at the gate.

Lila's eyes slid up to the power line before forcing a smile. "Can I help you?"

"I'm Ross Davies from RGE. I'm looking for—" he glanced at his clipboard. "Jonathan or Kelly Cox?"

Even as he spoke, Lila shook her head. "Sorry. They're not here."

"Is there any way I can get in touch with them? I'm investigating the incident last night for RGE. He clicked his pen before asking, "And you are…"

"Lila Homstad—Kelly's sister."

"Were you here?" Ross asked as he scribbled down her name. "Is that H-o-m-e—"

"No e. S-t-a-d. I wasn't here. I met them at the clinic last night."

"So you saw them—talked to them? What did they say happened?" So Lila began the first of many recounts of the story. Ross listened, shaking his head. "It's bad enough for something like this to happen, but a kid so little…"

As she finished her story, Lila told about the bird, pointing to the trash can. "I didn't want the kids to play with it so I tossed it."

Ross nodded. "Is it okay if Melissa takes a picture of it and where it was?"

The idea revolted her, but Lila shrugged. "Sure. It was laying down there—you can't miss where it was." As the woman, Melissa, stepped through the gate and strode to where the trash cans were, Lila called out, "Watch out for the flies."

Ross snickered. "Sorry. She hates files. This'll be good." He glanced at his notes and said, "Okay so you said that they're in Manchester—Cunningham?"

Dread washed over Lila as she realized that this man—this man from the *electric company*—knew the name of a burn unit two hours away. "Yes. Cunningham."

"And do they have a phone number—"

"No, sorry. Jon lost his job last fall, so they've been cutting back—wait. My sister's there. I can give you her number."

Ross waited. Lila smiled. Ross smiled back. At last he said, "And that number would be..."

"Oh, sorry." Flushing, Lila rattled off the numbers, corrected him when Ross had one wrong, and tried to think calm, cooling thoughts before she made an even bigger fool of herself.

"And your sister's name?"

"Breanne." Lila hesitated and then spelled it out for him. "B-r-e-a-n-n-e."

"Same last name?"

"Yeah. We get that a lot, but yeah." Ross gave her a questioning glance but didn't ask. Lila shrugged. "Lots of kids means people assume lots of dads or moms or some combination, but it's just Mom, Dad, and us kids."

"Dare I ask?"

"Nine."

"In the family or nine kids?" Ross looked almost afraid of the answer.

"Kids. Well, unless you count Jon. He'd make ten—legally speaking."

A smirk appeared around the man's lips, but Lila didn't allow herself to wonder. "Okay, well thank you," Ross said as Melissa reached the gate. The woman tossed him a dirty look making him smirk again. "I think we've got what we need for now."

"We," the woman growled. "Yeah."

Lila strolled back to the house, looking over her shoulder a few times as she tried to decide what to think. As she slipped through the side gate, she pulled out her phone and called Breanne. "Hey, so the RGE people are here. They wanted a number for Jon and Kelly, so I gave them yours. I hope that's okay."

"Yeah. They'd better take responsibility for this. It's—well, it's just bad. There's so much damage. I keep hearing surgery for this and procedure for that. We're talking thousands and thousands of dollars every day and no insurance."

Before she could reply, Mrs. Cox's car pulled into the drive. "Hey, she's here. Gotta go. Let me know what the RGE guy says. He was pretty nice. Didn't like hearing about Nathan getting hurt."

"Well, who would?" Breanne retorted before disconnecting.

9:58 a.m.

Breanne stretched and moved to try to quiet a screaming machine again but failed. Before she could go in search of a nurse, a man stepped in the door. "Hi, I'm Dr. Smith. Are you Nathan's mother..."

From the corner, Kelly waved. "I'm his mother." The doctor stepped forward to shake her hand as Kelly introduced Jon. "This is my husband, Jon."

A nurse bustled into the room to adjust the monitor and stop the alarm as Dr. Smith introduced himself as Nathan's surgeon. "I'll be working with Nathan to get him back on his feet."

Jon and Kelly exchanged glances, and Breanne skirted behind them and out of the way, listening. Nathan gave the doctor a weak smile and said, "Doctor Who!"

The surgeon sent them all quizzical looks, but before Breanne could explain, Kelly spoke up. "The bow tie."

"Bow ties are cool."

And he's Doctor Smith. How cool is that? Breanne mused as she listened.

Dr. Smith smiled and tweaked his tie. "I like them... so Doctor Who wears bow ties. That *is* cool." As he spoke, Dr. Smith flipped through several photos and frowned.

10:19 a.m.

Mary Cox pulled into her son's driveway and turned off the engine. Fumbling for her purse, she stepped from the vehicle and glanced around her. Lila's car was there, but the girl was nowhere in sight. *Did she find the spare?* Mary blinked as the sun's rays blinded her for a moment. *What an absolutely ordinary thought on a very un-ordinary day.*

Lila rounded the corner of the house just as Mary pushed open the door. "Morning, Mrs. Cox."

"Hi. Hope you haven't been waiting too long."

"No, I just went out to see what happened. There's some guy and a girl from RGE out there. They were looking for Jon and Kelly, so I gave them Breanne's cell number. I hope that's okay..."

"I think that's probably wise." Mary glanced around her at the piles of unfolded laundry and the remnants of the previous night's dinner. *Poor girl—didn't even have time to wipe down the table.* "I think I'll take care of the dishes while you pack what you need. If I can help, let me know."

Minutes later, with Mary's arms were deep in sudsy water, Lila brought her list in. "Can you tell me where Jon keeps his vitamins or whatever this stuff is? I can't pronounce it."

Mary glanced at the list. "Oh, Homocysteine Redux. It's probably in that cupboard right—no, that one," she said as Lila reached for the door next to the correct one. "Right. I think it has a green lid."

After reading half a dozen bottles, and pulling two others from the shelf, Lila shook one. "Got it. Thanks. I just can't find Kelly's nursing shirts anywhere. The drawers are empty and so is the closet."

"Could still be on the line, or in the dryer," Mary suggested. "Or maybe in those baskets of laundry by the couch. They look clean…"

"This would have to happen when they have a new baby and Kelly is lucky to get half the sleep she needs."

The comment seemed strange to Mary. *Does she really think it would have been easier in a year when Anna's walking or in five when Kelly has another child to educate? When is it ever "easy" to have a tragic accident?*

"Do you need help? I could fold the laundry…"

"I'll get it. You need to get the suitcases to—was it Breanne's boss?"

"Yeah. Shelli said she'd drive it up on her way to a wedding." Lila pulled out her phone. "Yikes. They're leaving at eleven. I'd better hurry."

Lila never did find the shirt Kelly wanted. After frantically tearing apart the living room, bedroom, and laundry room, she grabbed a couple of basic t-shirts, shoved them in the suitcase, and tore out of the house. Mary stood at the living room window, drying her hands, and hoping that the girl didn't end up wasting time getting a lecture and a ticket for speeding.

Laundry covered the couch, coffee table, and armchair. Mary turned away, forcing herself to finish cleaning up the kitchen before tackling the laundry, too. She emptied the garbage, packed up anything from the fridge that might spoil in the next day or two, and mopped the floor. That accomplished, she worked her way clockwise through the house, picking things up, folding the piles of clothes, and putting away anything she could find.

Well, it's not perfect, but at least she won't be behind when she comes home.

12:01 p.m.

The scent of powerful hand sanitizer preceded the arrival of a stocky man with a great smile. Short cropped silver hair, tanned face, and a British accent that sounded out of place in a Midwestern hospital—Ian Brenner introduced himself and smiled at Nathan. "Hey, buddy. I'm Ian. I'm a fireman here in Manchester. I heard you had an accident. What happened?"

Kelly shifted Anna in her arms, smiling as Nathan's eyes widened with genuine delight. "A bird died."

"A bird died. Wow. That's sad..." His eyes slid to Jon and Kelly, questioning.

"Hit the power line, transformer blew..." Kelly explained. "It all went down from there. Literally," she added with a weak attempt at sleep-deprived humor.

"Well," Ian said, handing Nathan a little bear with his legs wrapped in bandages. "I'm really sorry to hear that. I brought you someone who understands. See, he has bandages on his legs too."

Nathan smiled for one brief moment before his forehead furrowed. "He doesn't have arms."

Kelly pointed to the bear's limbs. "See. There's one—"

"No..." Nathan pointed to his own bandaged forearms. "He doesn't have them like mine."

"We can fix that," Ian promised with a silent request to the nurse who waited to check Nathan's vitals—again.

"Sure. I'll be right back."

In minutes, Nurse Allison had the bear's arms appropriately bandaged and ready for Nathan's inspection. "How's that?"

He nodded.

"Okay, good. Now, let's check your blood pressure—the squeezy bandage, okay?"

Nathan whimpered until he saw her move for the arm without the IV. Ian used the opportunity to speak to Jon and Kelly. Breanne cleared the double chair-turned-bed of their lunch debris and turned it around to make room for him, saying, "Sorry. It's kind of awkward in here."

"Did you guys get set up at the Ronald McDonald House across the street?"

Jon and Kelly exchanged questioning glances. "Um… no…" Jon didn't seem to know how to answer.

"We'll take care of that for you. You'll need a place to get some good sleep. Just go over there when you need to. They've got rooms and laundry facilities—everything you can need."

"Thanks." Breanne offered an exhausted smile. "I'm sure that'll be great."

Nathan began crying as the nurse soaked his bandages again. Breanne jumped up to soothe him, leaving Kelly and Jon to talk to Ian about what happened. "Shhh… she has to do it so you'll get better."

"Noooo…"

As Nathan's wails grew louder, Kelly handed Anna to Jon and went to help. Ian Brenner stood, offered his hand, and said, "I'll get out of your hair. Don't forget the RMH. I'll get right over there and set that up."

No sooner had he left and Nathan's bandage soak ended, a hospital social worker arrived to go over financial issues. Upon hearing that the Coxes did not have health insurance, she began asking other questions—Jon's income, the number of people in the family, Kelly's income. "Oh, yeah. You definitely qualify for state assistance. I'll bring the paperwork a little later."

Breanne watched Jon and Kelly exchange glances and knew what he'd say before he spoke. As much as she respected his convictions, part of her screamed, *Noooooooooo. You guys will be in debt until you die. Just do it.*

"Thank you for the offer, but we're not interested. We'll find a way to pay cash."

"Are you—I mean, do you have any idea how expensive this is going to be?"

Jon shook his head. "I don't. But I know it's a lot more than I think I'll ever make, but I've got to try. I appreciate you trying to help, but we just can't."

"That's fine, not a problem. I'll let the financial office know so that they can set up payment arrangements. Right now, though, you worry about getting him well. This stuff can wait."

1:39 p.m.

The hospital room teemed with people. The surgeon and pediatrician spoke with nurses regarding the upcoming hydrotherapy. Kelly tried to listen in, but with nurses coming and going, Anna screeching to be fed, and Nathan objecting to each new poke and prod, chaos reigned. Breanne took the baby for a walk in hopes of quieting her down, but returned minutes later on the heels of another man and woman. Kelly listened, eyes widening, as Breanne whispered, "I overheard them tell the nurse out there—they're from RGE."

"Oh!" Kelly stepped forward, her attention diverted from descriptions of the upcoming tortures for her son, and introduced herself. "I'm Kelly Cox."

"Ross Davies—this is my associate, Melissa. We're from RGE. We just wanted to stop by and see how everyone is doing—well, and ask a few questions about what happened." He glanced around the room. "We could come back..."

"No, you made that trip already..." She took the baby and murmured to Breanne, "Can you get Jon and stay with Nathan?"

As Ross introduced them once more, Melissa took notes on a clipboard. She seemed detached, but pleasant enough. Kelly couldn't decide what that meant, but she listened to each word, each inflection—every nuance she could find in Ross' voice in the hopes of gleaning more than why they'd come. "Mr. Cox, have you been examined? Touching someone during electrocution usually transfers the current to the second person."

"I didn't feel anything. I think it was too fast or something," Jon assured him.

"I'd feel better if you had an EKG to be sure."

Jon shook his head and Kelly repressed a sigh. *Not that I thought he would, but it would have been nice to know for sure...*

Ross didn't push, although Kelly suspected he wanted to. Instead, he began asking questions. Hospital personnel jostled for position around Nathan's bed as different needs arose, but between answering questions about wet Pull-Ups and trying to help soothe Nathan through another bandage soaking, she listened as Jon told the story from his perspective.

"—was just leading him back to the house—away from the fire—when he just fell and started writhing and screaming. I jerked him off, but it was too late."

"Were there sparks?"

Jon nodded. "Yeah. Quite a few, actually. I just didn't see it—the wire that is. The shadows in the alley, and it was almost dark by that point—I just didn't see it."

"And you say a transformer blew and started the fire?"

"That's what it looked like—after that bird hit the wire," Jon clarified.

More questions. More answers. More moments reliving something she'd rather forget. Kelly fought the rising urge to scream, "Just leave us alone—all of you—and let me wake up. This can't be happening!"

Instead, she forced herself to smile, reassuring Ross that she didn't blame the power company. "It was an accident. We know that."

"It was my fault," Jon repeated for what seemed like the hundredth time since it happened. "I should have seen it."

Ross assured Jon that no one could have prevented it. "I wish we could have. I hate to see a little guy like that hurting." The surgeon and the pediatrician stepped out of the room, leaving a little space by the bed. "May I talk to him?"

Kelly nodded. "Sure."

Melissa followed on Ross' heels but still said nothing. Ross offered his hand to Nathan and Kelly winced as her son tried to shake hands. Her heart squeezed as she watched Ross hunker down a bit lower to put himself at eye level with Nathan. "Hey, buddy. My name is Ross."

"Hi."

Kelly found herself exhaling slowly as Nathan spoke without a whimper or whine. *Medication must be working. Good.*

"So what happened to you?"

Nathan's big brown eyes stared at the visitor, blinked once, and then he said, "A bird died."

1:41 p.m.

"Mom, the Facebook page says they set up a PayPal account. What is it? Mrs. Allen wants to know." Drew's voice reached Dee long before his body entered the room—as usual.

"It's Dad's account. That way we pay the taxes."

"What's the email?"

Failing in her desperate attempt *not* to roll her eyes, Dee rattled off the email address. Curious, she opened a new tab on her browser and typed in their login information. The balance astounded her. "Wow."

"Wow what?"

She turned her laptop screen so Drew could see. "Over three hundred dollars already."

"Cool," Drew muttered as his thumbs slid around the keypad on his phone. "There. Thanks."

"I talked to Breanne…"

"Yeah, me too. Glad he's doing a bit better," Drew opened the door. "Be back later. I'm late."

Left alone once more, Dee ruminated over her conversation with Breanne as she typed the next update.

** UPDATE 8**

Talked to Breanne. The nurses are in love with Nathan. Spoiling him rotten. He is absolutely unfazed by them wanting to do blood draws etc. Someone found out he likes firemen and made a call. A fireman came, talked to Nathan for a bit and then talked to Kelly, and Jon. I guess he asked if they were at the Ronald McDonald house yet, and when they said they didn't know anything about it, he took care of it. Got them a room and everything. It's amazing.

The pediatrician wanted Nathan caught up on vaccines—particularly tetanus. Offered something that's supposed to ward it off but not the vaccine—something like that. He was courteous about it but strongly recommended it. Jon and Kelly were researching information about it when the surgeon came in. When they asked his opinion, he said the chances of tetanus are pretty much non-existent, so they didn't need to consider it at all.

A social worker came in to talk about state medical assistance, asked a couple of questions, and instantly said they qualify. Jon thanked her but said he wasn't interested, and the woman said she understood.

RGE spoke to Jon as well. We'll see. There is a chance that there was a malfunction of the power line. When the explosion happened, the power should have been cut off.

Interesting aside, it turns out we had a brownout here when it happened—just a second or two of flickering. That sickens me when I think about it, but it is interesting.

She remembered that brownout—that flicker. On hot summer evenings—usually July or August rather than June—when the grid became overloaded with appliance usage and air conditioners battling the temperatures, brownouts were quite common. "I think," she murmured, unaware she'd spoken aloud, "it's a blessing we didn't know then."

"What, Grandma?" Aiden stood in the doorway, a cup in his hand.

"Just thinking aloud. What'd you get?"

"Fair-Berry Blast."

Dee laughed. "Audrey's good with the names. What kind of berries?"

"Dunno. Did Mom call? How's Nathan?"

"I said you'd call Breanne when you got home. They're going to Skype on her laptop. I'll get mine set up. Why don't you call?" Dee searched her laptop for the program and pulled it up. While Aiden chatted with his parents and his little brother, Dee went to find the phone. *Guess I'd better let Mom know what's going on.*

1:57 p.m.

As if designed to torture those daring to interrupt the tranquility of the home, Dee listened, wincing as her parents' phone rang three— four— *What's going on? They always answer by four—five.* Just as she pulled the phone away from her ear to hang up, her mother's trademarked, "Heee-ello!" stopped her.

Dee fumbled. "Mom?"

"Hey there!"

"Hi. How's everything?" *What kind of stupid question is that? If everything wasn't okay, wouldn't they be calling to let us know? Kind of like you're doing right now?*

"Good—there?"

"Not so good." *That's why. Segue. It's weird how our conversational patterns are designed for this stuff.*

"What's up?"

That's Mom. Get right to the point. Do not beat around the bush, do not pass go; do not pass up a chance at two hundred dollars—or something like that. "There's been an accident—Nathan..."

"Oh, no. What?"

How something could feel like déjà vu and yet be the first time she had to articulate the story, Dee couldn't understand, but she found herself recounting the events of the previous night in as much detail as she knew. "Breanne's with them now—will be until they come home, I expect. She got the week off, so maybe she'll just go home with them for a day or two."

"Is Jon okay? I mean, if he was holding Nathan's hand, he couldn't have missed getting a jolt too, could he?"

"I don't know. He didn't think so, but..."

Dee listened as her mother told the story to her father and heard her father's response. Her father's voice came on the line a minute or two later. "Can you have them check him out? With adrenaline going at a time like that, he might not have noticed it, but it can do a lot of damage that doesn't show up right away."

"Kind of like the burns. They said his legs can keep burning for two days!"

"Well, it's not actually still burning," her father corrected.

It's always the same—that cool and fascinating feeling of knowing that your father knows everything—even if, or maybe especially when, he doesn't. Do you ever get too old to feel the wonder of it? "Right. The damage continues. That's what I meant. It's all so jumbled when they talk to us—so much information all at once."

"How is Aiden—and that baby? Are they okay?"

Dee assured him that the other children were fine. "They've got Anna with them at the burn center, but Aiden's with us."

"Well that's good. I'll give you back to your mom. We love you."

"Love you too, Dad."

The boys burst into the room just as Dee started to say goodbye. "Hey, want to talk to Grandma Josephs?"

Aiden grinned and took the phone first. *He's a neat kid, Lord. I mean, he's never actually met them, but look at him. Most kids his age wouldn't be... what's the word. Eager. Most kids his age wouldn't be eager to talk to great-grandparents just because they're related. Jon and Kelly are doing a good job—even if he is a juvenile delinquent in the safety law department.*

After Aiden finished, Logan talked for a few minutes and then passed the phone back to her. "Grandma said to call again when you know something. She said they'll be praying for the surgery on Monday."

Aiden's eyes whipped over to meet hers. "He has to have surgery? Why?"

"I think that's what they're calling it when they go in and clean out all the burned skin and stuff." She'd assumed Jon and Kelly would tell him about it, but it seemed as if they hadn't. Aiden pressed for information, and when she found that they'd had to postpone the Skype conversation for half an hour, Dee found herself describing what the doctors had said about needing further care over the years as he grew. "I don't know what all it means, but your dad will tell you when you guys talk in a bit."

"'Mkay."

"Hey, Mom!" Logan waited for her to acknowledge him and added, "The neighbors were asking about Nathan. Mrs. Kilgore said that people all over town are talking about it. Someone said something about The Deli doing a fundraiser—twenty-five percent of whatever they make next Saturday going to help pay Nathan's bills."

"That's great!"

Logan grinned. "So can we eat there?"

"You do know—" *It's futile,* Dee thought to herself. *Just let them. They'll feel like they're helping.* "Sure."

"Aiden too?"

"If he's still here, of course, but he'll probably be home by then, so you'll have to get permission from Jon and Kelly."

Aiden's face fell. "That's okay."

"Well, you ask," Dee insisted. "Make sure they know we'll send food home for them too. They probably will like having a night off from cooking after a few days in the hospital."

It worked. Aiden heard the silent message loud and clear. *We'll pay for it.*

"Thanks, Grandma. That'll be great."

4:09 p.m.

Nurse Allison arrived and glanced around her. "Where's Jon?"

"He went for a walk." Kelly watched the expressions flicker across the nurse's face. "Is something wrong?"

"It's time for hydro..." Her eyes slid over to where Nathan lay flipping through a book. "I was going to have Jon carry him but—"

"Should I go find him?"

"I... no. I'll see what Dr. Smith wants to do. We usually just wheel in the bed or put patients in a chair, but he's so little and he's going to be terrified." With one last glance at Nathan, she slipped from the room, leaving Kelly there with her heart in her throat.

Breanne and Kelly's eyes met. "Should I try to find Jon?" Breanne asked.

"I don't think so. He needed that walk. If he gets back in time..."

Kelly was interrupted by Allison's arrival. She wheeled in a plastic wagon and pulled back the privacy curtain. "Okay, Nathan. It's time to go for a ride in the wagon."

Nathan's eyes, dulled by rising pain as his medication wore off, hardly glanced at the wagon. "Noooo..."

"Hey now..." Kelly tried to keep her tone kind but firm. *He can't get used to protesting everything, but Lord, I know I'd protest! He's hurting.*

"It's important, buddy," Allison said as she lowered the rail on his bed. "We're going to take a walk around the unit and then we'll go to a special room and try to help your leg."

Despite the nurse's assurances that all would be well. Nathan balked. Allison glanced at Kelly and said, "Maybe we'll forgo the walk and just get it over with."

Kelly nodded and passed the baby to Breanne. "I'll be back in a bit."

As she adjusted the half-asleep baby, Breanne asked once more, "Are you sure you don't want me to go find Jon?"

Of course I do! I don't want to do this! They said he'll scream. **Scream!** *What mother wants to endure that? But why should Jon have to?* "No…"

"If you're sure…"

She wasn't sure, but Kelly refused to admit it. She followed the nurse to the hydrotherapy room, trying to encourage her son as she went. "They're just going to give you a shower—just like at home." At the nurse's confused look, Kelly shrugged. "The bathtub in our second bath leaks, so we don't use it. We just have a stand alone shower unit for all of us, so they take showers."

As the medical team prepped Nathan for his "hydro," Kelly donned her own "rain coat," shower shoes, and shower cap and prepped herself for the pain. Jon arrived just before they began the procedure, and as much as her brain screamed for her to leave, she found herself riveted to the spot. *What if he needs me?*

Once more, the pungent stench of decayed and dead flesh permeated the air as bandages dropped into basins. The burns, what she could see of them, looked so much worse than they had before the bandages. *Maybe they should let them air dry—like a cut. Should they look worse? Surely not.* The doctor's explanation of continuing damage reminded her that the forty-eight hour window wasn't up yet. *Just prepare yourself for worse for a few more times,* she admonished herself, trying to ignore Nathan's ever-increasing protests at the medical team's interference.

However, nothing could have prepared her for the heart-rending screams that erupted as warm water sprayed on her son's legs. Jon held the boy's head and arms while the doctors and nurses worked quickly to remove all the dead tissue they could. Tears poured down Nathan's cheeks and great wracking sobs shook his little body. "Don't hurt me, Daddy!"

The medicinal scent of the anti-bacterial wash combined with the water and dead flesh sent waves of nausea through her. Minutes—how could they only be minutes—upon minutes passed as the screams ripped through her. *This is going to kill me before we're done. How can they do this every. single. day?*

The doctors and nurses spoke in hushed tones as they worked. Allison tried to comfort Nathan, but the boy was beside himself with pain, terror, and what Kelly suspected was a sense of betrayal. She could almost hear her son screaming inside, *Why are you letting them hurt me? Why won't you stop this, Mommy? Why is Daddy hurting me?*

The fifteen minutes of gentle spraying and scrubbing felt much longer than any lifetime Kelly had ever imagined. For the first time, II Peter made sense. *"One day is like a thousand years..." Yeah, I get it now. I've just aged a thousand years in the span of fifteen minutes,* she whimpered to herself. *Imagine how he feels. He'll be old beyond his years by the time this thing is over.*

The cries of baby Anna sent her on ahead of Jon, Nathan, and their benevolent torturers. She entered their room and found Breanne sitting in the chair, clutching the baby with tears pouring down her face. "Is it over?" Breanne whispered.

"For today."

Breanne nodded. Their eyes met as Kelly took the fussy baby and settled down to nurse. Seconds passed with unified thoughts unspoken until Breanne choked out, "Don't hurt me, Daddy?"

5:25 p.m.

A knock on the door was interrupted by a nurse in the hall. "Be sure to use the hand sanitizer before stepping in the room."

Jon glanced up from his place next to Nathan, surprised. "Naomi—Pete."

"Hey," Naomi said as she and her husband entered the room.

As she stepped from the bathroom, her hand reaching for the sanitizer in what had already become second-nature, Kelly froze and blinked. "Naomi? How—"

"Mom and Dad called—thought you might like some fresh fruit..." Naomi offered her brother the bag she carried. "We just wanted to see how you all were. See if we could do anything..."

Kelly hugged her sister-in-law and glanced around her. "I guess Breanne is still out with Anna." She led them to the bed and said, "Hey,

Nathan. Look who's here! Aunt Naomi and Uncle Pete."

Nathan giggled. "Hi."

"Hi." Naomi said, her eyes sliding toward Jon in a questioning look.

"He's high on morphine," Kelly explained. "After the hydrotherapy, they gave him something for the pain and he's been a bit giddy ever since."

"What do they do in hydrotherapy?" Pete stepped closer and grinned at the boy. "Hey, buster. Whatcha doin'?"

"They basically give him a shower—"

Nathan's eyes widened. "Nooooo…"

"Not now," Jon agreed. "We're just telling them what happened." While Breanne distracted him with her phone, Jon explained the procedure.

They all choked up as Kelly recounted Nathan's cries and pleas for no more pain, but the news that he had to do it every day made the story that much worse. "And the bandages? Do they have to soak those every day?"

Jon nodded. "Every six to eight hours—according to Allison."

"He doesn't like that either, but it's more of a protest and regular pain than hydro—"

As if attuned to the word, no matter how softly spoken, Nathan began whimpering again. Pete distracted him by asking about the toys on his bed. At the news that a fireman had brought the bear, Pete's eyes widened. "Wow, a *fireman*. That's cool."

Kelly's heart warmed as she watched her brother-in-law interact with her son. Jon and Naomi discussed their stay, the procedures planned, and the upcoming surgery on Monday, but Pete and Nathan just hung out at the bed, discussing the merits and demerits of the bear, the toy truck, the books, and the rest of the toys and paraphernalia that littered Nathan's mattress. Nathan moved wrong—again—and the monitors freaked out. Again.

A hospital aide entered the room with food for the Cox family and left again, promising to send a nurse to quiet the protesting machine. Naomi wrinkled her nose at the plastic trays of food. "Um, why don't I try to bring something tomorrow—maybe fresh salad and some chicken or something not so…" She glanced around her before adding, "Institutional."

"You don't have to do that—"

Naomi cut Kelly off with a smile. "No, but I can. What else can you use? I have fruit and some water bottles in the bag, but—"

"Jon? Is there anything we need?"

With a forkful of mashed potatoes paused in mid-air, Jon tried to think. Nathan, impatient to be eating, grabbed Jon's wrist and brought the fork to his mouth. Chuckles rippled through the room, giving things a lighter feel after such heavy discussions. Breanne entered the room with Anna, juggling the baby as she tried to rub hand sanitizer into her hands. "Oh—hi! Naomi, right?"

Naomi nodded, introduced her husband, and took baby Anna from Breanne. "How's my chunky monkey? Wow, she gets bigger every time I see her."

"That's what babies usually do, hon," Pete remarked without much inflection.

"Ha. Ha." Naomi rolled her eyes and murmured something about obnoxious uncles into Anna's ear. "We were just asking Mommy and Daddy what you might need." She glanced up at Kelly. "What about diapers—wipes?"

"Breanne went to a store earlier. Got 'em. We could use some of Jon's protein bars, though. Something to keep his blood sugars level." Kelly fumbled for her purse and pulled out her wallet. She dug through it but only found a five and a couple of ones. "Jon… don't you have cash? I'm down to nearly nothing."

Jon pulled out the wad of cash Drew had given him and peeled a twenty from it. "Thanks," he said as he passed it to his sister. "That'll help."

Nathan reached for the piece of chicken on his plate and took a bite, obviously unwilling to wait any longer for the adults to quit yammering about unimportant things like food for them.

6:34 p.m.

Chad Tesdall's truck bounced over the rutted drive. At the living room window, his wife watched smiling to see him dragging up the steps. Thunder rolled somewhere, but the skies overhead looked clear from her vantage point.

Willow turned to greet him, but Chad didn't look her way. He went straight for the library and the gun safe. "Hey, Chad. Dinner's almost done. I'm grilling steaks."

No response.

Kari rose on still wobbly legs and staggered toward Willow in the drunken-sway she'd mastered in recent days. Willow grinned. Nothing would make Chad smile faster than the sight of Kari. She scooped up the beaming child and carried her to the library where he'd emptied his gun belt into the safe and slammed the door shut. Eager to see him smile, Willow deposited Kari a few feet from Chad. She made it two steps before he knelt before the tottering little girl, engulfing her in a boa constrictor-like hug. Willow's smile wavered and dissolved as she saw his lip quiver.

"Chad?"

"Where're the boys?"

"Becca took them with her to change pastures—why?" She stepped closer. "Chad?"

"Aiden Cox—"

Her heart sank. "No... I thought he wasn't riding things right now."

"His little brother. Nathan. Ele—" Chad choked, the words disappearing behind a wall of emotion.

"Nathan what?"

Kari protested, fighting to get out of her father's confining arms, but Chad didn't notice. She waited for him to release the child, but he didn't. His shoulders shook with repressed sobs until Willow knelt beside them and tried to take Kari from him. Nothing could have prepared her for his reaction.

"What! Can't a guy hug his kid and be grateful she's safe? You're such a control freak!" As he pushed away from them, Kari, startled by his outburst, screamed. Willow lifted her daughter in her arms and stared at the retreating form of her husband. The front screen slammed shut prompting a fresh round of wails from Kari.

Willow wandered through the house, to the kitchen, and into the pantry where her phone sat charging on the windowsill. *Is it hypocritical to get frustrated if your spouse talks to his parents before you but you want do the same thing once in a while?* Kari's sniffles subsided as Willow smoothed her hair and debated within herself. Before she could second-guess herself further, she picked it up and selected her father-in-law's number.

"Hey, how's my favorite daughter-in-law!"

"Your only daughter-in-law, but I'll take it," she teased, but even she could hear that her tone gave away trouble.

"What's wrong?"

"I think something happened at work today. Remember Aiden?"

"The helmet kid? Oh no..."

Willow swallowed hard. "Something happened to his little brother, but Chad won't tell me. He just hugged Kari until she turned purple, so I tried to get him to loosen his hold, but he just blew up at us—yelled, stormed out of here. I think he's mad that Becca has the boys too, but I can't figure out why."

"Let me check Fairbury news... Marianne, have you seen anything about an accident in Fairbury—probably involving a car and a kid on a bike or scooter or something?"

From her kitchen, she listened as Christopher and Marianne called back and forth. Marianne's cry of, "Oh no!" told Willow she'd found it.

"What is it?"

"Hang on, I'm looking—oh, it's bad. Nathan—he's three, right?"

"I think so—around there."

Christopher started to speak and stopped again, making his words sound like, "Hgroldown."

"What?"

"Sorry." Willow heard him take a deep breath before he said, "Yeah. You'd better find Chad. He's going to take this hard. Nathan was electrocuted last night—third degree burns. That kind of thing always tears him up—remember the last time there was something that reminded him of Aiden? How he shut you out and overreacted to things? It's happening again, and that same family—"

"And we're closer to them now. Jon worked for us for several weeks. That poor family. What can we do—"

"Right now, the most important thing for you to do is get to Chad and get him talking about it. He'll do much better if he can just get the images out of his mind."

"But he wasn't working last night. He was home. I don't understand."

"Then it's probably guilt," Christopher surmised. "He's just so connected with Aiden and that first accident. He was probably relieved not to be there, and then felt guilty—none of it makes sense, okay? This kind of thing never does. He just needs you not to let him withdraw. He'll probably yell, push you away. Heck, he might even become paranoid about the kids for a couple of days, but just be you. Stick with being you. You're good for him. We'll pray."

She found Chad leading the boys back from the pasture with Becca following behind looking very bewildered. "Chad—"

"I don't want them out there. They're too little—too unpredictable."

"Too vulnerable," she whispered.

"That's right."

She debated within herself for a moment and then passed Kari to Becca. "Will you take her and the boys please?" Chad's head whipped around, but Willow ignored the glare in his eyes. "We have to talk."

Chad protested, but Willow noted that he did allow her to lead him away from Becca and the children. She slipped her hand in his, feeling the tension in his body rise with each step. She forced herself to ignore it and focused on keeping her body language relaxed. As they neared the stream, she steered him toward the pool.

"I talked to Dad…" Chad stiffened. "You don't usually yell at me like that—not for trying to keep you from smothering your child with love and affection…"

"Yeah. Because it's a crime to love on your kids."

"No… because no matter how much love is meant, squeezing to death still results in a death," she corrected. "Dad told me what happened with Nathan—well sort of."

"What do you mean, sort of?"

"Dad told me that he was electrocuted and had some serious burns. Then I came to find you. Wanna talk about it?"

"Since when does *my* wife say 'wanna'?" Chad muttered.

No matter how grouchy he sounded, Willow heard a softening in his voice—one he'd deny if she bothered to mention it. "Since she spends so much time with her semi-illiterate husband…"

"Who's the one with the degree here?"

Willow attempted to raise an eyebrow, but both rose. Chad didn't notice. Her silence, however, must have spoken louder than any raised eyebrow, because he threw his hands up in mock surrender.

"You're right. I don't even want to try to go head to head with you academically. Point taken."

They sat cross-legged facing one another. Willow picked at the dirt, drawing pictures and erasing them as soon as she finished. How long she waited before she asked, "Did you go see him?" she didn't know.

"Can't. They transported him."

"You could have gone to town…" She reached to touch Chad's knee, but he stiffened again. Her fingers dropped centimeters from their target.

"He's in Manchester."

Willow hadn't heard anyone mention Manchester before. "Where's that?"

"Two hours north. They have an excellent burn unit there. The clinic transfers everything but first degree either to Rockland or Manchester." His eyes rose to meet hers. "Manchester gets the worst cases."

Her throat tightened. "Oh, Chad…"

"He's so little. Joe said—" Chad frowned. "And Aiden was on a bike today—with Logan."

"Helmet?" Why she asked, she didn't know. Aiden had been wearing a helmet. Of that, she was certain.

"Yeah. It just seemed to—oh, lass…"

Seemed to be the death of childhood innocence—that confidence Aiden always had that he was invincible. After his little brother was hurt, it would be gone.

"I know…"

"How will they pay for this? I sent money, by the way. They have a PayPal account set up, so I sent a couple hundred dollars."

"What's PayPal?" Willow scooted next to him and leaned her head against his chest.

"A way to email people money."

"But two hundred dollars isn't going to pay for them letting him enter the clinic. I've seen how fast bills add up. My leg, your hand, the babies…" Willow shook her head. "We've got the money to pay it, don't we? We need to do that, Chad. I can call Bill; he can set it up with the hos—"

Chad's arms pulled her closer, squeezing her much as he had Kari. "We can't do that, lass. The money would be gone in no time, and then what would we do if something happened to one of our kids? We can help," he added as she began to protest, "and we'll do whatever we can, but we can't cover everything all by ourselves. We just can't."

"I could ask my grandmother—"

"They don't have anything, Willow. They spent it all trying—"

"No," Willow argued, jumping to her feet. She offered Chad her hand before tugging him toward the house. "I mean my *other* grandmother. Maybe they can do something decent with their money for once—or she can anyway."

"I don't think she has access to it. You can't profit from your crimes. The money that should have been hers is probably tied up in court with other relatives now."

"Then we'll give them what Steve gave us. It'll be a start," Willow insisted. "We'll still have the interest, your salary, whatever money the farm makes. Becca can expand again if she—"

"How about we wait and see what the need is before you try to save the world—"

Willow shook her head. "I can't and I know it, but I can help the Coxes!"

"Okay," Chad said, starting over. "I'll talk to Keith Homstad—let him know that we're prepared to help as much as we can. Is that a decent compromise?"

"Keith is..."

"Kelly's dad." When a light bulb didn't switch on in Willow's eyes, Chad added, "The guy who taught the boys to say, 'Mr. Homstad is brilliant and handsome, too?'"

"Gotcha. Yeah. Talk to him. I like him."

Chad gave her an odd look. "Because he goofs off with the boys?"

Willow shook her head. "No... because he'll agree with me. He's intelligent."

"I don't even want to know what that says about your opinion of my intelligence," Chad groaned.

7:36 p.m.

A busy Saturday morning prevented Claire from checking Facebook until late that evening. Ice slowly melted in her glass of water as she scrolled through dozens—maybe hundreds—of well-wishes and prayers for the Cox family. Friends and neighbors—strangers. The town had already rallied in support. "Beautiful."

"What's that?" James Rhodes paused as he walked past.

"The way this town is just going all out to support the Coxes. The prayers—"

James rerouted himself to the couch. "Any updates?"

"Let's see... hard to find among all the other posts, but here. It says, 'Nathan has been doing great! He's getting spoiled by all the nurses. They've brought him tons of toys to play with, and they're having firefighter come and visit him this afternoon.' That sounds good, doesn't it?"

"Sounds better than 'He should be dead.'"

"True—oh, here's another. 'Nathan (and his parents) got to video chat with his brother, Aiden, this afternoon, which seems to have boosted his spirits. All he wanted to do was show off his new toys. I think he's in a good mood. —Breanne.'"

"Still better," James agreed. "Is that all?"

"Not sure..." Claire leaned against her husband's shoulder and closed her eyes. "How will they pay for all this? They don't have insurance anymore. That part-time thing he's been doing keeps them fed, but..."

"I don't know. Maybe the PayPal thing will help."

"Well, sure it will help, but a few hundred dollars here or there keeps them in groceries or gas for doctor visits, but they have a mortgage and they're racking up thousands upon thousands of dollars every day. Every surgery—everything." She sat up and scrolled some more. "Oh, look."

James and Claire read the next update, their hearts choking them.

```
Quick Update—looks like Nathan will need to stay
here for at least a week. He has two surgeries
scheduled so far. They'll need to see how the first
goes before they decide if they need to do any more.
They've said from the moment we arrived that they
(the hospital) would be like family for a lot of
years, as Nathan will need continued care long after
he goes home. Thank you all for your love and
```

prayers. Every one is such a blessing!

Just as Claire started to speak, a new post loaded. James and Claire read it, laughing.

Me: "How does your balloon float?"
Nathan: "God created it to float. He created all balloons to float."

Too cute!

"Doesn't that just sound like him," James murmured as he dragged himself off the couch. "Gotta water the backyard plants. That kid is something else."

8:04 p.m.

In the dim light of his living room, Ross Davies sat with an abandoned glass of wine beside him. The dishwasher sent gurgling noises through the house, making him wonder, yet again, if they'd be buying a new one soon. His wife Denise paused in the doorway, purse in hand and ready to take off for work. "Everything okay?"

He glanced up and forced a smile. "Rough day—kid electrocuted last night."

Compassion filled Denise's eyes as she crossed the room and knelt beside him. "I'm sorry. Is he—she—going to be okay?"

Ross shook his head. "Is anyone who gets whipped by a power line ever really 'okay' even if they do survive? This kid's got years of surgeries ahead of him. I don't think the parents even get it. They spent half the time we talked reassuring me that they didn't blame the company. 'It was an accident.'" Ross closed his eyes. "I'll never forget that father's voice. 'It was my fault. I should have seen it.'"

"Seen what? Oh, the power line?" Denise pressed the palm of her hand against his cheek and turned his head to face her. "Ross, it's not your fault."

"I know. It's not anyone's 'fault.' It just happened."
"What happened?"
"From what I can piece together," he began in a review of his

notes and observations from the day, "a raven hit the power line and blew the transformer. At that point, the power line fell. At the service station, the computers detected the line disturbance and shut off the power, but when nothing else came, the computer switched it back on." His wife's sharp intake of breath told him she knew what had happened. "Yeah. The line wasn't at full power yet by the time the boy stepped—fell—I'm not sure which—on it. If it had been, he'd be dead."

"Why didn't it stay off?"

Ross clicked into work mode as he explained the process. "It's just the protocol. Any disturbance to the line gets it shut off. If nothing else affects it, it comes back on because that could have been a bird, a tree branch, the wind whipping it just right. If they shut off and kept it off every time it happened until someone came out to check it to be sure, people would be without power for hours several times a week. It's usually just something benign. When a down occurs, it usually shows up differently."

"Major lawsuit coming, isn't there?"

"Yeah. They have no insurance. I can't imagine that they won't sue—they'll have to in order to pay for the bills, but they seemed adamant against the idea—kept saying they weren't blaming anyone."

"It's easy to say that before you get that first envelope demanding every penny you've made for the last year or two—and then realizing it's only the first of many for one hospital stay," Denise mused. "No one would blame them for trying to get their bills paid."

"Right—it's just that kid. He's so little—only three."

The pain in Denise's eyes told Ross she now understood his pain. "Steven's age." Her eyes slid toward the bedroom where their small son slept in comfort and safety—slept without pain killers and machines waking him every few minutes, without bandages covering what should be smooth skin over growing, active legs.

A glance at the DVD player told him she'd be late. "Better get to work. Walmart would fall apart without you overseeing the night shift."

"You going to be okay?"

Ross shrugged. "I'll have to be, won't I? And then again—"

"What?"

"Well, it's easy for me to say that—to feel that. But my 'I'll have to be' is so much easier than theirs. I have to live with knowing about it. They have to live *with* it."

Once Denise pulled from the driveway and rolled down the street, Ross shoved himself up from the chair and grabbed his glass. The fruity aroma of the liquid gave away his lack of interest. "Too young. Should have known better than to try it," he muttered as he poured the liquid down the sink and rinsed the glass.

His eyes slid toward the hall, but he turned away and stepped out into the back yard to feed the dog instead. Sitting on the back steps, he tried to ignore the tug his son's room had on him. After a minute or two, the dog chose dinner over a few absent scratches behind the ear and left him alone.

Ross stood and returned to the kitchen. A pile of bills waited by the phone. He flipped through them in a worthless gesture. His eyes remained riveted on the darkened hallway. Despite every effort to avoid it, Ross found himself shuffling down the hall to their son's door. He peered into the room and watched as the starry night light sent wavering shadows across his son's face. *Man, how can they stand it? How do parents deal with this stuff? They were so nice, too—didn't demand to know what we were going to do about it. Actually, they didn't seem to think we* **should.** *I'd be demanding a settlement ASAP.*

Ross crossed the room and laid his hand on his son's back—just as he had when the boy was an infant and needed comforting in the middle of the night. Steven, though asleep, relaxed even further at Ross' touch. *Nathan Cox won't relax like that for months.* Heart breaking for a child he'd only seen once, Ross crawled into bed beside his son and wrapped his arm around the boy. In his mind, he saw Nathan's brown eyes staring up at him. *Strange how kids think. Instead of talking about his owies, the kid tells about a bird.*

DAY THREE

Sunday, June 7, 11:04 a.m.

All around the Rockland loop, Christians gathered in churches. In Brandt's Corners, Marcus Vaughn sat in his usual seat, praying as the opening song slowly finished. A few stray amens warmed his heart, but it chilled as William Markenson stepped up to read the announcements. "Good Morning—or it is for most of us. Before I read the rest of the announcements, I wanted to share one that people here might not be aware of."

A murmur rippled over the room. Marcus heard it, but his eyes stayed riveted on William. *It's got to be big if William is deviating from a prescribed list.*

"Friday night, a small boy was electrocuted in Fairbury. He's been transferred to Manchester with third degree burns. Now, the Cox family doesn't have health insurance. There's been a Facebook page set up so people can read updates on little Nathan's condition, and there's a link to a website where you can donate if you'd like. But more than anything—"

An uncharacteristic moment of repressed emotion choked William. Marcus, lost in prayer and concern for the Cox family, almost missed it. *Lord, take a cop or a fireman—the toughest one around—and show him a child injured or emotionally scarred by something and they fall to pieces. It never ceases to amaze me.*

As William read off the rest of the announcements, Marcus stole a glance over the congregation. Mac squeezed his son tighter than usual. Aggie and Luke exchanged pained glances. Mrs. Dyke sat with head bowed, already praying for the little guy. *She'll bake cookies and con William into getting them to the kid—even if it means he has to drive them himself.* And in the row behind Aggie's family, in the corner, one young woman sat, eyes riveted on William, as if bolstering him with her mind. Tina Warden cocked her head ever so slightly. William faltered as he reminded the congregation about the Wednesday night singing the following week. And Tina smiled.

We've got a good family here, Lord. Thank you, Marcus prayed as he prepared for the next song.

11:07 a.m.

Gerry Arnett stood at the pulpit at The Assembly in Brunswick. His eyes rested on his wife—his son. Jason had been three once. *Yesterday—or maybe the day before. Certainly not nineteen years ago.* "We're going to do something a little different today. I had my topic planned and my notes written." Gerry waved them. "Just in case you all think I'm schluffing off."

The room must have sensed something had happened to

interrupt their usual service. He saw in several faces that some knew what. "For those who hadn't yet heard, Friday night, a freak accident in Fairbury left a three-year-old burned by a downed power line." A gasp went up around the room. Nolan Burke's arm tightened around his wife's shoulder. Christine Dawson sat up a bit straighter and glanced at the man beside her. Gerry sighed. "The boy's name is Nathan Cox. His parents are Kelly and Jon Cox, and they have two other children as well. They also do not have insurance. I've already had a few people ask me if I know if there is some way to donate to the Cox family, and there is. We'll, of course, forward any donations left with us for them, but there is also a PayPal account set up to receive funds as well."

Heads nodded and pens scratched. *Good. It's amazing how good people feel when they know they can* do *something.* "So what we're going to do is pray, read comforting Scripture, and sing this morning. This is a time of praise for the Lord sparing Nathan's life. From what I've read, the medical establishment all agree that Nathan should be dead." A second gasp rose in collective astonishment. "This is also a time of prayer—whether through supplication, song, or Scripture— that the Lord would comfort the Cox family and provide for their needs. Now, let's ask John to lead us in a song before we start praying."

11:08 a.m.

The eclectic collection of congregants at the Rockland Mission all sat in their metal folding chairs and listened to the morning's scripture passage. As the reader stepped down, Barney stood and carried his Bible to the front of the room, but a man beckoned to him. *What does Matt want that can't wait?* He listened, concern filling his face. "Why isn't it in the paper? That's big news!"

"Not sure. But, I thought you should know."

Barney nodded, thanked his friend, and returned to the front of the room where he stepped on the low risers. "Okay, well, I had planned to continue our discussion of the fruits of the Spirit, but Matt just told me about something I'd like to pray about first…"

As he told the little information he had, Barney looked out over the room. Business professionals sat next to people he knew sold drugs on weekends. The mission's biggest contributor—an elderly woman who looked more suited for a southern garden party than an inner city mission—sat two seats down from a man whom Barney knew had spent time in prison. For rape. Faces faded out of focus as he prepared to pray, but a strange thing happened once he opened his eyes again and said, "Amen."

Faces became clear. The former rapist had tears in his eyes as he dug through his pockets and pulled out a couple of dollars. He passed it to the woman, and Barney thought the man said, "For the kid—can you get it to him?"

All over the room, similar things happened. Homeless men and women who usually only came to Sunday services to get out of the heat or the cold fumbled for the little bit of change they had and passed it down to those sitting on the center aisle. Barney, choking back emotion, nodded to an Indian man in the back. "Looks like we've got an impromptu offering going on here. I think I'd like to read a couple of verses while you and Matt collect that."

Barney flipped through his Bible, debating between Mark and Luke, and finally let it stay open in Mark. "Mark chapter twelve, verses forty-one through forty-four. 'And He sat down opposite the treasury, and *began* observing how the people were putting money into the treasury; and many rich people were putting in large sums. A poor widow came and put in two small copper coins, which amount to a cent. Calling His disciples to Him, He said to them, 'Truly I say to you, this poor widow put in more than all the contributors to the treasury; for they all put in out of their surplus, but she, out of her poverty put in all she owned, all she had to live on.'"

11:11 a.m.

His voice choked with emotion, Vince Lanzo of Westbury Community Church tried again—tried and failed. Shaking his head, he beckoned for one of his elders to come forward. He whispered a few words, wiping tears from eyes with the back of his hand, and pointed to his wife. A minute later, David Weeks stepped up to the pulpit, a pained smile on his face. "Well, this is awkward. Our tenderhearted brother is so moved by what I have to tell you that he can't get the words out, but I'm chuckling because it's just so *him*. I love this about him. I think we all see a bit of Jesus' care and compassion for His bride when we see Vince 'weeping with those who weep.'"

A few "amens" echoed around the room before David continued. "I'm sure some of you have already heard about this, but Vince received news from the Tesdall family about a little boy in Fairbury…"

11:59 a.m.

The Church at Marshfield rustled in their seats as the sermon ended. Dan Shatternmann sank into his seat as Ron Senior rose, moved to the front of the building, and began the week's announcements before the closing hymn. His heart constricted at the news of the accident in Fairbury, immediately praying for the boy, his family, and the medical team entrusted with his care. As Ron recounted the words of the paramedics, "He should be dead," praise flowed from his heart to the Lord. As he heard where they'd transferred Nathan for care, his eyes slid across the aisle to where his wife sat. Her head turned and her eyes clung to his. In that moment, he knew they'd be making the journey to Manchester that coming week. *We'll probably have to stop and grab a fire truck on the way too, won't we, Lord? Man, I love that woman.*

12:06 p.m.

"So, we've decided to meet here half an hour early tonight to pray for the Cox family. Everyone is welcome, but we do ask that you try to keep children quiet during this time of prayer. We know that's not always easy—" James Whyte's infant son let out a wail as if to provide comic relief. "—as is evidenced by Jared's protest at the idea of being among Hillsdale Christian Assembly's family and not having everyone's attention on him. It'll be character building—either for him or for Jan and me; I'm not sure which." A few weak chuckles told him the congregation understood. "I hope to have a little more news tonight. For those who can't make it, please be in prayer tomorrow morning. I understand that's when they plan to do the first surgery to remove dead skin and tissue. Let's close in prayer…"

12:09 p.m.

The First Church of Fairbury was unusually subdued that Sunday morning. They'd prayed for the Cox family—twice. A note passed to him from one of the ushers told him that several envelopes had been dropped in it marked "Cox Family." He'd chosen a selection of Scripture passages that showed the Lord's provision for children all throughout the Bible. It had meant he went over his sermon time, but no one seemed to mind. For the first time in all his years as a minister, Tom Allen didn't see one hand pull up a sleeve as the wearer glanced at a watch. Not one head turned to glance at the clock in the back, and not a single person—not even the teenagers in the back row—had pulled out a phone to check the time on it.

But the faces throughout the room showed the effect one accident had on an entire community. Tom fumbled as he closed his sermon. "You know, I don't know if I'm even making sense this morning. My only consolation is that I don't think anyone here noticed and if you did, I doubt you mind. We're all a bit shell-shocked. I understand this and sympathize. Trust me; I've spent enough time of my own in prayer, asking the Lord why. But I'm going to go out on a limb and tell you why I think this happened."

The lazy, half-interested faces shifted. Eyes widened. Shoulders squared. Women pulled small children onto their laps and men squeezed the shoulders of elementary-aged kids who had gotten a little restless. The congregation waited—looking for the kind of encouragement that Tom feared he couldn't give. *Lord, help me out here. If I'm wrong, either stop me now or give me the humility to admit it when I know—but stopping now is preferable.*

"I believe that God allowed this to happen to glorify Him. Those are some pretty harsh-sounding words, but look at Job. Righteous man. He lost his house, his possessions, his servants, and *all of his children*. Why? Because Satan had something to prove—and God was glorified. Even in the pain and misery of it all, God was glorified."

1:29 p.m.

"*Look, I don't know how, this will bring God glory—only He does. I just know that somehow it will. Even if it's because the Cox family stands firm in their faith through it all, or because we all pull together to help them stand strong.*" Tom Allen's words tumbled through Karyn

Bryant's mind as she puttered around her house. Inexplicable restlessness made it impossible for her to settle. She washed the lunch dishes and loaded them in the dishwasher before she realized that they were already clean. Her son strolled in with his dirty plate and turned to go.

"Gonna go get that new game from Walmart," he muttered as he pulled on his shoes. "Need anything?"

Out of habit, Karyn almost said no. But an idea struck her in full force, setting new wheels in motion. "Yeah, actually. I need a Starbucks gift card."

"I thought you liked The Grind better?"

"I do. It's for Kelly. I know how much she likes their iced stuff, and I can reload it online any time I see it getting low."

Todd grinned and gave her a quick hug. "You're the best. I'll bring one back. How much on it?"

"Get fifty. She shouldn't have to worry about running out if she needs one every day while she's there."

He froze at the door and turned. "You think she'll be there for ten days?"

As a nurse, Karyn knew all too well just how long burn victims could spend in hospitals. "I've never worked a burn unit, but I'm pretty sure it'll be a long process. Ten might be conservative."

"The Facebook page talked like just a few days."

"Either they aren't sharing everything," Karyn insisted, "or they haven't been told everything yet—maybe not until they do the first surgery. I mean," she added at the sight of Todd's impending protest. *He's sooo...readable!* "I don't think they're *keeping* anything from them. They told them that they'd all 'become like family.' I just think they may not be stressing the length of stay until they have a better feel for how deep the damage is. It still hasn't been forty-eight hours. The damage can continue that long."

"I guess. Still, you'd think they could at least warn them."

Karyn sighed. "I think they're probably doing what is best, and that probably means that the Coxes understand a lot more than they may even realize. We just don't know yet. Now go get your game. I'm going to run down to the shop."

A snicker escaped and Todd didn't even try to hide it. "Something for Nathan? A book about firemen perhaps?"

"I was thinking that and some cute pajamas too. Maybe

something for Anna. Who knows if they brought enough for her too? People did their packing, I presume. If they don't know how messy babies get—"

"And they're at a hospital. It's not like there's a washer and dryer," Todd suggested with a smirk around his lips.

"Oh, go away. I'll give 'em what I want to. You don't have to mock me."

"I'd nev—okay. Bye!"

"Don't forget my card!" Karyn called as the door slammed shut behind him. "And learn to shut the door without rattling the house!"

Karyn grabbed her purse, dug out her keys, and slung the purse over her shoulders. She hesitated. *Would Dale want to come? Should I ask?* She sauntered down the hall where her husband should have been enjoying his Sunday afternoon nap, and found him snoring. *Guess that answers that question.*

She stopped at Bookends first. There the problems began. *I thought I'd have trouble finding something. Ha. Limiting choices is harder. Maybe this book...* From books and DVDs to keep Nathan's attention occupied and off his painful legs, Karyn "shopped" from her shelves until she had a pile more than twice the size of any reasonable one. Indecision plagued her until she grabbed a shopping bag and began piling things in it.

Three books, four DVDs, and a toy train later, Karyn left the store, a pile of rejects left on the counter for Todd to put away the next day. *I can always send some of that stuff later if they stay longer than expected,* she consoled herself.

At their boutique clothing store, Karyn pulled out two pairs of pajamas and a few fun pairs of socks. Three outfits for the baby followed as well as a stuffed bear. *Nathan will want something to cuddle, too.*

A mother's journal caught her eye. *Kelly likes journals, but that one's all wrong. I bet there's one at the bookstore, though.* With that thought, she hurried to the door and hesitated. "Cash." Her voice echoed in the empty store, startling her. "They'll need cash. I wonder..."

The register held their usual morning till of a hundred dollars in bills. Hesitating only for a moment, Karyn pulled out her personal checkbook and wrote a check to the store. Cash in hand, she locked the store and hurried back to Bookends. Officer Brad waved.

"Everything okay, Ms. Bryant?"

"All good. Just getting a few things for a friend."

"That's nice."

She glanced back at the officer as he rounded the corner of the square. "Hot out there," she muttered as her key fumbled in the lock. "Especially in those navy uniforms. Could get him a cold soda from the back..."

Once inside, she hurried to a display of journals and chose one with a butterfly. *Kelly loves butterflies. It's perfect.* A display of blank cards by the front register gave her an idea. She pulled one from it and wrote out a quick note. As she shoved the cash in it, her eyes fell on the register. *Why not? They need it more than we do.* Her inner self put up a token fight. *Business is lousy right now.* The truth of the words did little to stop her. She unlocked it, pulled the cash from it, and wrote another personal check to cover it. *Yeah, maybe so, but they still need it more than we do.*

Minutes later, Karyn stepped from the store, a large gift bag swinging from one hand and a cold Coke for Brad in the other. She tossed the bag and her purse in her car and crossed the street just as he reached the corner opposite her. "Thought you could use something a bit refreshing right now. Have a good one."

"Thanks, Ms. Bryant. I appreciate it."

DAY FOUR

Monday, June 8, 11:03 a.m.

Emails flooded Dee's inbox. "Spam, spam, spam, skip, spam..." Her kids chided her constantly about using spam filters, but she'd lost too many legitimate emails to it to bother. "It takes three minutes max to delete them all, and I never miss one I need. That's just worth it to me," she murmured.

Once the spam had been relegated to the trash where it belonged, she scrolled through several prayer requests, several PayPal notices of payment—most of which should have arrived days earlier—and three business offers. "Oh, good."

"What?" Logan looked up from his video game. Aiden's eyes

followed.

"Just got a blog-site to do. Big one, too—nice."

"Cool."

Dee hardly heard him as she read the specs for the job. She hit the reply button, attached three documents to it, and typed out a reply, thanking the motivational speaker for considering her and assuring him that she could easily meet his deadline. *That's just what I needed, Lord. Thanks!*

The next offer left her mind spinning with possibilities—full-time work. *Oh, wow. It could cover medical payments—significant amounts of them. I'd be making more than Jon did* **before** *he lost his job. An entire year's salary going to pay off nothing but medical debt.* She glanced at her youngest child—just thirteen. *Logan still has five or six years of school left. It'd be hard to work full-time and school him and his sisters. I don't know…*

While she mulled that idea, she opened the third one, smiling. Logan must have noticed because he asked, "What?"

Is that the only word he knows? Sheesh! "Just got another one—big one. It'll take a few weeks, but payment is excellent." *Of course, if I accept the permanent position, I can't do it. I won't have time.*

As she pondered the options, Dee hit forward on the job offer and typed in her husband's work email address. Above it she typed,

```
Keith,
What do you think? They gave me a deadline of a week
to accept or reject it. I don't want to make rash
decisions, but this could be the answer to paying
the medical bills. I also got two other jobs today.
One's a seventy-two hour turnover—no biggie. The
other will take a couple of weeks. It's good pay
too—three thousand for that one. That'll help, but I
can't assume I'll make that every month. The steady
income would make setting up payments so easy.
I just keep thinking of Logan, Reagan, and Jamie.
How would I keep school up with them and manage a
full-time job?
Dee
```

While she waited for a reply, Dee clicked over to Facebook to see how Nathan's surgery had gone. *Can't keep avoiding it. If things were* **too** *bad, they would have called—surely.* Still, Dee found it odd that no one had called.

The Facebook page had dozens of new "likes." Half a dozen messages filled the message box, and offers of prayer and help covered the wall. *This town—okay, people elsewhere, too—but this town is amazing. Wow. Car wash, Deli fundraiser, coin cans—people are going all out to help. It's just cool!*

Dee scrolled down to read updates in proper order.

Nathan is about to be prepped for surgery to remove all the dead skin and tissue. We all had a really hard night last night as the poor little guy was in so much pain that all he could do was cry, and all his parents and aunt could do was watch. It was heartbreaking. Your prayers would be so appreciated. Thanks! - Breanne

Bleeping noises, exaggerated crashes, and cries of, "Aw, man!" as the boys competed in their electronic car races tried to register, but Dee forced them back and stared at the screen. *I knew there was dead tissue—in my head. It just takes on a new level of "real" to see it actually happening.* Taking a deep, steadying breath, Dee she scrolled up to the next one.

They haven't gone into surgery yet. He's been the OR for a while now, but the nurses have said any minute. Daddy is with him as only one parent was allowed in the room. We are looking at, at least two more hours of wait before we know anything. —Kelly

Dee glanced at the time. Three hours earlier. Surely... her index finger jabbed at the up arrow key until the next update showed.

They just brought Nathan back. He is still out of it (thankfully). Hubby went to get breakfast... now we're just in the waiting mode. Emotionally, we are all stable. This is all we can update right now. — Kelly

What "waiting mode" meant, she didn't know, but Dee suspected Kelly meant waiting to hear what the doctors discovered. *Good news, Lord. We could use some good news.*

Dee's email chimed. She glanced at the sender. Keith. Taking a deep breath, she clicked on it, praying that his answer was one of those rare, put-his-foot-down, moments where she didn't have to make the final decision. She read the five word message, confused. *"Pretend they're a drug dealer?"* Understanding dawned and she laughed. "Just say no. I love it. It's so him."

1:21 p.m.

Kelly watched her son as he rallied after his surgery. Nathan laughed, made goofy faces, and regaled them with incomprehensible stories of firemen and the men from the movie, 'Courageous.' "I watch 'Courageous'? Can I?"

"Maybe in a little while if Aunt Breanne doesn't need her laptop," Kelly promised. She glanced at the other side of the room where Jon slept. "But we can't play it too loud. Daddy's resting."

In his trademarked, happy-go-lucky sing-song, Nathan chanted about watching his favorite movie until Breanne brought him the laptop and connected it to their online movie account. "I like 'Courageous,'" Nathan insisted. "It's funny. I want to watch the police car."

With a heart swelling with gratitude, Kelly rested in the chair, nursing the baby and eying the roll left on Nathan's plate. *That looks sooo good. It wouldn't be too much for her if I just ate a bite or two, would it?* She glanced over at Breanne. "What do you think? Can Anna take it if I eat a couple of bites of his roll? I'm still starving."

"I could go down and get something else if you like." Breanne shifted as if ready to spring to her feet.

Guilt hit Kelly in the gut. *She hasn't been able to get any real rest since we've been here. Just try it. How bad could it be?* "I think I want to test it. It's probably fine now."

"If you're sure..."

Kelly nodded. "Yeah, it was probably just postpartum hormones or something weird combining with an immature digestive system."

Jon's better, though. It made a difference in him, too—avoiding the gluten. Why? The doctor never said anything about avoiding it for Chronic Fatigue, but he has been better. Her thoughts were interrupted by the nurse's arrival.

"Time to soak the bandages," Allison whispered.

The words filled her heart with dread. Nathan hated the seemingly constant moistening of the bandages. Jon moved to Nathan's side in preparation for the process, proving that his nap hadn't been an effective one. "Let's move the stuff off the end of the bed for Miss Allison, okay?"

Nathan nodded, smiling at his favorite nurse, but his expression changed as he realized what came next. "Noooo…"

"Shh…" Jon murmured, stroking his boy's head. "It's going to be okay. We just have to do what will make you get better."

Jon's gentle tones rose and fell as he tried to calm his son's rising panic. Nathan protested, crying, begging, wailing for relief. Monitors beeped and alarms sounded as the boy's movements set off one after another. When he still couldn't be calmed five minutes later, Allison returned to give him morphine.

"That makes me happy."

"What?" *How can it possibly make you happy to have to give a child drugs? I don't get it.*

"He smiled again when I came in. He hasn't given up. That's the big thing—that he doesn't give up emotionally."

3:19 p.m.

A woman wearing a hospital badge—one that Kelly couldn't read—knocked on the door. "Hello, I'm Christine. I just stopped in to see how you're doing…"

Jon and Kelly exchanged glances. As he introduced them, Jon stepped forward to offer his hand while Kelly fidgeted with the hem of her shirt. *So this is the social worker that Allison mentioned. Why do we need a social worker? We didn't do anything wrong! It was just an accident.*

"—job is to make sure that you are taken care of physically and emotionally. I understand you don't have insurance?"

Seriously? This is about insurance? Kelly wanted to scream. *With the unemployment rate rising every quarter, you're surprised? So help me if this becomes about our inability to provide adequate care—*

"No we don't." Jon's calm, confident tones soothed Kelly's spirit. "Is that a problem? We've already spoken to the financial office—"

"Oh, no. We just want to ensure you have everything you need—you know, access to programs and such."

The conversation rambled. Kelly had trouble following what all they discussed. One minute they were talking about life in Fairbury and the next she found herself sharing all the overwhelming support they'd already received. Jon mentioned their financial arrangements, and Christine asked about physical therapy and if they needed counseling to deal with the trauma of it. Somewhere in the middle of the informational maze, Christine discovered their income for the year and her eyes widened. "Whoa. You qualify for quite a lot more than I imagined—such as everything available. How are your assets? House, car, bank accounts?"

At that moment, everything changed. What had been a gentle ramble through topics became a very focused financial assistance consultation. The final verdict astounded Kelly. "Get rid of it—all. Get rid of that savings. It'll kill your opportunities."

"What?" Jon stared at his hands. "You're telling us that we need to get financial assistance and the way to do that is to take the money we've worked hard for and saved and 'get rid of it?'"

"Look," Christine said, lowering her voice, "I can't tell you exactly what to do with it. I can only say that having that much money in the bank will end up penalizing you for being wise with your money. Surely you have family members who might need a... temporary loan."

Kelly sat, jaw agape, her eyes bouncing back and forth between her husband and the well-meaning woman before them. *Seriously? This is how our "system" is run? They decide that people who don't squander their money are simply not needy? No wonder people on welfare are considered to be bad stewards. They're penalized if they don't. So they can slowly save a few thousand dollars and work to get themselves out, or they can follow the guidelines and have expensive TVs and take trips because those don't count as "assets" that make them ineligible. Crazy!*

"We're not interested in that kind of assistance," Jon said, choosing each word carefully in his characteristic way. "But we'll remember that."

Christine stood and reached into her pocket. She pulled out a stack of what looked like business cards and handed them to Kelly. "Meal cards. As good as cash down in the cafeteria. I can at least help with that. If you run out, just let me know. I'll get you more." She shook hands with both of them, holding Kelly's for just an extra minute, but her eyes were on Jon. "If either of you need to talk—about the accident, how you'll manage, what's coming, anything—I'm on the first floor. Just ask for me at the information desk."

Breanne, looked up from the corner of the room—forgotten by all as they talked. "That was weird."

"I've always thought of social workers as people who come out when kids are abused or neglected—the enemy of decent, law abiding parents. I never thought of hospitals as having them. She was nice."

"A little overeager to sign us up for government assistance," Jon mused. "But well-meaning."

Breanne hopped up and came to stare at the stack of meal cards before plucking one from the top. "I'm going to go get something to eat. I missed lunch. Anyone want anything?"

6:14 p.m.

They sat across from one another, plates of food growing cold as they read the pages of printed advice. Some suggested; others almost demanded, but the conclusion on nearly every front, by every person they trusted and by a few they didn't remained the same. "Get a lawyer."

"I don't want to sue anyone," Kelly insisted. "I don't understand why we'd need one if we weren't going to sue."

"Right here," Jon said as he passed a page printed from the message board. "This family didn't 'need' one, and decisions for their own child were taken out of their hands. We can't risk that."

"I don't see how that can happen, though."

Jon shrugged. "It shouldn't be *able* to, but that doesn't mean it can't and won't. Then again," he added, "at what point does all the 'protecting yourself' stuff move into the lack of faith category?"

"Mom thinks the electric company is responsible for the accident."

"It was just that. An accident."

"Right," Kelly said. "She says that while it couldn't have been prevented, it is still their equipment and that puts the responsibility on them."

"She doesn't want us to sue…" Jon stared at his wife, shocked.

"No! Mom? Sue? No way. She's totally against that kind of thing." Kelly picked at her chicken. "She said that they might force it, though."

"Force a suit? How can they?"

"She was talking about that thing with Alice on the board— where her son ended up in a lawsuit even though they didn't want it." She chewed a bite, took a swig of her water, and sighed. "I wish they *would* just offer to pay his medical bills. It would make everything so much easier. We can't pay for this stuff, Jon. We don't have it—we'll *never* have this kind of money."

"I know. It seems like they should, but I can see why they wouldn't. I mean, if they did, it would be like admitting fault and open themselves up to a massive multi-million dollar lawsuit."

"But we *wouldn't!*" A few glances in their direction made Kelly wince and drop her voice. "How could we? We're just not—"

"They just don't know that. Even if we signed a paper releasing them of all liability, they still couldn't do it."

Her eyes widened and Kelly shook her head as she sawed at her now rubbery chicken. "Why on earth not?"

"That stuff doesn't hold up in court anymore. People sign all kinds of things that say they won't sue and then turn right around and do it—and win."

"That makes me *really* not want to get a lawyer. I don't want anything to do with that stuff."

"Trust me, I don't want one." Weariness coated every word. "I just don't know how wise it is not to have one."

"How would we even pay for one? We can't pay the bills we have now."

Those words cut Jon—visibly aged him with the faint breath it took to speak them. "I don't know," he whispered.

6:53 p.m.

Laughter filled the Rhodes kitchen as someone made a joke. In the living room, one man tuned a guitar, and another hummed a bar of music before asking a question. Claire listened to it all, grateful for a house full of friends and family who love the Lord.

James passed and she grabbed his arm. "We should pray for

Nathan first."

"We'll do that. Still waiting on Steve."

As if his cue, Steve knocked and opened the door. "Everyone here?"

Booming laughter from the other room cut off Steve's reply, but he waved at Claire and hurried to join the group. Cup in hand, Claire followed the rest of the group into the other room and waited, her heart praying and her hands itching to do more. James gave her a smile before he spoke. "Hey, I don't know how many of you know about what happened the other night—" His eyes roamed the room and Claire's followed. Some faces fell instantly while others grew confused—concerned. James went on to explain the accident and gave an update of the day's happenings. "He's doing good so far—came out of the first surgery still full of energy. Breanne said he was being a bit of a goofball even."

A group chuckle broke the otherwise pained silence. "So, we thought it might be a good time to start with prayer for them. There are so many needs—medical, spiritual, financial, emotional. It's just overwhelming."

One man in the corner of the room spoke up. "He had surgery today? For a burn?"

Claire stepped in and shared all she'd learned on her Internet research regarding the process of cleaning out all the dead tissue. "It's just a lot for such a little guy."

What began as a simple, audible prayer for strength and healing became a desperate appeal of a dozen hearts unified in spirit for the entire Cox and Homstad families. Silence wrapped the room in a warm cocoon of fellowship, leaving everyone still lost in their private moments of prayer long after James finished with "Amen."

At last Joy Rhodes, seated at the front of the room, asked the question burning in Claire's heart. "What can we *do*? How can we help? I don't even know how to pray. Did you notice that?" she continued as those around her nodded in agreement. "None of us knew what to pray *for.*"

"I know how you feel." Claire listened to a few others who expressed similar concerns before she added, "I just know that the best we can do is stay out of the way and pray—even though we really don't know what to pray *for.* I don't know about you all, but I don't even have enough information to know which way to direct my prayers."

"So we just pray anyway?" Joy pressed.

James' low, deep, rumbling voice answered their daughter before Claire could. "'In the same way the Spirit also helps our weakness; for we do not know how to pray as we should, but the Spirit Himself intercedes for us with groanings too deep for words.'"

Nods and murmurs of agreement echoed throughout the room. Claire smiled as she added her own nod of agreement. "That's right. That's exactly what I was thinking. All I know to do is offer my home and services if needed, but I'm not the kind of person who pushes."

Another woman nodded her own agreement. "Right. I do that too. The offer is there, but I won't get in the way of anyone who is already overwhelmed."

Claire listened, nodding. "Exactly. I feel totally useless. I've just spent the day keeping up on the latest news and praying—for what, I don't even know."

Steve, seated near Claire, gently strummed random chords that slowly morphed into the tune they'd been practicing for weeks. Joy, making her way to the piano, began singing on the second line. Her fingers picked up the melody by the fourth, and several other voices joined until the house swelled in song. Claire listened, taking her time before joining in with the rest of the group. *This is good, Lord. What you've given us—it's good.*

7:38 p.m.

Dee read the latest Facebook status, clicked open a new tab, and logged onto her message board. She read the most recent prayers before clicking the "modify" button and adding the latest update.

```
**UPDATE 9**
He had a much better afternoon than anticipated. We
are all so thankful. He had to get morphine at one
point, but we're back to Tylenol for the most part.
At this point, we're in "time will tell" mode.

They have to keep the bandages moist, and that is
something Nathan really does not like. He gets very
```

upset by it. The one nurse explained that it's important that he not give up emotionally... basically getting to the point that the sight of a nurse will make him cry and whatnot. He goes up and down a lot emotionally, but he is, overall, doing very well. We are just so thankful.

The surreality of copying and pasting that message hit home once more. Each update, each setback, each milestone—everything into one thought. *This can't possibly be happening. It's too unreal.*

Drew burst through the door, with Jamie hot on his heels. "Hey! Any news?"

"He had a good day after surgery. Sounds like he was pretty high on drugs," Dee said. *Why add the part about the bandages? They'll read it soon enough.*

9:54 p.m.

She'd avoided it all day, but as she checked the message board, several posts asking for updates prompted her to set aside her work on the website and share the latest update. *What can I say, Lord? I mean, really. What can I say? The kid hurts, he breaks our hearts, and the first of what sounds like many surgeries is over. How do I share that without sounding unconcerned or melodramatic. There is no "happy medium." There's nothing happy about any of it.* Her conscience pricked her spirit and forced her to amend that thought. *Okay. He's alive. He'll survive this. Everything **will** be okay. That is happy news. **That** is the happy medium.*

With those thoughts to buoy her up, she hit the modify button once more and then hesitated again. *But it's not really an update.* Instead, she scrolled through the main forum, looking for a thread with a title that would likely garner the most notice. The words, "How are Kelly and family REALLY doing?" caught her attention and she opened it.

Several failed attempts prompted her to close out and set the laptop aside. She brushed her teeth, washed her face, and turned out the lights as she made her way through the house to her bedroom. Keith's snores stopped her at the door. *If I can hear him over the fan already—* She forced herself to close the door behind her and fumble through the room to her side of the bed. She crawled in and kicked him.

Five, four, three, two— Keith rolled over. Snores ceased. Dee closed her eyes and tried to relax. She failed. She attempted every "fall-asleep-technique" she could remember. They failed. The clock taunted her with each minute that passed—at a pace that made snails look like NASCAR racers. Still, sleep refused to come.

It's what you get for trying to go to bed at a normal hour. Your body doesn't know what to do with it. Just go finish the website. Forget the update. You can do that tomorrow. Another glance at the clock said **10:12**. *Yep. Get up while you still have your sanity.*

Lights flicked on again as she made her way back to the living room and settled in "Keith's" chair. Thanks to necessary "updates," the laptop took an extra ten minutes to download them, install them, and restart again. "Can't even get back to work without a delay," Dee muttered as she shoved it aside and shuffled into the kitchen for a glass of water and a bowl of watermelon cubes.

Five minutes into the website's stylesheets, Dee gave up and opened a new browser tab. She navigated through her website, to the abandoned thread, and opened it. Without second-guessing herself, she wrote.

```
**UPDATE 10**
Nathan is doing okay. When the pain meds wear off,
he cries and all they want to do is cry with him. As
Breanne said, "It's super hard." She says he was
talkative today, which is great, because he hardly
said anything yesterday.
In surgery, the doctors were able to clean out all
of the dead skin and tissue, and they want to do
another surgery on Wednesday or Friday... we'll see.
```

Dee hesitated again, hating herself for the uncharacteristic indecision that seemed to have overtaken her. *Just how much is too much? How much gives an accurate picture without just playing on people's emotions?* Determined to get the unpleasant task over and back to work on the website, she typed the final words of the day's update.

Breanne said that he was "back to his goofball self for a while today." We'll take "a while." It's better than not at all.

DAY FIVE

Tuesday, June 9, 5:09 a.m.

Kelly felt Anna stir and struggled from the fog of semi-consciousness. *Get up now or she'll wake everyone.* She grabbed the diaper bag and laptop and crept from the room. The night nurse, Liz, smiled. "Restless?"

She nodded. "Yeah. After the night he had, I don't want the baby to wake him."

"He's almost due for another dose of Tylenol. I'll probably do that in about thirty minutes."

Through the doors, down the hall, into the elevator, and onto the first floor—the hospital hadn't yet come alive with the bustle of the morning routines. Kelly changed the baby in the bathroom, washed them both up a bit, and then settled herself into one of the lobby chairs. As Anna nursed, Kelly opened the laptop and scrolled through her email subjects. *Nothing of vital importance yet.*

Her mom's message board was flooded with prayers, offers of help, and requests for more information. A gift consultant offered an online "party" with all profits going directly to the Cox family. Kelly choked as she read the lists of people buying to help. Statements such as, "*I was going to get this for my sister for Christmas, so I'll buy it now to help Nathan*" and "*I've always wanted to try their lotion—what better time to start than now?*" filled post after post.

Kelly took a moment to type a one-handed response of gratitude, finishing just in time. Anna pulled away, belched, and began rooting again, anxious to continue her early morning snack. Unwilling even to try to type with her left hand only, Kelly surfed the web, reading blogs, news reports, message boards, and Facebook.

The well-wishes on Facebook never ceased. Each time she had a moment to read, she found a dozen new "likes" and even more posts from friends and strangers who cared about a little boy in a

Manchester hospital. People asked questions and offered suggestions, but the posts that brought the most guilt and anxiety were offers of fundraisers. It seemed as if every perusal of the "Help Nathan and Family" page brought a dozen new suggestions. Spaghetti dinners, recyclables, catalog parties of every kind, car washes, bake sales. All had one thing in common—a desire to help.

Anna finished her meal, snuggled up against Kelly's chest, and promptly fell asleep. After several minutes passed and she still remained fast asleep, Kelly forced herself to type an update.

```
Bit of a rough night pain wise, but they are keeping
on top of it with his medications. Snuck downstairs
with my early bird baby here and am catching up on
all your notes and messages. Thank you so much. I
know I'll be writing them down. They will be
treasured in the time to come.
```

There was so much more to say, but Kelly couldn't find the words. She closed the laptop, leaned it against her chair, and allowed her eyes to close. Several minutes later, the whoosh of the front doors announced the beginning of a new day and jolted her awake. "Well, time to go back to the room, eh Anna?"

11:23 a.m.

Aiden read the Facebook page again. *It could work. If Grandma lets me. I mean, if I can't go—* That thought did it for him. "Grandma! Look!"

Dee glanced up from her place on the couch. "Hmm?"

He carried the laptop to her side. "Look—coin cans at the stores. I can do that. I could make up cans and take them everywhere—to all the stores."

"Well…"

"Oh, c'mon. They didn't let me go, so if I'm going to stay, why can't I do something to help?"

"Aiden…"

He'd gone too far. Grandma didn't put up with arguing. "I'm sorry. I just want to *do* something. I earned all that money last summer with the parking meters. I can do it with this, too. People like me."

She didn't answer, much to Aiden's frustration. Still he waited—waited and tried not to look impatient. He'd reconciled himself to a resounding no when Dee asked, "Where would you get the cans?"

"The dollar store? They should have something, shouldn't they? Or Grandma Cox? They save peanut jars and things. Maybe—"

"We'll go in a bit."

"Go where?" Lila stepped into the room, smiling. "I've got to go get some nail polish remover—just spilled mine." She wiggled a hand with two fingers missing the nail polish.

"Can you get me half a dozen—"

"A dozen—or two!" Aiden insisted.

"Fine, a dozen containers—something clear or at least translucent."

Lila shook her head. "What?"

Laughing, Dee explained. "Look, just find something we can cut a slit in the top for change to drop through. Aiden is going to put them all over town."

"Oh, smart! Cool. I'll get some." She smiled at him. "Do you want to come with me?"

Going to Brunswick—even Ferndale—would be more fun than staying, but Aiden shook his head. "I'll make posters to put on them—something that says what it's for. Can I use one of the pictures of Nathan from Facebook?"

Lila nodded. "Sounds good. I'll get some clear tape too."

Aiden stared at the wagon, disgusted. "Kids my age just don't drag wagons. It's embarrassing!"

"We don't have anything else to carry them with," Lila insisted.

Logan eyed it critically. "Why can't we—"

"Me. This is mine. You can do something else if you want, but this one is mine."

"Fine." Logan looked more amused than affronted. "Why can't *he* just put them in a backpack? He can come back to refill it if he unloads all the first ones.

Why does he have to have a good idea when he's being all

superior again? It's like the minute you're a teenager you suddenly think you're so mature. "That'll work. I've got my backpack from home."

Aiden started to leave—had made it to the sidewalk—before his grandmother called him back. "You've got to eat lunch first."

"I'm not hungry."

"I didn't ask if you were hungry. I just said you have to eat your lunch first."

Aiden recognized the words as "Grandma-ese" for "Get your butt in here and eat, young man" and chose to comply before his afternoon plans became someone else's. "Coming…"

The clock struck one o'clock as he seated himself at the table and one-o-three as he shoved back his chair and tossed the breadcrumb covered paper towel in the trash. "I'll be back before dinner!"

At the sidewalk, he hesitated before turning toward the edge of town and the mini-mart. People smiled at him. Some had smiles that looked sad, others that looked uncomfortable—like they needed more fiber in their diet or something—but few people gave him a genuine, happy-to-see-you smile. *It's like he died or something. Sheesh.* By the time he reached the mini-mart, Aiden was ready to turn around and go home. Lila would do it for him, and she didn't care what people thought or did.

Aiden had no doubt that the big gal behind the counter would help. *She likes kids—likes Nathan. Thinks he's the cutest thing ever. It'll be perfect,* Aiden thought as he pulled open the mini-mart door. But it wasn't. Flora Ghant shook her head. "Sorry. We're not allowed to do it—franchise policy. But, lemme have the paper from the front—to show people, y'know. I'll collect myself—keep it in my pocket. You can pick it up every time you come this way. People will give. You'll see."

And, as if to prove the veracity of her words, the next customer who came in handed over the two dollars and thirteen cents change she gave him after he'd paid for his gas. "See? Just go find some stores that have cash paying customers—places like The Deli and The Grind. People will give their change after paying for what they buy."

At the corner of the square, Aiden swept his eyes over the various stores. For the first time, he knew what his father meant by, "Asking for a handout makes you weak—dependent. *Earning* your money brings respect." He shifted his backpack and hesitated. *What will Dad think? Is okay to ask for a handout* **for** *someone? What if it's* *your little brother? Is that too close? I'm willing to work for it. Should I add that?*

A woman stopped mid-stride on her way to The Deli and turned. "Aiden?"

He recognized her, but his mind refused to produce her name. "Yeah..."

"When you talk to your mom, let her know we're praying for you all."

"'Mkay. Thanks."

She smiled at his backpack. "You forget there's no school?"

Aiden shook his head and pulled off his backpack. He unzipped it and pulled out a plastic container. "I'm taking these to the stores. People keep asking what they can do, so we thought..."

Even as he spoke, the woman pulled out her wallet. She dumped her change into her hand, removed all quarters, and handed the rest to him. A dozen coins dropped into the container. "Sorry. Have to keep quarters for the meter." She stared at the bottom and fished a few dollars out too. "Put that in there. People give more when there's something in the bottom."

Those words echoed in his mind as he left the can in the hardware store. "Thanks. You can call Grandma's if it fills up. We'll come get it." Even as he spoke, Aiden frowned. "Yeah. It won't fill up but—"

"Just come in every couple of weeks," Lindsey said. She smiled at him. "Larry will have it ready. Actually, stuff is so slow right now, I might roll them for you myself."

Gary Novak called out from the other side of the store, "Hey, I'll take one."

"Gary," Lindsey retorted, "No offense, but no one goes into your place. You go to them. How—"

"I'll take it in my truck—keep it in the window. People can dump their change when they sign their release forms. You'll see."

Aiden didn't, but he pulled out another can and handed it to Gary. "Thanks."

The door jangled and Charlie Janovich entered as Gary exited. "H-h-hey A-aiden. Wh-wh-atcha doin?"

"Putting up cans for my brother—for change."

Charlie dug his hands in his pockets and pulled out a large handful of change. "I-I-I've got change."

"Might want to save the quarters," Aiden said as he saw the fistful of coins. He didn't want to; in fact, he'd almost kept his mouth shut, but the idea of what his father would say forced the words from him.

"N-n-ah. I-I-I'll just have t-to..." Charlie grinned. "G-g-et more."

"Thanks." Aiden unscrewed the top of the can and handed it to him. Coins filled the bottom. "You sure carry a lot of change."

"Looks like his laundry money," the store owner Larry commented. "Good man, Charlie."

"You don't have—"

"D-d-didn't say I-I-I did." Charlie turned to Lindsey. "C-c-can you order m-me some m-more of that n-n-non-caustic—"

"Paint remover," Lindsey filled in for him. "Yeah. I'll get some. Be here Friday," she snapped.

Charlie laughed at the shocked expression on Aiden's face. "Sh-she doesn't like m-m-my stutter. B-bugs her."

"I—"

Larry stepped in. "Stop insulting my customers and just go order the stuff." To Aiden he added, "You get along. Make sure every business in town gets one of them things. Trust me. People are dyin' to help. They'll be glad to see something they can do—even if it's just toss some change in a jug."

Larry's words proved true. People welcomed the can at nearly every store. Logan rode by with a backpack on his back and handed it to him. "I thought you might want to have it—keep it on your handlebars or something. Mom wants a couple of cans of beans. Want me to take it to the grocery store while I'm there?"

No, he didn't *want,* but Aiden nodded. "Yeah, thanks." He jogged up the steps to The Confectionary and pushed open the door. Audrey Seever waved. "Hey! How's your little brother? Been praying for him!"

Aiden shrugged. "Had surgery yesterday. They're going to do another one in a couple of days. Even Mom says she doesn't really get what's going on."

"I'm missing her around my place already. One missed day and I feel like my house has become a pig sty." She leaned forward, "I think I've let myself become lazy because I know she'll come in and make it look amazing."

Panic gripped him. *What if Mom loses her job? We **need** that money.* :I—I could do it for you. I could—"

"No worries. I know how to clean up after myself. I just like having her do it. I'll be glad when she's back again, but not—" Audrey smiled again. "Hey, I'm not looking to replace her, Aiden. I'll be glad when she's back because it means Nathan's doing better more than because I want someone to scrub my toilet."

Ew. Yeah. Let her wait. Toilets. Why didn't I think about the fact that she has to scrub toilets? Ew. "I just brought in..." He fumbled with the zipper. "—one of these cans. People keep asking, so we thought—"

Taking it from him, Audrey read the cover and plopped it next to the cash register. She reached into the machine, pulled out several coins, counted them up, and wrote something on a slip of paper. As she dumped them in the can she grinned. "There. People always give more when there's already some in there."

"That's what—can't remember her name. The woman who married Miss Lexie's brother. That's what she said."

"Heather. She's right, too." Audrey smiled. "Got a minute to try my lemon ice bon bons? They're in the back. I can't decide if there's enough lemon or not."

Aiden nodded, unfooled. Audrey always asked him if he liked things, but she didn't ask most of the other kids. *It's just because Dad's not working—much.* Half a minute later, she slid a pale yellow confection across the counter. "Do you like lemon?"

"Yeah." Aiden took a bite. He started to say it needed more lemon when a burst of it in the center filled his mouth. "Oh! Yeah. That's really good. Wow. Didn't expect that."

"So it works?" The excitement in her eyes made him doubt his previous assessment. *Maybe she does care about my opinion.* Then, as if the final proof, she grinned.

"Great! It's always good to know what the older kids think. Little kids love everything with sugar in it, and teenagers try to be critical of everything—especially if they love it. Kids your age are just honest—well, if you can trust them to be honest."

The implication that she could trust him buoyed his spirits. "Thanks. I like it. It's really good. I bet Mom would *love* it." He shook his backpack. "I've gotta hurry. Lots of places to go."

"Don't forget Mr. Goldberg at The Deli. He's so excited about his fundraiser. Told me, 'I scooped the whole town. That's the first and last time anything like that ever happens.'"

Aiden didn't forget The Deli, The Grind, The Fox, The Pettler, or any of the other stores. Mrs. Bryant at Lil' Darlin's insisted on taking two cans. "I'll run one over to Bookends as soon as Shannon gets back from her lunch. Did anyone go up to Manchester yet?"

He heard the question Mrs. Bryant wouldn't ask. *Has anyone taken Nathan the bag of stuff I sent?* "I think so. Grandma took the bag out to a car yesterday morning."

Karen Bryant smiled. "Great. And you—if you have any books you want to read, you just go over to Bookends and grab 'em. Tell Todd I said I've got 'em covered."

"Thanks, but you know Grandma. If they wrote the book any time in the last two hundred years, she probably owns it."

At the door, she called him back. "You know what? We just got in a new series—just released last week. I know for certain Dee hasn't bought it yet. Go get it and leave it laying around the house. It'll drive her crazy."

Aiden grinned. "Good one."

Several businesses asked him to come back when the owner or manager was there to approve it. Even still, with both backpacks, he ran out long before he ran out of stores. He'd saved one, though—one that he hoped would bring the biggest donations of all. Marcello's. *Everyone eats there—and they have to have money to do it. It'll be perfect.* The lunch rush had probably ended a couple of hours earlier and it wasn't even close to the main dinner crowd. Only a couple of tables had diners seated at them.

The hostess smiled and called for Mr. Simon. His wife, Anna, followed. "What is this about?"

Aiden choked back a sigh. Ramon Simon sounded ticked. "I'm Nathan Cox's brother—the kid who got electrocuted." He waited for recognition to form, but Ramon just nodded. "Well, people keep asking what they can do to help, so I made donation cans, see?" He held up the can with the picture of Nathan in a hospital bed, arms and legs bandaged. "I wondered if you would put one up by your register..." Even as he spoke, Aiden saw that there was no register at the hostess station.

"We don't have a register. The money is all handled in the back." Ramon shook his head. "I'd like to help—I'll talk to the owner about a donation from the business or maybe talk to the employees about a donation from us, but that really isn't appropriate for—"

Anna Simon's hand slid over her husband's as it rested on the hostess station. She didn't speak a word—not to him or her husband—but her action changed everything. Aiden tried not to gape as he saw the man visibly soften. "Well, I think we'll put it up here after all," he said at last. "People have to wait here for a table sometimes. If they don't donate *before* they're seated, they'll have all through dinner to let the picture influence them. I bet they'll leave something by the end of the meal."

"Thanks!"

Before he could leave, Anna Simon opened her wallet and removed every penny—every dollar—and dumped them in the jar. "People are more likely to give when someone else already has."

Dee's fingers hovered over the keys—again. *How many times have I done this now—just sit here and wonder how to try to say what I think or share some bit of information that never comes out like I mean it to?* If it had been her child, she might not have wanted to do it, but grandchildren are different; she couldn't deny that. *Especially at a time like this. People keep asking how to help. Is it tacky to let them know he's done this? Seems like it.* She frowned. *Yeah, and it seems just as tacky **not** to.*

Love won out over pride and Dee typed in her update on Nathan's Facebook page.

```
Aiden (Nathan's older brother) wanted to do
something to help, so he's spending his afternoon
making donation cans and leaving them all over
Fairbury. Proud of that kid.
```

There. That's benign enough. Just as she started to close out of the page, a new post appeared.

```
Nathan had physical therapy this afternoon. It was
pretty hard for all of us, but we're hoping it gets
better soon. His therapist said Nathan will have a
lot of work ahead of him. We'll hopefully find one
in Fairbury, or even Rockland, so we don't have to
```

make the two hour trip every week. Prayers for that would be wonderful—Kelly.

Dee eyed the permanent job offer once more. *No. They might need me for other things. I can't do that. I just can't. I need to have more faith.*

Allison arrived with the wagon and tried to speak, but Nathan's panic drowned her out. Jon frowned. "Nathan. Stop."

"No hydro!"

"No hydro, Nathan. Not today. That's over already, remember? We did that earlier?" The nurse turned to Kelly and sighed. "I should have known better to do that first one with the wagon. Bad idea. He's going to associate this with that forever." To Nathan, she put on her brightest smile and pointed to the wagon. "We just thought we'd take a walk."

"Can I take my Thomas?" Nathan held up the little wooden train.

"Sure! I bet he'd like to see something other than this room. We'll go around the halls, downstairs, and maybe outside for a few minutes."

Nathan beamed. Breanne, carrying Anna, stepped into the room just as they loaded him into the wagon. Her eyes widened. "Another hydro?" she mouthed to Kelly.

Kelly shook her head and took the baby. "We're going for a walk. Want to come?"

Breanne nodded.

Outside the room, Jon took the handle of the wagon from the nurse and pulled it. After several steps, Nathan leaned over the side and held his train as it rolled along the floor, propelled by the movement of the wagon. Kelly snickered and Allison smiled.

Breanne videotaped it, following behind as the shirtless little boy in an orange baseball cap rolled along the hospital corridor to the elevators. In the lobby, she allowed the others to go ahead of her as she uploaded it to the **Help Nathan & Family** Facebook page.

Having a great time with his Thomas Train! — with

Kelly Cox @ Manchester Community Hospital—Cunningham Memorial Burn Unit.

The status made her smile. *Something upbeat for a change.*

That night as he Skyped with his mom, Aiden told about his day. "Everyone was so excited. They *wanted* to help."

"Well, I think when it's a little guy especially, people feel helpless, so even if it's just a handful of change, it's something to *do*," his mother mused.

"You know what was really weird?"

"No, what?" Baby Anna bonked the screen, making Kelly dive for it. "Sorry. What was weird?"

"Okay, you know that guy at Marcello's—the one everyone says is mean to his wife?"

"Yeah... but don't listen to that kind of gossip. It isn't fair. People don't really know what's going on."

Aiden tried again. "You're right! I mean, he was all, 'I don't think this is an appropriate thing for my business,'" Aiden said, deepening his voice for effect.

"I can just hear him. He's so formal!"

"Well that's where it got weird." Aiden took a sip of his soda. "So when he was talking, his wife just touched him—his hand—and it's like he totally changed. Kind of like you do when Dad rubs your hair. He just—"

"Melted?"

"Yeah, kinda. It was so weird. He can't be too mean to her if all she has to do is touch his hand and, bam! He's changing his mind, right?"

"Doesn't sound like it to me. How many cans did you put up?"

Aiden counted. "Okay, so there were fifteen at first, and then Lila went to get more... I think twenty-two—almost every business in town."

"Wow. That's impressive."

Nathan began fussing, his murmurs of discomfort growing into pleas for help. "I've got to go. Nathan needs me. Sorry."

"That's okay," Aiden insisted. "I need to unload the dishwasher. Grandma said I couldn't watch 'The Avengers' until Logan and me—"

"Logan and I..."

"I'll never get that right," he groused. "Logan and *I* get the kitchen clean."

A minute later, Aiden closed the laptop and carried it back to his grandfather's chair. "Thanks, Grandpa."

Dee skimmed the thread titles on her message board, checking to make sure she hadn't missed anything important while being absorbed in her own little family world. The prayer forum had several new requests. As usual, she paused by each one, praying both for the actual request and for a reminder to continue to pray once she clicked out of the forum. The main forum took longer. Good news about a potential job, funny story about a child, the search for a pair of shoes to match a dress for a wedding, packing help needed—the topics were almost endless and varied widely.

One post nearly escaped her notice—likely would have on an ordinary day—but hypersensitivity to the name "Nathan" brought it to her attention.

`Electricians in Alaska Are Talking About Nathan.`

Dee clicked and began reading. Her eyes widened. "Hey, Keith. Listen."

"What?"

"Lori on the board. Listen." Dee began reading. "'*Jimmy works for an electrical supply company. Some of his customers from the local power company were talking about a little boy out in the Rockland area that survived something that they all fear and even went into some details about Nathan's accident. Jimmy listened for a minute to make sure it really was Nathan they were talking about and asked how they had heard about him. They said that they received a report about the accident. They said that he is such a fortunate little boy and that he survived is absolutely amazing.*

"'*So, even though we all know that God is amazing, it's just really touching to me that God is using a precious little boy and absolutely beautiful family to His glory all of the way across the country.*

"'Cox and Homstad families—as hard as things are right now, I pray that you will all feel God's hand as He carries you what He has planned for you and know that He is using you for His glory in ways that you may never even know about.'"

"Wow." Keith shook his head. "So there are reports of the accident being circulated in Alaska, but our local paper somehow didn't get the memo. Interesting."

"I know, right?" Dee sat up, shoving her laptop aside. "I mean, it's insane. You can't sneeze in Fairbury after midnight without making the front page as someone spreading swine flu, but a kid is electrocuted and not. a. word. I mean, the FairBlog will scoop the paper!"

"Well, to be fair, Michael Cox's wife's family does own it..."

"But it came out today—today! The paper had Saturday and yesterday to do it. It's just weird."

"True... I mean, even guys at work asked why it wasn't in yesterday's edition," Keith mused.

"And I can't go to the store—even in *Brunswick*—without *someone* stopping me and asking if Nathan's my grandson and wanting to know how he's doing. I don't know these people, and I'm not I'm wearing a t-shirt that says, 'My grandson was electrocuted. Ask me how.'"

"And it's not like there's a gag order on fire stories—headline today was about them responding to a call about smoke down on Cedar." Keith and Dee exchanged curious glances before he added, "We could call, I suppose, but—"

"But is right," Dee interjected. "We have no idea if this is some kind of protection the Lord is giving the family. I'm not sure I *want* it in the paper. It's just bizarre that it isn't. I'm almost at conspiracy theory stage."

"Frank would be proud..."

Silence hovered between them for a moment before laughter filled the room. "Poor guy. Everything is a conspiracy—especially those things which can't possibly be," she chortled.

A new thought occurred to Dee. Grabbing her laptop, she typed in the website for the *Fairbury Gazette* and clicked on the police logs. Her eyes skimmed the dates—third, fourth, sixth... "Hey. The paper doesn't even have the police logs up for the fifth! What's with that?"

"Probably just a delay." Keith stood and held up his glass. "Want a refill?"

"Sure." Dee passed him hers before adding, "But they have the sixth up—just not the fifth."

"Okay, that is weird—very weird."

"I wonder..." Dee typed in the town's website and clicked on the police tab. The police logs were on the left. With one click and a few scrolls, she found the entry. As Keith returned with her drink, she turned the screen toward him. "There it is."

```
20:24 GENERIC FIRE CALL/NOT SPECIFIED 338746216
Occurred on Linden St, Fairbury. Second call
requesting medical and fire. UNK if associated with
previous call 338746218.
Disposition: Duplicate Call Entered.
```

"That's it. That's all they say about it? It doesn't even mention Nathan's injury. Someone called and asked for a paramedic, right? Isn't that what Kelly said?" Keith settled into his chair and began searching himself. A minute later, he said, "Okay, scroll down two. See the one on Tanglewood. That's it."

Dee looked, her gut twisting as she read such a life-changing moment reduced to an inch on a website page.

```
20:26 HAZARDOUS CONDITION 338746218
Occurred at Tanglewood/Woodlawn, Fairbury. Cellular
E911 Call: power line down, bird hit
wire/transformer
blew, hit fence and sm child.
Service Class: W911.
Disposition: Referred To Other Agency.
```

"Think we should get a copy of that police report for them?" Keith sighed. "And maybe suggest a lawyer?"

"Lawyer? They're not going to sue, Keith. It was an accident."

"Who said sue?" He closed his laptop and slid it aside. "I just think they need to find out what kind of legal protection they need. For all we know, the neighbor's homeowner's insurance will come after them or their insurance. RGE could even decide that they destroyed RGE property by allowing their son to 'play' with the power line—"

"Oh, come on..."

"It's insane," Keith agreed, "but you've heard of stupider lawsuits. They need to know what they need to have in place to protect themselves. Even the neighbor with the fence—Franklins?"

"Yeah."

"Well, they could name them as part of their lawsuit—assuming their insurance company did that—and they'd still be brought in. It's just best to be prepared and not need it than to be scrambling at the end." Keith insisted.

Sinking, swirling, dizzying emotions filled her as even more changes settled over their lives. "I never even thought about it being taken out of their hands. Oh, Keith..."

DAY SIX

Wednesday, June 10, 8:03 a.m.

Lila arrived at work to find her charges still asleep. *Being a nanny can be an awfully cushy job.* She remembered potty training and amended that thought. *Sometimes.*

Facebook announced three birthdays, two changed relationships, and a dozen funny and not-so-funny memes popped up addressing everything from the latest political snafu to men's ability to commit to everything but women. "This is such a stupid site. There's really nothing—"

Just as she started her semi-regular rant against the banal narcissism of social media, a new update appeared on the **Help Nathan & Family** page. "That'll teach me," she muttered.

```
Nathan had his best night yet! Only woke up twice
with pain. Mommy, Daddy, and Auntie managed to get
more than just a couple of hours of sleep. Yay! —
Kelly
```

"Only twice with pain. It's sick that this is good news."

Lila jumped as a voice at her elbow said, "What?"

She gazed down at four-year-old Zain. "You scared me! What, 'what?'"

"You said something is sick good news," Zain insisted. "What's that?"

"Oh, I just don't like hearing that Nathan hurts. It's sad when less hurt is good news instead of no hurt."

"Then I'll just pray that he has no hurt," the boy quipped as he skipped to the breakfast bar and climbed up onto the barstool.

When Jesus talked about the faith of children, He wasn't joking. Geez Lois! I wish I had that kind of confidence. "I'll just pray all the pain's gone." Problem solved.

Fairbury Notes & News
Wednesday, June 10, 9:00 a.m. *(Rachel Delman-Cox)*

A three-year-old is on the long road to recovery after a freak accident last week left him with third-degree burns covering his legs.

Late Friday evening, a raven that apparently flew into some power lines in the alley near the 400 block of Linden Street apparently started a fire on a property near Jonathan and Kelly Cox. Jon saw the fire and rushed out to extinguish it.

The Cox's three-year-old son, Nathan, who was helping his dad in the alley at the time, attempted to follow his dad down the street. Jon spotted his son and began jogging back to remove him out of harm's way. Before he could get to him, Nathan tripped on an exposed power line. Jon quickly pulled him from the wire, but the electric jolt was enough to severely burn the boy's feet and lower legs.

An evaluation by medical staff at the Fairbury Medical Clinic yielded an early diagnosis of second-degree burns. The child was transported to the Cunningham Memorial Burn Unit of Manchester

Community Hospital in Manchester for further analysis and treatment.

At the burn center, the family learned from a specialist that the burns were in fact third-degree. The first two days were spent determining whether the jolt had caused nerve or organ damage. The family learned that although treatment would be long, and painful, Nathan could make a full recovery.

Jon was also evaluated, and cleared, of any damage caused by his contact with the current.

During the first several days in the hospital, family and friends of the Coxes began a Facebook campaign to raise support for the uninsured family. So far, Jon and Kelly are staying with Nathan and their two-month-old daughter, Anna, in the same hospital room as their son.

"We were offered a place to stay in the Ronald McDonald House, but it was just too far away," said Kelly.

She told the *Fairbury Notes & News* that while the effects of Nathan's burns have been managed somewhat by pain medication, even relatively noninvasive treatments cause her son tremendous pain.

Several procedures have indicated that the best-case scenario for Nathan's release will be Friday after his first skin graft. Kelly noted, however, that they have been cautioned to wait until it is clear he is free from fever, infection, or other risks.

"It's a two hour trip if we have to come back, so I think they want to be on the safe side."

In the meantime, she is making her son as comfortable as possible in his temporary surroundings.

"I'm not sure he really understands," she said. "He asks why we can't go home, why he can't go out and play, why he can't see his brother," eleven-year-old Aiden, who is staying with relatives in Fairbury.

But Nathan usually has times during the day when he is playing, laughing, and enjoying the company of his family, visitors, and the hospital staff.

"They have been so amazingly compassionate," said Kelly.

The treatment calls for skin grafts every six to twelve months. Physicians will take skin from his upper leg and move it to his lower legs. "They say it will be like getting a burn all over again," said Kelly.

Because of Nathan's age, the procedures will probably take place regularly over the next fifteen years.

The family is clinging to the silver lining that came with the unexpected trauma—an outpouring of love, prayers, best wishes, and even donations to the family.

"I feel so blessed," said Kelly. "People have been very generous to us."

Already an "extreme couponer" and do-it-yourselfer, Kelly said that she is making it a personal challenge to honor those donations by making the most of them.

Friends of the Coxes can follow the progress and recovery of Nathan, as well as make donations to his PayPal account, at **Help Nathan & Family** on Facebook.

"The love and care people have shown us has been amazing," said Kelly. "We just hope that we can repay that—if not to each of those people, then to someone else who needs it."

Claire Rhodes—Wednesday, June 10, 9:12 a.m.
Excellent article. I am absolutely astounded that our weekly Blog managed to scoop the town paper. It has been six days since the accident. At least three of those days have been opportunities for our town to have a real headline—the first since the Plagiarist Killings. I'll be curious to see what today's headline is. Will the *Gazette* finally have news about this?

Karyn Bryant—Wednesday, June 10, 9:57 a.m.
I too am flabbergasted to read this here. I'm not saying that this blog shouldn't post this news. It should. It just shouldn't have almost week-old news before the daily paper. I'm totally befuzzled.

Wayne @ The Pettler—Wednesday, June 10, 11:11 a.m.
Does anyone know why the *Gazette* doesn't have anything about this? There are people in this town who might not have heard—hard as that is to believe. They shouldn't have to wait a week to get basic news. I mean, the headlines two weeks ago had to do with someone's irresponsibility in leaving their sprinklers on all night. How is that any more important than the life of a child!

Tait Stedtmann—Wednesday, June 10, 12:21 p.m.
Okay, this isn't funny. I appreciate the integrity of the Doman family in their reporting, but it does call into question the bias that the *Fairbury Gazette* has shown in this incident. Why have they not printed anything? I know when the Wilcoxes owned it, they would have had daily updates if they could get them—even if only taken from the Facebook page. Now that it has been bought out by a syndicate, what do we get? Nothing. Well, nothing of substance when a major corporation is involved anyway. Curious.

Gary Novak— Wednesday, June 10, 2:03 p.m.
I would like to point out that we do not know the reason that the paper hasn't done an article. Perhaps they do not have the connections to be able to interview the Coxes that the Delman-Cox family does. After all, the local reporter—or is it reporters—aren't all related to the Coxes. So, as much as I'm sure we'd all like answers, we do have to be reasonable about our speculations.

Claire Rhodes— Wednesday, June 10, 3:30 p.m.
I was prepared to come back and agree with Gary until my daughter pointed something else out to me (As did Tait above). The *Gazette* DOES have equal access to the family. They can use the contact button on either the Facebook page OR the blog it links to. In a town this size, there just is no excuse for ignoring real news in favor of what flavor ice cream is the most popular at The Confectionary. (No offense to Audrey Seevers, but that is nothing compared to what now looks to me

like a major cover up.) Does RGE really fear a lawsuit so much that they're leaning on a small town newspaper? I think I will go call and ask.

Adric Garrison—Wednesday, June 10, 3:41 p.m.
Please do let us know what you learn. I too am torn between trying to give the benefit of the doubt and letting my history-riddled mind to see unsavory reasons for the silence.

Claire Rhodes—Wednesday, June 10, 3:58 p.m.
They declined to comment. When I asked when I could expect our TOWN PAPER to report TOWN NEWS, they informed me that they "strive to offer the best in balanced reporting of everything relevant and of interest to Fairbury residents."
I guess they get to decide what is relevant and interesting to us—that must be that "balance" thing. They balance what we want to know with what they think we should know. Aw… reminds me of when I was a little girl at home. Not. Cool.

Karyn Bryant—Wednesday, June 10, 4:08 p.m.
My paper arrived today. Cover story? How the fire department had to spend two hours to get a cat out of "a" tree because it jumped from limb to limb like a squirrel instead of staying put so they could get back to their dinner. Amazing. When the Fire Department actually does an emergency response call to try to save a life, they get ignored. What a way to support the men who risk their lives every day.

Tabitha Allen—Wednesday, June 10, 4:12 p.m.
Or, at least they (the firemen) would (risk their lives) if we'd bother to have any real fires around here. Apparently electrocutions don't count.

Fran Tillney—Wednesday, June 10, 4:21 p.m.
I'm disgusted. I've never seen such a blatant cover up. This is appalling at best. My mind goes to the criminal. If RGE thinks they're going to avoid a massive lawsuit by bullying papers into keeping it quiet, they're crazy. This kind of cover up just

explodes these days. It'll be viral in hours if the right people say the right things in the right places. I just wish I was that person.

Rachel Delman-Cox—Wednesday, June 10, 4:21 p.m.
I would like to remind people that while this country does allow for freedom of speech, people can be sued for libel and/or slander. I would just caution people to consider that the average person does not have the resources to defend him or herself in such a suit.

Arlene Paulson—Wednesday, June 10, 6:43 p.m.
I think the fact that Jon Cox allowed his son in a dangerous situation like that calls for police investigation into child neglect. There is no excuse for that boy to be in that alley with a fire and a live power line on the ground.

Faye Hartfield—Wednesday, June 10, 7:02 p.m.
Shame on you, Arlene Paulson. Shame on you. Accidents happen. That you would even make a comment like that shows ignorance and unChristian character. Shame on you.

Chrissy Santina—Wednesday, June 10, 7:27 p.m.
OMGoodness. That's just totally retarded. I can't believe you'd even write that. Kids just do stuff before you can even see them move. I babysit all the time and I can't even pee because if you turn away for a second, they're out the door and in the street. They totally don't need this from people.

Bentley Novak—Wednesday, June 10, 7:32 p.m.
Chrissy, I agree with the spirit of what you said, but I would really appreciate it if you would reconsider the use of the word "retarded" to refer to stupidity. It is as offensive as "nigger" to many people.

Chrissy Santina—Wednesday, June 10, 7:38 p.m.
I think it's stupid that we act like "retarded" needs to be saved for people with special needs.

They don't use it for themselves, but not using it just gives it more power. People with special needs aren't retarded. Stupid people are.

Rachel Delman-Cox—Wednesday, June 10, 7:41 p.m.
I would appreciate it if Chrissy and Bentley would take their semantics discussion to a more private and/or appropriate forum. This is for Fairbury news.

John Dalton—Wednesday, June 10, 8:12 p.m.
I'd say that The *Gazette* has the right to print anything they like—or not. I'm surprised at the words of some of the commenters—people I know who believe that businesses have the right to run things as they please. If the paper chooses not to get involved in printing this story for whatever reason they don't, that's their business and we have no right to demand they do it any other way.

James Rhodes—Wednesday, June 10, 8:29 p.m.
Mr. Dalton made an excellent point. The paper is not obligated to print anything. And I am not obligated to continue my subscription to such an obviously biased periodical. Thank you for that reminder.

8:41 p.m.

Dee read the comments and her mind churned with ideas. *Okay, Lord. What gives? I mean, I don't even think I **want** this in the paper, but isn't it weird that it isn't? That just seems so bizarre to me. If Kelly goes with a lawyer, he might want to know this, but then he might take it as another way to push for a lawsuit. Maybe not. Still, it's weird.*

2:12 p.m.

The phone rang. Dee eyed it with suspicion. *Once upon a time, if I didn't feel like answering a phone, I didn't. Now look at me. I'm hesitating. This craziness has changed everything—even the inconsequential things like whether to answer the phone or not.* She snatched it up and sighed. "Hello?"

"Hey, Mom. It's me."

And aren't I glad I did it. Whew. This is still insanity, but whew! "What's up, Breanne?"

"I'm down in the lobby with Anna. Jon and Kelly are in the room talking with a lawyer."

"They're doing it?" The thought cut, but Dee couldn't imagine how they could avoid it. Reading about Alice's son had sealed the deal for her. "I mean, I would. Did she show you what Alice on the board said about their accident?"

"Yeah. I think that's what did it—that and because they don't want to end up being held liable for stuff that isn't their fault."

"Still... is Kelly okay?"

"I think so. They both look worn out—I mean they are. We all are." Breanne shushed a fussy Anna before adding, "Actually, I think that's also part of why they're doing it. They need help making decisions. We're all just too tired to think clearly. Next comes the Medicaid."

"They're doing that?" *Oh, man. What a blow. I'd be going crazy at the thought. That's gotta hurt.*

Breanne made noncommittal noises. "—just hard to know. I mean, they can't pay these bills, and it'll start three days before the accident, so I'm hoping they will."

"Ugh."

"Mom!"

Dee tried again. "Look. I get it. Okay, you may not see why it's such a big deal, but it's about principle. If you're against government funded charity when you *don't* need it, then consistency demands that you remain against it when it benefits you. I can understand that. They've always been against it, and their need isn't going to change their political convictions."

"Convictions don't pay the bills."

*Oh, the idealism of youth. An exception here, another there—no biggie. They forget that **someone** has to pay for it, and in the long run, it means more taxes for their neighbors—for themselves.* "Look, I'm torn, okay. I absolutely understand their position. I support them. But I also know that if they don't, logically speaking, the doctor and hospital will never get paid. Jon and Kelly will scrimp by on next to nothing until they die and still not pay half the bills. That's reality. So there is a part of me that says, 'The law requires them to provide emergency medical care so why should they be penalized?'"

"Exactly my point. Dr. Smith is amazing. The nurses say that he writes off so much of his patients' bills. But he has bills to pay too."

"Yep." Dee had spoken to enough doctors over the years to know that the idea of all doctors being rich was idealistic at best. "The malpractice insurance alone is more than a lot of people make per year. I've seen numbers anywhere from ten to two hundred thousand a year. The guy needs to be paid so he can actually afford to work."

"I just hope they'll do it."

As Breanne shared her opinion on the subject, Dee tried to estimate the bills and failed. "There's a part of me that hopes so, too," she said at last. "I just hope they only do it if they can live with that decision. I'd hate for them to feel bullied into it—either by friends and family or by circumstance. It's easy to say it'll solve a problem, but it doesn't if it creates a new one."

"Well, if RGE just decides to pay the bills, all of it will be moot."

"That," Dee agreed, "would be the optimal solution."

3:30 p.m.

Breanne sat in the corner chair, patting Anna's back as Nathan's screams of pain and fear ripped through the room. Her laptop lay open beside her as she read the latest installment of a fan fiction story. Her attention flipped back and forth between the drama on the screen and the drama playing out before her eyes. The baby squirmed again, but didn't open her eyes. *How does she sleep through all this? It's crazy!*

Kelly tried to encourage her son, but watching him proved almost too much for her. She winced with each wail, choked back tears at each sob. Jon tried to remain calm and firm, but the tension in his jaw, the way he clenched it between admonitions to try one more time, told the real story.

The baby popped her thumb in her mouth, let out a sigh that Breanne managed to hear between gasps and screeches, and continued to snooze unfazed by the torturous sounds echoing around them. Breanne reached for her laptop and pulled up the **Help Nathan & Family** page.

Oh, so hard right now for us… Nathan is doing physical therapy, and while it's hard to distinguish pain from being scared about pain, we know there is some, so it's just hard for everyone. He is a trooper, though. Prayers for strength for us all— much appreciated. It's hard to cause pain to make him feel better in the long run.
First bath after surgery #1 is coming up shortly. We (parents/aunt) will see the wounds for the first time since the surgery. I am praying for a strong stomach. —Breanne

4:04 p.m.

After Nathan's bath, Breanne settled back in with her computer. The wounds still churned her stomach. She downloaded them to her computer and considered emailing them to her mom. *Mom can't take it. She'd kill me.*

Nathan lay relaxed in bed, his hands behind his head and looking very content. Breanne clicked on "the page" and typed in a quick update.

After his bath. He's high—life is good!

She snapped a quick picture and uploaded it. Just a few seconds later, Kelly commented on it.

He's got his Thomas PJs and his Thomas train… he's all good…

Their laughter made Jon pause at the door. "What'd I miss?"
"We just posted basically the same thing." Kelly smiled. "Taking your walk?"
"Yeah. Thought I'd get one before dinner."
Breanne inched closer to Nathan, recording him on her phone as she listened to him chattering about something. "What did you say?"
Kelly shifted Anna from one arm to the next. "What?"
"He was just talking about something, but I couldn't get it."
"Can I play with that?" Nathan reached for it, already

accustomed to having his little whims granted.

Breanne held it up so Nathan could see himself in the phone. "Say hi…"

Nathan waved. He watched the phone for a moment and then blew raspberries into it. Breanne and Kelly giggled, but Nathan didn't seem to notice. He stared at the phone again and asked, "Can you talk?"

Kelly giggled.

"Can you talk?"

"That's you in the camera, Nathan," she said as she giggled again. Breanne nodded. "That's you!"

"Can you talk?" he repeated.

"Can *you* talk?" Breanne asked.

As if fixated, Nathan asked again, "Can you talk?" A pause. "Daddy?" Another pause. "Taaaalk!"

Breanne and Kelly giggled, shaking their heads at one another.

Nathan pointed to the screen. "It's on his nose."

The women exchanged amused glances. "His nose?" Kelly mouthed.

His finger tapped the screen. Again. And yet again. Confusion and amusement mingled in his expression as he tried to interact with the little boy on the phone screen.

Kelly giggled again. "It's like, 'why isn't he responding?'" As Breanne put the phone away after one more "Can you talk?" Kelly said, "You know, that's what he says when he talks on the phone."

Just a little while later in the Homstad house, several people crowded around Dee's laptop and watched the video. Once alone again, Dee stared at the screen, a smile forming as she read the caption.

```
Nathan watching himself while high on meds.
Nathan's a bit high… and he can't seem to grasp that
the little boy in the video he's watching is
him. :P— with Kelly Cox. ("Can you say hi to me?"
when talking to himself.)
```

DAY SEVEN

Thursday, June 11, 9:11 a.m.

Claire stretched. The house echoed with the blissful silence of empty rooms and peaceful moments alone. Her eyes slid to the corner of her computer screen. *Thirty minutes before I have to start walking.*

With her emails read, filed, and deleted, she moved to check her calendar. *It's all work. I'll deal with that there,* she decided. A familiar click of a gate latch preceded the creak of the mailbox lid. She leaned, craning her neck, and watched as the mail guy exited through the gate again, carefully pulling the latch shut. *Too bad your substitute isn't so careful. Roxie got out last week thanks to her.*

Comfortable couch cushions urged her to stay—not to bother with silly things like mail. *It'll all be bills anyway. People don't send **real** mail anymore.* Still, despite a dozen internal protests, Claire dragged herself off the couch and to the door. Just outside, their old-fashioned mailbox boasted three letters. "All bills," she murmured as if speaking outside wouldn't mar the perfection of peace and quiet inside.

She stuffed the bills in the organizer by the back door and glanced at the oven clock as she passed. *Five minutes. One last check in case there's news of Nathan, and then I've got to get my clothes changed and head out the door.*

The page loaded instantly with one new update.

```
"Can you help me? Because my legs are hurting."
He learned this early on, LOL!—Breanne.
```

As the laptop closed, so did Claire's eyes. *Can't he just have one relatively pain-free day?*

10:42 a.m.

He picked up the phone. "Ross Davies for the Cox family in 2014." The doors swung open, welcoming him. Ross squared his shoulders and tucked the small fire truck under his arm. His wife's teasing filled his memory.

"A toy? Really? Ross, if you ask Steven to pick out a toy for this boy, he's going to think he gets one."

"Then we'll give him one too, but I want to be able to tell Nathan that my son picked it out for him." Ross led his son down the aisle. "So, if you got hurt and a fireman helped you, what toy would you want?"

Denise threw up her hand. "Ross! That's just what I'm talking about. It's like saying, 'I'm going to give you a toy. Pick it.'"

A little finger pointed and then a hand reached—a small fire truck. "That one, buddy?"

"Yeah. Mine."

The "I told you so" look on Denise's face didn't faze him. Ross grabbed two of the trucks and tossed them in the cart. "Thanks. Let's get the Pull-Ups and go."

"I play with it?" Steven begged.

"At home. You can play at home."

At the door of room 2014, and after taking a calming breath, Ross knocked. "Excuse me, do you have a minute?"

The woman—Kelly?—looked stricken. *Oh, no. Did something else happen? Is he okay?*

Jon stepped forward. "I am very sorry, but to protect ourselves from liability issues, we've retained a lawyer, and he has insisted we talk to no one without him present."

And I thought they were different...

Defeat hit Ross in the gut and forcibly expelled all oxygen from his lungs. Unable to speak, he nodded, plastered an understanding smile on his face, and turned to go. Kelly's voice reached him before he'd taken a second step. "Jon, why didn't you tell him we're not suing? He's got to think we're some money-hungry family or something."

"I—"

Ross slowed his walk, ignoring the guilt that tried to condemn him for eavesdropping.

"I don't see how it can hurt to let him know that we're just protecting our right to make decisions regarding Nathan—that we don't want to get sued ourselves for somehow damaging their property when Nathan fell on it. How can that hurt?"

The tears that came next propelled him out of the burn unit and into the elevator. As he punched the button for the first floor, the doors closed, further separating them from him. *So maybe they are different. They're nice anyway. He looked genuinely sorry not to be able to talk to me. Poor woman—she's worn out and overwrought.*

Ross remembered the posts he'd seen on the Facebook page and sighed as he stepped from the elevator. *I hope their faith encourages them as much as it seems...*

1:24 p.m.

Dee locked herself in her room where the noises of crazed teen and preteen boys on a rampage through digital warfare couldn't drown out her mother's words. She dialed, waiting to hear her mother's usual "Heee-ello!" but her father's low, gentle, "Hello?" followed by a tender, "Hi there," brought an unexpected smile to her face.

"Hey, Dad. I was just calling with an update on Nathan..."

"Let me get your mom. She'll want to hear this. Hold on."

Though he made it sound like her mom would be picking up another phone, she knew he'd pass it over; her parents didn't have two handsets. As her mother's voice came through the phone, Dee found herself relaxing. "Hey, Mom."

"So what's up? Anything new since his surgery?"

"Let's see...he has had his first physical therapy, his first post-op bath, and he enjoyed a ride around the hospital and outside. Then let's see... the town blog scooped the newspaper, they hired a lawyer—"

"Wait, lawyer? Why?"

Dee flopped on her bed, feeling very much like a teenager again, chatting with a girlfriend about the latest school gossip. *That's why Mom always said talking was a waste of time—gossip. Wow. How did I miss that until now?* She blinked as she tried to pull her thoughts back to the conversation. "Well it boils down to them needing to protect themselves. We keep reading about kids being named in homeowner lawsuits and such as injured parties and the parents lose all control over whether their child is even involved. So, they decided to do it so that they aren't caught in the middle of a lawsuit they didn't ask for and don't want."

"That actually makes a lot of sense. Have they heard from the electric company about it all? Will the company take financial responsibility for the medical bills?"

"We don't know. The lawyer said not to talk to RGE without him present—probably to protect them against saying anything that might be construed as being at fault." Dee sighed. "Mom, the bills already are staggering. From what I can see online, they've got to be close to one hundred thousand—if not over—just for the hospital alone. That doesn't include the Fairbury clinic, the pediatrician, the surgeon, the anesthesiologist, the lab—"

"It's gonna get pricey, that's for sure."

"I got a job offer…"

"A job—"

"Full time—working at home, of course—but for some serious money." She hesitated. "I don't see how I'd have time to do that *and* do everything else I have to do, but it could cover so much of the medical bills…"

"But then you'll just end up spending more on take-out, tutors, and housekeepers. That's not sound logic."

"The bills, Mom! Where on earth are they going to come up with the money to pay these bills? Jon hasn't been able to get a job for almost a year—not a real one. He's making below poverty level and they have no insurance anymore. Who's going to insure them now?"

"Someone will. If that's what God wants, it'll happen."

It sounded so good but simplistic—too simplistic. "Mom, I know that, okay. I really know that. But I can't ignore the fact that at the rate things are going, they could be looking at a million dollars' worth of medical bills and no way to pay them. They'll be in debt for the rest of their lives and that poor doctor and that generous hospital will never see a fraction of it. They'll pay," Dee added quickly. "They'll live on nothing, own nothing, work themselves to the bone to exist while paying, but they'll never get close!"

Dee's mom spoke. What she said at first, Dee never remembered, but four words burned themselves into her mind. "God's got this covered." If she said anything else, Dee missed it.

"What's that?"

"I said," Mom repeated slowly, "God's got this covered. We don't know how; we're just waiting to see how, but He's got this covered."

6:21 p.m.

A neighbor waved as Ross stepped out of his car. He tried to smile as he gave a half-hearted move of his hand. A flutter at the window caught his attention and his heart squeezed as two eyes and a nose appeared over the edge of the couch and peered through the sheers. They disappeared. Even over the noise of the lawn mower down the street, the screeches and splashes of kids in a pool somewhere, and extra heavy-duty insulation they'd gone into serious debt to pay for, Ross thought he heard his son giggle.

Wishful thinking, but you know he did.

Before he could reach the door, it flung open and little legs streaked across the distance. Small arms wrapped around his legs, and big blue eyes stared up at him. "You're home!" Before he could respond, Steven added, "How come you took my toy?"

"I didn't. This is for the little boy who was hurt, remember?"

"Yeah." Steven dragged him into the house. "Lookie my fort."

The couch, chairs, entertainment center, bookshelves, coffee table—every inch of the living room that could possibly hold one edge of a blanket—had been draped with what looked like every blanket in the neighborhood. "Did Mommy help?"

The boy's eye twitched—just as it did every time the kid was tempted to lie. Steven opened his mouth—and clamped it shut. Once more... and shut again. Defeated, he crossed his arms over his chest and nodded. "Mmm hmm."

Ross hunkered down on his heels to peer into the bedding abyss. "Bet you had to really help her know the best place to put each one, huh?" He glanced back at Steven. "Moms have bigger arms, but they're not always very good engineers."

At the sound of a throat clearing across the room, Ross raised his head to meet the glowering glare of his wife. "Um, well you've always said that you're no engineer... I was just quoting!"

The glower didn't fade. "Bigger arms?" Denise crossed hers across her chest in a perfect imitation of Steven. *I guess it's the other way around, but it doesn't look like that now.*

"Longer arms, then. I was using kid-friendly vocabulary."

"He knows what longer means." Denise grinned at her son. "Don't you, baby?"

"I'm not a baby."

"Okaaay..." Denise tried again. "You do, don't you—know what longer means?"

"Yeah." The boy tried to shove his hands in his pockets. And failed. "It means I gotta wait."

Ross didn't even try to hide his smirk. "Yep. That's it all right. That's it indeed." He skirted the room, squeezing between the couch and the wall, and reached his wife's side. Steven had already made it.

"It's faster through the fort, Daddy!"

"I see that." Ross saw the "oh no" look in his wife's eyes and relished every second as he added, "I guess I took the *longer* way." He tried to kiss her. Denise shook her head and stepped back.

"Nuh, uh. No kisses for you."

Steven's indignant retort blasted through the house. "Mommy! Daddy needs his kisses!"

"Yeah, Mommy," Ross echoed. "Daddy needs his kisses."

Denise, outnumbered, leaned in for her kiss and froze. "Why do you have that toy still?"

"They got a lawyer."

"Oh."

He stepped into the kitchen and dropped the toy on the counter, staring at it. Unable to meet his wife's gaze he whispered, "I get why—I do. The poor people are just terrified that they'll get sued themselves. The woman practically begged him to come out and assure me that they're not trying to make money on this thing."

"Then why—"

She didn't hear me. Ross tried again. "Something about protecting themselves in liability issues."

"What? They seriously think RGE is going to sue them? What for, being in the wrong place at the wrong time? That's ridiculous!"

"My supervisor said they're probably being taken in by an ambulance chaser who knows how to spin things in a way to get him to do what he wants. He knows they're not interested in a lawsuit, so he terrifies them with stories about people getting forced into one or whatever."

"That's just sick. Those poor people have enough to deal with without some shyster taking advantage them." Denise jerked open the oven and reached for the casserole inside.

"Oven mitts!"

She stared at her hand. "Yikes! Thanks."

Hours later, as Ross turned out the kitchen lights on his way to bed, he paused by the little red bubble-shaped fire engine and ran one finger over the yellow ladder.

WEEK TWO

DAY EIGHT

Friday, June 12, 1:51 p.m.

Homstad road trips usually consisted of license plate games, impromptu eruptions into song, and someone getting irritated that someone else didn't answer a question due to the blissful noise-reducing qualities of a little invention otherwise known as ear-buds. Dee often read or, when the mood struck her, spent her ride doing needlework of some kind or another.

A silence too dull to be described as eerie and too unusual to fit into the realm of dullness and ordinary permeated the vehicle. Dee's hands sat folded in her lap in a deceptive appearance of calm and tranquility. Behind her, Lila fidgeted with her backpack strap. *She's nervous*, Dee thought. *Lord, let her be exactly the kind of help they need during this exact time. Don't let anyone expect her to be another Breanne. They're two different people with nearly opposite strengths. I just pray that this is the time that they need someone like her.*

Keith's usual relaxed posture while driving had been replaced with the stance of a man on a mission. *You'd think this is the last hour of a long vacation—gotta get to the destination. Conquer the journey and arrive the victor.* A small smile tried to form. *People are so predictable—even when they're not.*

The Internet directions sent them the same way they'd sent Jon and Breanne. As they reached the appropriate exit in Manchester, Dee redirected them the other way, hoping that the road didn't split into some odd one-way thing that meant a reversal wouldn't work. Street signs assured them that they'd gone the right way.

"Okay, up here—oh, there it is. Turn right at that light."

With a parking space so close to the front that it felt like valet parking, the Homstads, accompanied by Aiden, descended on the Manchester Community Hospital en masse. Nine bodies filed through the sliding doors and were blown in by the whoosh of the fans. Nine bodies crammed into an elevator and rode to the fourth floor. As the doors slid open, Breanne stood there holding Anna.

"Okay, so two can come at a time, but that's about it. Mom?"

Dee took the baby and beckoned for Aiden to follow. "C'mon. Let's go see everyone." The rest of the family found chairs or places against the wall and sat on the floor.

Over two giant doors, a sign announced the Cunningham Memorial Burn Unit. Dee swallowed hard as the full impact of what that title meant assaulted her. Breanne picked up the phone. "Room 2014 Nathan Cox—family."

The doors opened. Outside the room, Breanne pointed to a dispenser on the wall. "You can't enter without it," she said as she pumped a glob on her hands and rubbed it in. "They're fanatical about it."

"Probably necessary," Dee agreed as she waited to see that Aiden used it properly.

Kelly's weary face did little to reassure Dee that things were going well. Happiness lit Kelly's eyes. "Aiden!"

"Hey, Mom!" Aiden glanced at the bed where Nathan lay surrounded by toys and books. "I got fire truck, Aiden!"

After a quick hug, Aiden wriggled out of his mother's arms and went to see what Nathan had to share. Dee rubbed Anna's back as she asked, "How's he doing today?"

Kelly nodded. "Not too bad. Hydro..."

Nathan's head jerked in their direction, but Aiden distracted him with a burst of noise from the truck. Dee quirked an eyebrow at her daughter. Kelly rolled her eyes and said, "That's the least obnoxious. I kid you not, we've had one delivered every day for the past seven days. Some are small, some are big, and all are loud. All."

"Sorry it took so long to get up here. We kept thinking we'd hear, 'Coming home tomorrow' every morning. But Aiden needed to see you and *really* needed to see Nathan."

Kelly's eyes softened. "Really? He always treats Nathan like a barely-tolerable pest—the little kid who breaks his Lego creations and interrupted our perfectly happy little home."

"Yeah, I don't think you'll see much of that. It's surprised him too. I can see it in his eyes as he asks about what's happening now or what'll come next. He's a bit taken aback that he misses Nathan so much, but he does. He's always loved the little guy—"

"Oh, I know that. He was so excited when Nathan was a boy, but you know. There's such an age gap…"

Once she'd greeted and hugged her son-in-law, Dee took the baby and sank back into the corner, out of the way. Even with people coming and going every day, they'd developed a rhythm. *I can sense it. We've disrupted that—just like when someone drops in unannounced at home. They're not unwelcome, but they have disrupted your day. It's weird. They **have** a "day" here.*

Naomi and Pete entered within half an hour of their arrival. Dee smiled up at them and offered sleeping Anna, but Pete moved immediately to join in the fire truck play and Naomi shook her head. "We just brought water bottles and protein bars—oh, and strawberries. There were some on the way that looked so good, but they haven't been washed."

Dee started to mention that they could wash the berries there when she realized what that'd mean. *Lord, they're washing their food in a hospital bathroom! This is just too much. Ugh!*

Keith appeared in the doorway and crept around the back of the room. His hand trailed over Anna's downy head before he made his way to Nathan's bed. As he listened to Nathan explain all the features of his fire truck, Dee glanced around her. *Breanne must have stayed out. Still, the hospital is being very accommodating. That's nice.*

Jon's sister and brother-in-law didn't stay long. After a bit of persuasion, Kelly handed over a bag of laundry and promised to pick it up the next day when they came for showers. Curious, Dee waited until they left and then examined the bathroom. No shower of any kind. *How did I not know they had to leave just to take a shower? What a pain.*

As if her thoughts were a silent cue, Nathan began fussing. Kelly watched him for a moment and stepped outside the room. Dee strained to hear what she might say but failed. However, a couple of minutes later, the nurse stepped into the room and adjusted monitors, took vital signs, and gave Nathan a dose of something—pain medication from what Dee could tell.

Dee watched Kelly and Jon with concerned eyes before murmuring something to Keith. He nodded. She pulled Kelly aside and said, "Let's go get you something to eat—something not hospital or fast food. Dad'll take Jon and Aiden and a few of the others when we get back."

She hesitated—Dee knew she would—but after a moment or two of indecision, Kelly nodded. "I could use something that at least *feels* like real food."

"What sounds good?" She listed off every restaurant she could imagine, and nodded as Kelly latched onto a seafood chain. "I'll look up how to get there. Gimme a minute on Breanne's laptop and we're good to go."

"Make sure she comes," Kelly murmured. "I know she's been craving something better, too."

"Where do you think Jon would like to go?"

"There's a steakhouse just up the road. I think he'd like the big salad bar they have. His sister was telling us about it."

"Gotcha. We'll go see who wants to go where. Why don't you feed Anna so she can sleep and you can eat in peace? Come on out when you're ready." Dee and Keith stepped from the room and exited the burn unit. In the hall, they polled the kids to see who wanted surf and who preferred turf. Only Drew would be the uncertain vote. *He'll choose to come with us,* Dee finally decided. *He's probably aching for a bit of quiet.*

But he didn't. By the time Kelly arrived, ready to go, Drew announced his preference for the steakhouse and went to take his turn spending time with Nathan. "Well," Dee said as she watched him and Lila disappear behind the burn unit doors, "he never ceases to amaze me."

All the way to the van and across the city of Manchester, Dee listened as Breanne and Kelly shared the details that they hadn't had time or inclination to post online. "It's been just one thing after another. You don't know what to say because you don't know the last thing you said. If you skip something, it won't make sense, and if you don't..." Kelly sank back against her seat, closed her eyes, and sighed. "Mom, it's just one thing after another. We never get a break."

Breanne spoke before Dee could find any words that would be remotely encouraging or comforting. "I think you're doing fine. People don't expect you to sit around with your hands ready to type out his latest reaction to antibiotics, his latest Pull-Up change, or his current blood pressure levels." As Kelly started to protest, she added, "And the few who do are just jerks, and you don't need to worry about them."

"She's got a point," Dee agreed. "As much as I know you want to keep people informed—"

"People who have already donated over a thousand dollars!" Kelly interjected. "I can't just say, 'Thanks for the money. I'll let you know what we did with it if I feel like it.'"

"Actually, you can." Dee turned into the parking lot, put the vehicle in park, and turned off the ignition. She turned to her eldest child and smiled. *When did she become a woman who has to bear these kinds of burdens, Lord?* Aloud, she said, "People don't give with strings—not most, anyway. Those who do can just deal with it. You do not have the time or the emotional strength to add that burden to your plate."

"Tell that to the people who want me to make a million decisions on things like fundraisers. They're planning all kinds of stuff, but I can't help. I just can't handle it." Tears filled Kelly's eyes.

Dee led them inside, waited until they were seated, and chose the first thing that looked remotely good on the menu. While Kelly, Breanne, and Jamie tried to decide on what they wanted to eat, Dee organized her thoughts. The moment Kelly set aside her menu, Dee spoke. "Okay. I'll take care of the fundraiser thing. Some people will ignore it, of course, but it'll take care of most. At a time like this, people are dying to *do* something, and they can't see that pressure on you to help them decide what to do is just that—pressure. You can't say anything without being ungracious, but I can."

"They'll just say you're interfering or—"

"Dee shook her head. "No, Kelly. Even if they do, that's fine. Let them focus their frustrations on me. It's okay. It's what moms do."

Jon hardly spoke a word as they drove to the restaurant and waited for a table. Once seated, he talked to Aiden, asking questions about what the boy had been doing. "You rode down to the Confectionary, eh?"

"I wore a helmet," Aiden assured him.

Lila listened, smiling at the way her nephew knew exactly what to say to amuse his father while not saying anything to concern Jon. *Kids learn this stuff so young it's not funny. Whew.*

Once food arrived, Lila noticed Jon slowly drooping. He ate—methodically and with little interest—but every bit of him exuded exhaustion. *Is it mental or physical?* It felt like an age-old and unanswerable question. *Probably both,* she concluded. *They've been through so much in just a week. It's crazy.*

Although several of the Homstads tried to engage him, Jon only interacted with Aiden. To everyone else he was polite and answered direct questions, but otherwise, he just ate. Despite the reasonably fresh food and the change of atmosphere, Jon just couldn't disconnect.

It's almost like he blames himself. The moment that thought occurred to her, Lila knew. *He is—does. He blames himself. Great. How do you convince a guy that his son's accident isn't his fault? How?*

"Dad?"

Lila glanced up at Aiden, watching.

"Hmm?"

The boy waited until Jon looked up from his plate. "When do you guys get to come home?"

"I don't know. Surgery on Monday. Then we'll know."

Aiden stared at his half-empty plate. "What are they going to do—in the surgery, I mean?"

"I don't know. They say it depends on what they find when they get in there." Jon tore his roll into shreds as he spoke. "I know Dr. Smith said sometimes it takes a couple of the one kind of graft before they can do the final one, but he's hopeful for as few as possible." Jon shook his head. "What a way to state the obvious."

"And then you'll come home."

For the first time since they'd arrived, Jon smiled—a genuine grin that reached his eyes and made the corners crinkle.

8:34 p.m.

Kelly slid the memory card into the laptop. A dozen pictures filled the screen as she opened the folder. Her dad holding Anna. Drew teasing Nathan. Pete, Logan, and Aiden laughing at something Nathan said. Breanne's tearful goodbye. One picture brought a big smile to her face. Aiden and Nathan lay side by side, their hands behind their heads—a picture of relaxed camaraderie. She clicked it and clicked the "upload" button on Facebook. As it uploaded, she typed a caption.

Hanging out with his big bro!

Nathan fussed as Lila tried to get him to straighten his leg. "C'mon, just try for a minute—"

"Noooooooo…"

Kelly's heart constricted as she listened to the ineffectual attempts to convince her son to cooperate. At last, Lila crawled up beside him and spoke soft and low until Nathan settled into a restless sleep. Kelly grabbed the memory card, shoved it back in the camera, and took a picture or two before going back to her previous updates.

Friday's Update: We had a good day. The day started off well for Nathan. Then we did physical therapy, and that was really hard for both him and us. We need to try to do it every hour. Best times, of course, is right after meds.
We also did hydro again, and that was horrible. We could hear him screaming in here, and all I could think about was that it sounded like he was getting electrocuted all over again. :(
They gave him more meds when they got back and they kicked in REALLY well. He definitely seemed better after that. As you can see by the videos, we like him on meds… makes us laugh and helps his pain as well.
Family came down this afternoon. It was WONDERFUL to see my oldest again after so many days! This is the longest I've ever been away from him. :'(And Nathan loved seeing him and the rest of the family.
So Aunt Breanne went home with Mom and Dad and Aunt Lila is staying here to help us. So, you may see updates posted by Aunt Lila—this would be why.

I just wanted to take this time again to thank you all for your support—so many ways. It is all sooo appreciated and sooooo helpful.

The lights dimmed as Jon readied the room for the night. They closed the door most of the way, drew the curtain, and pulled pillows down from a shelf. Kelly yawned, closed the laptop, and grabbed her pillow. "Night."

DAY NINE

Saturday, June 13, 6:32 a.m.

Bleary-eyed, Lila fought to wake up as the children roused the family. As consciousness arrived, her eyes flew to Nathan's bed. *Is it pain again?* She glanced at the clock. *It's been four hours. Is that kind of pain medication the same as the home stuff? Does it wear off in like four hours or something?*

Unable to decide, she asked Kelly about it.

Kelly nodded. "Yeah. They're just awake—"

The nurse interrupted them. "Here to check his vitals, see what the monitors say. How are you doing, Nathan?"

The boy shrugged. As the nurse checked him, Lila tried to get Nathan to stretch out his leg as Breanne had explained, but he wouldn't have anything to do with it. "Maybe after breakfast," she conceded. *Did Breanne get him to do it?* Lila wondered. *Because I'm failing—big time.*

And so the morning went. Nathan objected to every attempt to touch his legs. Anna, in what felt like a commiseration attempt, fussed as well. Exhausted, Jon went for a walk while Kelly and Lila distracted the children. Breakfast came, went, and still moods were low and irritation levels ran high. Lila tried cheerfulness, distraction, firmness, gentleness—everything. Nothing worked. Nothing. Well, leaving him alone worked. As long as they didn't touch him, didn't try to interact, Nathan remained quiet—subdued.

As the hours passed and hydrotherapy loomed, Lila became nervous. All she'd heard and read told her that even from the comparative comfort of the hospital room, it would be a horrifying experience. *Maybe this once will be better... I can hope...*

She hadn't counted on being in the room. However, when the nurses arrived, Jon rose and glanced at Kelly who wrestled with a starving but unwilling-to-nurse Anna. Lila cringed before she spoke. "I'll go."

Kelly's eyes met hers and asked a silent question. *Are you sure?*

Lila nodded. "Just take care of the baby."

Nathan watched, understanding dawning. The moment he saw his father reach for him, the protests began. Pleas, heart-wrenching pleas, echoed in the hallway as they made their way past the supply room to the hydro room. Once they stepped in, the protests escalated and then exploded into terrified screams. *Oh, Lord, why? Why don't they give him something to stop it? This is horrible!*

The nurses turned on a TV set and pointed to Sponge Bob. "See... look at Bob..." but Nathan continued to scream, too loud and non-stop. *I thought Breanne prepared me, but man, no one can prepare you for* **this.**

As the doctors soaked bandages and slowly pulled them off, Lila and Jon worked to try to calm Nathan but to no avail. With the bandages removed, Nathan saw the horrible wounds and screamed even louder, fighting and protesting. No amount of distraction worked—the more he saw, the louder he screamed.

Tears coursed down Lila's cheeks as her heart broke for the little terrified boy. *Helpless. I've never felt so helpless.* Her eyes sought Jon and what was left of her heart squeezed at the pain on his face and his eyes. *Look at him. I think I feel helpless? He's still blaming himself—I can see it. Can't someone make him understand this isn't his fault?* Time lagged, crawled, dragged them through the procedure until forever seemed such a short time.

Long after they returned to the room, Nathan's sobs continued in intermittent and ever-slowing cycles. Then, as if to see how much torture one three-year-old boy could take, a man entered and smiled at Nathan. "Are you ready for some physical therapy?"

"Nooooooooo," Nathan wailed. Lila's heart wailed with him. *Noooooooooo! Hasn't he been through enough already?*

"Okay, Mommy, do you want to help me here?" The man smiled at Lila, beckoning her to come.

Kelly waved from the corner where she nursed Anna. "I'm

Mommy... that's Auntie."

"Oh." The man fumbled for words, evidently confused.

*Do I **look** old enough to have a three-year-old? Do I **have** a wedding ring? I don't think so. Geez Lois!* But despite her internal protests, Lila stepped up, forcing herself to help when all she wanted to do was order everyone from the room and lock it. *That's not real protecting, you twit. That's just making things worse to make 'em easier for you. Suck it up and deal.*

They pushed him, forcing the leg straight. It bent again—straightened. Repeatedly, over and over, until Nathan had worked himself up once more. With a weak smile, the physical therapist squeezed Nathan's arm, saying, "Good job, buddy. See you tomorrow."

With the room left to themselves again, the rest of the day crawled to a slow, steady pace. Lila used every opportunity to continue the expected therapy. She put on a movie, waited for him to be engrossed, and tried to straighten his leg. Nathan was not amused. They played with puzzles, and each time he concentrated hard to get a piece in the right place, she straightened it.

Books—everything they could think of to distract him failed. With each attempt to straighten the leg, Nathan cried, begging Lila not to do it. She stood firm—resolute. Twice she lost her patience. "Listen, Nathan Samuel Cox, I have to straighten it. It's good for you. If you keep bending it, we're going to have to start all over."

It worked, albeit a bit slowly. Though still reluctant to have her touch him, Nathan tried to relax—tried to control his instinctive desire to resist. Still, Lila felt it as a sense of betrayal came over him. She had become one with the enemy. Aunt Lila had been relegated to the ranks of nurses, assistants, therapists, doctors, and other torturers. That realization cut her even deeper. *I can't be soft-hearted about it. He needs to do this.* Her eyes slid over to where Jon and Kelly tried to relax and drown out the ever persistent objections of their son to his therapy. *I can make him do it—be the big meanie. If I do it often, they won't have to. They can stay the "safe place" for him to go when it's over.*

A woman power-walked through the alley between the back

fences of houses on Linden Street and Tanglewood Drive. She passed the partially charred fence and the place where a power line once sparked. However, a wilted-looking garden arrested her attention. *No rain for days—two weeks isn't it? It looks like it's dying. All that work they put into it. And Nathan loves working in there—digging in the dirt.*

Her morning exercise almost forgotten, she let herself in the back gate and jogged across the yard to the spigot at the corner of the house. A hose lay coiled beside it. With water spilling from the end of the hose, she rushed to the garden and laid it in the furrows. A slow trickle flowed down the row.

The rate of water flow assured her that she had time to make it around the neighborhood once before she had to move it to the next row. And so went her morning workout. After each row, she walked the block a time or two and moved it again. Whether it was reality, her imagination, or just wishful thinking, by the time she finished with the last row, the first looked less withered.

The grass looked half-dead as well. *Don't they have sprinklers for that? I thought I saw the previous owners put them in—at least out front.* She jogged to the front of the house but it too looked parched. The sun now shone high overhead. *After sundown. It'll be better after sundown.*

As much as it hurt to hear her son as he fought Lila's attempts at his physical therapy, having someone else do it was always a welcome relief. Several times, Kelly started to tell her sister to let him alone—let him relax after a hard day of constant pain, but she knew her weakness would only harm him in the end.

She sat with her laptop, reading messages of love and support from friends and strangers. The PayPal balance had already passed the next milestone and crept toward a third. *Do people realize that they're paying the mortgage so we don't lose our house? They're paying the utilities we're not even home to use. They're providing us with gas to drive to Naomi's for showers or food that we need but otherwise wouldn't be able to purchase. Because of them, Anna sleeps and doesn't explode out of every diaper we put on her—because she can't handle gluten or dairy. I can do this because of them, and I don't even know how to say thank you. It's all so inadequate.*

Her thoughts were interrupted as Nathan cried out, "I did it! Look, Mommy, I did it!"

"Good job! Yay!" Kelly clapped, not caring that she'd probably wake the baby. Nathan needed it. As the laptop tried to slide off her lap, she grabbed it and began typing an update on her personal Facebook page.

```
"Mommy, I did it." Mommy is so proud of her son, who
conquered    his   fear   of   physical   therapy    and
straightened his leg.
```

As the sun fell in the evening sky, a woman strode up the sidewalk on Linden Street. From his porch, a man watched as she crossed the lawn and began rooting around the side yard. He stood, abandoning his bottle of beer and jogged down his steps, shoving his hands in his pockets. Just as he started to call out—to ask what she was doing there—he saw her find a sprinkler valve key and insert it into the head of a sprinkler.

He paused, watching. *Is she supposed to be doing that? Then again, it is looking dry...*

The woman glanced up at him. "Hey, do you know if they have sprinklers in back? I didn't look earlier."

"Why?"

"Because their grass is dying? My husband has watered our yard twice in the time they've been gone."

"So... it's okay for you to be dinking around their yard?"

The woman dropped hands on her hips. "So if your kid ended up in a hospital two hours away, you'd want your neighbors to let your plants and grass die because you didn't think of or didn't have time to run around the neighborhood asking for someone to come keep it alive?" She pulled out her phone, offering it to him. "Why don't you call the police? I'm—"

"Whoa, I wasn't trying to say—just curious. I've never seen you before, so—"

"Sorry." She shoved the phone back in her pocket. "I'm Janie. I live over on Tanglewood. I just saw the garden dying this morning, and I know all the work Kelly put into that thing, so I watered it and then I saw the grass..."

"Dan," the man responded. "I'm Dan. I'll go get my yard sprinkler. They don't have regular sprinkler heads back there—just a hose attachment. I doubt it's in the back anywhere. Jon's pretty good about putting that kind of stuff away each time he uses it."

"Oh... yeah, I didn't see anything like that. Makes sense though. It's just an old yard. Their house is the last one in this neighborhood to be renovated." Janie glanced up at the little house with its double-doored detached garage and sighed. "I doubt it'll get an upgrade now."

"You don't think there'll be some kind of settlement? I mean, people get millions for this kind of thing."

"Even if they did, and I doubt it," Janie mused. "It would probably be held in trust for him or something—no way the parents could touch it for something like their house."

"True..." Dan glanced over his shoulder. "Be right back with that sprinkler. You can just leave it back there. I'll get it later or I could—"

"Thanks, but I've got it."

Thirty minutes later, Janie paused on her way down the street. "If you could turn off the water in another fifteen minutes, that'd be great. My daughter called." The woman rolled her eyes. "Teenagers. Anyway, I've got to go rescue her from a party gone wrong."

"Got it. No biggie." Not until she was out of sight did he wonder, *Why isn't she going through the alley instead of around the long way?*

As had become her habit, Claire picked up the laptop and signed into Facebook. Her finger slid across the mouse pad until the cursor hovered over the **Help Nathan & Family** page link and her thumb clicked. Several updates had been posted. Starting from the back, she read:

```
Sniff. Another "bath" to wash the wounds, and I can
hear him from several doors down—screams that break
your heart and words like, "No! Please stop! Daddy,
it hurts!" God give me strength. —Kelly
```

Tears choked her heart and stung raw wounds still festering from the last news. *How much can one little guy take?*

Regarding fundraisers (garage sales, dinners, car washes, etc.): The family appreciates the suggestions of ideas to help raise money. We're grateful for the offers of help. We are aware that there are YEARS' worth of very expensive trips back and forth to Manchester, surgeries, therapies, etc. And we do not want to seem ungrateful for all that people want to do for us.
However, at this time, we just do not have the physical, time, and emotional resources to help with these things. If people choose to do this for us, we will, of course, be quite grateful, but for the present, we just cannot be involved. We hope everyone understands. -Dee Homstad

As she read, Claire nodded. It was a lot to handle for people already swamped and two hours away. "Everyone just wants to help and their help is making more work for the family. That's just hard."

Across the room, James looked up from his Bible. "Hmm?"

"Just thinking out loud. I don't know how they're all holding up with everyone wanting something from them, but they need the help people are offering too."

"They being the Coxes?" James clarified.

"Yeah… the updates. They actually had to post and ask people not to expect too much from them in regards to fundraisers."

"That must have been hard to do."

Claire nodded. "Especially for Dee. Having to even mention that people are doing fundraisers would be hard for her." Without elaboration, she continued to read the next update.

Today's update: Long day for everyone. He no longer has to be monitored with constant IV and a monitor. We had a lot more physical therapy today including lots of stretches and emotional stress for everyone. On the upside, he's only had two shots of pain killers—one before his bath and the other right before bed. We were also able to go outside for a bit. Nathan LOVED it! —Kelly and Lila.

Hearing of Nathan going outside made her smile. She sat back, the laptop abandoned beside her, and tried to imagine him outside, pointing at birds or butterflies. Did they let him play on the grass? Did he run his little train along the ground beside him again?

The fundraisers still niggled at her, worming their way into her heart and taking up residence there. All the fundraisers around town helped—every dime helped—but if they could somehow organize them for the family and take that burden off the Coxes and Homstads... "There's got to be a way."

"Hmm?" James murmured, but his wife didn't hear.

DAY TEN

Sunday, June 14, 9:24 a.m.

Father's Day—no matter how much the sun shone, no matter how chipper the staff or how many cards and balloons appeared, the day dawned with a dreariness clouding it. Kelly watched her husband, concerned. *How long will he blame himself? What can I do to comfort or reassure him? I just don't know what to do.*

Still, despite efforts on every side, their family was fractured on Father's Day. That hurt. *Tomorrow. He's coming tomorrow. We had to do Father's Day a day late once when I was a kid. It didn't kill us or ruin Dad's life forever. Why does it feel so monumental now?*

As Jon fed Nathan and Lila wandered the halls with Anna, Kelly checked Facebook and her mother's message board. A late night post from Dee brought a lump to her throat.

Another long day from the way it sounds. They had a lot of physical therapy and a lot more is ahead of them. Please pray for a good night's sleep and as nice of a Father's Day for Jon as we could hope for. He'll not get to spend it with Aiden. We're taking Breanne up tomorrow as it is, so we just decided to do one trip. I'm kind of regretting that now.

Lila arrived with Anna just as Kelly finished eating her own breakfast. "If you're done, I'll go down and get something. I'm starving."

No sooner had Lila left than the cellphone rang. Kelly fumbled for it. "Hello?"

"Hey, Mom! I wanted to wish Dad a happy Father's Day before I left for church."

"Sure! Hold on." She leaned forward, stretching out the phone as far as she could. "Aiden."

There it was—that flicker of normalcy in Jon's features. Momentary happiness. *Lord, thank you again for that phone. I've got to thank Rachel for sending it. What would we do without it? They'd be calling Breanne, but she's not here, so she'd give them Lila's number, and Lila would have to run back—craziness. I am so grateful for that thing right now.*

How long Jon talked, she didn't know, but it did both of them a world of good. Kelly basked in the residue of relaxation that hovered around her husband, and Jon drank in his son's words. A nurse appeared mid conversation—one Kelly didn't know well. Nathan whined as the nurse examined the bandages and prepared to soak them. This effectively ended the conversation and prompted Kelly's own internal whines to the Lord.

Why? He finally gets to relax and be himself again and this has to happen? Couldn't that guy have come in fifteen minutes later? This is crazy.

Her thoughts came to a screeching halt as she heard the nurse say, "—bandage slipped."

What does that mean? Wh—

"—s'nt going to do hydro today, but—"

"Noooooooo not hydro. Nooooooooo please, Daddy!"

"Shh..." Jon began, trying to soothe the child's rising fear.

In a misguided attempt to be helpful, the nurse tried to explain to Jon that fear of hydro is a perfectly normal emotion, and children often protested, but Jon stopped him. "We'll handle it, thank you."

"Well..." The man's eyes bounced between Kelly and Jon. "I'll go let Dr. Smith know what's up then."

The moment they had the room to themselves again, Kelly pounced. "What was *that* about?"

"Nathan's bandages slipped," Jon explained. "If you look, you can see the protective sock is stuck to the wound. They'll have to soak it off…"

"Nooooooo…"

Again, Jon shushed Nathan, assuring the boy that he would be right there. "Sometimes we just have to do what we don't like."

Tell me about it.

Dr. Smith examined the bandages and shook his head. "Yeah… we'll have to do something about that." He caught the nurse's eye and said, "Let's add Versed® to his pre-hydro pain meds—see if it calms him a bit."

"What is that?" Jon asked, leaning closer.

"It's a calming agent. It'll help him handle his fear a bit better, I think, and it tends to produce a bit of amnesia of the procedure. We'll also try to get him to walk down there." The doctor's eyes slid to where Nathan fiddled with the pages of a book, uninterested in the contents. "We've got to do something to keep him from giving up. I can see him close at times."

"If you think it's best…" Jon stared at his son, uncertain.

"I think it's almost imperative. He's got to try, and the body is fighting with him for self-preservation. We need to give him the tools to be able to overcome it."

Jon nodded. "I can see that."

"We'll be back in about twenty minutes." Dr. Smith leaned close to Nathan and smiled. "I hear you slept good last night. Glad to hear it."

Nathan grinned. "I did it, too!"

"Did what?"

"Straighted my leg!"

Smiling, Dr. Smith squeezed Nathan's hand. "Good job. I knew you could do it."

Jon followed the doctor to the door and said, "We put him on his stomach last night. After he relaxed, his leg straightened. It was straight for most of the night, but today—"

"It's okay. He did it. That's what matters."

The great plan to help Nathan walk to hydrotherapy failed.

Despite everyone's concentrated efforts and the extra medication, Nathan balked, refusing even to try. At the doctor's nod, Jon picked him up and carried him. Once inside the room, everyone "suited up" again. Shower caps, backwards "rain coats," shoe covers, and gloves. Lila suggested they try a different TV program—one Nathan had seen—but to no avail. The screams still echoed in the room as the medical team soaked the protective sock from his wound, irrigated it, and prepared the fresh bandages. Still, it did seem less traumatic for him.

As he carried Nathan from the room, the boy's sobs already subsiding, Jon gave Lila a weak smile. "Seems like it helped, doesn't it?"

"Yeah. Helped." Lila squeezed Nathan's hand. "You did good. You did really good."

Immediately after lunch, two physical therapists entered the room, Nathan's nurses on their heels. Lila looked up and her heart sank as she realized what was coming. A sidelong glance at Jon caught him squaring his shoulders for the procedure. "Do you want me to call and see if Kelly is almost here?"

"No... it's hard on her. Maybe missing it's for the best."

Yeah, well you missing it would probably be for the best too, but I don't see that happening. But Lila nodded and moved to Nathan's side. "Hey, buddy. Look who's—"

She didn't have a chance to finish. Nathan took one look at the torturers in doctor's clothing and whimpered. The man from the previous day held up a plastic bat and ball set. "I brought you something..."

The glassiness faded a bit from Nathan's eyes as he sat up. He reached for it, but the therapist pulled it back slightly. "You have to walk for it—come get it."

Nathan's eyes slid from his leg to the bat as if weighing the trauma of physical therapy against the benefits of the toy. He grabbed his bear, stuck it on his head, and checked out. Laughter surrounding him sent his eyes sliding toward his father. Jon moved the bear and helped Nathan sit up. "Sorry, it's not an option. Let's try it."

The first few attempts failed. Nathan leaned all his weight on his "good" leg as he kept his "bad" one bent back and away from the pain-inducing floor. "Nooooooo... don't make meeeeeeeee............ noooooo...."

The distinct scent of the hospital's hand sanitizer drew Lila's eyes to the door where Kelly stood rubbing it into her hands. Kelly's eyes asked the question at hand. *"Did he try?"*

Lila shook her head.

"C'mon, now. Try to get the toy..."

How anyone could see if he even tried, Lila couldn't imagine. One therapist held Nathan's body erect, while the other worked to straighten the child's leg. Jon's hand held Nathan's hand, and nurses stood ready to help or cheer depending on the outcome. *He needs encouragement!* "Good job," Lila insisted, not knowing if the boy's attempts were any good at all.

Something in the child's demeanor shifted. Lila pulled out the camera and began recording the procedure as Nathan tried to move toward the toy. Though he didn't straighten his leg, he did occasionally add a bit of pressure to it, whimpering with each step.

"You're almost there," one therapist said.

"Pleeeeeaaaasssssssssssssseeeee. No more. Stop! Ow! Ooooowwww! Noooo... Pllllleeeeeeeaaaaseee..."

"You have to do it. You can get the toy if you just try. I know you can," the therapist insisted.

Nathan seemed to take that quite personally as he pulled his hand free and pushed away the fingers that constantly worked to straighten his leg. A nurse wiggled the toy in continual taunting torment. His father encouraged him. The therapists fought to keep his leg straight, and Nathan, weary of it all and with his leg screaming for relief, screamed with it.

Jon murmured admonitions to calm himself, but Nathan had endured enough. He fought to cross the room, but Lila suspected it was to get the ordeal over more than to earn the toy. Several steps produced further screeches—both in protest and in pain, but at last he collapsed in Kelly's arms, spent.

The therapist offered him the bat, but Nathan didn't even notice. His eyes glazed over and he shook with exhaustion. After a few more rounds of praise from everyone in the room, the medical personnel left the Coxes alone. Lila smiled at Jon. "Happy Father's Day, Daddy. He did it."

Before Jon could respond, Allison came in with morphine. "Let's make you feel better, okay?"

Nathan beamed up at her. "I walked."

"You are so his favorite nurse," Lila mused. "I think he would have told anyone else, 'You made me walk, you meanie.'"

"Did the video turn out?" Allison asked as she helped Nathan wash down the medication.

"I'm about to upload it. Just as soon a—"

"Where's my bat? I want to show her my bat."

Lila looked on the bed, under the bed, under the covers, on the table—she looked everywhere. Kelly began moving the things on the chairs, but Jon spoke up. "I think he took it with him."

"Who?"

"The therapist. I'm pretty sure he had it in his hand when he left."

"What!" Fury filled Lila, and in an uncharacteristic fit of self-control, she bit back the words she wanted to say. *They promise the kid a toy and then just walk off with it? What are they thinking?* "I'll be back. I've got to walk before I say something I'm not supposed to."

Kelly and Jon stared at one another, shocked. Allison smirked. "I can see my summary of the day's events. 'Physical therapy: Two doctors. One baseball bat. One screaming kid. One heartrending video. One ticked off aunt when they don't give the kid his toy.'"

"Mom! They didn't give him the toy! I mean, c'mon! He worked hard for that! I don't know what to do!"

"Just go get one. Just take the van, find the nearest dollar store, and buy it. Usually I'd say that he's gotten enough toys and gifts—"

"Someone comes up from Fairbury every day," Lila interjected. "It's just so cool how people we don't even know care about him."

"That's my point. Usually with all the toys he's been given, I'd say just forget it."

A murmur from someone interrupted Dee. Lila waited impatiently until her mom returned. "So just get one?"

"Yep. Just go. And upload that video. I want to see him walk."

"You don't want to see it, Mom. It is horrible. I'll upload it for Breanne because she'll 'get it' but—"

"I can't avoid all unpleasantness. But go get the toy first."

She seethed all the way to the room for the van keys. "Mom wants to see the video—or she thinks she does. Can you upload it?" Without waiting for Kelly's response, she added, "I'm going to the store. Can I take your van?"

"Sure, but—"

"Need anything?"

Kelly shook her head, but Lila didn't see it. She'd already zipped out the door and down the hall. Kelly heard the great doors clack open and snap shut behind her. Jon chuckled as he muttered, "Woman on a mission."

"Where's Aunt Lila? I want to sing. 'One little, two little, three little Nathans...'" He paused. "Happy Birthday, Daddy!"

"It's not Daddy's birthday," Kelly said. *Didn't take long for those meds to kick in!*

"But he got balloons." Nathan giggled. "Can I play with your balloons? They go wheeeeeeeeee in the air, but you have to hold the toy."

"What toy?" Kelly reached for Jon's Father's Day balloons and passed them to her son.

"This one. See!" Nathan held up the plastic, monkey-shaped weight on the bottom. If you hold it..." The balloon rose. "See. Goes right up! Up, up! Whee..." The balloon jerked to a stop as the ribbon grew taut. "Hey... we should take the toy off. It can't go up anymore."

"Maybe you should jerk it back down and let it rise again. If we take the toy off, we won't be able to get it back down. No ladder," Kelly explained.

"The fireman can come. He has a ladder!"

Kelly snickered "I don't think that'll work. Their ladders are much too big—and attached to the truck, remember?"

"Oh." The boy stared at the balloon. "Sorry. You have to stay with me."

While Nathan chattered to the balloon, the blank TV—"Will you tell me a story?"—and nearly every other inanimate object within sight, Kelly pulled the memory card from the camera and tried to figure out how to upload it to the Facebook page and Jon rested, clearly spent after his long morning.

It took a few minutes for all thirty-seven seconds to upload. Kelly laughed at yet another goofy comment by Nathan and typed the status update.

<u>Nathan walks in therapy (11:53 a.m.)</u>
Warning! May not be suitable for young children to see.

Nathan working on physical therapy. It was a long, exhausting morning, but we are making process.

Immediately, with hardly enough time for anyone to have even watched it, the comments flowed in.

Bentley Novak (11:54 a.m.)
My heart goes out to you guys.

Chrissy Santina (11:54 a.m.)
Made me tear up! Poor baby. Hang in there, Nathan! (((Hugs)))

Karyn Bryant (11:56 a.m.)
Kelly, is it at the ankle that he is afraid to bend? I don't know how much of each leg is burned… totally from toes on up?

Tait Stedtmann (12:01 p.m.) He is an incredible little guy. The prayers won't stop.

Kelly answered the one question, not trusting herself to respond to the influx of well wishes while they still toyed with her emotions.

Help Nathan & Family (12:07 p.m.)
He has burns behind the leg, at the ankles, and toes. On the right leg, every place it bends (except at the torso) is where the burns are concentrated. It is a mobility issue, so he has to straighten them.

As more prayers, well wishes, and empathetic posts of astonishment and pain flooded the video's comment log, Kelly closed the laptop and shook her head. "Can't take much more."

"I was going to go for a walk," Jon murmured. "I could take Anna—"

"She'll sleep a while longer. You go ahead. I'll hang out with Nathan," Kelly insisted. "Do you want me to go down and get dinner when Lila gets back?"

"I'll get it later. Thanks."

Baseball from a hospital bed isn't the sport of kings, but Nathan adapted it to an odd combination of golf and croquet. Just as Lila settled in with Anna and tried to give Kelly a chance to rest, Christine entered the room, waving another stack of meal cards. "Thought you might be getting low. I'm off tomorrow, so I wanted to stop in really quick today." She passed them to Kelly and pulled something from her pocket. "Look what I brought for you. I thought you and your bear might need masks for your next therapy. Keep the icky germs away."

"I did therapy. I walked. Lila got me my toy because they stole it."

Lila blushed. "Can't say anything around that kid."

"Stole it?"

Throwing caution out the window and into the street, Lila scowled. "They make the kid work, do painful and terrifying things while promising him a bat and then walk out of the room with it? I don't *think* so!"

"But I got it," Nathan insisted. "Lila got it. But this one is red and the other one was blue. I like red better."

"Well that's good," Christine said. To Lila she mouthed, *"Why did they take it?"*

"No idea. Lame if you ask me."

"So..." Christine glanced around the room. Kelly, barely keeping her eyes open gave her a half-smile. "Is Jon having a good Father's Day?"

Lila shook her head. "Would you if you had to send your kid through hydro and physical therapy in one morning?"

"Lila!" Kelly shot the social worker an apologetic glance, but Lila didn't care.

"Well! It's true. How's it supposed to be good?"

"I'll see what I can do about that," Christine promised. "I think maybe what everyone needs is a chance for some fresh-air therapy."

"Not therapy," Nathan protested. "I did it. I walked. I'm done."

"That's right. Until you do your practice after dinner, you're done," Lila agreed, rolling her eyes as she tried to tie masks on Nathan and the bear. It failed, eyesight being essential for such tasks. "There."

"I'm all safe!" Nathan pulled down the mask a bit. "Do you need one?" Kelly shook her head, but Nathan said, "No. Mask lady. Does she need one?" Then, as if he hadn't already asked a question, he turned to Lila. "Can I watch 'Courageous'? I want to see Javier in the car."

Christine and Lila exchanged amused glances before Lila said, "Well, okay then!"

The hospital grew hushed around them as Lila attempted to write the evening's Facebook update. She typed it in three times before giving up hope for a cohesive and coherent message and went for "done" as sufficient to her purpose.

```
Lots to share tonight. First, we uploaded a video
earlier of Nathan's physical therapy. It's hard to
watch, but he walked! Woohoo!
Later, we went for a walk in the wagon around the
nurse's station and then outside for a Father's Day
picnic. Nathan enjoyed eating on a blanket and
having a grass war with his favorite nurse, Allison.
Time will tell who the victor truly is. Right now,
both sides claim that title.
They're about ready to try to put an IV line in him
again, which means reinserting another needle. :'( .
Thankfully, his favorite nurse is still on duty and
it's after a really good time outside. —Lila
```

An hour later, Kelly read over the previous messages and added her own update.

```
I am sorry to report that they couldn't get an IV in
him tonight. The blood vessels burst every time. Two
different nurses tried and in three places—even
```

going into the hand. Sniff. I don't know what that means for tomorrow and his surgery. I mean, they have to do it, but how they will manage it, I don't know.

I wish I had the time to personally write each one of you for your kindness and encouragement and support in all the ways we have received. While I don't have the time, I just want you to know that it means a lot to us.—Kelly

Blissful silence of a sleeping house gave Dee time to do much needed work on her website project. She tried one color, then another. She adjusted the margins, the padding, the header, and recreated yet another logo banner when a fresh idea came to her. Lost in the project, she jumped as Drew and Jamie burst into the room, her laptop skidding halfway to the floor before she caught it.

"Mom!"

"What!" Dee took a deep breath. "You just aged me by at least two years. You owe me."

"Go to the Help Nathan page."

"Yes ma'am."

Jamie had the decency to cringe. "Sorry. But look, seriously. I'm so ticked I could—spit."

"Do it outside. I don't have time to mop the floor and you should be in bed," Dee muttered as she clicked on the Facebook tab and slid her finger to the link to Nathan's page. "What?"

"Go to the video where he's in the wagon. Look at the last comment!"

Her eyes rose and sought what she hoped would be the less indignant face of her son. "Seriously?"

He nodded.

Dee fumbled through the site, clicking into photos, then albums, then videos. "Man, they make this complicated."

"Right?" Drew shook his head. "It took me forever to find it."

The comment jumped out at her before Jamie or Drew could say another word.

Tilly Fremont (9:31 p.m.) I can't help but notice that this is a page to "help" a family supposedly in need after a traumatic accident. But this video clearly shows that this family can't be in too much need if the father is walking around wearing expensive running shoes. These crooks should be ashamed of themselves, fleecing people like this.

"No way. How ridiculous!"
"Can we delete it? That's just wrong!" Jamie leaned forward as if to do it by sheer mental power.
Dee shook her head. "No, no. Leave it. We'd make it look like we have something to hide. People will know—will see just how petty this is. We—wait. Naomi just posted." Dee's laughter filled the living room and Dee turned the laptop so her kids could see it.

Naomi Wardoff (11:42 p.m.) @Tilly Fremont. I've spent almost an hour rereading your comment, trying to decide if you're really that stupid or that insensitive. I'm going for stupid. I think it's better than being cold-hearted. It's really none of your business, but since you insist on knowing, the shoes do not belong to Jon. He was wearing dirty, torn shoes for working outside when the accident happened and needed something a little more sanitary for the hospital. So, if you base need upon the quality of shoes a person wears in a video, I'd say a guy who doesn't even have his own shoes and has to borrow them definitely fits in that category. Please keep your ugliness to yourself next time. The family just doesn't need this kind of garbage.

"Oh, that's good," Drew said, snickering. "If this Tilly isn't a friend of the family, she won't even know that Naomi is Jon's sister. Too funny."
"Sad that it even came up—just really sick, if you ask me." Dee sighed. "Meanwhile, you should still be in bed. Go!"
"Okay... Night, Mom!" Jamie waved and shuffled off toward her

room. Drew hung back and asked, "Why do people even do stuff like that?"

Dee shook her head as she reread the original comment. "I think some people are just that unhappy—or they've been burned by people who *did* take advantage and can't see anything outside that experience."

"I guess. It's not funny, then—not really. It's just sad."

You aren't kidding, kid, Dee mused as the room once more became enshrouded in silence.

DAY ELEVEN

Monday, June 15, 6:54 a.m.

"C'mon, Nathan. I know you're tired but you need to eat. You can't have anything after this until after surgery."

Still groggy from interrupted sleep, Nathan shook his head.

"One more bite..."

He opened his mouth... and yawned. Lila took the opportunity to shovel a full mouthful of food in while it was open. Nathan's expression—priceless. Still, he chewed the food and downed the water Lila offered him. Kelly pulled the carton of soy milk off the tray and shoved it in the ice chest under the chair.

Was it only four days ago that she did that and I didn't know why? How weird—that odd things like saving milk becomes normal in a place like this. Aloud she asked, "Think Naomi will come today?"

"Yeah. They were in Fairbury for Father's Day yesterday, so she'll come today." Kelly's eyes slid automatically to the ice chest. "Good thing too. That thing is getting full."

"And you're running low on water. I should have got some more yesterday. I was a bit out of it."

Kelly snickered. "Yep. But it was funny."

Nathan yawned again, and with a glance at the clock to be sure it wasn't past seven o'clock, Lila shoved one more bite into his mouth.

"Hmphaaay..."

"Forgot I said last one. Sorry. Chew it since it's in there." *Okay, Lord is it wrong that I'm glad I forgot? I mean, I **did** forget, but I'm not* *sorry I did. He needs the food. Long time until he can eat again.*

The night nurse stepped into the room to take away the tray. "No more for him. Sorry." Though she'd never been Nathan's favorite nurse, he beamed at her as if his rescuer—the patron saint of sleepy boys who don't want to eat.

"Okay, so we're going to go in for his bath—"

"Nooooooooo…."

Kelly's eyes widened. "Before surgery? Won't they be doing everything in there anyway?"

The woman shrugged and handed Jon a clipboard. "I just have orders for hydro before his surgery, so we'll take him in in about an hour." She nodded at the papers. "You just need to sign those—consents and whatnot."

Jon nodded and began that arduous task of reading the paperwork before him. He pulled out a notebook and began writing down questions for the surgeon. Lila carried clean clothes into the bathroom and tried to clean up a bit. *You'd think they could get him that paperwork sooner—so he doesn't have to try to think about everything right away. Not everyone just signs paperwork and lets people do whatever they want to their kid. Some people agonize over every decision.* The moment she thought it, Lila nodded and sighed. *Unless that's why they do it—to save people agonizing over something that has to be done anyway. They mean well, I suppose.*

By the time they were all dressed for the day and the room cleaned up, the team came for Nathan. "Time for hy—"

The poor nurse hardly spoke before Nathan began his objections. Kelly glowered at the nurse. "We'll take him in, thank you."

"I—"

Lila spoke up. "It's hard enough that he has to go through it. You don't have to rub it in."

"Lila…"

She whirled to face her sister. "What? It's what we're all thinking. Geez, Lois! Give me a break."

"Sorry…"

"You should be." Lila glanced up at Kelly to see if she'd spoken aloud, but Kelly passed her the baby without any kind of response. *Well, she should. Someone has to tell them or they'll never stop it.*

Alone in the room with the baby, Lila waited, nerves taught with dread, for the screams to commence. The baby blew out a diaper, proof that Kelly must have had gluten or dairy in the previous twenty-four hours. The change distracted her long enough to realize that over five minutes had passed without a sound. *Did they take him to surgery instead? Did I misunderstand? Did I chew that guy out for nothing?* That thought made her shake her head. *He still said the "H" word. Jerk.*

Though there were evidence of tears on Nathan's face, Jon carried him in the room without a whimper. Lila stared at Kelly, shock stealing her voice. Kelly grinned. "Didn't scream once. Cried—but didn't scream."

"Nice!"

Kelly slid her eyes sideways and leaned closer. "They're coming in soon to try the IV again…"

The next Facebook updates followed in quick succession.

```
11:24 a.m. We are about ready to take Nathan into
the next room to be strapped to a board to try to
get an IV in. :'( It's obvious that Nathan is scared
and his favorite nurse isn't on duty today.
Horrible quote of the morning. "Mommy, I don't want
a needle. I can't be a big boy." Oh, my sweet one. —
Kelly
```

The next said only:

```
11:42 a.m. After sweat and tears (literally), we
finally got an IV in his hand. :'( It was a
struggle, but they did it!
Nathan's second surgery is scheduled for 3:30 this
afternoon. Please pray that it goes well! —Kelly
```

In an attempt to distract Nathan from the burgeoning approach of hunger pangs, the nurses brought several visitors in to entertain them. A musician carrying a guitar and harmonica came first. Nathan cheered as the man began asking about songs—songs Kelly and Jon had never heard of. After a moment or two, Kelly suggested "Danny Boy." Nathan clapped, Lila swooned, and Jon and Kelly grinned at one another.

"What else do you like?"

Nathan looked at his mom before saying, "Celtic Thunder!"

The musician raised one eyebrow. The second followed almost immediately. "A three-year-old who knows Celtic Thunder… interesting."

"I'm impressed that you guessed his age right," Kelly mused.

"I'm good. What can I say?" He blew a riff and rolled his eyes. "Okay, so the nurse told me."

"We would never have known," Lila joked. "You totally failed that one."

"So what song do you like by Celtic Thunder?"

Nathan began singing, "'I wanna spend my life with you…'"

And so the music continued until a dog appeared in the doorway. The musician waved as he left the room, but Nathan, absorbed with the dog, hardly noticed, stopping only to wave and say "Thank you," when bidden. As he played with the dog, telling the animal all about his grandma's German shepherd, Captain, Lila worked to straighten his leg. He objected, but in a more absent way than had been his habit.

However, all the distractions they managed didn't completely destroy the dread Nathan felt as they prepped him for surgery. Kelly and Jon followed him as far as the hospital would allow, and Lila, desperate to do something, took the baby down to the gift shop to buy him a balloon.

```
3:32 p.m. Nathan just went into pre-op. He wasn't
very excited—Lila.
```

Twenty minutes later, Lila sent a text message to Breanne. STILL NOT IN SURGERY.

Breanne wrote back minutes later. JUST STOPPED IN CHATTSVILLE. BE THERE IN AN HOUR.

Twenty minutes after Kelly arrived to say they'd taken him back, Aiden, Dee and Breanne arrived. Lila gathered her things and packed them in the car, arriving back to the room in time to hear Nathan was out of surgery and in recovery. "How did it go?"

Kelly shrugged. "We don't know." She sighed. "We never know anything. One of the nurses said something about them not doing anything, but he's wearing new bandages, so…"

As Lila and Dee sped back to Fairbury, Breanne waited with Anna while Kelly and Aiden walked the halls, watching for Nathan's return.

4:59 p.m. Nathan is in recovery! He'll be back in his room in a few minutes! —Breanne

Later that night, Kelly posted a new update.

8:32 p.m. Nathan made it back to his room at twenty past five. He is in pain—you can tell. We're waiting for the meds to kick in well. He was sooooooo happy to see his brother Aiden, and we were happy to see him too. Aiden will be here until Friday. It's nice to be together again.

9:19 p.m. We haven't heard from the doctor yet. Waiting to hear what, if anything, happened and where we're at now. Since it's 9:20, most likely we'll hear about it all tomorrow. —Kelly

7:21 p.m.

The soulful sounds of a popular song faded slowly into an improvisation of "It Is Well with My Soul." The Rhodes family joined the harmony of the rest of their Monday night regulars. As the room quieted, Steve asked the question on many hearts. "How is Nathan?"

"Surgery today," Claire said. She shrugged. "Don't know how it went. There was nothing up before everyone came—just that he was out and one nurse thought they didn't do anything." Her eyes lit up as she remembered something. "But Aiden is there. That's got to feel good."

"Times like this make me tempted to get a Facebook account." Steve murmured. "Anything else? Does the family need anything?"

"What they need is a serious fundraiser." James spoke from behind Claire. She leaned back and gazed up at him.

"Serious? What do you mean? People keep coming up with fundraiser after fundraiser."

"But nothing substantial," he objected. "The Coxes need one that will really bring in a significant amount of money."

Joy interjected her opinion as she brought bottles of water to pass out amongst the musicians. "The problem with things like that is that it costs so much to make anything. No one in town has those kind of resources—well, except maybe Alexa Hartfield."

"We do."

Claire's heart squeezed. *If he thinks our savings would cover the costs of a big fundraiser… we'd be better just to give them the money and hope it grows some other way.* "Not really—"

"My Daddy owns the cattle on a thousand hills. He's one rich Dude. And if we gather together and pray, He's here with us. He can do this."

"Do what, though?" Claire shook her head. "I don't know what it is that you think should happen."

"Well, I've been thinking—"

Joy and Noelle glanced at one another and burst out singing, "'—thinkin' over, thinking over, thinkin' over the things that you've said…'"

Claire laughed. "They are your daughters…"

"Well, I have…" James insisted.

Steve laughed. "That's obvious. We're just interested to know about what."

James leaned back in the chair, his hands resting on his guitar neck. "We get together like this—we sing. We've done the open mic at the USO building…"

"Which got us invitations to other things like the Midsummer's Faire and the Cancer March—right… I get it," Steve prompted in a clear attempt to speed James along.

"Well, since we've done these kinds of events for other people, why not set up our own? Why can't *we* do this?"

"Yeah! The USO guys might let us use the building," Joy interjected. "They like us!"

Claire's mind had already begun to organize it. She reached for a notebook under her Bible, folded half back, and grabbed a pen. "When?"

"I don't know, how long does this kind of thing take?" James' eyes bounced from one person to another.

Joy pulled out her phone and scrolled through a calendar. "Well, we couldn't be ready by next month—"

"Six weeks," Claire said. "We need a minimum of six weeks. You've got practices, we've got work to do to get the word out—no matter how small or big it is, we need at least six weeks."

Noelle and Joy spoke in unison. "August fifteenth is a Saturday…"

"Do we need two months?" James waited, anticipation making his leg jostle.

Claire stared at her paper, trying to imagine the work necessary to plan and execute a large fundraiser. "You want this big—as in raise a thousand dollars or more?"

"Several thousand—at least."

She nodded and began writing. "Then we need two months. Let's do it."

"Where? Where will we do it?" Steve asked.

"I'm sure any of the churches in town would—" someone began.

James shook his head. "No. This needs to be a community event—not just a church one. Some people will be turned off by it. We don't want to alienate the very people we hope will help. This isn't the church asking the church to support its own. This is the town asking the town to do that."

As James spoke, Steve nodded, catching the spirit of the idea. "We'll go down to the USO on Friday night at Open Mic—talk to them. If they let us use the building and don't charge too much… Steve unscrewed the cap of his water and took a swig. "Hopefully they won't be outrageous."

The impromptu planning session swung into earnest discussions on what they'd sing, how they'd get out the word, and what kind of publicity they'd need. Claire caught Joy's eyes over the heads of the others in the room and jerked her head toward the kitchen in a silent request. *Start dishing up the ice cream?* Joy nodded and beckoned Noelle to follow.

DAY TWELVE

Tuesday, June 16, 6:40 p.m.

The grass looks bad—too tall. If it gets any taller, mowing is going to be hard. I could do it. Dan stared at the house, wondering how much longer the grass could go before it became a jungle. *Then again, if we don't get rain…*

He pushed himself off his front step, grabbed his empty beer bottle, and shuffled off to his garage, dumping the bottle in a recycling bin in the process. *They won't have time to deal with it when they get home anyway.* He rolled up the doors, wrangled his mower from its corner, and pushed it into his drive. The gas tank looked low and his can proved empty.

Dan pushed it back in the garage, grabbed the gas can, and fished his keys from his pocket. His neighbor laughed. "Outta gas before you start, eh? Sounds like a good excuse not to bother. You're not looking very tall there…"

"Thought I'd get the Coxs' yard before it gets too tall."

The man blinked. "The—" His eyes shifted to the Cox house and back again. "That'd be nice for them. I've got gas in here. Hold on."

The evening air soon filled with the sweet scent of cut grass. Each pass of the mower overpowered the petroleum odor that the machine belched at every turn. Back, forth, up, down. The tiny yard didn't take long to finish—and he'd only begun. Dan found himself outside with weed trimmers, a trowel, a rake. Once the mess he'd created had been relegated to empty garbage cans on one side of the Coxes' house, he wandered through their back yard, examining it. The grass grew even higher there—likely fed by the semi-frequent watering of late.

The temptation to turn around and ignore the much larger area that now called to him grew with each passing second. He glanced at the sky, hoping for some indication that there wouldn't be time to finish, but the sun hadn't set and wouldn't for some time. That excuse gone, he turned and went to retrieve the mower.

This time, Dan just made one pass across the yard. *No need to go overboard. Just trying to prevent a jungle.* As he neared the edge of the lawn, out by the garden, he let the mower die and stared at the rows of plants. In the fading light of the sun, he began pulling everything that looked different than most. *Man, if there are more weeds than plants, I'm going to kill everything good and save everything bad, but weeds don't usually have roundish leaves—do they?*

He waved as the woman—Janie—powered past as quickly as possible. "Been looking at those. Just haven't had time to get to them. Thanks!" she called as she hurried down the alley and out of sight.

9:12 p.m.

The phone rang. Dee's natural dislike for telephones had increased exponentially since the ordeal began. The new primary objection came with her inability to let one ring without answering it now. *What if there's something wrong—if they need something. I just have to answer the dumb thing—especially after nine o'clock at night. It's just annoying!*

"Hello?" *How can I sound so cheerful when I want to throttle the person on the other end of the line?*

"Dee? It's Janie—Kelly's neighbor? We had that garage sale together a month or so ago?"

"Right. Janie. How are you?" *And why are you calling me at this time of night?*

"Good, good. Any new news on Nathan? I saw they didn't do the skin graft, but—"

You seriously called me at night to ask what you could find out from the Facebook page? Are you nuts? "Nope. That's all we know right now."

"Oh, well, I figured. Anyway, I just thought you should know, in case someone saw it and thought something was wrong, Kelly's neighbor, Dan, was mowing their yards tonight. He did a bit of weeding too. I just thought if anyone reported seeing someone going in or out around dark, you should know it's okay—nothing wrong."

"Oh—the garden." Dismay filled her. "I forgot about it. Kelly was counting on it. She asked Willow Finley all kinds of stuff about how to make sure they got enough to get them through part of winter—tilled up over half the back yard!"

"Yeah, it's pretty big. I was impressed. I kept meaning to go over, but I've been so busy—"

"And with no rain, it's gonna die. Thanks for telling me. I'll go over and see that it's watered tomorrow."

"Oh, no. I've been watering during my walks. It should be good. And with Dan weeding, it should be fine," Janie insisted as she disconnected the call.

"Thanks..." Dee stared at the dead handset in her hand. "Wow..."

When Mom said You've "got this," she wasn't joking. You've taken care of everything before we could even ask—before we even knew to ask. Wow. Just... wow.

DAY THIRTEEN

Wednesday, June 17, 2:53 a.m.

Anna screamed. A fresh diaper didn't help. A full belly did nothing. Several burps seemed only to increase the child's protests. Jon stirred. Breanne shifted, and Aiden's eyes stretched open for a fraction of a second. "What's wrong?"

"Just cranky. Go back to sleep." She stared down at the pallet on the floor and wondered why they'd thought it was a good idea to let him stay overnight. *Because we're a family! This is what families do. We sleep together under the same roof.*

Kelly stepped outside the room, intent on riding down the elevator to pace the lobby where no one would be disturbed, but the night nurses pounced. "Oh, I'll take her!"

The other nurse balked. "Nuh, uh. You got her last time. It's my turn."

How do they know that I need to hear this—need to know that we're not a crazy burden? Though it niggled at the back of her mind that it might all be a charade to make her feel better about them taking the baby so she could sleep, one look at the nurses' eager faces told her no one could act that well at that time of morning.

"Okay, I don't care who gets her first," Kelly sighed as she held out the wailing child. "I'm just grateful for sleep."

Long, slim chocolate fingers reached for the baby and wrapped around the little body before the other nurse could move. Something about it reminded Kelly of a song her grandfather had sung about a gunfighter who shot down another man in a barroom brawl before that man could even unholster his weapon. "I guess I win," the woman crowed, snuggling the baby to her chest.

Anna, now on the Cox family traitors list, gurgled and popped her thumb in her mouth.

3:12 p.m.

Once more, Kelly's eyes slid toward the clock. *Where's Lynn? It's a good day. He'll want to paint today.* Even as she waited for the hospital artist to arrive, Kelly wondered, again, what had inspired her to do it. *Twice a week. But why?*

Mid-thought, a knock came at the door, and Lynn entered, rubbing sanitizer into her hands. *I am not going to miss that scent,* Kelly thought randomly.

"Hey! How's my friend, Nathan? Are you ready to paint today?"

Nathan beamed. "Yes!"

"Excellent. What will we paint?" She pulled something from her bag. "I made this for you—for your train." Unfolding a papery fabric revealed a road—a hand-drawn railroad with hills, valleys, tunnels, and trees.

Without hesitating, Nathan dug his train out from beneath the covers and sat up straighter in bed. "Whooo-oooh..."

"I thought we were going to paint..." As Lynn laid out her supplies, she talked about what he might like to paint. "You did a frog... and the bird. So, what today?"

"Candy!"

Kelly laughed. "Someone brought him a jar of candy. He gets one piece per day, so he's a bit obsessed with candy now."

"Well, I'll just get him a jar and he can put in lots of candy."

The Coxes watched as Lynn taped a thick sheet of paper to a food tray with blue painter's tape. She squirted several colors of paint onto a paper plate and pulled out a wide brush. "First, let's color the whole background of this... what do you think? Blue or yellow?"

Nathan pointed to the blue paint. "I like blue." He accepted the brush and swiped it in and out of the paint and then brushed it across the paper. Occasionally, Lynn dropped a single drop of yellow, white, or black into the paint, just before he swiped the paper plate, giving the wash a bit of highlight and depth. Once finished, she wiped the tray free of excess paint and pulled out her portable hairdryer.

"Let's just dry this off, and we'll draw a jar on there, okay?"

"I had a jar with fireflies last year. I like jars."

Kelly and Jon snickered. "The things he says," Kelly mused. "He had a jar of fireflies, so he likes jars. He got electrocuted after a bird died, so 'what happened' is that a bird died. He has a unique perspective on life."

With a few flicks of the brush, and a few more long, deliberate strokes, a jar appeared on the page. "Now, we'll take these..." She pulled out several small tubes with foam at the end and pressed one into the paint. "And all you have to do is do that—push it into the paint—and then press it into the jar somewhere. Like this." One round gumball-looking piece of "candy" appeared in the jar. "How's that? Can you do that?"

Nathan nodded. With his tongue sticking out of one side of his mouth, Nathan alternated colors, filling the jar with individual pieces. "Is there purple? I like purple candy best."

Lynn added just a bit of blue to the red and stirred. "There. Blue and red make purple." She pointed to the plate. "I can make orange too. Look at this..." One by one, she combined basic colors into different hues to add variety. "That's right..." she encouraged as Nathan worked to fill a hole. One candy ended up outside the jar near the bottom, but she urged him not to worry. "I'll add a couple there like some spilled out. It's okay."

Piece after piece appeared on the paper, until the jar was filled. Lynn helped him sign his name and moved to tape the picture to the wall next to the one from the previous week. Kelly took Nathan's distraction from the painting to ask about Lynn's program at the hospital. "What made you decide to do this? How did you get started?"

Lynn stepped back to admire the picture and pulled her camera from its bag. "My husband, actually. Before he died—"

"Oh, I'm so sorry," Kelly interjected, ready to kick herself for asking.

"No, it's fine—really. It's nice when people ask about it. I get to talk about him. People who don't know him, don't know to ask, and people who do, often think I don't *want* to talk about him."

"So your husband encouraged you to do it?"

Lynn nodded. "Just a couple of weeks before he died, he said, 'Lynn, you need to paint. You love it. I want you to paint when I'm gone.' So, after the funeral, I was talking to his nurse—she came, isn't that sweet? Anyway, I told her what he said and admitted that I didn't know what I'd do with it. I didn't want to be a traditional artist. It's not my thing. I like being with people. She suggested this."

"The patients love it." Kelly insisted. "I've heard other patients talk about it. Even when Nathan doesn't want to do it, he's so happy to see you. And he loves the cards we bought with his picture on them. My whole family loves them. Mom keeps asking if there are new ones. She buys them every time she hears that the gift shop has added another one."

"The card idea was genius. Did anyone tell you they're using the money to help fund the new cancer wing?"

Every time we buy one. Aloud, she said, "I think that's just awesome. The gift shop lady said you'd made over three thousand dollars already."

"Yep! It's just fabulous, and the kids love to see their picture in the racks in the gift shop. That was the hospital program coordinator's idea. It just made everything come together."

From the bed, Nathan called, "Is it a card now? Can Mommy go buy one? Grandma likes my picture cards!"

DAY FOURTEEN

Thursday, June 18, 10:19 a.m.

A customer entered Lil' Darlin's just as Karyn pulled up the **Help Nathan & Family** page on Facebook. She stepped around the counter and smiled at the woman. "Good morning. Can I help you find anything?"

"No, I'm just looking, but thanks…"

Before Karyn could step back and give the woman space, she asked a question—and another. For the next thirty minutes Karyn showed one outfit after another, made shoe suggestions, matched hair accessories, and pulled out catalogs for coordinating outfits. The woman deliberated, considered, reconsidered, and left saying, "Maybe I'll just try Gymboree. They do all the matching for you."

And what did I just do? Frustrated, she rehung the dozen or two outfits, put back the accessories, and reshelved the catalogs. She refreshed the web page and read the morning update.

```
10:47 a.m. Nathan has had a fantastic morning, which
we're all excited to see as he has another surgery
tomorrow. There is a good chance they won't be able
to get everything done they need to do in this
surgery, so they will most likely do another one on
Monday as well.
Nathan's still doing a lot of physical therapy and
```

it's still very hard and painful for him. They will have to put in an IV tonight, so prayers for this would be appreciated! We're all praying it won't take five times like the last time. This means Nathan will need to stay really calm (HA!) as they get the needle in him. Thank you for your prayers and support! They mean so much to us! —Breanne

More surgeries. More procedures. When would it all end? *I've seen it too often. Optimistic doctors who expect things to follow a prescribed table and it doesn't. They want to give good news. They want to believe they can do anything.*

The door chime jangled again and a man entered, glancing at his watch. "Morning."

Karyn put on her best "customer service" smile and stepped forward. "It is. May I help you?"

"Niece's birthday. She's turning four, but she's small for her age. Her mom said I can't show up with a toy unless I bring clothes too."

"So... uncle spoils her?"

The man shrugged. "What can I say? She's a good kid and my sister's a single mom. Kid needs a male influence."

Karyn selected a few outfits, but the man shook his head. "No offense, but I want stuff that looks like a little girl—not a teeny bopper. She's just a kid."

Grinning, Karyn put the outfits back and led him to a less prominent corner. "Something like this, perhaps?"

Slow nods told her he'd already begun the process of elimination. "The blue dress and the pink top and pants."

"Hair accessories? Bows, headbands—"

"Whatever you think." He glanced around him. "Don't suppose there's a toy store in town? I was trying to avoid the Rockland traffic…"

"Bookends has a good selection—mostly educational, but a few classic things." Karyn smiled. "I guess I should admit that I own it, too. So I've got a vested interest in sending you over there."

The man nodded. "I'll have to stop in. Been wanting to get Sarah—my sister—Alexa Hartfield's latest. Maybe if I tell her I bought it here, she'll forgive me for forgetting it every time I go."

"They're autographed over there. Ask Todd if he's seen her today. If she's around town, she'll personalize it for you."

"Really?"

Karyn nodded as she assembled complete outfits for his approval. "Yep. She's great that way. She keeps us in business, actually."

"I guess bookstores are a dying breed, aren't they?"

A lump formed in her throat. *Tell me about it.* "Yeah, well. Between affordable overnight shipping, volume discounts, and eReaders, people just don't pay retail anymore, and little guys can't compete without retail."

The man nodded as she stepped back to let him decide. "Perfect. Do you gift wrap?"

As she removed prices, folded, boxed, and wrapped, the man asked about Fairbury, the other shops in town, and how the economy was affecting the local businesses. Before she could answer his last question, he spied the "Change for Nathan" can beside the register. "Who is Nathan?"

"Local little boy. He was electrocuted a couple of weeks ago. He's in the burn unit in Manchester with third degree burns on all his leg joints. The bills—no insurance." Karyn gave him a weak smile. "—you can imagine."

Curiosity melded into thoughtfulness as the man read the label on the container and asked, "How old is he?"

"Three."

"Are people donating?" The man peered into the bottom of the container as if mentally counting the dollar bills and coins scattered across the bottom.

"Some. Food establishments get more, of course. People usually pay with credit in here—not much change and they have to save quarters for the meters, so…"

Karyn tried not to watch as he pulled out his wallet and shoved a bill into the jar. She tried not to look as she swiped his credit card and handed him his box. Feeling nosier than she had in years, she drummed her fingers on the counter until he disappeared from sight of the window and lifted the container. She'd expected a five—maybe even as much as a twenty—but a hundred dollar bill lay half-folded atop several ones and a pile of change.

Thank you, Lord. I needed that.

1:32 p.m.—Brunswick

The meeting at the Brunswick Salvation Army drew to a close, but Captain Mark White pulled another memo from his folder. "We have one final thing to consider." The chatter around the table ceased. The secretary picked up her pen again, and several others leaned forward, listening. "The Cox family."

Understanding nods followed. One woman blinked back tears. "He's so little. We took up another suitcase last week and brought home some dirty clothes. Did you know they had to buy clothes because they didn't have time to wash? That's crazy."

"And he's been completely out of work again for a full two weeks now. And they can't get unemployment for it... he just couldn't go. Mortgages don't go away just because you're not home," Mark said unnecessarily.

"So what are we going to do?"

"I had planned to ask for suggestions—give days' profits from thrift store sales, a percentage of the month's donations—whatever we could get approved, but my wife had a suggestion and I think it's perfect—something that can be on-going, which will be helpful for the long term."

The woman at his right drummed her fingers on the table. "And that is?"

"If everyone agrees, we're going to begin a recycling drive. People can bring us their recyclables and we'll handle everything for the family."

"That is brilliant—a way that almost everyone can afford to give. I love it." The emotional woman dropped a few more tears as she beamed with excitement. "How will we advertise?"

"*The Fairbury Notes & News* has promised to do a special report tonight, and we'll put in an ad at the *Brunswick Independent.* If we could get fliers put up around town here and in Fairbury and announcements sent out to the churches, that would help immensely."

The division of labor began immediately. As they prayed the meeting to a close, Mark couldn't let the idea of no income go. Jael Higgenbotham's—well, Garrison, now—husband owned an automotive repair business, and Jon did have some mechanical experience. Maybe…

Wanda McCord grabbed the keys and shuffled around the counter at the Fairbury Water District office. The clock showed three minutes after five o'clock. Time to close and go home.

A car pulled up to the front parking space—the handicapped, no less. Wanda scowled as she saw Neal Kirkpatrick step from the vehicle. *You are **so** not handicapped and you are definitely a jerk. I should lock this door fast.* But she didn't. She opened the door, allowing the keys to jingle in her hand as a hint that he was late.

Neal pulled out his phone and shoved it in her face. "Four fifty-eight." He glanced up at her clock. "It's five minutes ahead."

"Well, we go by *our* clock. You're lucky I didn't lock it anyway."

The man hesitated, his jaw working in a rhythmic motion that could mean anything from anger, amusement, or disgust. Wanda suspected amusement could be removed from the possibilities. Still, he shook his head, pulled out a checkbook, and stepped up to the counter.

"I haven't gotten a bill yet—"

"That's because they don't get mailed until Monday."

"—but since I know the closing date is the fifteenth, I want to take care of it," Neal ground out.

"Goin' somewhere?"

Neal shook his head. "The amount?"

"Let me see… Kirkpatrick on…"

"Linden Street." He clicked his pen open and shut for effect.

Wanda's hands clicked over a clunky, ancient keyboard. "Um…Sixty-two thirty."

The pen scrawled across the check. Date, name, numeric amount, handwritten amount— "Invoice number?"

"Don't have one. You can put the month it's for. I'll give you a receipt."

Check written, he passed it across the counter and began writing another one. "I'd like to settle the Coxes account as well."

"The who—"

"They live on my street," Neal clarified. "Number 412."

Wanda shook her head. "I'm sorry; I cannot give out personal informatio—"

"I didn't ask you to. You can mail the receipt to them. That's fine. Just leave my name off it." He clicked his pen once more. "The amount?"

"They haven't paid May's bill yet. It's not due until the thirtieth."

"I said settle the account. Let's get June's paid too."

"That'll be ninety—yeah, ninety-eight even." Wanda glanced at the check number and typed it into the program. "That's really nic—"

"I didn't ask for commentary. I just asked for a total. See that they get a receipt." With that, Neal turned and exited the building, leaving Wanda gaping at the space he'd occupied seconds earlier.

It took three seconds of intense deliberation for her to snatch up the phone and run her fingers across the computer keys, searching for a number. As she found it, she punched in the number. "Dee?"

"Yeah?"

"It's Wanda over at the water district."

"I—" Silence. "Um, we're on auto-pay, Wanda. What's wrong?"

"Oh, no. Sorry. Nothing to do with your account. You know Neal Kirkpatrick?"

Dee groaned. "Kelly's neighbor, yeah? What complaint is he making now?"

"None. That's just it. He was just in here and paid Jon and Kelly's bill—last month and the one coming out on Monday."

"He did—you're serious?" Dee mumbled something to someone and several surprised voices told Wanda she'd told them.

"Yep. He came in to pay his bill—the one we haven't mailed yet—and then said he wanted to settle their account. I tried to tell him how nice it is of him to do it, but he got all mad and said, 'I didn't ask for commentary. I just asked for a total.'"

"Sounds like him. Still, that's pretty amazing that he'd do it at all. He despises Aiden..."

"The kid is happy. Of course he despises him." Wanda knew something sounded off but was too tired to try to discover what. "Anyway, I'm exhausted and need to get out of here before some other crank comes in and tries to convince me that there's no way watering their lawn every day of every week could possibly use 'that much water.' I'll see you 'round. Just thought you'd like to know."

Outside the office, Wanda stared at the handicapped space once more. *Maybe he is handicapped—in the heart. But today... today he behaved like a human. That's pretty neat.*

WEEK THREE

DAY FIFTEEN

Friday, June 19, 10:08 a.m.

Breanne sent out a Facebook update as she watched the nurses wheel Nathan off to surgery. The simplistic words did little to express the weight on her heart.

```
They just wheeled him off to surgery... - Breanne
```

The waiting began. Minute after very long minute of hoping for some news and knowing there would be none until he was out and in recovery. Jon walked—still lost in a world that blamed him for the unavoidable. Kelly cuddled her baby daughter, cooing reassuring words that meant nothing to the baby but everything to her.

Naomi arrived with the day's water rations, a hot crock-pot casserole, and a pile of clean clothes. While Kelly filled her in on the lack of news, Breanne filled the laundry bag with mini-cartons of soy milk. She rattled the crock-pot lid and the scent of chicken, spices, and vegetables made her stomach grumble. *Real food. Man, I miss real food.*

Much sooner than expected, and later than desired, a nurse peeked her head in the door. "Got the call. They're coming out, so you can go be with him in recovery in a minute." Allison grinned. "Doctor's words were, 'surgery went great.'"

Breanne traded soy milk for a baby and waved as Naomi

followed Kelly from the room. She placed the baby on a thick pallet—the one Aiden had used. Her eyes widened. *I never told people that Mr. and Mrs. Cox took him shopping with them. People probably think we're ignoring him. Oh well. Later. He'll be back in time to see Nathan after he's back in the room.*

She typed out several pathetic attempts to explain why they hadn't mentioned Aiden in her update, but all seemed like damage control for something that hadn't even happened yet. Hitting the delete key, she tried again.

```
Kelly just went into recovery with Nathan. The
surgery went great, which means there's a
possibility that they will be able to do his next
one on Monday instead of Wednesday (or that's what
the doctor said yesterday if today's went well).
Yay!- Breanne
```

Aiden entered the room with the Coxes right behind him just minutes later. "Where's Mom?"

"She went down to be with Nathan as he came out of recovery." Breanne leaned forward. "The surgeon said it went great."

"So they can do the next one now, right? Because there's the whole weekend for this to heal. Right? This is good for Monday too?"

"Someone's been listening," Martin Cox teased.

"That's right." Breanne beamed up at Mary Cox. "Man, we needed good news right about now."

Mary's smile—how had she never noticed that Aiden had that very smile?—said it all. Good news from the doctor. *Good news!* "Maybe now we'll start hearing something about coming home."

Aiden's eyes widened. "Really?"

"They still have surgeries, buddy, but still. It's possible now that we're hearing 'went great' instead of 'couldn't do anything this time.'" Breanne watched Mary's eyes slide toward the baby and picked up Anna, offering her. "Wanna hold her? I could use a quick walk break. I feel like my legs are numb from sitting so much."

By the time she returned, she heard Kelly's voice in the room, talking about Nathan screaming as he came out of anesthesia. She expected pain in the boy's eyes as she stepped into the room, but nothing would have prepared her for the sight of Nathan's undressed foot. *Oh, that's just—ugh. Poor kid, no wonder he was screaming. Oh, man. But it doesn't smell. That's got to be good. Really good. Nice!*

She didn't talk—didn't ask questions. Instead, Breanne moved back to the corner with her laptop and listened, waiting to hear everything she needed for an update. When the topic moved from Nathan to things at home, and Jon arrived to see how everything went, Breanne began typing.

```
Nathan is back in his room. Kelly said when she went
to see him in recovery, he was screaming in pain.
They left his left foot undressed, as it has healed
up enough to be exposed, but it sure looks nasty!
Nathan's other grandparents are here to visit and
take Aiden back to Fairbury now that the surgery is
over. We'll miss him. He's kept our minds off things
when it got to be too much. Love that kid. - Breanne
```

The Rhodes, Steve, and another friend, Eli, met in the USO parking lot and prayed before going in to talk to the director of the historic building. Frank Welch glanced up as they entered and grinned. "Hey, here early, aren't you? Need the mics turned on?"

Claire and James exchanged glances, and a silent agreement passed between the group. James would speak for them where possible. "Actually, we were hoping we could talk to you about a plan we have..."

"Sure." Frank grabbed a chair, turned it backwards, and sat down, his arms draping over the back. "What's up?"

"We want to do a fundraiser for the Cox boy."

"Nathan? Kid who got burned? There's cans all over town. I've got one in the gift shop, but not very many people come in here—"

"Right," James agreed. "That's why we want to do something bigger. Everyone wants to help, and I think it's a good thing to let them. Bake sales, car washes, deli dinners—I've heard of a lot of stuff being planned, and I think it's good for the community to get involved and do whatever they can for the family."

"I hear a but coming."

The group laughed. "Got that right," Steve said.

"We just know that it's all helpful but still not enough. They need a lot of money and they need it fast. Claire talked to the hospital financial office and asked for a rough estimate of what a week in the burn unit would cost—didn't say who for. She was just trying to get a ballpark."

"Fifty K?"

James shook his head. "Double that. Per week. Minimum."

"Ouch. Can't they get assistance?"

"Sometimes hospitals do hardship reductions and stuff—"

Frank waved his hands, "No, no. I mean state."

Claire listened, shaking her head almost in rhythm with Frank's words. "This is the Cox family. They won't do state assistance. He'll work until the day he dies and still not make a dent in it. So we want to do a big fundraiser—huge."

"What kind of huge?"

"Concert—benefit concert. We'll have music, food—the works. This would be a community event. We'd even advertise in Brunswick, Rockland—all the communities nearby."

Frank sat lost in thought. "I like it—I like it a lot." His eyebrows drew together. "So how can I help?"

"Tell us what it would cost to rent out the building for the night?"

"You want this place?" Frank glanced around him and called out, "Hey Rob, can you come in here?"

Another man appeared, wiping his hand on a towel. "Yeah?"

And so they began again, telling their story and sharing the vision for a benefit concert that would raise a significant amount of money. "Maybe," Claire added as James finished his presentation, "people will even continue to give once it's over—make a monthly subscription to the account or something."

Frank and Rob exchanged glances and Rob scoped out the room. "This would be a great place to serve food and have the displays you want, but it's not big enough—not nearly big enough. We could use the park though. We have the chairs for it, and what we don't have, we can get."

"Isn't that kind of impersonal?" Claire's eyes slid back and forth between James and Steve.

Eli spoke up for the first time since they'd entered the building. "Isn't that why they added those sliding walls?" He pointed to the enormous glass dividers that separated the two main portions of the building. "Can't we use every inch of this room and the next for seating and then put all food and stuff in the entry?"

"Excellent." Frank turned to Rob. "And we're not sending people outside into a muggy August evening."

"Good point. So what do you need from us? How can we help?"

Claire grinned at her husband "Give us a great discount on the rental?"

"I'll go you one better," Rob said, smiling. He paused as if waiting for confirmation from Frank who nodded. "You've got the place—no charge."

As the quartet left the building, James chuckled. "Well, if we had any doubt—any at all..."

"We don't now," Claire agreed. "The Lord's got this."

DAY SIXTEEN

Saturday, June 20, 9:24 a.m.

Breanne read the message again, a sick feeling in the pit of her stomach. Once more, she scrolled through the other missed messages, trying to decide what to do. The clock on her laptop taunted her. Mom wouldn't be awake. *But this is really important. Would she want me...*

One look at Kelly's face as she got on her laptop made up Breanne's mind. "Ignore it. I'll talk to Mom."

"Scam?"

Breanne stuffed back a scream of irritation. "Just ignore it. There's a lot of garbage out there. People are just being careful." *God, please let it be that.*

Breanne jumped up from the chair and inched her way to the door as she dug out her cell phone. Kelly's strained voice barely reached her ears, "Breanne, why would someone think that?"

Pain filled the eyes of both sisters—their lives now bound even deeper together through the shared experience of Nathan's recovery. "God's got this, Kelly. We don't know what He's doing, but He does." With that, Breanne eased through the door, holding her breath as she pulled it almost shut behind her. A glance through the crack showed

Kelly wiping away a runaway tear. She poked her head in the door once more. "Go on Home-Bodies, read about a new baby walking or another kid getting accepted to college. Ignore Facebook until I get back." With that, she strode from the burn unit, her parents' phone ringing in her ear. "Logan?"

"Yeah. What?"

"I need Mom."

"She's asleep," her little brother protested. His words were code for, *I don't want to die before I hit fourteen.*

"Trust me; she'll want you to wake me—um, me to wake you up—um. Just wake her up."

"Is Nathan—" Logan swallowed loud enough for Breanne to hear.

"He's fine. Just get Mom."

From the muffled protest, Breanne didn't expect a chipper, "Hello!" She didn't get one either. However, Dee didn't growl much either. "What's wrong?"

Only in our family would people assume something is wrong if the mom gets a call before ten-thirty in the morning. "Can you get Logan to bring your laptop? I meant to, but—"

"Logan! I need my laptop!" Seconds ticked past. "Lo—oh, thank you. Okay..." she continued. "So, what am I looking for?"

"Messages."

"I haven't been reading those," Dee admitted. "I assumed they might be private."

"Yeah, well, I did too. Then I saw the first words of this one and read it—and then read a couple of others..." Breanne forced herself to remain civil. "I told Kelly people were probably just being careful. There are a lot of scam artists out there."

"Oh great. She saw it?"

"I couldn't stop her. She opened it up before I knew—"

Dee interrupted. "No, that's fine. Just post a response for the page. I'll respond to this. We'll take care of it." A moment passed before Dee asked, "So what's on the agenda for today?"

"Well, they have a vacuum on the back of his knee. It's supposed to help with circulation. If it does what they think it will, he'll be ready for the next surgery on Monday."

"And that's it? That'll be the end?"

Breanne demurred. "Not sure about that... I've seen stuff change too fast. Even the doctors are being more careful about what to expect. It's frustrating, but I guess it's what it is."

Her mother sounded distracted. "Yeah…"

"Well, I should get back and write that update. It'll make Kelly feel better anyway."

"I'm already working on the reply to that woman. I'm sure it'll be fine soon enough."

"Be sure to let me know if they actually donate. That would make Kelly feel better."

As Breanne entered the room, she saw the Facebook screen on Kelly's laptop and sighed. "Mom's going to take care of it, and I'm going to put a statement on the page explaining why Dad's name is on the PayPal account instead of yours."

"That'll make sense. I didn't think of that. If people don't know us, they won't get that at all." Kelly sighed. "But the financial gal said not to use our account."

"Right. But people don't know that." She clicked on the status bar and began a new update. "We'll get this straightened out."

```
Hello all. A quick update regarding our donation
page…
All the money IS going to Jon and Kelly. Funds are
being collected by Nathan's grandfather (Keith
Homstad) via his PayPal account. That money is then
being given directly to Nathan's parents to help
with expenses.
This page is directly connected to the Cox family
and the link above is to our site. This is not a
scam. Please continue to donate whatever you can,
but above all, please keep praying for Nathan.
Nathan now has a vacuum attached to the back of his
knee and it is helping the healing process. We
continue with physical therapy as much as possible—
```

Dr. Smith entered the room and startled her. Her finger hit the "enter" key and the status appeared. She started to delete it, but the surgeon's words distracted her. She listened and her heart sank. Once more, she tried adding a complete update.

```
The surgeon is here right now. Sounds like he will
NOT have surgery on Monday after all. Possibly
```

```
Wednesday (crossing fingers!) but it's not yet in
the  schedule,  so  we're  in  wait  and  see  mode.
Hydrotherapy  tomorrow  morning.  We  are  kind  of  back
to  square  one  on  the  walking  part.  Because  his  one
toe  is  not  bandaged  at  all,  I  think  he's  hesitant  to
put  pressure  on  it.  But  we're  still  working  with
him.
```

The surgeon's parting words prompted her to add one more line to the update before she hit the enter key.

```
It sounds like Nathan will be going to get a child's
walker here shortly—Breanne
```

A remote controlled fire truck rolled into the room, sirens blaring. Dr. Smith laughed. "That oughtta keep the nurses hopping!"

Pete's head peered around the door. "I thought it was time for a *real* fire engine!"

Naomi followed seconds later, shaking her head. "It's for *Nathan*, not for Pete, of course..."

8:27 a.m.

As the Farmer's Market set up on the west side of the town square, a group of young people unloaded panels, boards, mechanical pieces, and a motley assortment of unknown pieces from a pickup truck. Officer Joe Freidan stood off to one side, watching the proceeding with a skeptical eye. "Do you guys have a permit for that thing?"

Tabitha Allen dug through her purse and fished out a paper, handing it to him. "I've got a contract with Mr. Garcia too. Need that?"

"Nope," Joe passed the permit back to her. "Just making sure. Who's paying for the insurance?"

Caleb dropped a large coffee can full of nuts and bolts before answering for his sister. "Mr. Garcia. He's paying the taxes too—just like he was running it himself, but it's for Nathan Cox."

As if further proof, Logan Homstad and Aiden Cox arrived, unrolled a big banner across the grass, and stood back to admire it.

"Look! Isn't it great!"

"That had to cost a fortune," Lila protested as she began organizing the pieces jumbled all over the grass.

"Free. Michelle Ferguson made a big mistake on someone's—did it on the back instead of the front. So she airbrushed that black and did this on the front. Perfect! We can let anyone having a fundraiser use it!" Aiden pointed out the benefits to each thing as he continued. "See, his name, the accident, what the funds will go toward, but no name of the fundraiser so we can use it for years to come!"

Logan leaned over and muttered, just inside Joe's hearing radius, "Guess who listened very carefully to every word Ms. Ferguson said?"

"Yeah, well she's right."

Joe stepped in before a good project turned sour before it could get started. "Sounds good to me. So, who are we dunking?"

A familiar voice behind him made Joe's mustache twitch. "I was fixing to get up there and challenge the fire chief to a 'who's all wet?' campaign, but if you wanna represent Fairbury's finest…"

"I think," Joe said after a moment, "The town would enjoy the battle of the chiefs more."

"Figures." Chief Varney stretched. "Anyone bring a towel?"

Aiden scrambled for the truck and pulled a stack of towels out. "See! We're totally prepared."

Nine o'clock came and went, and they still hadn't managed to set up the booth. Logan stared at the hinge pins in his hand. "Are we supposed to have all these leftovers?"

Caleb grabbed the socket wrenches and began unscrewing the pieces again. Chief Varney hauled himself out of his lawn chair and began barking orders. As Joe passed on his rounds, he found the group working, with the chief rigging the mechanical assembly while a group of kids stood around him looking suitably impressed. "Okay, now who's gonna blow up that pool?"

"The birthing pool?" Aiden glanced around him. "Where's the air compressor?"

"What? Birthing what?" Caleb Allen stared at the pile of vinyl with suspicion.

"That—" Aiden said. "That's a birthing pool, isn't it? Like when moms have babies? My mom used one just like that."

"For…"

"Having the baby in? You know—" Aiden made a few revolting

groans followed by a screech, and Caleb tackled him.

"Enough! That's disgusting. How—are you sure?"

"Now, boys. Doesn't matter what it was designed for—if it's a dunking pool that people use for birthing or a birthing pool that people use for dunking—either way, it does the job."

"But—"

The chief glared at Aiden. Joe moved closer, listening as Aiden muttered to Logan, "Mom rents it from Mr. Garcia. She says it's cheaper than going through the midwife."

"So Kelly had Anna in this—" He erupted in laughter. "Oh, man. I can't wait to tell Caleb—after I get him to let me try it out on him at the end of the day."

A voice called out from behind Joe as they began filling the pool with water. "Is it ready?"

"Will be in about forty-five minutes," Aiden said. "That's how long it takes—"

Logan kicked him.

The chief pointed to another spigot. "If you fellas find a few buckets, you might could fill 'em and start a brigade—fill it faster."

They tried and it worked—shaved just over fifteen minutes off the filling time. By ten-fifteen the chief sat atop the board, jeering at well-wishers. Nodding to Joe as he passed, the chief called out, "Go tell Terry Marsh that I challenge him—if he's not too chicken. We each sit for an hour. One with the least dunks wins. Loser buys lunch."

Joe nodded. "I bet he'll be here within the half hour. Terry never misses out on a free meal."

"Hey!"

"No worries, I'll be sure to get the guys to come throw at him. Forget that," Joe added. "I'll call Judith—and maybe Willow Tesdall. Terry won't have a chance."

"That's my boy. You do that."

He ignored two speeding tourists and an expired meter before rounding the corner and meandering up the drive to the fire station. A couple of the guys waved, and one called out, "Lose your way? Police station's on the other side of town."

"Very funny. No, I've got a message for Terry from the chief."

"Terry *is* the chief," another teased.

But Joe didn't respond. He pulled open the door to Terry's office. "Hey!"

"Joe! Problem?" Terry started to rise.

"No... not really. But you might have one."

Terry leaned back, suspicion in his eyes. "And why's that?"

"Because the chief says you're too chicken to accept his challenge."

"And what challenge would that be?" Terry crossed his arms over his chest. "Oh, this is gonna be a good one."

"They've set up a dunking booth—fundraiser for the Cox boy. Chief says you'd get dunked more than him inside an hour. He says loser buys lunch."

Terry jumped to his feet. "Oh, he's on." At the door, he grinned at Joe. "If for no other reason than it's a valid excuse to avoid Mark's spaghetti—nothing more disgusting than Mark's spaghetti."

With five minutes to go, the score was Varney five, Marsh four. Willow Tesdall raced up to the booth, plopped down her purse, and shoved a fistful of dollars into Logan Homstad's hand. "Whew. I made it. I didn't think Becca would ever get to the house to watch the children, and I knew I'd never make it if I brought them. How many balls do I get?"

Logan counted the bills. "Eight."

Three minutes. The first ball hit. "Tie," she crowed.

She started to throw the next ball, but something in Aiden's eyes stopped her. *What is it? Do you want Terry to win? Is that it? He's a fireman. Nathan—ooh...*

"I did what I wanted to do," she murmured, dropping the next ball back into the basket. "Someone else has a minute to get Terry in, otherwise it's a tie."

The dunk-off began at twelve forty-five. Five-minute increments. People abandoned their produce shopping in favor of hosing the fire chief and assaulting the police chief with a soakly weapon. What had begun as a friendly rivalry between police and fire chief became almost a war between their men—and women. Judith arrived in time to knock Terry Marsh down twice. Mark, the terrible spaghetti chef, managed to even up the score again.

For Terry to win became incredibly important to Willow—so

much so that she dug through her purse again but failed to find any more cash. Failed to find a checkbook. She eyed her credit card but shoved the wallet back into the purse. "I'm broke."

"There's only two more minutes," Aiden said, chewing his bottom lip. "It's still a tie."

No one stepped forward. Willow glanced around her and frowned. "Will anyone loan—"

"You didn't use all your balls. You don't need to pay for more," Aiden insisted. His eyes pleaded with her. "One minute left…"

Willow threw. The police chief splashed into the pool with one throw. And Terry Marsh cheered.

DAY SEVENTEEN

Sunday, June 21, 2:31 p.m.

"Have you checked the PayPal balance lately?"

Breanne looked up from her laptop. "No, should I?"

Kelly nodded. "It's over three thousand." While Breanne squealed, Kelly added, "Mom called."

"About…"

"They did the thing with the dunk tank yesterday. Mom counted the total." A tear spilled down Kelly's cheek. "It's too much. Three thousand in PayPal, almost two hundred fifty in dunk tank…"

"Too much? That's great!"

"We can't do this. We can't. They're planning car washes and bake sales—Mrs. Rhodes said a concert." Kelly glanced over where Jon slept beside Nathan and lowered her voice. "We can't keep taking people's money. We can't do this."

"You don't have a choice. Remember how Grandma always says, "God's got this?"

"Yeah…"

Breanne shrugged. "Well, it looks like that's how God is doing it this time."

"I wish you didn't have to go home…" It was the first time Kelly had allowed herself to vocalize her dread of being without the continual support her sisters offered.

"Just until Wednesday. I'll bring Aiden too."

"How will he get home this time? It's too much to stay—"

Breanne interrupted before Kelly could talk herself out of a visit. "Lorena is coming here Thursday after her class and then she's driving home. She'll take him with her—just one night. Mom said he came home much less jittery after being here last time."

The words had been chosen with perfect precision to make her feel better; Kelly knew that. Still, they wrapped her in comfort and prompted her to nod her agreement. "That's good. I slept better after seeing him." She giggled. "Mom said Aiden dunked Caleb Allen in the tank."

"He's got a good arm. Have you considered softball?" Breanne glanced at her phone and shoved it in her pocket.

"Need to get that?"

Breanne shook her head. "Nah, just a text from someone wanting me to have a game night. I'll call later. So, softball?"

"Dunno. No, the funny part about the dunk tank is that Aiden told Caleb that it's the same pool I used when Anna was born. Caleb is so grossed out by that. Mom said that Lily told her he took three showers in the space of an hour when he got home."

DAY EIGHTEEN

Monday, June 22, 7:49 a.m.

Christine arrived with more meal cards and a stack of paperwork. "Okay, did you get rid of your money?"

"Get rid of it?" Kelly frowned.

"Right... like I said, put it all on bills, pay down your mortgage—anything. That money has to be gone or they'll reject this. What about the vehicles? Did you put them in a family member's name like I told you?"

Jon shook his head and knotted his hands as he worked out how to tell her they wouldn't commit fraud—even if she did mean well by suggesting it. "We can't do it. It—"

"It goes against our religion," Kelly interjected, hoping the woman could understand it that way without feeling condemned for trying to help them.

"Well, then this is what's going to happen today. I'm going to plug in this information. It's going to reject you. I'll have an appointment set up for you so that you have a ticket number there. It'll mean you don't have to leave as early."

Kelly nodded and pulled out her pen. "Where is there?"

Christine explained where the welfare office was, and those words alone sent a bit of panic over her. *Are we really doing this? Welfare? I mean, that's what it is. It's just so foreign. Jon works hard— always has. We've always paid our own way. Is God rooting out some kind of pride?*

"—then you'll be sent over to the Children's Medical Fund office where they'll process with different software and get you signed up."

"Wait—why can't we just go there if you and the welfare office are going to reject it?" Kelly looked to Jon for support. Jon only nodded his agreement.

"It's how it's set up. I better hurry down. Can one of you come with me in case I missed something?" Christine hesitated by the door and then smiled as Jon rose. "Sorry for the inconvenience, guys. It'll be okay. We'll get you set up. We do it every day."

The moment they left, Kelly pulled out the cellphone and dialed her sister-in-law. "Hey, what are you doing today?"

"Laundry... want some of yours done?"

"I'd love it, but I don't have time to get stuff together. We need someone to come stay with Nathan while we go talk to the Medicaid people."

"Jon's going to do that?" The excitement underlying Naomi's words belied her disbelief. "I never thought—"

"Yeah, we didn't either. It's horrible. I don't even want to think about it, but we don't want to leave Nathan alone either."

"I'll come. What time?"

Kelly sighed. "I don't even know. All I know is this morning. I'll have to call you back."

"That's fine. Whenever. Do you want to leave Anna?"

"Probably not—she might get hungry." Kelly stared down at the sleeping baby and prayed that she slept all the time they were gone as well.

"True. Okay. Just gimme a call."

Before Kelly could put her purse away, Nurse Allison stepped in.

"I overheard."

"Yeah... I don't even want to think about it."

"Well, the decision is yours," Allison insisted. "Don't feel bullied into anything, but I felt like I had to say something."

"About..."

She glanced behind her and then stepped closer. "I wouldn't take my baby to the county building. I—" One more glance. "Look, she's already in a hospital full of recirculating germs. I mean, we have powerful filters and stuff, but still. There are hospital infection scares for a reason. You don't have a choice for this, but to go from here to a county building where people have to bring sick kids, come in sick—I won't even mention the smoke outside that place..."

"Oh. Yeah. Good point. I'll see if Naomi—"

"If she needs help, you know we'll fight over who gets to hold the baby." Allison snickered at Kelly's eye roll. "You've got help. Just don't risk overloading that poor kid's immune system—especially since you can't vaccinate."

An alarm went off somewhere, sending Allison scurrying from the room. Kelly stared after her, grateful. *"...can't vaccinate." Most people say won't, as if we're just too lazy or stupid. At least someone gets it.*

9:39 a.m.

Breanne's phone rang just as she pulled up to work. While she parked the car and pulled the key from the ignition, she dug out her phone, her heart in her stomach. *Why is Kelly calling this early? What happened?*

"Hi............. It's meeee. I'm me, well not me because I'm Nathan, but hi."

"Yeah, you sound high all right," Breanne joked.

Silence. Several seconds passed. Then familiar words came through the phone. "Can you talk?"

"What do you want me to tell you? Why don't you tell me something?"

"What?"

"Um..." Breanne thought for a moment and said, "So what did Thomas the Train do today?"

"He rided all around… wooooohhhhooooooowwooooo… and then his wheels got tired so he rested."

"The train's wheels got tired?"

"Mmm hmmm," Nathan murmured. "From riding. Like when you walk too much. The wheels got tired. So he rested."

"Makes sense to me." Breanne tried again to come up with something to keep him talking, but exhaustion after several weeks of interrupted sleep hit her hard.

"He saw other Thomas the Trains. They all went to see 'Courageous.'"

"Do they like Javier too?"

"Yes." Nathan murmured something unintelligible in response to something Kelly said. Breanne understood none of it but laughed when he came back and said, "Javier was going to eat their smoke stack." He giggled. "Smoke stack. Kids can't smoke. It's against the rules."

"You're silly, you know that?"

"Mommy said I'm a silly Billy, but I'm a Nathan, not a Billy—or a goat. Like Grandpa's. Billy goat—goat—gooooooat," he sang in an off-key sing-song.

A few muffled shuffling sounds preceded Kelly's voice. "Isn't he hilarious? He's been talking like that for the past half hour."

"And I'm missing it. Ugh."

"I'll record him if he keeps it up. The pediatrician is here now. He said surgery on Wednesday and then maybe one on Friday or Monday. Gotta go."

Once inside her boss' house, Breanne said good morning to the boys and asked for a moment in the bathroom before her boss left. She stepped in and began typing out a new status update on her phone for the Facebook page.

Just got a phone call from the little man. He's super high on meds right now, which made for a hilarious conversation! He should be having a surgery on Wednesday and then another one on Friday or maybe later. —Breanne.

10:03 a.m.

Kelly glanced nervously at the clock on the corner of the laptop. *Will they be late? We can't be late.* Her eyes slid to where Jon assembled various stacks of papers, ordered them in some fashion, and then put each stack into a file folder and stashed it all in the laptop case. *Time to close down the laptop, I guess.*

Pete and Naomi entered with twelve minutes to spare. "Sorry—accident down the road. They had to reroute us. You'd better hurry now. Take Mason Parkway—" The confused expression on Jon's face arrested Naomi's explanation. "Okay, go out here, turn left. Take the second right and that'll take you to the parkway. Just follow that until you get to Turner Ranch Road. Then take all rights until you get to the building."

Even as Naomi spoke Jon kissed his son, took sleeping Anna from Kelly's free arm, and passed her to his sister. His eyes spoke for him. *Let's go.*

"Coming." Kelly turned to Naomi, ready to thank her for watching Nathan, but Naomi pushed her from the room.

"Go. We've got this. You just get that kid some insurance."

Kelly fidgeted all the way to the appointment. "Is this the right thing?"

"I don't know."

"Mom pointed out that if we don't, the hospital and doctor are going to be out a lot of money."

"They don't *have* to help. They can send us home."

"But they do," she objected. "The law makes them, so why should they be penalized because of that. But Medicaid…"

"I know." Jon's jaw clenched as he spoke. "I figure we have to talk to them."

"Breanne says that she's glad that all the taxes they pay are finally going to something she can support." Even as she said it, Kelly knew how ridiculous the words were. Jon pounced immediately.

"But they haven't paid hundreds of thousands of dollars in taxes. They probably only pay for enough in taxes to cover road usage and the IRS employees who process that return."

"But it's probably true of lots of people."

"Then they should be able to choose to do it," Jon argued. "People should be able to *choose* if they want to donate—like they're doing with Nathan."

"So you're saying we should stop complaining about needing the assistance?" A sly smile accompanied that little barb.

"Okay, fine—wait, is that it?" Jon pointed to a building they'd just passed.

Kelly craned her neck to read the giant numbers on the building and nodded. "Yep, it was."

Allison hadn't been joking. Long before she reached the doors, a cloud of smoke from the dozens of people puffing on cigarettes from several yards to just a couple of feet away attacked their lungs. Kelly fought the urge to cough, not wanting to be rude, but her lungs couldn't take it. One man turned away, trying to redirect his smoke, as if it would help, but she smiled, hoping he'd see that she appreciated the thought.

As they pulled open the doors, Kelly looked up at Jon. "So, what are we going to do?"

Jon's miserable eyes told her before he ever said the words. "I don't know."

The waiting became horrendous. Kelly twice tried to force herself to use the restrooms as they waited but couldn't bring herself to do it. The building was filthy. *Why don't they clean this place? It's like they **want** to drive folks away, but is this really the way to do it? What about the people who have to work here? Why can't they keep it decent at least for them?*

Then, as if an explanation, a baby spat up, splattering the floor at his mother's feet. The woman stood and moved across the room to one of the few empty chairs available without a second glance. Jon got up and left the room, returning with paper towels to clean up the mess. *Is that it? They don't bother because people don't care, or do people not care because they don't bother? Or both? Or neither? But how could you just move like that? Your kid made a mess.*

Never had she ever seen anything like it. Just as she'd decided that the least the county could do is require those receiving aid to help keep the offices in shipshape, another child made a mess of his diaper, the contents oozing out of his shorts and down his leg to the floor. The mother sprang into action, grabbing the child and rushing him off to the bathroom. "I'll be back in just two minutes to get that. So sorry."

Once more, Jon went to find something to clean it up, but she heard the mother protesting outside the restrooms. "No, no. You leave that alone. I wouldn't want you to get whatever he's got. I didn't want to bring him today, but if you don't come…"

What the woman said next, Kelly didn't hear, but she did smile as Jon returned with several paper towels. "I'll get wet ones."

"Thanks."

As she scrubbed her hands in the bathroom, the woman mopped up her son. "I've probably got an extra diaper in the van. Would that help?"

The woman nodded. "Oh, please. It would. I just got a new one on him and he just exploded again. I wish I had someone to leave him with, but…"

"Don't worry about it. You have to do what you have to. Be right back."

The morning passed like that—long into the afternoon. Twice Kelly drove back to the hospital to feed Anna, and twice she returned to find very few people had gone through. When their turn did finally arrive, it took exactly six minutes of answering questions for the computer to spit out its verdict. "Denied. You have too many assets. Too much in savings, the house, the vehicles… income wise you qualify for everything we've got, but not with those kinds of assets. Take this over to CMF—"

"What's that?"

"Children's Medical Fund. They are for families with higher income or assets, but they can't take you unless you've been denied by us. It's a smaller pool of money, basically."

"Right. So where is that?" Jon put the paperwork back in his laptop case and closed it. "Thank you for your time."

"I'll call over there and get you an appointment—hold on. Sometimes I can get people in with Jessica if I call at the right time."

But she didn't. Jon and Kelly drove back to the hospital more confused than ever and with an appointment for nine-thirty the next morning. Naomi looked up from the puzzle she and Nathan were doing and asked, "So…"

"So, tomorrow we find out. After another appointment."

"Is the building really as gross as Kelly described?"

Jon nodded. "I've never seen anything like it. It felt like it belonged in a third-world country."

"I suppose," Naomi mused, "it is *our* country's *'third world'* so to speak."

"You know, we've been told a million times since we got here that we're under the poverty level. Well, from what I saw today, we can't possibly be. We have a nice house, decent vehicles, plenty of food and clothing. Those people were there for rent, food, basic necessities. I don't think numbers on a chart mean anything." As she spoke, Kelly looked to Jon for confirmation, but he sat in the corner, head in his hands, lost in thoughts she didn't even want to imagine. *It's not his fault—none of it is. I just don't know how to make him see that.*

DAY NINETEEN

Tuesday, June 23, 4:43 p.m.

The phone rang, and Dee snatched it up, hoping it would be Kelly with a verdict on the medical assistance. "Hello?"

"Hey, Mom..."

Kelly's defeated tone told Dee that they'd signed. "You okay?"

"No—yes—I don't know." Silence hung between them before Kelly whispered, "We refused to sign."

Shock filled Dee—and relief. Disappointment followed on a wave that crashed over it all. "You did?"

"Couldn't do it, Mom. We've given out every bit of personal information imaginable, and they still want more. They talked about what they could do to lower our assets legally so we could do Medicaid instead, and while it would be legal, we just couldn't. Jon just stood up and said, 'We really appreciate all you've tried to do, we're sorry for wasting your time, but this isn't for us. We just can't do it. We tried—for the doctors and the hospital, we tried—but we're not going to sign. Thank you.'" Her voice dropped to a whisper. "I've never been so relieved or so proud of him."

"It probably didn't help that you were in such a discouraging place. Breanne told me about the building."

"No, different place. This place was bright, clean—even an older building, I think—but they just took better care or something. The people—Mom, they didn't look so hopeless or jaded. I don't know what the difference is, but it was marked. I just have never seen anything like that last place *or* the difference between it and the one we went to today"

"I'm proud of you, Kelly."

"I thought you wanted us to do it!"

Unsure how to explain herself, Dee did try. "No, listen. You did what you thought you had to do, and when it came down to the wire, you held firm to what you believe—that the taxpayers shouldn't be forced to pay your medical bills for you. I'm proud of you for that. God's got the rest handled. Somehow, some way, that doctor and that hospital will get paid, but I'm proud of you for sticking to your convictions." As Kelly disconnected the call, Dee finished her sentence, unspoken. *And I would have been proud of you if you'd done it too. It would have been a hard pill to swallow to decide to set aside those convictions for the benefit of those who might have to wait a very long time to get paid.*

The phone rang again, and Kelly's voice filled her ear. "Forgot to tell you, recovery is still taking longer than expected—two more surgeries at least."

"I was just clicking on the page. There it is. I'll let the gals on Home-Bodies know."

She selected the text, copied, clicked onto the next page, and pasted words she didn't even want to read.

```
Always hope for the best… but be prepared for the
worst.  Recovery  is  taking  longer  than  expected.
Expect  to  be  here  for  two  more  scheduled
surgeries. :( —Kelly
```

DAY TWENTY

Wednesday, June 24, 9:03 a.m.

Adric Garrison answered the phone. "Fairbury Automotive, Adric speaking, how may I help you?"

Routine questions. How much is a smog? What if repairs are necessary? Does the DMV offer extensions if repairs take too long?

Adric answered them as he washed his hands in the shop sink and went into the office to schedule the service. His eyes noted the time as he ended the call. *Just in time to see what's up in Fairbury,* he noted to himself as he clicked the town blog's link on his browser toolbar. There it was "Toddler Still Hospitalized."

Fairbury Notes & News
Wednesday, June 24th, 9:00 a.m. *(Rachel Delman-Cox)*

More complications, necessitating more surgeries have cropped up for a local three-year-old boy recovering from third-degree burns after being electrocuted two weeks ago.

Nathan Cox and his family expect to remain at the Cunningham Burn Unit in Manchester for at least another week, extending a stay that began in the early hours of June 6th.

Nathan was electrocuted by a downed power line, the result of a freak accident after a raven flew into the wire and blew the transformer near his Linden Street home.

Mother Kelly Cox said that Nathan has his third surgery on Friday and that his surgeons plan another one for later this week.

"Nathan is doing all right—some days are better than others," she said. "Sunday he had a really good morning—almost his normal self. It was really good to see that."

Kelly said that the constant procedures and physical therapy were taking a toll on their son, but that the professionalism and the compassion of the staff made their stay as comfortable as possible.

She also expressed her gratitude to all the people who have supported them through the trauma. Her family has been helping with the care of their older son, while Kelly and father Jon take care of Nathan and ten-week-old Anna at the hospital.

"We have our own little Ronald McDonald House," she joked, referring to Jon's sister, Naomi, who has opened her Manchester home to the family for occasional showers, laundry facilities, and hot meals.

"I am grateful for the prayers and support and everything people have done to help us," she said. "Every little note has left me with a smile."

Friends of the family created a "<u>Help Nathan & Family</u>" page on Facebook to post periodic updates. There is also a link to a PayPal account for anyone wishing to make donations.

"Town's slow on the uptake. It's almost ten after and not a single comment."

His hand hovered over the phone again, hesitating as the word "PayPal" burned into his brain. He grabbed it and dialed home. "Hey, got a question."

"Got an answer," his wife retorted, mimicking his usual response to the same opening.

"How would you feel about delaying that vacation—maybe indefinitely?"

"Ohhh," Jael cooed. "This is gonna be good. Why?"

"I'm thinking about using it to bring on Jon Cox. Retroactively starting—"

"June fifth perhaps?"

"Sixth. He'll get paid for the fifth, and sixth and seventh are weekends. So actually, eighth." He swallowed hard, knowing how badly Jael had looked forward to the Florida trip.

"I think I want to know why you haven't called him already."

Adric chuckled as he said, "Too distracted talking to a pretty lady?"

"That'll work. I'll start cutting coupons. We'll go next year. This'll work."

"You sure?"

Jael exploded. "Just call already!"

"Got the Homstads number?"

"No, but you could message them on Facebook," she suggested.

Adric disconnected the call and navigated the Facebook website to find the web page. "I don't know how people can stand this thing. It's such a mess."

There it was. Message in the top right corner. Adric thought for a moment and then typed.

This message is for Jon Cox:

Jon,

This is Adric Garrison over at Fairbury automotive. Since we lost Leo, we've been looking for a good, dependable guy to join our team. I just learned recently that you know mechanics. So, I'd like to offer you a job. You wouldn't need to start until July 6th, but if that didn't give you enough time, we might be able to make things work until you can. I know you've got shift work in Brunswick, but I thought it might be nice to work nearer home—and not to have whether you still have one up in the air.

If you're interested, I'll email an application to you and you can fill it out, sign it, and fax it back at your convenience.

Thank you for your consideration,
Adric Garrison
Fairbury Automotive

While on the Facebook page, Adric read the latest updates.

Nathan went into surgery this morning. Praying for the little guy. Can't wait to hear that he's out and well—Dee

A shout from the bays drove him away from the computer and out to see what the trouble might be. Not until lunch did he get a chance to resume his perusal of Nathan's page. As he did, a new update appeared.

Just arrived with Aiden. They're all happy to see him again. We will be spending the weekend here, which will be the longest period the Cox family has had with their son/brother in a while.
In other news, there is a possibility (thought every time we say that, something else happens, so who knows?) that Nathan will have his last surgery on Friday. Praying the doctors are right! —Breanne

"Adding my prayers to that, Lord. Adding mine. It's time for them to come home."

A head popped over the divider between Ross's and Melissa's desks. "Whatcha doing?"

Ross jumped. "Wha—"

"'*Fairbury Notes & News.*' Are you serious?"

"Just checking in on him." Despite the nonchalance he tried to infuse into his response, Ross knew he sounded defensive.

"It's not your fault—"

"I know. I just like seeing that he's doing better. Look, they're hoping to go home soon."

Melissa glanced behind her to see that no one could overhear and murmured, "We're not supposed to get involved. If the family knew this bothered you—"

"Well, they won't, will they?" Ross punched the monitor off button and shoved his chair back. "There is no way for that family to know that I've ever looked."

"C'mon, you're the only one who has posted on that blog saying 'Sending positive thoughts your way.'" She scowled at him. "And I traced it to the Brunswick library, so anyone else can too."

"There are lots of people in Brunswick. I kept it private. I just wanted to *do* something, even if it was just send a good vibe their way. I'm allowed to do that on my private time—which this is my lunch, so this counts, too—as long as I don't bring the company's name into it. Well, I didn't bring my name into it, so it's all good."

"Man, I don't know. I don't think Troy would be too happy—"

"Then why don't you go ask him about it," Ross growled. "Show him exactly what I've done, and if that's not okay, then let him fire me. I've gotta live with who I am as well as with a job. And if this job doesn't allow me to send good thoughts toward a hurting little boy—" Ross realized his voice had escalated. He glanced around and saw a bunch of shocked faces staring at him. "—then," he said a bit quieter, "this isn't the job for me."

DAY TWENTY-ONE

Thursday, June 25, 1:32 p.m.

Anticipation filled the Coxes—well, most of them—as a man arrived carrying a child-sized walker. Nathan, absorbed in a game of Angry Birds, didn't pay much attention to it. In fact, his now finely honed "zone-out" skills helped him ignore anything that didn't interest or overwhelmed him, and apparently a walker fit that bill. Jon took away the tablet, promising Nathan he could finish his game later, and showed him the walker. He stared at it with disinterest.

"It's for you to try to walk. See. You hold on and push it."

Nathan's disinterest dissolved into disdain. "Wagon."

Kelly's eyes met Jon's and slid over to the therapist who stood there beaming. "You'll love it. You can go down the hall, and outside…"

Once more, Nathan shook his head. "Wagon."

"Just try it, Nathan," Kelly cajoled.

Disdain erupted in distress. "Noooooooooooooo…"

They tried everything, understanding, encouragement, compassion, direction, firmness—nothing worked. Nathan refused to cooperate. The therapist pointed through the door. "Maybe if he had more room—didn't feel closed in…"

It couldn't hurt, so they carried him and his walker out to the hallway and set them both down. Nathan refused to stand. Bonnie, a nurse in training, disappeared just as they needed her help, prompting a few grumbles by the therapist and the other nurses. By the time she returned, they'd barely managed to get him to lean on one leg, his hands gripping the walker. He still refused to put down his foot.

"Just take one step. We'll start with one," Kelly suggested.

Bonnie stood back a way, holding a bright, Mylar balloon. "Or you can walk over here and get the balloon."

Something in Nathan shifted. His desire for the balloon kept him on his feet, but he still resisted putting down his foot. His eyes slid right then left. His hands gripped the walker. He hopped forward, traveling at least an inch and a half. The self-satisfaction on his face sent up a row of laughter around him. "Is he proud of taking that so-called step, or because he found a way around taking a real one," Kelly whispered to Jon.

Six feet away, Bonnie shook her head and inched backwards a tiny bit. "I said walk, not hop. That doesn't count. If you want the balloon, you have to get it."

Tension filled the air. *Will he protest? Does he remember the fiasco with the bat and ball?* Dread filled Kelly as she imagined her son deciding the effort wasn't worth it. *How much do we insist before we make him give up mentally? I don't know the answers to the questions I'm afraid to ask.*

But he did. He took one step—then another. He whimpered, cried, and paused long enough to make them think he'd never go again, but he did. And as he worked, they encouraged, cajoled, cheered, and held collective breaths in anticipation as he neared the "finish line."

Weariness plagued him for the last two feet. Kelly feared he might not be *able* to make it. She telegraphed her concerns. Bonnie nodded. The silent plan worked. Kelly called to Nathan. As the boy turned to see why his mother had moved back, Bonnie moved almost a foot closer. "Good job. I am so proud of you. Look, you can almost reach it. Go get it, son!"

He turned, saw the prize, and almost managed a face-plant in his eagerness to go. The physical therapist caught him just in time. "You still have to take reasonable sized steps. Let's save jumping for later, okay?"

Bonnie hunkered down on her heels. "Two more steps. I think it'll only take two more steps and then you can reach it. C'mon. I knew you could do it."

Nathan took one step more. The group clustered in the hall cheered. A man, his face almost completely covered in bandages, stood in the doorway of his room, a tear sliding out of the corner of his eye and into his bandage. "You go, little guy. You go."

Hesitation came again, but this time it appeared to be prompted by weariness rather than reluctance. Nathan's legs shook. His arms shook. Perspiration beaded his forehead. Kelly almost gave in—had the words ready to speak—when he forced his bad foot forward. Forgetting that he needed the walker for support, he reached for the balloon and collapsed in Bonnie's outstretched arms.

"Good job, little man. Very good job."

With the balloon ribbon tied around his wrist, and comforting arms wrapped around him, Nathan glanced around him. "Where's the wagon? You said we could go outside."

WEEK FOUR

DAY TWENTY-TWO

Friday, June 26, 6:01 a.m.

After a restless night with Nathan up almost every hour on the hour, Breanne collapsed in her bed-chair, too tired to think, too awake to sleep. The sight of her laptop made her realize that she hadn't had a chance to update the Facebook page. Nathan slept in his bed, Kelly and Jon slept in theirs, and Aiden slept peacefully at his aunt's house. *No uncomfortable pallet for him this time,* she mused as she grabbed her laptop and dragged herself out of the bed and down to the elevator.

The hospital would come alive in the next hour—a hotbed of busyness. But in the last moments of the late shift, things remained quiet. Only one other person occupied the lobby—a Latino man with kind eyes and a weary expression. "Good morning."

The man nodded, giving her a half-smile.

Maybe he doesn't speak English. Yeah, probably.

A new thought crossed her mind. *This'll be the last time I come down here to write an update—or probably do anything down here. Wow. He's coming home!* Foolishly, Breanne decided to take that moment—that time when physical exhaustion would acerbate any emotions—and review the past weeks' statuses—from that first one telling of what happened, to the first surgery, the hydro, the videos and Kelly's weak attempts to hide how very much it all tore at her as a mother. *I always hated it when I saw someone saying, "I know that hurts your mommy heart," but I kind of get it now.*

Despite every effort, tears coursed down her cheeks, a few daring ones splashing on her laptop in an act of defiance to her "no liquids near my laptop" policy.

By the time she reached the top, Breanne ached to write something good—upbeat. Something that said, "This is horrible, but it's not, because God and His people are awesome." Still, everything she had to say she'd said before. Visitors, physical therapy, great nurses, compassionate doctors, loving church family—*That'll do it.*

```
Yesterday Nathan had visitors! A family from The
Assembly in Brunswick stopped by with gifts and
cards from members of the church. Thank you all so
much! You have no idea how happy it made Nathan to
see all the cards (and of course, the toys were a
hit as well). Our lives have been touched by so many
people—Thank you, The Assembly at Brunswick.
```

She had to leave one more post—something to remind people to pray. Her message box filled daily with people asking how to pray, what needs had arisen, and if this or that other thing. *I need to go home. I need to be able to sleep before I post anything else. I am too tired to sleep, too tired to be awake, too tired to drive, too tired **not** to drive. I need to leave now before I get worse.*

As Breanne pushed through the door, her laptop case almost dragging and her backpack slung over one shoulder. Keith's eyes widened. "What are you doing home? I thought you were coming after the surgery."

"I was tired and knew I wouldn't get any rest, so I came home." She glanced at his laptop. "Any news on surgery? I wasn't there when they came in to say what time."

"Just read Kelly's latest—thought it was yours."

"Gah! What?" Breanne snapped.

"What what?"

With more patience than she thought she should need to use,

Breanne asked, "What does the latest update say?"

"Oh, 'Prayers that today would be Nathan's last surgery would be very appreciated! —Kelly.'"

"Can you type something in on my account?" Breanne opened her laptop case and withdrew her computer. She opened it, signed in, and passed it to her father. "I'll brush my teeth."

"What do you want me to say?"

As she dug through her backpack, looking for toothbrush and toothpaste, Breanne dictated an update. "Just say, 'Nathan walked around with his walker yesterday! He didn't go far, but he was putting weight on his right (bad) foot, which is fantastic and something he hasn't done often. I also got to go in for his hydrotherapy yesterday, and he did so much better than in previous ones.'"

"Whoa… '…did so much…'"

"Right." Breanne waited for him to look up at her and then added, "Then just say, 'Today he has surgery. I'm not sure what time as I am no longer in Manchester, but I know they wanted to try to do it early. Thank you all for your prayers. Keep them coming! God Bless— Breanne.'"

Exasperated, Keith snapped, "Wanted what? Try to do it early?"

Breanne repeated the last of the message, wishing she had just done it herself if it meant delaying sleep any longer. She inched her way to the bathroom, correcting words as she went, and then locked herself in. She accepted her laptop on her way out the door to her room and hesitated, trying not to be as outwardly disrespectful as she felt when her father called out, "Wait."

"Yeah?"

"Kelly just posted. 'He's headed into surgery! Hopefully it will be his last for the foreseeable future!'"

"Great! Thanks. Night."

She slogged her way across the concrete drive, wondering a bit incoherently why it felt like mud, and up the steps to her room. Several piles of clean clothes sat at one end of the bed, but Breanne just shoved them off and collapsed. Her phone buzzed notice of a text message, but Breanne never heard it.

Breanne's first coherent thought came hours later. "Where am I?"

Lila stood over her, pointing at the clothes on the floor. "Seriously? I clean your clothes, fold them, and you just shove them on the floor?"

"I was tired—still am. What time is it?"

"Two o'clock." Lila began picking up the disheveled piles of laundry.

"I'll get it. Is Nathan out of surgery?"

"Mom posted an update a while ago—something like, 'Yay! He's out of surgery!' Real informative."

"Probably because Kelly doesn't have someone there to do it for her. She's got a kid right out of surgery, another one demanding to be fed, and another one in the way but not. Give her a break."

"You're grumpy. Geez."

Breanne grabbed clothes from the top of Lila's piles. "Yeah, I am. Not enough sleep'll do that to you. I'm gonna try a hot shower. Do we have any real food?"

"Not now, but Mom said she'd make *pico de gallo* for dinner tonight—fajitas too."

"Good." Breanne stared at the clothes in her hands, trying to remember what she'd planned to do with them. When they did nothing to enlighten her, she flopped back down on the bed and rolled over, clutching them to her chest.

DAY TWENTY-THREE

Saturday, June 27, 2:13 a.m.

Fists shoved in his pockets, Aiden sauntered down the street toward the center of town. Cars passed, a jogger waved, but lost in thought, Aiden almost didn't notice. Someone called his name. He turned toward the voice, searching for who called him. "Oh, hi, Mrs. Allen!"

"Any news about the surgery today?"

Aiden crossed the street and leaned against a fence post. "Yeah. He's out. They didn't do the skin graft though—not the… auto—yeah. I think it's auto they wanted to do. The homo-graft is the one he's already had." After a pause, he added, "I think."

"Right, that's what I thought. So they didn't do the one where they took his own skin?"

He shook his head. "No… maybe Monday."

"Okay. I'll keep praying." He turned to go, but Lily stopped him. "Wait. Hold on." She raced inside and hurried back out again. "I got this gift certificate for my birthday—to The Confectionary."

"I—"

"It's just enough for an ice cream or a few cookies. Someone put it in my Secret Sister card at church, but I'm on a diet, Tom is avoiding gluten right now, and there's not enough for all the kids, so take it. Enjoy something for me." He hesitated, searching her eyes for some hint of insincerity, but she met his gaze frankly. "If you don't want it, I can give it to the paper kid. You just came by first."

His hand reached out for it. "Thanks. I was going to get me an ice cream there. Grandma gave me money." He pulled a wad of bills from his pocket. "I'll put this in Nathan's jar instead."

"Great idea! I love it."

By the time he reached the town square, half a dozen people had stopped him, asking about his brother. As he stepped into The Confectionary, he just wanted to be left alone. Audrey Seever peered around the corner of the back room and grinned. "Hey, there. I have a box of cookies for you and your grandparents. I tried out a new recipe—good, but not what I was looking for. Not cinnamony enough. Want 'em?"

"Sure, thanks." He grinned. "I want…" Aiden peered at the denomination on the gift certificate. "Two scoops of Star Spangled Freeze in a waffle cone."

"Good choice. I love that stuff. Pop Rocks on top?" Audrey reached for the scoop, waiting.

"How can it be 'spangled' if there's no pop to it?" Aiden grinned. "I've been waiting all year for this. When Grandma overheard you say you started making it, she said Logan and I could come get one."

"And where's Logan?"

Aiden grinned as he dug the dollars out of his pocket and shoved them in Nathan's jar. "He had someone call him to mow their lawn. He might come later, but…"

"But you didn't want to wait. Smart kid." Audrey pointed to the jar as she handed over his besprinkled cone. "What's that all about?"

"Mrs. Allen gave me this." He slid the gift certificate across the counter. "So, I thought I'd put Grandma's money in the can. She'd like that."

"I like that you gave your treat money to your brother. Good move." Audrey leaned across the counter, her eyes never leaving his. "You okay? It's been a long time without them."

"I just got home this morning. I got to see them for a few days."

"That's good," Audrey said, but she didn't move. "Still, it's gotta be weird living with Grandma and Grandpa—no matter how much you like 'em. Wait." She leaned back and crossed her arms over her chest. "Weren't you supposed to stay until tomorrow night?"

"Yeah, but Grandma and Grandpa Cox came this morning for a while so I went home with them—saved Lorena driving back here before going back to school again."

"Her classes aren't out yet?"

Aiden shrugged. "She's always got classes—so does Breanne. Oh, and Lila. I think they're doing summer school. Doesn't make sense to me," he admitted between bites. "They keep talking about 'maintaining a 4.0 average,' but I thought that was good. So why do they need summer school?"

"You didn't ask them?"

Audrey looked like she wanted to laugh, but Aiden couldn't figure out what he could have said that would amuse anyone. "I didn't want to make them feel bad."

"You ask them. I'm pretty sure they won't feel bad at all."

His teeth crunched into the cone. Aiden eyed her as he chewed and frowned as he swallowed. "They're gonna laugh at me, aren't they?"

"Not meanly, no. But yeah, they might find it funny. Trust me. They'll love it." She saw him inch toward the door and added, "Hey, let me get you those cookies. Tell your grandma they're good with vanilla ice cream between them."

"'Mkay."

As he pulled open the door, Aiden realized that she hadn't asked about Nathan. *She asked about me. That's weird. Nice. But weird.*

Wayne-the-daisy-man loaded more daisies into the barrel outside his shop as Aiden passed. "How's Nathan? That surgery go okay?"

Normal's good too. I know how to answer normal questions. "Yeah. Went good, but they didn't do the one thing they wanted to, so he has another one on Monday. The doctor said maybe the last one before they come home."

"That would be swell!"

What does that even mean? Swell? Is it good or bad? Sounds good. Weird. "Yeah, well Mom said she's got her fingers crossed but not counting on it or packing their bags yet."

"Smart woman, your mom." Aiden made it several steps away before Wayne called out to him again. "Do you know how he did coming out of the anesthesia? I read the last one didn't go so good."

"Mom said better." Aiden choked on a piece of cone, hacking until it flew out of his mouth and onto the ground.

"You okay?"

"Ugh. Yeah. Anyways, she said he didn't want to wake up so they didn't make him. He was in a lot of pain, though—after he came back to the room. Mom made them give him the good stuff. Then he got funny."

"Well, you come by when your mom gets home, and I'll have a big bunch of daisies for her. She probably needs them about now. She's always telling me that they're the friendliest flower. Guess that's why I use 'em, eh?"

Aiden scanned Wayne's face, but could see the man didn't get it. "You know why she says that, don't you?"

"Because she likes 'em?"

"Well that," he agreed, "and the fact that some girl says it in a movie—the one about the people who met online."

"Figures. Your mom doesn't speak in riddles, she speaks in movies."

"Gets it from Grandma and Grandpa," Aiden agreed. "I never know if they're talking or quoting. It's weird."

DAY TWENTY-FIVE

Monday, June 29, 7:09 p.m.

As musicians tuned their instruments and debated song choices,

Claire passed out water bottles and told of their success thus far. "Okay, so we have the USO building—it's reserved for August 15th. They're not charging us anything, so that's amazing right there. I was just hoping for a delay in payment until after the fundraiser, but the Lord took it one better and got it for us free!"

Murmurs of excitement and gratitude filled the room. Another few song choices were added to the growing list, but James hesitated. "Having a single song like 'Amazing Grace' or something—that's something people are comfortable with, but this is supposed to be for the community. Let's try to keep our choices less revival meeting and more general concert."

"That's right. I had several businesses agree to print fliers, and one actually asked up front if this was a church concert or one for 'everyone.' I think we can let the Lord shine through without blinding people with our unbusheled lights."

James blinked. Joy laughed. Noelle snickered, and James finally found his voice. "That doesn't make sense."

"Well, you know what I mean. We can share the love of Jesus without beating people over the head with Him. This is a way for the community to reach out to one of its own. The churches have already done that. It's just—"

"We get it, Mom." Joy winked at Noelle. "Yep... she's on a mission."

The work began in earnest. They chose songs, decided on singers, made rough practice runs, and started over again, new options, new combinations—making a final decision on exactly two numbers. "Well, it's a start," James said as the night drew to a close.

Several people left, but Steve stuck around for root beer floats. "This is going to be good. I bet the Deeter family comes up with something good—probably country, of course—and Joy and Eli always sound great together. Gotta get them to do something."

"'My Life with You,'" Claire said. "Someone has to sing that. He loves that song—from that Irish group. Kelly was showing me one day. It's hilarious that a kid that little would love something like that over some Disney junk."

"That's a good song... that's a *really* good song, actually." Steve went for his guitar and began picking out notes. "Can someone get me that on a laptop or something? Let's try this once—just to get a feel for it."

James printed out lyrics for himself and Joy while Claire pulled up the music on YouTube. Steve shot her a strange look as decidedly Irish flutes filled the room. "It's just the opening. They do that with their video—see." Applause thundered from the laptop and then the singer crooned the opening line. Jon followed along with the lyrics while Steve picked up the melody on his guitar. At the chorus, Joy joined in, harmonizing.

Claire listened, her eyes closed and a slow smile forming. *This is it, Lord. This is what it needs. This is gonna be great.*

DAY TWENTY-SIX

Tuesday, June 30, 1:14 p.m.

I want to thank everyone who is doing fundraisers for Nathan. Kelly and Jon really appreciate it. However, I would like to remind everyone that the Cox family is unable to keep up with it all. If you have any questions, feel free to contact me, and I'll try to help you out as best I can, or please wait until things settle down a bit for the family. At this time, they're just trying to keep their family together and make it through each day. Again, thank you for your generosity and consideration! —Breanne.

It's really sad when I know exactly what prompted that post. I'm not in the middle of all these fundraisers, and I hear people complaining that they aren't more involved—like they can be from Manchester. Kelly's family is right there, helping all they can. The churches are helping all they can. But people want Jon and Kelly to make decisions about whether this or that happens. That would be hard enough in the best of circumstances. Adric sat lost in thought as he reread the message. In a fit of frustration at not being able to be a buffer for the family, he dug out his wallet, reached in, and pulled every bill from it, shoving it in the donation can on his counter.

Isn't this the second time they've had to post this kind of request?

He reached for the phone, tempted to ask his wife to see what she could do to help organize people. *I bet half the time they just want someone to sign off on an idea so they don't have to take responsibility for it.* She could do that. But as he thought about it, Adric knew it wouldn't work. *We're not family, and people want family. And I guess that makes sense.*

Another update appeared just as Adric finished his lunch. At that precise moment, the deep, country voice of Chase Ashton filled the bays and the office as the man sang, "I'm Gonna Miss You."

Nathan had a great morning being towed around the hospital grounds in the little red wagon by… country music star Chase Ashton!! (Yes, the ignorant mommy here didn't know who that is and had to YouTube it.) Dang! That guy has such a deep, soothing voice. Nathan was in heaven. He got to hang out with his fireman buddies (all fifteen of them) AND a cowboy. They were filming an episode of America's Great Heroes and the Manchester Fire Department, along with the Cunningham Burn Unit, were filmed today. Nathan will be on TV on Halloween!

10:14 p.m.

After a busy day running around with the boys, helping Jamie with a writing assignment, grocery shopping, and the phone ringing almost incessantly, Dee flopped into Keith's chair the moment he shuffled off to bed, and flipped up her laptop. The page needed updates, and Kelly had begged her to do it in one of those many phone calls. She began with the words they'd waited to hear and share for over three weeks.

Yay! They're coming home tomorrow. Lily Allen will be putting together a meals list for a while, so please message Lily if you'd like to bring the family a meal. Note: Due to the baby's sensitive stomach, gluten and dairy-free meals are preferred. Kelly can't eat anything containing either. Thanks everyone. This is just such a great day!

Almost immediately after she posted, one from Kelly appeared, dated several hours earlier. *She must have given up on me. Poor kid. Well, I did it when I could. That's all I promised. Still, at least their Internet is working again.* Despite her inner justification, a twinge of guilt plucked at her. She read the words once—twice. Then read them all over again, still grinning at them. *Phase one—and the worst one—of this ordeal is over. On to better days!*

```
Taking apart what has been our home for the last 3+
weeks. Still a journey ahead of us, but this is one
move I am really looking forward to. It'll be
strange not to see Pete and Naomi almost every day,
though. What they've done for us while we've been
here—words can't possibly express what I want to
say.
Oh! Nathan is now using his walker without much
resistance. So proud of him!
```

The thought occurred to her—this could be Kelly's last update. Would people still want to know his progress when there would be days, weeks, even months between updates? Probably not. Still, they'd want to know about fundraisers—like the one Claire Rhodes was planning. They'd still planned a car wash, several home sales demonstrators had scheduled "parties" with proceeds going to Nathan and family. *The page will stay active with the results of those kinds of things for a while. People will still get good news. And, there's always him walking again. I know people will be excited when he finally gets out of the walker and wheelchair. That'll be a fun status. Kelly will enjoy writing that one. Heck, we all would!*

Kelly's email had become buried among the day's junk mail, notifications, and well-wishes and prayers. Dee scrolled through the inbox, looking for the email Kelly had sent from her phone. After several tries, she found it, buried in her trash. *Not the one to accidentally delete. Sheesh!* Before she could make an even bigger mess of it, Dee checked the page to be sure Kelly hadn't posted the "thank you note" she'd composed, and then typed it out.

```
I got this from Kelly today:

Thank you for sharing in our tears of happiness as
```

well as sorrow. Thank you for all the financial support and fundraisers. We can't even begin to make our thanks sound adequate for all that everyone has done. It has all been and will be so very helpful to us. God bless each and every one of you as only He can.
Love, The Cox Family

—Dee

DAY TWENTY-SEVEN

Wednesday, July 1, 3:24 p.m.

The Homstad house pulsed with artificial normalcy. Keith and Dee washed windows, each standing on one side, pointing out minuscule smudges that no one else would ever notice. Breanne read chapter six of her Criminal Justice text—read it six times. Lila and Drew enjoyed a sudsy sponge war over the hood of her car. Logan and Aiden crashed cars regularly enough to convince any onlooker that total annihilation was the goal of the game.

All heads turned as the phone rang. Dee grabbed it from the couch cushion and answered. "Hello?" A voice spread a wide smile over her face. Aiden stood, inching his way to the door until Dee nodded. The boy bolted outside and down the sidewalk. Breanne tossed her book aside and rushed to the back of the house—the boys' room. *Getting his stuff, I suppose...*

Dee disconnected the call and rushed for the laptop, and her fingers flew over the keys. She sat back, satisfied. Grinning.

Psst… rumor has it, some adorable little boy is Home!!!

3:09 p.m.

How normal... Kelly couldn't imagine how this world—her world—should look so normal. The van rolled down Linden Street.

Neal Kirkpatrick trimmed his hedges with precision usually reserved for bonsai enthusiasts. Just in time, Kelly remembered not to wave. *He'll know you know about the water bill.*

Jon interrupted her thoughts as he pulled the van into the drive. "Someone mowed."

"Probably your dad."

The engine died as he pulled the key from the ignition and Nathan cheered. "Home!"

Jon and Kelly exchanged astonished glances. "Yep. We're home," Kelly agreed.

The garage door opened as Jon hit the button. As Kelly unbuckled Anna's car seat, Jon lifted Nathan from his. Before they could even step in the garage, Nathan pointed. "My tricycle! That's *my* tricycle. My wagon!"

"Let's try it," Jon suggested.

He's exhausted and his first words are, "Let's try it." He's a good man, my Jon. A good dad. I need to remember to tell him that more.

Cool air hit her as she unlocked the back door. Someone had come in and turned on the air conditioner. She set Anna's car seat down just inside the door and took a tour. Curious, she peeked into the fridge. A large salad, a container of grilled chicken, and a quart of goat milk told Kelly that her in-laws had been there. *At least I know who turned on the AC.*

The fingerprints of various people showed in each room of the house. The dirty dishes she'd left were gone—obviously washed, but not waiting in the drainer. *Mamacita Cox must have washed and then put away so they wouldn't get dusty.* Laundry that had been in baskets by the couch—she looked for it and found it all folded and put away in drawers. *Lila. That's definitely Lila. Mamacita wouldn't go into our drawers unless asked. Lila would finish it regardless—nervous energy.*

Mail sat in a basket on the counter, again a sign of Jon's mother's work. She stared at the back door, uncertain. Anna still slept in her car seat near the garage door. Her hand rested on the back doorknob, but she hesitated. Raw emotion slammed into her, knocking her breathless. Out there—out that door it all happened. *I can't avoid it forever...*

She opened the door and stepped onto the patio. Nathan's kiddie pool no longer lay in the grass. Someone had emptied and leaned it against the house. The backyard had been mowed as well.

Kelly waited for the tears, but they didn't come. She inched her way forward, glancing around her as she surveyed the yard, her eyes avoiding the back corner and the gate leading into the alley. The garden looked good—sparse in places, but alive and thriving. *No weeds. That's odd. Mamacita must have done that. I guess some of the plants died and she pulled 'em out.*

Jon and Nathan whizzed past, Jon pushing the boy on his trike. "I'm riding, Mama!"

Riding, but not cycling. Still, your foot is resting on the pedal. That's a start. "Doing good, too! Push with your feet..."

But they were gone, circling through the patio, down the side path to the front yard again. Kelly took another step toward the back gate. Another. She waited between each one, expecting that at any moment, her emotions would force her back again. They didn't. She leaned over the gate, staring at the ground where the power line had lain, sparking and sizzling in the ever-encroaching darkness. Her eyes rose to the bright sun overhead. *I think coming home midday is better. Feels less ominous or something.*

Still, a tear ran down her cheek as she saw where a dead bird once warned of coming danger. Another followed as she remembered the screams of her son, the neighbors rushing to help, someone calling 9-1-1. Kelly turned away, not as ready to deal with the emotions as she'd thought.

The sight of the yard again brought new emotions—happier, more grateful ones. *Lord, we thought we knew how much people had done for us. We heard about fundraisers, saw money in accounts and were just blown away by it all, but look at this. This is amazing. I knew Mamacita would do the dishes—clear out the fridge. I didn't think she'd have time for her garden **and** mine. I didn't think they'd fold and put away laundry. I didn't think they'd mow the yards. Wow. Now we're all home...*

That thought arrested her attention and sent her jogging toward the back door. She snatched the phone the moment she stepped in the back door and punched her mother's number into it. "We're home..."

WEEK FIVE

DAY TWENTY-NINE

Friday, July 3, 11:31 a.m.

Nathan called out as the doorbell rang. "Moooommmyyyy!"

"I hear it. I'm not deaf, no matter how hard you try to destroy my hearing." Kelly glanced at Aiden who didn't move from his new Lego set at the table. *Don't rush to answer it or anything,* she grumbled to herself as she wiped her hands on a kitchen towel.

Willow stood on the step. She made an interesting picture with one son wrapped around each leg, a daughter in one arm, and a large tote bag hanging from her other hand. "I brought meat."

"Wha—come in," she said as she recovered from the shock of hearing, "I brought meat."

"I just thought about Jon not being able to work for weeks and weeks and thought, "I've got all that frozen chicken and beef in the freezer—"

"Didn't you lose most of that in the fire?"

"We've butchered since then," Willow assured her. "We've got more than enough. This'll save you having to shop too—probably not easy with Nathan right now."

Kelly pulled a chair out for Willow and pointed out Nathan to the twins. "Nathan's in there. He's playing with his new fire trucks. There's enough for everyone—and their brother—so why don't you go let him show you."

"People like fire trucks?" Willow laughed. "Chad wanted to get one, but Joe swore the chief would kill him after the thing with Terry." The woman's eyes slid toward Nathan. "How's he doing home? Happy to be out of the hospital?"

As she talked, Kelly unloaded the meat from the tote bag and filled her freezer. "It's amazing. You can't imagine the difference. I thought after that first night, he'd be back to his detached self, but he's back to his *real* self. It's crazy. He actually chooses to get up on the walker instead of us making him. The doctors said it might take a week or two before he did that."

Willow listened, as she tried to keep little Kari from dismantling Kelly's kitchen. "And how long? How long should he have to use it?"

"The doctor says several weeks at least." Kelly offered Willow a glass of water. "It's all we have in the house…"

"Oh, I didn't plan to stay. I know you're busy and probably just want time to be together again. I just had a delivery down the street—Neal Kirkpatrick—so I thought I'd drop this off." Willow picked up Kari and called her sons to her. "Time to go, lads."

"I—" Kelly stopped herself. If Willow didn't want to or didn't think she should stay, then arguing wouldn't help. *Besides, I've got more laundry to do than I can finish in a day anyway.* "Thank you."

DAY THIRTY

Saturday, July 4, 8:19 a.m.

Kelly stopped short as she entered the boys' bedroom. Nathan sat on the floor, shoving his feet into his three-sizes-too-big boots. "Whatcha doin'?"

"Going outside."

"Oh." Unsure how to reply, she asked, "And how do you plan to get out there?"

"I'll walk."

Just like that. He'll walk. This is gonna be interesting. Still, she nodded and smiled. "Well, okay then. You do that."

If she thought he'd just stand up and walk, she had another think coming. He crawled across the floor in his too-big boots and turned down the hall. She hoped he'd stand at some point, but he didn't.

Once in the living room, he pulled himself up on his walker and pushed it toward the back door. "Can you help me?"

Like I'd say no. "Sure!"

Jon entered from the garage just as Nathan took off across the patio. With his hands settled low on his hips, Jon watched, shaking his head. "That's the kid who we had to force to use that thing just a couple of days ago."

"It's crazy. Crazy good, but still... crazy."

His arm slipped around her waist and his cheek rested against her hair. "It's good to see him almost normal. It's good to be home."

"Amen."

Aiden called for help, and Jon went to see what the boy needed, but Kelly just watched Nathan. The boy fell—twice—and both times were more likely caused by his over-sized boots rather than his injured foot. Even with that pain, he didn't cry. He just crawled back up and tried again. Kelly silently cheered.

She couldn't take it any longer. With a glance back to be certain he would be fine, she hurried to get the phone. She nearly jumped up and down, waiting for someone to answer. Her mother's groggy voice finally broke through. "Yeah..."

"Sorry, Mom. I thought someone else would answer. Didn't mean to wake you."

"No idea where everyone is. What's up?"

Kelly stood at the back door, watching Nathan decide to choose his yard toys over the walker. "You should have seen him, Mom! He just decided he wanted to take a walk so he got on his boots and grabbed the walker. Without being told to do it. He just did it!"

"That's great news! Wait—" Muffled voices drowned out Kelly's mother for a few seconds. "Lila wants to know if she can come by later—see him walk."

"Sure! Maybe after lunch would be best—after naps so he's rested."

"She'll be there. You should see her jumping."

"Mom, she's my sister," Kelly reminded. "I *can* see her."

Nathan scrambled for the door in his half-crawl half-walk as Lila entered. "I'm home! Did you see? I have a walker so I can walk!"

"Well, where is it?" Lila asked as she squeezed him into a bear hug.

"Over there." Nathan jerked his thumb in the general direction of the room—very unhelpful. "Look at my sword! I got two from the policemans."

"Where's the other one? We'll have a sword fight." Lila glanced around her and saw it on the couch. "Over there!"

Nathan hesitated, staring at the one in his hand for a moment. He passed it to her, stood, and hobbled to the couch to retrieve the sword. Kelly's jaw dropped. Lila's eyes widened. *"Get the camera! Video this!"* she mouthed as she prepared to battle Nathan.

"Okay, engarde!"

"What?" Nathan leaned against the coffee table, his knee resting on the top.

"That's what they say when they're going to do a sword fight—it's French."

Nathan thought, wrinkled his forehead, and then grinned. "'In my day, we were content to hate the French.'"

While Lila snickered, Kelly groaned. "That's what I get for letting him watch period movies. Kids always pick up on the worst quotes possible."

"C'mon, you love that movie." Another chuckle. "And at least he recognized the connection. That's got to be good as far as comprehension stuff goes."

"Sure," Kelly muttered with a sardonic twist to her lips. "Now I just get shredded by the PC police for letting my kid watch culturally insensitive material. Brilliant."

Unimpressed by the conversation that had drifted from exciting things like sword fights, Nathan waved the sword overhead and charged. Every other step was punctuated with a soft "ow," but he walked. Even with the semi-constant sway of the sword making him unstable, he advanced.

Kelly rushed for the camera. Lila took slow, deliberate steps backward, pretending to be scared. "No! Don't get me. Don't! Nooooo..."

Nathan continued his advance, swinging the sword and making a pathetic attempt at a diabolical laugh. "Haaaaaa..."

"He sounds like one of those yellow blobs in that movie," Kelly mused as she returned with the camera.

Jon stepped into the room, his eyes wide at the sight of his son staggering toward Lila and brandishing his sword in the process. Nathan tripped, crawled a few steps, but they encouraged him to get up again. "You can't fight on your knees! Come get me," Lila taunted, laughing.

And he did. He stood, stumbled forward, and fell—again. Once more he crawled. Again they urged him up onto his feet and he advanced. Engrossed in his play, the boy even forgot to complain about the pain that surely tried to register with each step.

```
Kelly Cox (4:32 p.m.) It's amazing what a few days
can mean when you're home. Nathan walked without his
walker today! (Video forthcoming) My heart is too
full. I'm so happy to be posting a fantastic update.
—Kelly.
```

Within minutes, Lila's video appeared—so few minutes that Kelly suspected her sister had driven home at speeds exceeding the legal limit. *Where's the local constabulary when you need 'em? Constabulary? Wow. I've been affected by period movies, too.*

```
Lila Homstad (4:40) Nathan's first time walking
without a walker!!! —with Kelly Cox. Gives new
meaning to "Independence Day!"
```

DAY THIRTY-ONE

Sunday, July 5, 5:02 a.m.

Milk dribbled down Anna's chin as the baby drifted back to sleep. Kelly nestled her into the "Moses basket" and set it on the floor. The quiet of the house in the early morning hours wrapped her in comfort—home. *That's why Mom likes to be up when everyone else is asleep. It's comforting to have the quiet and the dark—or semi-dark—when you're all alone.*

She raised the lid of the laptop and the date on the desktop calendar hit her, sending her mind reeling with the realization of what it meant. *One month. It's been one month.*

Tears flowed as the memories spiraled around her, spinning her into a vortex of emotions. *He went from "should be dead" to walking in a month. It's been one, horribly long month of medical procedures. He still shudders if he hears the word "hydro." Just days ago, he balked at the idea of using a walker, but look at him. He just chucked it aside yesterday. We expected to need that wheelchair, and he might never use it!*

The wheelchair stood to one side as if an ironic talisman against the need for it. *Cam sent that all the way from Alaska so we'd have one—so we wouldn't have to **buy** one. Now we won't even need it. That's just unreal. They talked about "limited mobility." He's mobile. If he's this mobile this fast, how long before you can't even tell he was injured? I never thought that was possible, but now...*

The vague hints that the doctors had mentioned when the wound seemed unwilling to heal—hints about the possibility of amputation—now felt ludicrous. *I was so scared—didn't even want to think about it. Now it just—how was it even possible that such an idea occurred to anyone?*

Kelly's fingers tried to type out a Facebook status, but the tears that filled her eyes and spilled down her cheeks created an odd pattern of red, wavy lines, indicating she'd misspelled about every third word. She mopped at them with the neck of her pajama top and tried again.

```
One month ago to the day… I haven't had a moment to
myself just to break down and cry—not until now. I
was just reflecting on all the love and support that
just keeps coming in, and that's all I CAN do right
now—cry. Thank you. May the Lord bless you and keep
you. Through the hills and valleys, you have been
there to support us, to pray with us, to cheer with
us. I can't put into words the gratitude we have for
each and every one of you.
```

That night, Breanne sat curled in the corner of her bed, a small lamp shining on her journal. After the day's entry, she added three short lines—lines unrelated to the lessons she'd learned in church that day.

```
By Sunday the 21st, Nathan had gone through three
surgeries. By the time he left the hospital—five
surgeries. He now walks around with a limp and says
"ow" with almost every step.
```

DAY THIRTY-TWO

Monday, July 6, 8:03 a.m.

Cheers erupted in the office at Fairbury Automotive as the men clustered around the monitor, watching Nathan walking without his walker. Jon stood a bit apart, but his smile told Adric he'd be a part of the crew in no time. "That is incredible! Didn't you say weeks?"

"That's what the physical therapist said. They were talking about us maybe needing to get him into a local practice a couple of times a week." Jon shrugged. "I think he just feels comfortable at home and this is what you do there."

"That actually makes sense," Adric mused. "I mean, if that's all he knows for home, it's natural to just revert back to that, isn't it?"

"Seems to be." Jon pointed to the clipboard on the wall. "Tune-up for the truck out there?"

Adric nodded and let him go. The other guys stared at him before one said, "What's with him?"

"He just wants to work. I don't think Jon's accustomed to being the center of attention—especially as a new guy with a new job."

"Well, we've been talking..." The other two men exchanged glances before the speaker continued. "When he has appointments and has to take off, we'll stay late—work his hours for him."

And this is why I love this town. Aloud, Adric said, "Will do. Just clock in on his card. We'll give him full credit for time worked." A new thought occurred to him as he pointed to the screen. "Go change the ticket on that tune-up. Mark it twenty-five percent off. I'm running a tune-up special. We'll give all labor profits to Nathan's fund."

"That's great!" one of the guys said, but the other looked nervous.

"Look, guys. This is my donation. Your paychecks won't be affected. I know you're giving your time for Jon, and that's more than I could ever ask. If you decide you want to give more at some other time, that's fine, but this is mine."

The relief on his mechanic's face would have been comical if the guy didn't look guilty for needing the money he earned. *Well, he shouldn't. It's his. No one should feel guilty about needing money to survive.*

"Now get back to work. I've got to call in a few ads, and once they come out, we're gonna be swamped, so we've got to finish up everything scheduled as soon as possible."

"Gotcha, boss. We'll handle it."

As the door to the bays slammed behind them, Adric picked up the phone and called the Fairbury Tourist Center. "Hey, Rachel. Glad I caught you. I need to place an ad in the blog—fundraiser for Nathan…"

The UPS truck pulled up to the house, honked twice, and Dan the "brown guy" jogged up the steps and leaned a package against the doorstep. Nathan hobbled to the door to answer it but struggled to stay upright and open the door at the same time. Aiden helped, something Kelly suspected wouldn't have happened pre-accident. *Not that he was mean to Nathan or anything, but this really brought us closer together than ever. We're more of a team now. I can already sense it.*

But despite Aiden's offers of help, Nathan insisted on carrying the box inside himself. Unfortunately, no matter how hard the little guy tried, he just couldn't lift and carry it. Aiden glanced at Kelly for approval, before picking up his brother from behind and carrying him to the couch. "Sorry. I thought you might want to get it faster. Look. It has your name on it. See that N?" Aiden pointed. "That N is for Nathan. It's for you." The phone rang, and Aiden dashed to answer it.

Kelly brought scissors and slit the packing tape. As she worked, she read the return address. *Okay, Lord. Those Home-Bodies ladies are amazing. I just can't—* Nathan's squeal interrupted her thoughts.

"Look, Mommy! Fireman boots! I've got real fireman boots! And—oh! A coloring book! I can color too. And a puzzle…"

One toy after the next emerged from the modest-sized box. Most were tiny, but all had clearly been chosen with great care. A small Lego set had Aiden's name on it. "That one is for Aiden," Kelly said as she pulled it from the box.

Nathan sent up a wail of protest—one that Kelly had dreaded. *I knew he'd become like this with everyone showering stuff on him. How could we have—*

"I want to give it to him!"

Relieved, she nodded, "Then how do you ask?" *Well that was easier than I thought. Whew!*

"Ca—May I give it to him?" Wide eyes stared up at her as a smirk formed on his lips.

"Very funny. Go for it."

Nathan hobbled across the room at what was meant for a run, although he'd once walked almost as quickly. *But he **thinks** he's running. That alone is just huge.*

As Aiden and Nathan assembled Aiden's new Lego warrior, Aiden showing much more patience than she'd ever seen him exhibit before, she couldn't help but wonder just how long it would take him to revert back to the sometimes-bossy older brother. *Well, he'd have been bossy all the time if I let him get away with it. Still, this will forge an even tighter bond. That's got to be good for a long-term friendship. Their age difference needs every single thing we can find to help them do that.*

As a diversion to getting caught up in yet another downward spiral of her perceived failures as a parent, Kelly opted to take a few pictures and post a thank-you notice on the message board. She carried the "loot" to the table, arranged it near Nathan, and ordered them to smile for a picture. "Say, wheeeeeeeeeeeeeeee!"

Nathan squealed his response, but Aiden just shook his head and smiled. Once the flash blinded them, Aiden muttered, "You're so weird, Mom."

"I come from a long, line of weird Homstads. Grandma always says—"

"Homstad is Norwegian for weird. Yeah, I know."

Caleb Allen let the last few notes fade naturally before covering the strings of his guitar. The others of the Monday night jam session nodded. "Great choice. I'm so glad you've decided to join us."

"I'm not a big performer, but a song like 'Blackbird' just lets you be quiet and let the music tell the story for you. I figured I could do that."

"And you wanted a Beatles song, Dad!" Joy initiated a high-five and turned back to the piano, her fingers rippling over the keys in a series of scales. Those scales morphed into chords, which melded into a melody of familiar notes. "I've been thinking of this one…"

"'Make You Feel My Love—' Good choice," Steve agreed.

"Well, we've got to get the final songs selected and get more rehearsals scheduled. We'll need to meet at least twice or three times a week until the concert," James interjected. "It's time to organize this thing."

Those words began a flurry of ideas, choices, and good-natured arguments over song choices and who got to sing what. Claire pulled out her notebook and passed it from person to person, asking each to write down which number they planned to do and with whom. "Okay, we need two places. That way twice the people can rehearse at once. One group can stay here, and I'll take the other to the church and they can practice there. I'll make a schedule while I'm there, so don't leave here until we get back. It's time to get this organized or one of us is going to be up there never having practiced something important."

Joy grabbed her mother's arm. "Don't go… please don't go…"

Steve joined in, along with Eli, "Don't go away…"

Claire and Noelle looked at one another and Claire sang back, "These…flops…" she kicked up her flip-flop shod foot and continued with Noelle. "—are made for walkin' and that's just what I'll do—"

"Don't go," James sang this time, joining his daughter and friend. "Please don't go.."

The "to go" group sang louder, "—of these days I'm gonna—" drowning out the first word of the "to stay" group's next line.

"—go away…"

Silence hovered for a moment before the group erupted in laughter.

DAY THIRTY-FOUR

Wednesday, July 8, 9:32 a.m.

In the kitchen at Rosita's Mexican Restaurant, Rose Alvarez pulled her laptop toward her, with one eye on the clock. *Got time. Let's see what's happening in the ever-exciting Fairbury.* A timer beeped, reminding her to stir the huge pan of refried beans simmering on the stove. "No customers for at least half an hour. We're good."

Fairbury Notes & News
`Wednesday, July 8th, 9:00 a.m.` *(Rachel Delman-Cox)*

```
Nathan Cox is home and doing well. On July 4th, in a
move some are calling "Nathan's Independence Day,"
the little boy tossed aside his walker and began
walking without assistance, something that doctors
didn't expect for many weeks yet. When asked about
it, Nathan's mother, Kelly, said, "We're just so
grateful to be home where he is comfortable and at
ease. We see the old Nathan again and it's nice."
A new fundraiser for the Cox family is creating
quite a stir on Facebook. People from all over the
community and from neighboring communities are
banding together in an effort to raise enough funds
to help pay the astronomical medical bills that have
followed the Cox family home from the hospital.
Those who want to help can visit the Nathan Cox
Benefit Concert page on Facebook or contact Claire
Rhodes at clairedeloony@letterbox.com or by calling
her home number at 555-312-1212.
```

She didn't hesitate. With a click of her mouse button, she found the Facebook page and began reading.

```
Claire Rhodes- (July 7th 8:00 a.m.)
Dear Lots of People.
I am in need of much help.
```

Saturday, August 15th we are putting together a benefit concert for the Cox family (Nathan Cox is the 3 1/2 year old boy who stood on an electrical wire and suffered severe burns) The event is going to be held at the USO building, and I am in need of people to help in several areas.

Refreshments: Someone to organize the providing of baked goods, beverages, plates, cups etc. Manning the table during the night. As the saying goes "many hands make light work," so if you belong to a group of people who are willing to provide baked goods then go for it.

Publicity: Poster and flier design (hint, hint Wanda Delman—you are the best publicist we know). Distributing fliers. Talking to newspapers and radio people. Contacting business, churches and organizations. Publicity is the key to bringing this all together.

Decorating: Setting up the room. Stage design. (We have a few ideas but need hands and props to pull it together)

Scrapbook maker: Telling the story including all the newspaper articles, photos of Nathan what happens next.

Videographer and photographer.

If you know of anything we may have neglected to think of, please let us know. And please feel free to invite people you know with talent in any of the mentioned areas.

If you have an interest in helping in any of these areas, you can message me here, email me at clairedeloony@letterbox.com or call my cell 555-312-1212.

Please don't feel pressured in any way. The best advertising for this event is word of mouth, so if you don't have an interest in any of the above then please just spread the word, and you will have done way more than we can thank you for.

Breanne, I've added you to this list simply so you can know what is going on and so you can keep the family informed if you wish. BUT, I don't want you

to feel obliged in any way to help. This evening is FOR you and your family. You guys deserve a break after all the stress and worry you have been through. (I will be asking you for some photos from your camera, though, so I can have them enlarged for the event)
Feel free to add people to this conversation as they come to mind—male and female.

Breanne Homstad (July 7th 1:12 p.m.) Thanks for adding me! I may be able to help more, but as I mentioned, I have a couple things I may have going on that day. However, I can definitely help! My mom and I could do all the scrapbooking bit—we have all the pics, newspaper clippings, story, etc.
BTW, did you want people responding to this message or message you personally?

Rose hesitated for less time than it took for her fingers to find their proper places on the keys. She typed out a message to Claire in record time and managed to be off the computer before the clock struck a quarter 'til.

Rose@Rosita's (July 8th 9:42 a.m.) I would be happy to take care of the food for you—whatever you want. Fruit, baked goods, coffee, sparkling juice, and water? Will that work? Just let me know.

Within seconds of posting, a reply appeared.

Claire Rhodes (July 7th 8:00 a.m.) Okay Rose, you're it. I'll send you a list of people who said they'd be willing to bake something. You can round up your own team. My hands are now FREE!!!!! Thank you SO much.

The "Open" sign flipped over at exactly ten o'clock. Rosita stepped outside to gauge the tourist presence and nodded, satisfied. *Should have it just about right. Now, to organize food for an undetermined number of people. That's not so easy...*

WEEK SIX

DAY THIRTY-SEVEN

Saturday, July 10, 9:13 a.m.

Breanne pulled two socks from her drawer and reached for her Converse while her laptop booted. As she adjusted the seams, she read Kelly's late night/early morning update.

Update from Nathan's mom: Nathan is doing fabulous—going back to being a little boy again. We're just so happy at the progress he is making. We went from three weeks of pushing him to use his walker (under duress and stress on all of us) to after one week at home, he's trying to run (imagine an "old man shuffle" and you have a good picture) ;)
We ask for continued prayers for his healing. We have an appt. Monday in Manchester and hope it's a successful one. We know we only see surface wounds and not what's underneath them, but I figure if it's healthy-looking on the outside, surely it's doing well on the inside.
We also ask for prayer for Nathan in regards to sleeping. He has been experiencing some horrible nightmares to the point where he is screaming almost like he is in pain, but it's just a dream. Thank you everyone for your continued support and prayers!

Lila burst in the room, calling for help in finding the bag of old towels she'd gathered and froze at the expression on Breanne's face. "It's horrible, isn't it? Nightmares. I can only imagine what those are like for him."

"I wonder why he didn't have them at the hospital—drugs, I guess."

Lila moved a blanket from the corner as she mused, "And coping? Now that he's home, he's relaxed enough to do it?"

"Yeah," Breanne agreed. "Probably." She jumped up and grabbed her purse. "Ready?"

"I can't find those towels!"

A memory niggled at Breanne. "Didn't you put them in your trunk last night so you wouldn't 'forget them'?"

"Oh, ugh. Let's go."

Tabitha Allen rotated out of the wash crew and into the "worker support" role. She dug through the ice chest for water bottles, filling her arms with as many as she could hold, and began passing them around to anyone willing to pause long enough to take a swig or two of water. "Drink up. Can't have anyone passing out from dehydration."

Lance Latimer took a bottle but drawled, "Who needs water with a drink like you around?"

"Someone all wet like you?" Tabitha tossed over her shoulder as she continued onto the next person.

Breanne took her bottle, asking, "What was that all about?"

"Oh, LoveLance Latimer is at it again. I swear, he hasn't done anything but harass the girls all morning. Why's he even here?"

Chad Tesdall wiped the back of his arm across his forehead as he accepted his bottle. "I don't know LoveLance."

"He thinks he's the world's gift to women," Tabitha snorted.

"Not God's?"

"He's an atheist." She muttered as she passed bottles to three firemen behind him.

"Sounds like he went to the Chuck Majors School of —"

Breanne interrupted Chad. "—Self-Proclaimed Stud Muffins."

The trio and two of the nearby firemen erupted in laughter, and

Tabitha glanced at Lance to be sure he didn't notice and feel bad, but the guy was otherwise engaged, annoying another girl. "Sounds just about right."

It took three trips to get all the volunteers fully hydrated again. Tossing the two extra bottles into the ice chest, she grabbed the sunscreen and began the rounds. "Okay, it's noon. Two hours since we started. Get yourself blocked against the rays." Lance opened his mouth once more, but Tabitha silenced him. "If you opened your mouth to drop another cheesy line, it's gonna get filled with this sunscreen."

"Can I get another bottle of water? I'm parched, and those dinky things—"

"Mean that people can get back to work after chugging a bit and half the bottle doesn't go to waste," she snapped. *Which wouldn't affect you since you still aren't **working.***

"Well, can I have one?"

"It's in the ice chest. Help yourself." She took the hose from a fireman and handed him the sunscreen. "You too."

"Hey, you handed out water last time…"

"To *workers*," Tabitha growled. "People not working can get their own."

"I would if there was anything to *do*."

Breanne stepped forward, accepted the sunscreen from the fireman, and said, "Well, let's see. You could gather up the wet towels and hang them on the line over there. You could grab a towel and help dry off cars. You could gather trash and put it away. You could give one of the guys a break—some of these guys haven't sat down for two hours. Just find something that needs to be done and do it. Sheesh, my three-year-old nephew—you know, the one we're doing this for? Yeah, he could figure out a way to help faster than you have. Just get to work or go home."

Lance shot Breanne a dirty look and shuffled off toward the ice chest. Lily Allen pulled up and called to Tabitha. "C'mon. We've got sandwiches to pick up at the deli."

Breanne smiled at the fireman beside her. "Well, Mark, looks like lunch is on its way."

"Lunch?" Mark Keating picked up the squeegee and began working on the back window of the car in front of him.

"Yeah. Lila just took Tabitha to get the food."

"Sandwiches for all of us?" Mark grinned and called out to the half dozen others nearby, "Food's comin'!"

"Then get to work. There are three cars ahead," Fire Chief Terry called out as he sank into the seat of the one before him and drove it out of the parking lot.

"Well, three to go and four in the lot. If we work fast…" Breanne stared longingly at the hose before her and shook her head. "I'm gonna get another bottle of water, want one?"

"Sure. Thanks."

She glanced at the other two firemen close to them. "What about them?"

"Hey, guys? More water?"

"Did you say lunch is coming?" one asked.

"Yep. Probably ten to fifteen minutes."

The other two shook their heads, but Breanne inched toward the ice chest. "I'm still getting me one…"

"Thanks. I appreciate it. I'd still like one, too."

She heard comments from the others as she left but chose to ignore them. *That's the problem with people—can't have a conversation with someone of the opposite sex without someone assuming it's flirting. And, if it is,* her analytical side insisted, *you don't even want to acknowledge it in case you're totally misreading them. It's just stupid.*

Sandwiches were delivered just as Terry arrived with a new car and drove off with the latest clean one. Lila appeared at Breanne's side a couple of minutes later with another bottle of water, a sandwich, and the "Car Wash" sign. "You go sit on the wall over there and wave between bites. I'm taking one to the other entrance."

"Good idea." She grabbed the food and sign and hurried to the bench. "I hope she got me something good—"

A shadow fell over her. "What?"

Breanne pointed to the wall next to her. "Sit down. You're blocking the sign." As Mark sat, she laughed. "I sound like my sister."

"The red head?"

"See, you just proved my point." Breanne choked on a swig of water as she saw his chagrined expression. "No worries. She just says it like it is. My mom always says 'Bushes are safe around her.'"

Mark blinked. "That's nice…"

So I've just convinced you that we're all nuts. Yeah, it's probably true, but still. "You know, beating around the bush. She doesn't do it, soooooooo..."

"Gotcha."

Talking around a bite of sandwich, Breanne pointed to the plastic bag-covered parking meters. "What's up with that?"

"Chief Varney did his part by covering all the meters on this side of town so we could park cars for the owners and not have to lose profits to paying for meters or customers who are afraid of parking tickets. They all say, 'Meters resume at 2:00.'"

"Well, that's cool."

"I think it was the kid—Aiden's—idea. He told Joe that no one would come if they had to worry about tickets, and there's not enough room in the parking lot for us to work *and* to park cars."

"Well, he's right. Kid's too smart for me to keep up with. I don't know how he comes up with this stuff. He's done it since he was tiny."

"But he won't wear a helmet."

Breanne shrugged. "Mom thinks it's some kind of sensory thing. Did you know ever since Jon lost his job, the kid won't ride anything at all? Only while he was at our house—and he wore a helmet then, too."

"For Nathan, I guess."

Breanne nodded. "Yeah... I guess." She wadded her sandwich wrappings up in a ball and propped the sign against Mark's feet. "You can advertise. I'll go work so someone else can eat."

"Did Sir LoveLance work while we ate?"

She laughed. No, she tried not to, but some things are just too amusing to resist. "Yeah. Sure."

Six minutes late, Dee posted the Facebook reminder and prayed her kids wouldn't sell her to gypsies or however that old saying went.

```
The car wash ends soonish! Hurry on over and get 'er
scrubbed!
```

Clean up—the worst and most boring part of any enterprise became a free-for-all of pranks. Few people managed not to wind up soaked and even fewer managed to resist the temptation *to* drench someone else in fresh and not-so-fresh buckets of water. Some dumped the little bits of water left in bottles on heads. Breanne avoided anything that looked like it had touched someone's mouth, shuddering at the thought.

Each volunteer was urged to pull his or her drying towels from the makeshift line and new ones were added as it emptied. Lila collected the Homstad buckets, ice chest, and hose, while Breanne and Drew cleaned up the signs and lingering trash. Aiden, in an apparent desire to stay on the good side of the law, raced down the street the moment it hit two o'clock and pulled all the meter covers off, dashing into each store as he passed and calling out, "Meters are running again!"

He arrived back just as Lila pulled the car through the parking lot entrance. "C'mon. Get in. Let's go."

Breanne shook her head. "Nah, Aiden and I have somewhere to be."

"Wha—"

But Breanne waved them off and grinned at Aiden. "I promised ice cream before this whole thing happened, and I heard that The Confectionary has Triple Berry Blast."

"Really? She said not for another couple of weeks!" Aiden pumped his fist. "That stuff is the best ever."

Nervous excitement made Aiden jittery. Weary from almost five hours of work, Breanne dug into her pocket for her cash and passed it to him. "Ask her to make mine a mini-smoothie, okay?"

"Thanks!" He took off, almost around the corner before she took her next step.

Crazy kid.

A car passed, slowed, and the right rear door opened. Mark jumped out and sauntered toward her. "Walking home?"

"Yeah. I promised Aiden ice cream a while back, and The Confectionary has his favorite again."

"He worked hard today. Harder than—"

Breanne laughed. "LoveLance." She gave him a sidelong glance before adding. "Is it horrible that I wanted to cheer when he gashed his leg?"

He waited—just a moment's hesitation—and then said, "Well, I think *someone* did."

"Lila. Yeah. She didn't bother to hide it. Never does."

"Not angling for a date with Lance Lothario, eh?"

Breanne snickered. "Yeah... not hardly." She turned the corner and scanned the street for Aiden, but the boy must still be inside the store. "I bet Lance might get why the fundraiser even happened now..."

"Speaking of fundraiser, did anyone add up the totals?"

"Lila will—or Mom will. We'll post on Facebook. It was nice of you guys to come help."

Mark shrugged. "You should have seen guys trying to switch shifts to get today off."

"Anyone change?"

"Nope." Mark laughed at the smug expression on her face. "What?"

"I just realized that it's Saturday. Who would choose to work on Saturday when they could have it 'off'? It's just a few hours of the day and then you're free."

"That too, but the guys just really wanted to help out," Mark insisted. "Some didn't get to go up to Manchester, so Dale *almost* got Tim to switch based on that alone."

They neared The Confectionary, and something in Mark's demeanor changed. Breanne felt the shift, glanced at him, and stifled a sigh. *Seriously? Why does everything have to boil down to a date?*

"So, I was thinking about the candlelight vigil at St. Michael's..."

"Is there one? What for?"

He stopped mid-stride and stared at her. "For Nathan..."

"At St. Michaels? Why?"

"Just praying for him..." Mark shoved his hands in his pockets and stared at their shoes for a moment before raising his eyes to meet hers. "I just wondered if you wanted to go with me."

"I'm not Catholic..."

He shrugged. "I'm not either."

"You don't go to the Community—"

"No, I go with my family to The Assembly—in Brunswick." A smile—bigger than any she'd seen yet, showed a hint of a dimple.

In an attempt to distract herself from that discovery, she asked, "So why would you go to a Catholic service?"

"Because they're praying for a kid I spent my morning and afternoon working to help. Seems like the least I could do is go."

Breanne heard the veiled rebuke. *The least **you** could do is go.* "Yeah… I could do that. What time?"

"Starts at seven o'clock. I—"

"I'll meet you there," she interjected quickly.

Mark searched her face for something—something he obviously thought he found. "I see."

"You see nothing."

"You want to make sure that I don't misconstrue you going as accepting a 'date.'"

"Like I said," Breanne repeated, waving as Aiden appeared with her smoothie. "You see nothing. I'm just not going to make too much of an invitation to a church I don't attend, with a guy I don't know."

"Coffee afterward?"

Aiden's eyes bored into her as he waited to hear her response. Breanne glanced at Mark and found his only slightly less intense. She smiled. "*That's* a date."

The congregation knelt—again. Breanne felt Mark slip back down to his knees and shifted uncomfortably in her seat. A minute or two later, long after the congregation had seated themselves again, Mark's discomfort made him shift. She nudged him with her foot. At seeing the congregation back in their seats, he slid back against the pew and stretched his sore legs.

"I'll never keep up," he whispered.

"Then don't try."

Mark's whisper, unusually quiet for a man, almost didn't register this time. "Just seems courteous to follow their customs."

She nodded. What else could she do? The service, much more formal than anything she'd ever experienced, did hold a note of reverence she couldn't deny. Some of the things the priest said bothered her, but others she recognized as pure scripture. The combination made for a confusing hour. She spent most of her time praying and tuning out her surroundings.

She greeted the priest once the rest of the congregants left, thanked him for thinking of her family, and discovered that the Mass had been "sponsored" by a member. "There have been candles lit for him on a regular basis since the accident."

"That's—very nice of—people. Thank you."

The priest seemed to sense her discomfort, because he turned to go inside again. "God bless you and your family—especially little Nathan."

The slow approach of sunset left a golden glow over town. "Beautiful this time of day," Breanne murmured. "I love it."

"Yeah...I like twilight."

"I did, but not a fan right now. Someday I'll like it again."

Mark murmured something that sounded like sympathy, but his mind seemed firmly fixed elsewhere. "Can I ask a question?"

"Sure."

"Why didn't you kneel?"

Breanne tried not to roll her eyes at what she could see was a sincere question. "Because I'm not Catholic. Because I don't know when I'm 'supposed' to. It seemed less distracting to people around me to stay put and pray than to try to follow a ritual that I don't know and has no meaning for me."

"Now why couldn't you have said that *before* I killed my knees trying to keep up?"

Laughing, Breanne turned toward Center Street and The Grind. "Why couldn't you have *asked* before?"

Stretched out on his couch, Mark scrolled through Facebook on his phone. Twice he hovered over the "Add Friend" button, and each time, he backed out again. *Too eager.*

Sore muscles plagued him. *I work out. I wash trucks all day. Why the heck am I sore?* The answer mocked him. *You don't know how to wash shorter stuff.*

Curious about the final tally, he searched for the **Help Nathan & Family** page and scrolled through the latest updates. The first made him nod with satisfaction.

Nathan is doing very well at home! He has another

appointment in Manchester on Monday and probably every Monday after that for a while. Thank you for all your support. —Kelly

The next frustrated him.

Just a quick thanks to all volunteers who showed up to help out with the car wash today. I heard it was a great time. Sorry to hear one guy hurt his leg. Nathan said to tell him that it'll get better and he is praying that "God won't make him (the guy) do hydro." Some kids fear bogey monsters. Nathan—torture masquerading as a shower. —Kelly

Poor kid. Still, where's the tally? We must have washed fifty cars—maybe more! The next scroll gave him the update he sought.

The results are in! We washed exactly seventy-six cars today for a total of $380 dollars, but the till shows $512, so some people must have donated extra. Thanks everyone for your help! —Lila

One response to the tally caught his eye.

Lance Latimer (7:12 p.m.)— Just this gash shows how painful leg wounds are. Big pain in the butt. I hope he's better soon.

Someone learned his lesson. A yawn interrupted Mark's thoughts. He started to lay his phone aside, but a small profile picture next to Breanne's response to the tally update made him hesitate. *Why not? It's what people do. Don't over-think it.* His finger hovered over her picture and he clicked. Beneath her cover photo, the button appeared again. "Add Friend."
Mark clicked it.

WEEK SEVEN

DAY FORTY-THREE

Friday, July 17, 6:54 p.m.

Kelly led Nathan into the auditorium at First Church of Fairbury. Jon followed behind, holding Anna and looking as exhausted as Kelly knew he felt. Nathan had wanted to come. Since he couldn't attend VBS, they thought they should bring him so he could see his friends do their program. They'd just started down the aisle to a seat up front where Nathan could have a good view, when a voice from across the room screeched, "Is that Nathan? Wow!! Look! He's just walking!"

Several others murmured, but a blur streaked across the front of the building and rushed up to hug Kelly. With tear filled eyes, the woman—one Kelly recognized but didn't know—choked back emotion as she watched Nathan walk to his seat and crawl up. "I can't tell you how happy that makes me. We've all been praying for him—all week. Well, okay," she amended. "Some of us have been praying for the last month and a half, but you know what I mean."

"He's doing great." Kelly tried to settle her restless son, but Nathan bounced, laughed, and waved at people he knew.

"Oh, let him move. It does us good to see it."

Kelly stuffed down the rising irritation that comes when another parent insists that a child be allowed to do what *his* parent tried to prevent. *She means well. She means well. She means well.*

Several others came up to talk, and the woman faded into the background. However, just as the program was about to begin, the woman appeared with her husband, pointing to Nathan. "See! He's here! He's walking and everything!"

"Welcome!" Tom Allen's voice boomed through the mic before Kelly could respond. "We're all here at The Son's Camp Out for our family night, and it's great to see all you parents here. The kids have been working hard on their songs this week—" Tom broke off awkwardly as he watched the strange gesticulations of a woman on the other side of the front row. "Oh! No wonder Tara's so excited. Nathan Cox is with us tonight. We've been praying for this little guy all week—missed having him, but we understand—"

"And he's walking! No walker!" Tara squealed again. "I just saw him walk right in!"

"While Kelly may be wondering why she came out tonight, after this, I think we can all say that Nathan walking is proof for our kids that God does answer prayers and sometimes very fast!"

Nathan poked her. "He said God answers prayer. He's supposed to. That's why He's God and we're not," the boy hissed loudly enough for everyone to hear, but just as he did, the music blasted throughout the room, announcing the preschoolers.

Well, no bell saved me, but the music... whew. Kelly gazed down at her son. *But he's right. He's God. We're not. And like Grandma always says, "He's got this."*

DAY FORTY-FOUR

Saturday, July 18, 2:13 p.m.

A bicycle rolled up to the Cox house. Willow Tesdall climbed off the bike and strapped her helmet to the back. Aiden watched from the living room window, wondering if the helmet was for his benefit. *I've seen her without it...*

She waved and beckoned for him to come out. He crept outside and shut the door quietly behind him. With a glance over his shoulder to be sure it remained closed, he hurried to her side. "Everyone's sleeping."

"Good. Your mom needs a break."

"Yeah..." He stared at the basket on the front of her bike. *Only she* would use one of those things. *It's weird—kinda cool, but weird.* "Soooo can I get you something?"

"I just brought eggs. Had extras."

Aiden felt his jaw drop, but he didn't bother to pull it into its proper position. "You rode here with eggs in your basket?"

"Yeah. Do you have a bowl? I need to unwrap them…"

He found her unwrapping eggs from cloth diapers as he returned with the requested bowl. The thought made him gag. "Um, here."

"You okay?"

"Sure… did they… survive?" He swallowed hard as she laid yet another diaper aside and reached for the next.

"Yep, diapers are amazing things. Cushion everything from a baby's bottom to the egg from a hen's—"

"Yeah. Here. I'll just take those…"

"Oh no," Willow said, pulling the bowl closer to her. "I've got more. I managed to fit two dozen in here."

"And none are broken?" *I've been on that road. It's horrible.*

"None so far. This is seven…" She half-eyed him as she worked. It made him nervous, but her next words didn't surprise him. "So, gotten any tickets lately?"

Aiden laughed. "Nope."

"Chad said you'd been riding while at your grandma's house…"

"Yeah, well, you don't really mess with Grandma. If she says go, you go. Mom doesn't make me ride if I don't want to."

Three more eggs filled the bowl before Willow spoke again. "Maybe your mom needs to make you do it more."

"She doesn't want the ticket and we can't afford it."

Willow leaned close, her eyes searching his face. "Then wear your helmet."

"I hate 'em."

"Me too."

He laughed. "I noticed. Why?"

"Makes my head sweaty and then I have to wash it maybe when I didn't plan to."

Still laughing, Aiden said, "And Dad says you hate to have your plans messed up."

"I hate gross hair more." She nodded at him as she unwrapped yet another egg. "Why do *you* hate 'em?"

"Feels like I'm going a bit crazy when I wear it—hats too." He frowned. "Except stocking hats in winter. Those aren't bad, but with helmets or baseball hats—I really want to take it off and throw it at someone. I'd rather work to pay off the ticket."

"Interesting. Stocking caps. You could wear one under the helmet maybe—in winter anyway."

Aiden hadn't considered that, but the idea intrigued him. "Maybe. I'll try it. Wouldn't that shock Chad—er, Officer Tesdall?"

"I won't tell him. But I will see if I can figure out something to make a helmet work in summer too." She eyed him. "Sweaty head bother you?"

"Nah… keeps you cooler." He accepted the bowl she offered and tried not to look at the pile of diapers she shoved in the basket. "Thanks."

Kelly met him at the door as he returned to the house. She waved at Willow and stared at the bowl in his hands. "She brought eggs on a bike? How?"

Aiden shuddered and handed her the bowl. "You do *not* want to know. Just be glad that eggs have shells. That's all I'm sayin'."

DAY FORTY-SIX

Monday, July 20, 11:39 p.m.

A whoosh of cool air from the air conditioner vents prompted Claire to reach for the throw blanket on the back of the couch. She tossed it over her toes and replayed the night's jam session. *They sounded better than ever, Lord. I'm just amazed at how perfect it all is. It's coming together and I don't even know how it happened.*

Mentally, she ticked off each area of planning, astounded at how many had already been assumed by others, completed, or were otherwise provided for—many with just a word to one person who took it from there. *It's just falling into place.*

Her phone buzzed with a text message from a friend, June. Claire ignored the late hour and dialed back. "What's up?"

"Got a videographer for you. He said he'll call tomorrow. Also, someone offered to print posters as soon as you have something for them to print."

Claire thought. "I'll find someone to do that soon. I don't want them up too early or people will get used to seeing them and forget, but too late means they'll already have plans. Gotta time it just right."

"How's everything else going?"

"I was just telling the Lord how everything's falling into place."

"You're doing great work," June insisted.

"But really, I'm not—no, it's not false modesty," Claire insisted as June began to protest. "Really. I just do the footwork, but God has already gone before me to prepare the way. Everything—and I mean *everything*—He's taken care of for me."

"That's just such an incredible testimony of His goodness. You'll have to share that with Kelly and Dee. That's the kind of thing they'll *need* to hear."

Claire nodded as she scribbled a note to herself. "You know, this I know and have great confidence in. When God orchestrates, there's no burden. His yoke truly is easy and His burden light."

"Amen. Preach it, sistah!"

"Well then," she added, laughing at June's pathetic attempt at a Southern accent. "I'll say this too. It may take a few minutes of your time, but God has already seen to the task."

"I should call you at midnight more often. You're profound late at night."

"I am, aren't I? Must be a fluke. Don't count on it on a regular basis." Claire leaned back, kicked up her feet, and listened as June shared what she'd learned about advertising.

"It's not going to be too hard. The radio station has already agreed to give us free spots, the *Notes & News* has something small on the sidebar and said if someone gives them the full information, they'll have their computer guy make an actual ad. The *Gazette* will probably give us an ad space as well."

"Right there," Claire said, showing great restraint in her opinion, "this is just proof that God is here and we do not believe in vain that He will help us in our need. We're getting to see and experience God at work in bringing all this together!"

"Because of advertisements…" June cleared her throat. "I think maybe it's bed time."

"No, because it's the *Gazette* offering—that and almost every need has already been met! This is such a visual, tangible, living reality that He is orchestrating every aspect of this thing."

"And you're right in the middle," June reminded her.

"That's what I mean! What an honor! What a humbling experience to sit here at midnight in my jammies and cold feet and realize that God is using *me*—lil' ol' me—to be His hands and feet in this project."

June screeched out a hallelujah that probably woke at least half the block on her street. "Kind of like His secretary or something."

"Whoa… that's deep. I actually get to work right alongside this living and loving God. Wow. How truly and literally awesome!"

DAY FORTY-SEVEN

Tuesday, July 21, 9:14 p.m.

Exhaustion taunted her—pushed her to close the laptop and go to bed. Even Aiden had crashed before nine o'clock. Jon soothed Anna back to sleep before stepping into the living room to see if she planned to come to bed before the Internet sucked out what brains she'd kept in reserve. *It really is a zombie—eating our brains while we stare mesmerized at the screen.* "I'll be there in a minute. Just have to give a quick update."

"It'll keep…"

"I know, but then I'll forget. These people have invested so much in us. I feel rude not acknowledging that."

"You're right. Just don't stay up too long. Anna's gonna be restless tonight, and I've got to be at work early."

Kelly nodded and finished reading the message board post she'd started. She typed out a quick response, just to feel connected to the online friends who had prayed them through so much, and then headed over to Facebook to post the update. *Surely Mom will share the update tomorrow if I forget…*

There wasn't much to say—just a quick thank you for gifts from others. It seemed so inadequate to say, "Thanks for the new toy." What else could she say, though? She didn't even know who had brought it. The package had been sitting in the back of Jon's truck when he got off work. *Thanks for the toy is better than nothing. Just do it and get to bed.*

The kids had a fun day today. Someone left a surprise gift in the back of Jon's truck for Nathan. He LOVES his new toy! Thank you, anonymous gifter. You made a little boy's day today.

Also, Nathan and Aiden received some awesome goodies from Kards for from Kids. Thank you to the organization and the parents who let their children participate. The boys loved everything!

Chad had arrived that morning looking very sheepish and holding a basket of produce. "Willow doesn't handle not being able to fix things well, so her solution is to feed you," he'd said. "If you can't use it, just pass it along or make compost. We won't miss it, and it helps her cope with watching you guys go through it all. I just can't tell her no."

After one look at the deep red tomato on the top of the basket, Kelly had insisted that he *not* tell her no. "No one in their right mind would refuse a tomato like that," she'd said. She meant it, too. *I hope mine look that good when they're ripe. They sure are taking forever.*

Kelly wondered if it would be inappropriate to mention the kindness of her "neighbors." *This is their business. People knowing that they've been generous is good for business, isn't it? Or would people expect freebies too? I could point out that Jon worked for them... somehow. It might be a way to thank them tangibly—with more business. I should try.*

Finally, I don't know how many of you have enjoyed produce from Walden Farm, but Chad and Willow have been sharing their excess with us—it pays to have friends in gardening places—and oh my goodness. Thank you so much! We've been having the BEST salads ever!

WEEK EIGHT

DAY FIFTY-SIX

Thursday, July 30, 1:01 p.m.

The Michigan Avenue Bridge began the Rhodes family's tour of the Magnificent Mile in Chicago. As they looked east over the Chicago River, obediently noting the series of mechanical bridges shared in their "walking tour" pamphlet, Claire's cellphone rang. She glanced at it, intending not to answer, but Rachel Cox's name changed everything.

"Hello?" Groans from Noelle and Joy sent her a few feet away, trying to hear. "What?"

"I said," Rachel repeated, "I got a call from a woman, JoAnn. She wants to donate—or her company does—to the fundraiser. Thrivent or something like that wants to do matching funds—"

"Matching funds? Wow."

"Right? Well, she wants you to call her back right away," Rachel insisted. "I didn't want to bother you on your vacation, but she says she's going to the board to get this approved and needs to talk to you first."

"Okay... so where do I call?" She glanced around her, but the others had continued to walk over the bridge, comparing the notes on the brochure to the sights before them. Claire scribbled the number onto a scrap of paper and disconnected the call. Her brain spun with ever-increasing speed. *How do you do this, Lord?*

Her joy bubbled over into laugher as she raced after her family. "Wait. You're so not going to believe this!"

Joy turned first. "What?"

With her hands on her knees and gasping for air, Claire tried to tell what Rachel had said. "Matching funds!"

"Oh wow! Thank you, *Jesus!*"

James' rich baritone rang out over the water, "'Jehovah Jireh, my provider, His grace is sufficient for me, for me, *for me!*'" Joy picked up the tune on the next line, and Claire and Noelle joined the chorus. "'My God shall supply all my needs according to His riches in glory...'"

Their group hug and glory-fest blocked the sidewalk, but Claire almost didn't care. "I've got to call this JoAnn back, but I had to tell you. Go on ahead. I'll meet you on the other side."

Claire pulled out her phone and dialed the number. JoAnn picked up on the first ring. "JoAnn Olsen, Thrivent, how can I help you?"

"Hello, Rachel Cox gave me your number. My name's Claire—"

"Oh, good. I'm so excited you called back right away."

Clare swallowed hard, tossed another prayer heavenward, and dove into the conversation. "She said something about matching funds at the Benefit Concert? I've just never heard of Thrivent."

"Well, I'm sure the Coxes have. Thrivent Financial for Lutherans is a Fortune 500 not-for-profit financial services organization that helps our members reach their financial goals. We also strive to give back to the community."

"I see. And the Coxes are Lutheran."

"Right. We want to help Nathan because members of the Lutheran church here have a great respect for the Cox family. We plan to match one-third of your fundraising—up to five hundred dollars."

"How does that work?" Claire asked as she tried to decide if that meant they had to earn fifteen hundred to get five hundred dollars or if Thrivent would only match one-third of five hundred dollars. *One hundred seventy? Or so?*

"Well, to receive the full amount offered, you would have to make fifteen hundred dollars. But that would make your total two thousand. However, we also want to present you with a thousand dollar check. Additionally—"

Claire's mind spun at the numbers. "Wait, what was that last part?"

"To be sure that you reach the fifteen hundred dollar goal for matching funds, Good Shepherd Lutheran of Ferndale is taking a weekly collection for you, but they're donating it at the actual event to ensure that you reach the maximum amount."

"Oh—oh wow. The Lord just keeps showering us. That's all I can say. What do we need to do for *you*?"

"All Thrivent asks is for a table somewhere to talk to prospective clients and five minutes of mic time to present the check."

"That's it?"

"Well, we would like our name on the fliers and posters if they haven't been printed, but we know we're coming in late on this."

"Consider it done," Claire insisted. "And thank you. I just can't tell you what an encouragement this is!"

"We're happy to do it. Now the woman I spoke to at the Visitor's Center said you were on your vacation, so go have fun, and I'll email you more later if you give me your email address."

DAY FIFTY-SEVEN

July 31, 8:12 p.m.

From: Claire Rhodes <clairedeloony@letterbox.com>
To: JoAnn <JoOlsen@fairnet.net>

Joni,
I've attached a copy of the fliers we will be printing up. I just had Dee put Thrivent's logo on it. Hope that is okay (I'm going to see if any churches are willing to print some out before I head to Brunswick).
We will also have an article in the <u>Fairbury Notes & News</u> where your group will be mentioned. I'm off to the *Fairbury Gazette* to see what they will do for us. I know my friend June said they were semi-lined up.
Have a great day,
Claire

WEEK NINE

DAY FIFTY-EIGHT

August 1, 4:35 p.m.

The Facebook page looked a little empty—the most recent update having been over a week prior. *I guess that's how it'll be, though*, Breanne thought to herself as she wiggled her sore toes. *Still, this one is too good not to share.*

She clicked on "Add a Photo" and uploaded the picture of Nathan, laughing at something his brother said, and added the day's update.

```
At a wedding for a friend: Quick share from Aunt
Breanne—Nathan is doing so well! His little limp is
getting less and less pronounced each week. Seeing
him run around with his little limp almost looks
like he's skipping, which is just utterly cute. ♥
```

The music swelled, tugging her away from her phone and out to the dance floor. She teased Aiden onto it, showing him a few swing moves she'd picked up before the music switched to a rollicking sixties number. "Do the twist, Aiden!"

The boy looked mortified, but he tried to follow her movements, making odd gyrations that looked nothing like any "twist" she'd ever seen. "I can't do this," he protested.

"You're doing great. Even Nathan's doing it!"

In the corner, hidden behind a canopy of wisteria, Dee

watched—watched and wept. *You're so good to us, Lord. Much too good to us.*

DAY SIXTY

Monday, August 3, 9:32 a.m.

Despite the muggy heat outside, a cup of tea sent steamy waves of aromatic bliss past Claire's nostrils as she typed. Several times she wrote, deleted, and tried again, but everything sounded either too stuffy and impersonal or too rambling and casual. *It needs to be perfect, Lord. What do I do?*

The answer came in an echo of what she'd always imagined the still, small voice of the Lord to be. *"Whatever you do in word or deed, do all in the name of the Lord Jesus." I can do that.*

She wrote, this time allowing the words to flow from her heart rather than over-analyzing every noun, verb, and adjective.

```
Hi there. This is Claire Rhodes and I am helping
to organize a concert to raise funds for the Cox
Family.
    I was wondering if you'd be willing to help me
with some advertising. I need to have several
thousand fliers printed up but cannot afford that
much. So I am asking churches and businesses if they
would be willing to print out 50 or 100 (or more)
sheets of the attached file (I will cut them
myself). Also, if you have the capability to print
some poster size that would be really, really,
really wonderful.
    Let me know if you are willing to help us in any
way in this area. I will come down and pick up
whatever you chose to print for us.
    Also, would you consider either placing it in
your bulletin or putting up a flier on your bulletin
board? All the information of the what, where, when
and why are on the attached flier.
    Thank you for your kind consideration.
```

Her finger slid across the touch pad and clicked on the attachment button. She chose the correct file and BCCed it to every church and business whose email she could find—at least any in Fairbury, Ferndale, Brant's Corners, and Brunswick that might have copying capabilities. As it whizzed its way into over a dozen places, she double clicked the flier once more and stared at the pictures of Nathan jumping before the accident, Nathan with his family, Nathan struggling to walk again.

Oh, Lord... please let us get enough fliers. Not having to spend a fortune on that would be a huge blessing.

The email cursor blinked as Claire tried to remember every name of every friend who had offered to help distribute fliers. *No time like the present to arrange helpers. If they're ready to go before we even have the stuff in hand, things'll go faster.* A knock at the door interrupted Claire's thoughts. Noelle hurried to open it. "Maybe it's my new shorts!" But as she opened the door, she called back, "Mom, there's a guy—I think Gerry Arnett? Yeah, Gerry Arnett—"

"From Brunswick," Claire finished as she reached the door. "Come on in..."

Even as she spoke, Gerry shook his head. "I can't stay. I was just passing on my way to Ferndale, so I decided to bring them now so you'd have them."

"You didn't need to rush..."

He laughed. "I didn't. Christine Dawson is filling in for our church secretary, and she's nothing if not efficient."

"Well, thanks—whoa. These are already cut!"

"Like I said," Gerry began.

"Efficient." Claire passed them to Noelle and asked her to put them on the desk. "Thanks again."

"If you need anything else—oh, and one of our men works in a printer's shop. He said he'd be bringing them to church in a couple of weeks—gone this coming weekend. Will that be enough time?"

Giddy with excitement, Claire almost forgot to answer. "Oh, yes!

Definitely. This is incredible. Thank you so much!"

"If you discover you need more, let us know. I just didn't know how many people you sent out requests too and didn't want to overwhelm you with more than you needed. We'll be happy to print more."

With that, Gerry turned and strolled down the walkway to the gate. Once it latched in place, he waved. "We'll be praying!"

Anna lay on the floor, kicking as if it was her daily workout. Nathan zoomed his train all over the mat Lynn-the-painter-lady had made him. After several failed attempts to roll over, Anna wailed. Kelly came to her rescue and pulled her upright onto her lap near Nathan. "See what he's doing? That's a train. He's taking coal all over the place so people can have heat."

"But it's summer," Nathan protested. "I'm taking them ice so they can be cool."

"Right. Ice."

Anna giggled and reached for the train as if she understood. Nathan hesitated before handing it to her. "Don't put it in your mouth. You could cho—."

Despite his admonitions, Anna promptly shoved the train in her mouth, a trail of drool sliding down the top almost before she finished speaking. Nathan wrinkled his nose. "Ew... Mommy!"

"I'll wash it off. You're good to share with your sister. She likes that."

These words, Nathan took to heart. He thought for a moment and slowly rolled up his pant legs. "See, Anna? These are my scars. That one..." The boy struggled to get the leg up high enough to show the scar on his upper leg. "—is where they took my skin off. It doesn't hurt as bad right now."

Anna cooed, showing appropriate interest. As she marveled—or so he thought—at his impressive display of skin damage, Nathan rolled his pant leg back down and said, "That's why I can't go swimming now—because it doesn't hurt as bad now."

Well, there's one for the Facebook page, Kelly mused as she rose to rinse off Nathan's train for him. *Where does he get this stuff?*

Before she could leave the kitchen again, the phone rang. "Nathan, if you want your train—" A semi-blur appeared and left, her hand now sans dripping train. "—aaaaand he's gone."

She answered on the third ring. "Hello?"

"This is Marla Johnson at Johnson Ranch in New Cheltenham. We're calling about your son—Nathan?"

"My son's only three… I think you have the wrong—"

"Right. He's the one who was burned by the power line, right?"

Kelly nodded before she remembered it wouldn't show through the phone. "Yes—yes. Sorry."

"We offer therapeutic riding sessions for children and adults who have undergone physical or emotional trauma, and we wanted to give your son twelve weeks of riding sessions."

"What?"

"We offer…"

"Sorry," Kelly interjected. "I was just kind of taken aback—stunned—flabbergasted. Whatever you call it. What would this cost us?"

"The gas to get here?"

"That's it?" *There has to be a catch. Insurance? Something?* "We can't afford—"

"We might be able to work out a fuel scholarship with some of our—"

"No, the gas we can afford. We'd find a way for that, but I mean insurance or riding clothes or—"

Marla's laughter filled the line. "Let me make this a little more clear. Our ministry is to help people. We do offer paid sessions, yes. But when I call you and say, 'I want to give you sessions' there are no strings to that. It's a gift. We just want to help, and we've found that horseback riding can really boost kids' confidence after accidents such as your son experienced."

"Horseback riding. Wow."

"So," Marla added, "when can we schedule the first session?"

The doorbell rang, adding a discordant chime to the rousing rendition of "Lean on Me" filling the Rhodes living room. Claire heard it and rushed to answer. *Who would be here and not just come in? Weird.*

Charlie Janovich smiled as she opened the door. "E-e-evning, C-c-laire."

"Charlie! Come in. We're just practicing for the concert."

"Th-th-at's why I c-came."

She carried a chair to the empty spot by Steve and smiled. "Join in if you like." *No idea how you'd keep up, but you do it anyway.*

"Th-thanks."

A strange look filled Steve's face as Charlie joined. Claire tried not to strain to hear the odd sounds of the worst stutter she'd ever heard blending with the final words of the song. Steve repeated the last few lines of "call me" as if unwilling to let it end. He and Charlie exchanged glances as if sharing a silent communication.

"Good to see you, man. How come you haven't come before?" Steve asked.

"N-n-ever thought a-b-bout it." Charlie smiled at the room. "I-I-I have a f-favor."

James leaned forward, resting his forearms on his legs. "To ask or give?"

"A-ask." He swallowed hard, the enormous Adam's apple that she'd often overheard kids at church make fun of bobbing like crazy. "I-I-wanted to know i-if I c-c-ould sing."

"Sure. Join right in." James glanced around the room. "We going to try that one again or—"

"A-at the c-concert."

Charlie's voice, so quiet and fractured almost didn't register with Claire. *He wants to sing at the concert? What? We can't say no. We can't say yes! What do we do?*

But before her thoughts finished, Steve beamed. "That's a great idea! We'll build it up big—surprise guest singer just for this concert."

A cockeyed grin gave Charlie's gawky features an even goofier look than usual. Claire looked to James for help, but her husband's eyes were on Steve. After a moment, he nodded. "Sounds great. What'll you sing?"

Charlie didn't hesitate. "B-b-bridge Over T-troubled Water."

Perfect song choice for this night, but honestly, he can't even say it. How will he ever get through it?

"Great! That's just perfect! I think you should do that," Steve agreed enthusiastically. "Do you play anything? Do you need accompaniment?"

"I-I was g-going to do it a-a c-capella, but…" His eyes requested the rest.

"I think a gentle acoustic guitar as light accompaniment would be perfect. Not too much. Just enough to carry…"

Claire didn't hear anymore. The uncertainty she'd first felt tried to form into a ball of dread in her gut, but she refused to allow it. *You've been in control of this since before we started. If You want Charlie to sing, then he's going to sing and we're going to support him in it.*

"This is great," she forced herself to say. Even as she spoke, Claire almost felt like she meant it already—almost. "I'm so glad you came."

To the room's astonishment, Charlie laughed. "I-I'm sure you a-are."

DAY SIXTY-ONE

Tuesday, August 4, 11:04 a.m.

Impatient fingers drummed the table as Claire waited for two people to arrive with fliers. The doorbell rang. She jumped up and rushed to the door, only to find Lila there. "Missy didn't go in today, so I thought I'd come down and see if you have fliers for me to put up. I can start canvassing whatever area you want."

Without hesitation, Claire reached behind her, grabbed a stack of the precut fliers waiting for distribution, and passed them to her. "Come check the map and tell me what areas you want."

Lila pointed to the town square. "I'll take that area and let you know where I was when I ran out. Jamie's going to come with me."

As Lila opened the door, Jamie strolled up the walk. "Ready?"

"Got 'em. Let's go."

Well, that's one area complete, Claire thought. *Now for the rest.*

Joy strolled through the kitchen a minute later. "Was someone at the door?"

"Lila and Jamie took fliers to pass out around town."

"Do we have enough yet? I thought we needed more."

"We do," Claire sighed. "We need lots more. I've only got enough here for maybe one quarter of town aside from the square. They took the square."

"I can take some around the downtown area of Ferndale before I go to work." Joy glanced at the clock. "If I finish getting ready right now, I'll have an hour to canvas the area."

Even by the time Joy left, the other fliers hadn't arrived. *Maybe it would have been better just to pay for them. I don't know. I love that people want to help, but I should have had them drop things off at the Visitor's Center so I wouldn't be tied at home. Good note for next time.*

Joy called within fifteen minutes after leaving. "Mom! I stopped at McDonald's on the way into town—figured they get a lot of Fairbury business, and the manager told me something people should know."

"What's that?"

"They're not allowed to put fliers up."

Claire's heart sunk. McDonald's would have been a great advertising opportunity. "Oh. I wonder—"

"That's why I'm calling. The manager said that most franchises have the same policy, but they *are* allowed to put up fliers in the break room. She said their more outgoing employees will likely spread the word when talking to customers and friends. So, tell people who go to distribute not to give up too easily. Ask about the break room thing."

"That was nice of her," Claire conceded. "Thanks for calling. Good luck!" Immediately, Claire sat down at the laptop and started typing out notes she could print to give with anyone distributing fliers. Point one: Ask franchises about break rooms if they say no to out front.

Lila stepped into the mini-mart and grinned at Flora Ghant. "Hey!"

"Hey there, sunshine. How's that nephew of yours?"

"Doing great. Walking and everything." She pulled out the flier and passed it across the counter. "They're doing a benefit concert for him—trying to raise money to pay the medical bills. I wondered—"

"If you can put one up in the window?"

The woman's sympathetic tones made Lila dig for the roll of tape in her pocket. "Yeah, we—"

"Can't do it, hon. The corporate office don't let us. But you give me a few of 'em and I'll pass 'em out to loyal customers. You watch and see. You'll get all kinds of people coming, and I'll be there. Even if I have to close the doors to get there. I wanna see that little guy walk. When I saw that video—" Flora choked, blinking hard and fast and taking gulping breaths. "Just heartbreaking."

As much as she hated to do it, Lila counted out ten fliers and passed them over the counter. Flora nodded. "I'll put one inside my car window too. It's only for a coupla weeks. I can do that much at least. Anything to do my bit."

Despite her disappointing beginning, the rest of Fairbury responded to the request with eager encouragement. Audrey suggested one on each side of the display window as well as the door. "That way if we don't get 'em walking in, we'll get 'em walking past."

The Market requested one for each window—a direct violation of everything owner Jill had ever said about previous requests, and the Fox Theater asked for a digital file of the flier. "We'll put it up on the screen between movie showings so viewers will see it before the preview starts."

As Lila stepped into Bookends, she heard a radio announcer give a thirty second spot to the upcoming concert. "Wow. Radio even." She slid the fliers across the counter. "I know Karyn asked for a bunch, but this is all I have left. I'll go get more, but this'll get her started."

"Thanks. Mom's been going crazy for these. I think she's called Claire about them every day."

"Yeah..." Lila shrugged. "My mom didn't get them done until last Friday I think. Churches just started dropping them off."

"Well, we'll spread the word," Todd assured her.

Empty-handed, Lila met Jamie at the corner and stared at the single flier in Jamie's hand. "Did you take one to The Grind?"

"Yep."

"The Deli, The Pettler?" At each nod, Lila tried again. "What about the library?"

"Not there." Jamie rolled her eyes. "What? We can do it on the way home. Why walk all the way there and back when we walk right past to go home?"

As Claire drove to several of the more outlying businesses, her mind whirled with the news about the theater. *Great advertising, Lord. Once again, you're one step ahead of me. And the bulletins! Two of the churches are definitely putting fliers in the bulletins.*

Her phone rang. Seeing the name Karyn on the screen, Claire pulled over and answered it. "Hey!"

"I just had two huge boxes of fliers delivered—cut and ready to go. You can start putting them in businesses for people to take with them now!"

"Oh, that's great! Perfect! I wonder if Lila and Jamie are still in town."

"Todd said they'd just been there when I talked to him," Karyn said.

"Gotta go. Don't want them to walk home if they can pass out more. Talk to you later. Thanks for calling." She slid her fingers over her phone until she found the right number for Lila and called. Hearing they were almost home, Claire started to say not to worry, but Lila said they'd already turned around. "We'll go back. It'll be worth it. People having one at home on their fridge will help keep them from forgetting about it."

The feed store loomed before her minutes later. Claire stepped out of her SUV and grabbed a stack of fliers. Inside, she asked for the owner. An employee pointed to the corner where an older man swept up spilled chicken feed from a broken bag. "What's his name?"

"Terry—" At Claire's pointed look, the girl added, "Boucher. Terry Boucher."

"Thanks."

Terry rose, dustpan in hand, as Claire approached. "How may I help you, missy?"

Missy is better than ma'am, I guess. How cute. "I was wondering if I could put a flier in your window. It's for a benefit concert we're giving to help Nathan Cox."

The man beckoned her to follow him as he dumped the dust pan in a trashcan near the front of the store. "Cox, did you say? Would he be related to Martin and Mary Cox?"

"I think so—his grandparents."

Terry nodded, a smile growing on his face. "Good people, those Coxes. What happened to the boy?"

So Claire began the first of what she realized would be many retellings of the accident and their plan, ending with a repeated request to post a flier in the window. "I have extras too, of course—if you'd like."

"I'd be happy to do that. Martin Cox is a fine man—knew him when I was younger. Some of his boys worked for me—Jonathan, Martin—"

"This is Jonathan's boy."

The man's eyes widened as if just connecting the words. "You put that right up there—right up front. And we'll pass one of those out with every purchase and put one in every receipt we mail. We'll get the word out."

That night, Joy and Claire told distribution stories around the dinner table. From store owners who choked up with emotion as they heard about such a little guy going through such pain, to others who asked for more fliers than Joy had to offer, the similarities in their tales became almost comical.

However, when Joy told about one woman who heard the name Cox and said, "Wait, Cox? As in the Martin Cox family?" Claire laughed.

"What? I thought it was cool. The minute I said yes, she was all over it. Asked for me to bring more tomorrow so she could spread them out to all the business owners she knew personally. I guess she's head of the Ferndale Chamber of Commerce."

"I'm not laughing because it's crazy. I'm laughing because it's good. Everywhere I went, I heard the same thing. Everywhere I went, the name of Cox drew favor and compassion."

James spoke, his voice almost a whisper in wonder beneath his breath. "'A good name is to be more desired than great wealth, Favor is better than silver and gold.'"

DAY SIXTY-TWO

Wednesday, August 5, 9:05 a.m.

Kelly logged onto her laptop and clicked on the **Fairbury News & Notes** blog, anxious to read the article about the upcoming Benefit Concert. It wasn't there. She clicked back a few, refreshed twice, and frowned. *Rachel's never late. This is weird.*

The phone rang and Aiden brought it into her. "Aunt Breanne wants to know about the news blog."

"Hey, Bree!"

"Did Aiden tell you? The article's not up. I thought they were doing a big thing on the concert. Mrs. Rhodes is going to be so disappointed. Do you know anything about it?"

"Nope," Kelly said.

"Why do they have to wait until Wednesday anyway? It's a blog!"

"The Delmans always thought it was a respectful thing to do for the town paper—show support and whatnot."

Clearly disgusted, Breanne snorted. "Well, the *Gazette* doesn't *deserve* respect after the stupidity they pulled with ignoring Nathan's accident. That's just stupid."

"So you said—wait. There it is."

"Oh, cool. I'll go read it. Thanks!"

Kelly stared at the dead phone in her hand. "Thanks for what?" she muttered.

Fairbury Notes & News

Wednesday, August 5th, 9:09 a.m. *(Lisa Holman)*

Local Musicians to Hold Benefit Concert for Injured Boy

Local musicians and singers have banded together to raise funds for Nathan Cox. Nathan, aged three, was severely burned when he stepped on a downed power line near his Linden Street home this past June.
The event will be held at the Fairbury Historical Society USO building on Saturday, August 15th. Doors will open at 6:30 p.m., and the program will begin at 7 p.m. Admission is free, but donations are

gratefully appreciated. Refreshments will also be available.

According to organizer, Claire Rhodes, the music will include selections from modern contemporary to classic rock and seasoned with a few gospel selections. When describing the event, Rhodes said, "We want this event to have a relaxed and comfortable feel." The group of singers and musicians does not have an official name, but Rhodes described it as a gathering of friends which includes the entire Rhodes family, Steve Burnside, and Eli Stillman. Rhodes also said, "We have just had a special singer come forward—totally unexpected. We're excited to have him with us." When asked about the singer's name, Rhodes refused to answer. "That's a surprise for everyone."

The group is composed of members of various local churches from around the loop who get together once a week to practice just for fun. They've performed at various events, including the March for Life and the Rockland County Fair last fall.

The group was thrilled to learn that Thrivent Financial, a not-for-profit organization based in Minneapolis that offers financial services through Lutheran churches, has offered to match one-third of funds raised for a maximum company donation of $500.00 for this event in addition to giving a separate check for $1,000.00 directly to the family.

Nathan suffered third-degree burns to both feet and his lower right leg. He spent almost four weeks in the Cunningham Memorial Burn Unit in Manchester where he underwent five surgeries, including several skin grafts. One of those skin grafts included removing skin from his own leg.

Unfortunately, this is only the beginning of Nathan's medical journey. Nathan will require regular check-ups and surgeries over the next fifteen or so years. "Basically, until he stops growing, we'll be going in every six months to a year," his mother Kelly Cox told Notes & News in a phone interview. "We don't really know what it'll look like until these first six months to a year are over."

The medical bills are already enormous and will continue to come until he is fully grown. Organizers of the event are asking everyone to join the effort to relieve this staggering financial burden.

For those unable to attend the concert, you can also follow Nathan's progress and recovery, as well as make donations to his PayPal account, at <u>Help Nathan & Family</u> on Facebook.

It's really happening. They're really doing this. Wow. Kelly reread the line regarding the surprise singer and tried to imagine just who it could be. *It would be so funny if it was Alexa—her off-key singing would be hilarious! Well, for a minute. Then again, having her there would be a draw.* That thought fell flat when she remembered that it wouldn't draw anyone if they didn't advertise her coming. *Well, still... it would be funny.*

With Steven dangled on one knee, riding through imaginary Indian fire to safety at Fort Whatalottahooie, Ross Davies read the **Fairbury Notes & News** blog. He eyed Denise as she unloaded the dishwasher for him. "Hey, hon?"

"Yeah?"

"What are we doing the fifteenth? You don't work that night, right?"

She glanced over at him and then went to check the calendar. "No, why?"

"They're doing a concert—benefit concert, I guess—for that kid."

"That kid?" She stared at him. "We both know you know his name."

"Fine. Nathan. They're doing a concert for him in Fairbury. We could go. It might be fun."

"What, some church thing? Really? You want to go to a church concert? I don't think so." Denise pulled several glasses from the top rack, nearly breaking two before she got them on the cupboard shelf.

"I don't think it's a church concert. They're holding it at the USO. It says, 'modern contemporary to classic rock and seasoned with a few gospel selections.' Gospel can mean almost anything."

"It's still church music. I'm not going."

"Fine. Steven—"

"Will stay here with me. I'm not going to have him watch them throw his daddy out for working for the enemy."

"Not the enemy," he protested. "I doubt they'll even recognize me. I only saw them a couple of times, and less than a minute the second time."

"I don't care. I know how I'd feel if my kid got burned by the power company's property, and I wouldn't want one of their so-called representatives there for something designed to help me pay those bills."

The truth of her words cut deeper than he'd expected, but Ross couldn't let the idea go. "Okay. Don't go. Maybe I won't. Maybe I will. But I'll stay in the background. Leave a little cash in the donation box."

"And hope they actually get it. Stuff like this is notorious for fraud. Those poor people probably won't see half what people donate. The organizers will keep half of it for 'expenses.'"

"When did you become such a cynic?"

Denise stared at him. "You're kidding, right?"

"No, I'm not. I—"

"I learned it from you, Ross. You're the one who is always telling me I'm too naive. Well this time, you're the naive one." She closed the door to the empty dishwasher and turned to face him. "I'm going to go get dressed for work. You might want to figure out if you want to live on a third of our income or not, because the kind of stuff you're doing is totally going to get you fired."

DAY SIXTY-THREE

Thursday, August 6, 10:03 a.m.

```
From: JoAnn <JoOlsen@fairnet.net>
To: Claire Rhodes <clairedeloony@letterbox.com>

Claire,
You did an awesome job! The Fairbury Notes & News
```

article was incredible! You had all the facts perfect. Oh, and the fliers—absolutely gorgeous. I was joking with my coworker that we didn't have a big showing on it, but we did get the last word!

I'm working with the company to be sure we have a good presence at the event.

So, to get a feel for what I am assuming is going to happen, I'll just type out an idea of how I picture this and you tell me what works and what doesn't. That's the disadvantage to not having attended your meetings.

I assume you've chosen someone to be the emcee. He or she will introduce the talent and after each or every two or three songs, he or she will say some words about the events of the night—perhaps about the donations. Are you going to share the donation totals as they come in?

Good Shepherd Lutheran Church plans to make a big donation, so that might be a good thing to save until the end of the concert. It's quite large and will ensure you will likely make the total needed for Thrivent to provide the full matching funds. Thrivent would also like to present the $1,000.00 from our local chapter. We have a HUGE check so we can get a good photo op. Although this is not part of the concert effort (can't count toward the matching donations from the corporate offices), we are grateful that you are allowing us to present it at the event.

I've been told a group of employees from a local business are also attending and making a group donation. They may want mic time as well.

Let's try to chat early next week. Oh, our chapter representative recommended that you have press releases from the family. From what I understand you know the family well and are aware of their wishes? Oh, and is there a radio station involved?

You've done a wonderful job with this event. We thank you for caring for others in our community.

Much respect,
JoAnn

From: Claire Rhodes <clairedeloony@letterbox.com>
To: JoAnn <JoOlsen@fairnet.net>

JoAnn,
Doors open at 6:30. The event begins at 7:00. Our tentative schedule for the events are as follows:
Opening song: Instrumental (designed to get people into their seats and settled down)
Introduction: I'll tell the story and introduce the family—bring them on stage (at least those who are comfortable doing that). I will also talk about Thrivent's offer to match one third of the funds. Then I'll bring the Thrivent representative(s) up on stage. AT that point, the floor is yours.
Thrivent: Here is your time to share what you want to about your services and what the company is doing for this event. The reason I'd like to do it as early as possible is twofold. First, I'd like the family to feel free to leave early if they need to get the children to bed. I'm assuming Nathan will still tire easily. Second, I want people to see generosity early on, hoping it will motivate and encourage them to give. If people have to leave halfway through the program, they won't have missed your name or the thrill of seeing the check being given. If we can start the evening big, then I believe we will have set the stage for even bigger. You can offer the big check at that time too.
Music: After your time at the mic, the music will resume.
Intermission: At about 8:15, there will be a fifteen to twenty minute intermission. We'll have refreshments available all evening, and your table will be set up near them so that people have to see it as they walk past.
We're all getting so excited. We've never done anything like this, but God keeps providing in ways we didn't expect. I feel like we're just along for the ride. We want the evening to be relaxed and friendly with much laughter and joy. It will be comfortable, fun, and oh boy it'll also be good when it's all over.
Claire

From: JoAnn <JoOlsen@fairnet.net>
To: Claire Rhodes <clairedeloony@letterbox.com>

Claire,
Everything sounds well-thought out and planned. My only concern was that I didn't want people to stop donating if they think the event has made $1500 early on. That would guarantee the $500 matching, but not the maximum donations. Either way, we will have the BIG CHECK ready, too!
Just for your knowledge, Good Shepherd Lutheran Church has a $1200 donation. I just thought knowing the amount might help you know where to put that presentation.
You'll have earned a long rest after this is over. Oh, and I am excited about the music choices. It all sounds exactly like the kinds of things I like best.
JoAnn

WEEK TEN

DAY SIXTY-FIVE

Saturday, August 8, 11:47 p.m.

Exhausted, sore, and in much need of a shower, Claire collapsed on the couch and stared indecisively at her laptop. *To update or not to update: that is the question.*

One thought overrode every objection she could formulate. *I'd want to know. I'd be waiting to hear.*

With that thought in mind, she opened the laptop and dashed for her room. While the computer booted and waited for her return, she showered, slathered herself with moisturizer, and shuffled back down the hall, combing her damp hair before the tangles overtook it. *Blow dryer when I'm done. That'll keep me from procrastinating.*

Each attempt to write a concise update failed. In desperation, as her hair dried without benefit of the taming influence of hot air, she wrote without attempting to rein in her words.

Just an update on the event: All fliers have been distributed. We ended up with so many fliers we couldn't possibly use them all. However, if you know anyone who needs one or a hundred, I've got them. The response was overwhelming. Aside from the *Gazette's* lack of follow through in printing it in the paper (let's hope they manage to get it in before the event, right?), the response has been-- overwhelming. There's no other word for it. People have bent over backwards to get things going for us. The community support for this event and the Cox family is absolutely beautiful. Fairbury Sparkling Water even promised all the free water we can use.

We're one week out from the event and the food coordinator, Rose, has assured me everything is coming along perfectly. We've been given or loaned all the props we need for decorating. I want to thank the Salvation Army for loaning us their tablecloths and the Visitor's Center for the display easels. The Homstad family has created a scrapbook to chronicle Nathan's journey, and we have a video that will be playing until the event begins.

I also want to thank people for all the wonderful ideas they've given me for ways to raise even more money. We'll use them for some for other event. We've already got five hundred dollars in gift certificates to the jewelry store, so we're working on a series of gift baskets to raffle off for Christmas! This is going to be amazing. Musicians, check your inboxes, I'm sending you a special note.

She pulled up the email program and typed out a quick note to the musicians. Just as she began typing, Claire realized she'd left out Charlie. *Oh, that would not be good! Thank you, Lord for bringing him to mind!*

Dear Musician Friends,
Please find attached the loose format for Saturday's performance. It is open to change if we see a better way. We really want this night to be upbeat and joyful. We want people to leave with a smile and a happy heart.
Thank you for the time and energy you are investing in this. (Let me know if you can't open the document)
Claire

DAY SIXTY-SEVEN

Monday, August 10, 9:12 a.m.

Dr. Smith's nurse, Sheila, ushered the Cox family into the examination room and closed the door. "So how is he this month? He looks good. Let's look at that leg," she said as she grabbed a camera.

"He's good. I mean, he's still just running around and being an active little boy. His run now looks a bit like a skip instead of a real run, but still." Kelly beamed at the progress she had to report. *He's doing so great. I can't believe it.*

Sheila rubbed a thumb over the welts covering the back of Nathan's leg. "Looks a bit thick—inflamed. The doctor will probably order a compression garment so it doesn't cause problems later."

With her heart sinking into her stomach, Kelly gaped at the nurse. *What happened to last month's "Hi, looks good. Okay. See you next month." Still, it's her opinion. Maybe the doctor will disagree.*

Jon and Kelly exchanged nervous glances as they tried to keep Nathan from going stir-crazy in the tiny office. Aiden stared at his shoes for a minute before he asked, "What's a compression garment?"

Anna squawked and settled in with her thumb as if to say, "That's what I think of 'em."

"I don't really know what they *look* like," Kelly began, "but they kind of squeeze the leg a bit so that it pushes everything into place. Sometimes pregnant women wear socks like that for those thick, bulgy veins they get on their calves."

"Like yours?"

Kelly glared at him in mock indignation. "Yeah. Like those." She raised her eyebrows.

"Well, you said it…" He stared at Nathan. "So, a sock. That's not too bad, is it?"

"I don't know. We'll see what Dr. Smith says. *Maybe it's not so bad. It **feels** bad. It feels like a setback. We've finally had some good stuff and now this.* Nathan walked around the examining table, exploring it. *Then again, he's walking. I can't forget that he's actually walking. That's good news. Focus on that. Focus.*

After what seemed like forever, Dr. Smith came in the room, his trademarked bow tie bobbing as he spoke. "Hey, there! How're you doing? I heard you could run. Can you show me?"

Nathan ran to him. "Your bow tie is blue—like the Tardis."

"That's right. I picked this one just for you." He smiled down at Nathan. "Why don't we take a look at that leg? I heard—yes..." Dr. Smith rubbed a thumb over the raised welts just as Nurse Sheila had. From the expression in his eyes, Kelly knew the verdict before he spoke. "It looks great—really great. I think we should get him a compression garment, though. The skin is thickening and the tissue is building up. It's also a bit inflamed, so let's put one on so it doesn't cause tightening of the skin. That'll prevent limited joint movement." He cocked his head and examined the largest welt. "I also want to give him steroid shots."

Kelly could feel her eyes as they bugged at his words. "Steroid shots? Why? How will that help? Where—"

"It's a simple surgical procedure. We'll give him some 'happy juice' and then inject cortisone into the worst of the areas."

"And what does that *do* exactly?" Jon asked. Kelly watched his jaw work as he considered the question.

"Basically, it helps with inflammation. That scar tissue is going to limit mobility if we can't get it under control."

As she watched her husband try to process the information, Kelly asked the next logical question. "So what do we do?"

"We'll send you over to Manchester Medical Supply and get him fitted for the sleeve."

Jon blinked. "And how long will that take to get?"

And how expensive are these things? Are we talking hundreds or thousands? The question she most needed to ask, stuck in her throat. Instead she asked, "Do we have to come back to get the sleeve..."

"You'll order it today and it should be ready next week." Dr. Smith began measuring his leg, to give them an idea. "It'll probably go from here to here."

Kelly's mouth went dry as she saw the doctor's hands stop at his upper thigh. "Won't that make it hard for him to walk?"

"Some, but kids compensate. Temporary limited mobility is better than permanent mobility limitations."

"And how long will he have to wear it?" Jon stared at the length line on his son's leg and swallowed hard.

"Probably about two years. He'll have to get new ones as he grows, of course." Dr. Smith anticipated her next question. "It'll be easier on him when it cools off. At first, in August, it's going to be hot. He won't like to wear it, but it's essential that he keep it on except when bathing."

Kelly choked back the rising urge to sob and nodded. "Okay, and this surgery? Would it be better to wait to do this until we see if the compression sleeve works? I mean—"

"It's inflamed now. We have to kill the inflammation. But yes, that's the point of the sleeve—to prevent future needs for surgery."

Breanne listened as Kelly explained the latest news, her heart constricting with each word. "Oh, no…"

"They keep acting like it's no big deal—that it's a good thing, but this just feels like such a huge setback."

Trying to keep her voice calmer than she felt, Breanne spoke the words she thought she'd want to hear. "I'm sure it'll be fine. Maybe they're just being overly cautious, and after the surgery they'll decide not to keep it on him."

"Well, Jon's got the kids buckled in. I've got to go. Just wanted to get you to get people praying. I don't know what happens at the medical place, but it just feels overwhelming. I could use the prayer just to get through it."

Her phone went dead as Kelly disconnected the call, but Breanne still sat with it up to her ear, lost in thought. The toddler she nannied stared up at her with his enormous blue eyes. "Call?"

"Yeah. Do you want to help me type something?"

Happy grins—just fiddling on a keyboard. *Little kids are so easily entertained!*

She typed.

```
Just got a call from Nathan's mom. Nathan had an
appointment today, and it turns out that he has to
get a compression sleeve. I don't really know much
more about it, but since Nathan's such an active
kid, I know wearing that thing 23 hours a day will
be awful. —Aunt Breanne
```

Stepping into the office of Manchester Medical Supply Group was nothing like Kelly expected. Instead of a pharmacy-like store with a clerk at a counter taking a special order for Nathan's compression sleeve, they were ushered into an examination room, much like the doctor's office they'd just left. *Why not just measure him there and order for us then? This is weird,* Kelly thought.

A man knocked and stepped into the room. "Good mor—" he glanced at his watch. "Afternoon now, I guess. I'm Oscar. So who—oh, yes." He smiled at Nathan. "I see what we're doing. Do you have the prescrip—" He smiled as Kelly handed it to him. "Thank you. I love people who are prepared. Were you ever a boy scout?" Oscar joked.

"Mommy can't be a *boy*! She's a *girl!*" Nathan protested.

Nervous laughter joined Oscar's hearty chuckles. He gave Kelly a reassuring smile. "We'll make this as painless as possible. I promise."

Oscar spent the next twenty minutes trying to create a sleeve that would cover as little as possible before he sank back on his rolling chair and crossed his arms. "I'm afraid if I don't just cover from ankle to thigh, he's going to get insufficient coverage. His wounds are just too scattered. I'd rather be safe than sorry."

"Do what's best for him. It would be such a waste of time if we didn't do it right," Jon agreed.

Kelly's heart just wept.

At the counter, Jon asked the price of the sleeve, and at the six hundred dollar price tag, Kelly's heart wept harder. *How will we ever pay for these things?*

Minutes later, she received a call from Dr. Smith's and immediately sent Breanne a text.

HIS NEXT SURGERY IS SCHEDULED for August 31.

WEEK ELEVEN

DAY SEVENTY-TWO

Saturday, August 15, 11:59 a.m.

Claire Rhodes stepped into the USO building, anticipation and excitement doing flips through her heart. A light flashed on in the entryway and startled her. "You're here right on the nose."

"Wow, Frank. Way to scare a woman." She laughed and stepped in further. "I thought I'd take another look around before I get started."

"Need to show you something. Come with me."

Dread inched its way closer, threatening to trip the continual somersaults of excitement that kept her usually placid self feeling almost giddy. "Is something wrong?"

"Well, I don't know. From what you've told me, I don't think so but there—see. Have a guy coming to perform on Monday. He's doing a one-man play and set up the stage on his way through to somewhere or another. Anyway, I was going to move it off for you, but then I remembered..."

"It's perfect!" Astonishment filled her as her eyes took in a small couch, chairs, lamps, pictures on the wall of the stage—even a hat rack. "It looks like someone said, 'Oh, I've got everything they could possibly want right here. I'll just fix it for them.'"

"Well, good. I didn't know about it until it was too late, but I could have moved stuff if I needed to."

"Can we move things around a bit—make room for the instruments?" Nerves tried to take over as she waited for Frank's answer. Seconds later she laughed as she realized he'd delayed just for that purpose. "I should be irritated, but I'm too happy to care. You know, our God is in the details. He keeps reminding us in every situation He is with us and still in the mix."

Rose Alvarez's "Anyone here?" from the front door kick-started the six hour preparation marathon. Food arrived in a seemingly never-ending stream. Crystal bowls and platters for fruit, plates of cakes, cookies, brownies, pies, tarts, pastries, and cupcakes slowly filled tables. Rose wove lights between the glass dishes, under cake domes, and around the crystal bowls. Fresh flowers donated by Wayne at the Pettler waited in the refrigerator with the cut fruit—waited to be put out at the last second before guests arrived.

Crews of people, some Claire had never seen before, appeared and began setting up chairs, moving tables, arranging the row of easels to create a path to the main rooms, and adjusting lights and decor. Each time Claire turned to do something, she found someone else there already taking care of it. *Lord, this is just **too** easy. Much too easy. Thank you.*

One woman stopped her. "I found the donation can. Where do you want that? Also, Rose wants to know if you want the baked goods money in the same can or if she should take it and put it in a cash bag and give it to you later?"

"No need to run back and forth, and I want the donation can right up front here where I can keep an eye on it. I can't imagine anyone stealing it, but I don't want to be foolish, either. So… just tell her to use her judgment." She glanced over her shoulder. "Does Rose have enough hors d' oeuvres? Selling the baked goods is one thing, but I want to be sure that no guest walks away unsatisfied."

"I think there's plenty. More bowls of fruit and more vegetable trays seem to appear every time I go back there."

Before Claire could thank the woman, another man interrupted. "I'm here to set up the video. Where would you like that?"

Kelly stepped from the van, nervous. Jon's eyes met hers as he opened the door for the children. *He's even more nervous than I am. It's just so strange to be here for something like this.*

"Is Aunt Breanne here? I want to show her my bow tie."

Trust him to be calm, cool, and collected. "I'm sure she is. Aiden, can you take him in?"

"Sure. C'mon, Nathan. Let's go find her."

Kelly waited until they were out of earshot before she sighed, saying, "He's different with Nathan now—more patient. I'd never say it was 'worth it' just for that, but it is a nice benefit."

"We truly learn to value things when we discover they can be taken from us." Jon hoisted Anna's car seat from the van and smiled. "Ready?"

"As I'll ever be."

They climbed the steps, Kelly feeling as though marching to her doom. *Why is this so difficult for me? It's crazy. I—* The sight of the entryway arrested all doubtful thoughts. A large photo of Nathan, taken just two weeks earlier at the wedding, stopped her. "It's great! I saw the little one, but look at it..."

Jon nodded. "I'm glad they showed a happy one first."

The next showed Nathan with both legs and one arm bandaged on his first night in the hospital. "I almost don't recognize him. It's so far removed already," she whispered.

One after another, the pictures of Nathan's progress led them from the door and into the main auditorium. Nathan in the wagon. Nathan with Fireman Ian. Nathan with Aiden and Anna. The whole family on the hospital lawn. Those first, painful steps. The picture that always tugged at her heartstrings—Nathan covering his head and eyes with his bear, shutting out the world.

Just as she started to step into the room, she turned and saw yet another row. "Look."

This row showed various aspects of the concert in progress. The fliers in store windows. The musicians practicing. Someone had even had a picture printed and mounted on foam board from that afternoon—a picture of the work crew setting everything up for the event.

People greeted them. Friends, strangers, family. Kelly's heart swelled with every well-wish, every assurance of hours of prayer on their behalf. "Thank you." She wanted to say more, show her gratitude for the deep well of appreciation it was, but the only words she could speak were a simple, "thank you."

Claire welcomed them and escorted them to where seats had

been reserved. "You don't have to sit yet, of course, but I wanted you to know you have front-row seats. There's fruit in the back, the video is playing over there..."

Her words drowned in the laughter and chatter of those around them. Kelly nodded, hoping she didn't appear to agree to something offensive. Something pulsed in the air—something she couldn't identify. While she unbuckled Anna from the car seat, her mind fought to drown out the cacophony around her and search out that something. When a dear friend rushed across the room to envelop her in a hug, she found it.

Love.

Just before she planned to give the signal, a woman stepped into the building. "Welcome. We're just about—"

"I can't stay," the woman insisted. "I just wanted to bring this." As she spoke, the woman pulled a folded check from her purse and handed it to Claire. "Please put this somewhere safe—not in the donation jar."

Cautious, isn't she? Still, Claire accepted it, thanked the woman, and stopped James on his way to the stage. "Can you put this in your pocket for me?"

The woman, satisfied that all was well, smiled, shared her appreciation for their efforts, and hurried outside again. "Well, that was interesting."

The musicians assembled on stage and took up their instruments. Singers stood behind mics but as the opening notes of "Lean on Me" began, the singers remained silent. Claire moved around the room, urging those she knew to take their seats as an example to others. It worked. The attendees found their seats and the opening notes started all over again. James opened the song with a solo line. "'Some... times in our life... we all have pain. We all have sooorrroooow.'"

Claire joined on the next line. The rest of the group joined in on the chorus. They sang with feeling—strength, love, support. Each note had been chosen, practiced, polished to wrap warm arms around the family—to make them *feel* the love shared, not just see it.

As she looked out over the room, Claire couldn't find a single empty chair—a single place that another person could stand. The wide open doors to the outside showed more people standing out there. Still, without even standing room, the homelike atmosphere permeated the event—exactly what she'd hoped for. *Only God can take a small, Monday night living room of people and make a **living** room of people.*

Rousing applause thundered through the room as the last notes died. When the emcee brought the family up on the stage, once more, the room clapped. Nathan stared out over the sea of faces and Claire snickered when he looked up at Kelly and said, "Are we going to sing now?"

The introductions over, Thrivent Financial took the stage, bringing the photo-op check with them. *Their hands are going to be sore tomorrow,* Claire mused as the room filled with more applause, a few whistles, and even more smiles. *We did it.* A second later, she amended that thought. *No, Lord. You did it.*

Ross Davies stood at the back in the shadows, his arms crossed over his chest and surveying the room with interest. The girl was there—the one who had answered his questions at the Cox home. As much as he tried, Ross couldn't remember her name. Kelly and Jon sat in the front row where Nathan scrambled from lap to lap, enjoying every minute of the concert.

He's looking good. Happy. That's good. Seeing the boy walk in had made every doubt about coming vanish. Denise still didn't understand—probably never would—but coming had been a good idea. *These people are real. Whatever they have may not be what they think it is, but it's real nonetheless. If it's God, well, he's not like any God I've ever heard of. This one might be worth knowing about.*

The number ended. The enthusiastic applause by the guests told him he wasn't alone in thinking the group had potential. *It's versatile without being all over the place. That's the best part. I thought it'd be all religious, but it's not. Just that one song after the big check. That was a nice touch.*

Knowing his company's stance on the accident, that check had been both a balm to his spirit and a kick in the gut. *It won't touch their bills. It's a payment rather than a payoff. But someone is doing **something**. That counts.*

Ross glanced at his watch. *Just one more song maybe before the intermission—or maybe it'll just be announcements.* He inched his way along the wall. Several people smiled at him. *You wouldn't if you knew I was the "enemy."* Even as he thought it, Ross admitted to himself that it wasn't fair of him to think like that. *Still, a lot of people would think that way. Maybe not all of these people, but I bet some. Maybe most.*

The emcee made a joke. Kelly laughed, her eyes meeting Jon's. *They won't. Even if they blame RGE, they wouldn't blame me just because I work for them.* His cynical side tried to argue—tried to tell him he was being ridiculous, but the memory of Kelly's words in the hospital, the pain in her voice as she agonized over following the lawyer's orders, it all told him she wouldn't. *You did the right thing. You have to protect yourself.*

The emcee introduced the next singer. As the man stepped up to the mic and began to share his reasons for joining the night's festivities, Ross winced. Disappointed, he turned and left the room. *They just ruined the night. Still, I hope they made a lot.* On the steps he hesitated, curious as the first faint notes of an acoustic guitar reached him, but he kept going. *Maybe I'll have a chance to talk to them again someday. Maybe.*

"Let's put our hands together once more for our surprise guest singer, Mr. Charlie Janovich!" the emcee called. "He's our last number before the intermission."

Applause rippled over the room—some confused, some enthusiastic, some hesitant. Charlie took the stage and hesitated. *Do I speak first? Not bother? I didn't think about that.* His eyes slid sideways to Steve. A slight nod gave him confidence. "I-I know that s-s-ome of you are p-p-probably wondering why I-I'm up here." He swallowed hard, told himself to keep calm and relax. "I-I just wanted t-t-o do something. I-isn't that why w-we're all here? T-to d-do something?" He gripped the mic as a signal to Steve, trying to ignore the murmurs and rustling that spread over the room. *You've got this.*

Several faces winced as they recognized the opening notes to "Bridge over Troubled Water." Charlie ignored them, paying careful attention to the melody and trying to lose himself in words he'd loved since he first learned them. "'When you're wear-ry… feelin' small…"

Gasps filled the room. Claire Rhodes' face—priceless. He slid his eyes sideways once more and caught the beaming smile on Steve's face. *He's enjoying this,* Charlie thought as he took a breath for the next line.

"'I'm on your side…"

From her place, Claire could see both Steve's and Charlie's expressions. *They planned this—deliberately. Oh, this is good. He is **so** good!*

The utter silence in the room told her that the same depth of emotion filled every person present. Even little Nathan sat staring up at Charlie, his eyes drinking in the sight of a scrawny man holding every heart in the room. "'…will ease your mind…'"

A slight hesitation—the merest of pauses—held the room for one brief moment before a standing ovation filled the house with applause and cheers. As if he did it every day, Charlie pulled the other musicians forward, stepping back into the shadows. Claire watched as he crept down the side stairs and made his way outside. *Aaaand… he's gone.*

Jon took the stage, tapping a microphone that seemed unwilling to cooperate. Feedback screeched through the room and he jumped back. "I think it knows I'm not much of an entertainer and it's going on strike." Chuckles and snickers rippled across the room. He started again, twice, until he found that sweet spot of audibility with no feedback. "I just wanted a moment to say something." Jon paused before continuing. "At times like this, words seem to fail me and thanks seems inadequate."

A murmur of understanding followed as Jon paused. Three rows back, Aggie gave Luke a pointed look—one he missed.

"We first need to thank Claire Rhodes for all the work she did to plan this event and the community who banded together to help make it happen."

Nods of agreement and approval punctuated Jon's words. Once more, Aggie eyed Luke and elbowed him with an obvious—to anyone who knew them—meaning of, "He's so like you it isn't even funny."

"—and of course, we must rely on Jesus for our ultimate provision. We appreciate your prayers and support." Jon swallowed and gave an uncomfortable but genuine smile. "Your generosity has overwhelmed us."

The last of the cleanup crew left as James and Claire walked through the building, turning out the lights. Frank stood with keys handy, ready to lock up. "Great totals! That eight-hundred dollar mystery check really took the total over the top! I can't believe you guys broke five digits!"

"I can't either," Claire admitted. "I would have been happy with five thousand. I mean, James kept talking big, and my big was too limited. God... He had something bigger planned."

A man approached, jogging up to the building. "Are you guys with the benefit concert?"

"Yes..." Claire glanced at the men beside her. "But it's been over for—"

"I know. I missed it. I just got off work, but I wanted to bring my donation." He dug his fist in his pocket and pulled out a few folded bills. "Here."

"Thank you. Sorry you missed it. It was great, but this—" Claire gave the bills a little shake. "This is what it's about."

"Yeah, I'm sorry too. I thought maybe I could trade with one of the guys, but they all said no." He turned and jogged back down the steps. "Thanks for doing it. This here—" He pointed to the sign announcing the concert. "This is why I live here. Fairbury is just amazing this way. Your concert showed that."

She rode home listening as James talked about the highlights of the evening. Just listening to his voice as he described the funny things

Nathan said, the camaraderie of the musicians—the God-orchestrated series of very blessed events—sent her mind thinking through her own journey to that moment. "Even more than the money, the building of community, the raising awareness—enjoying one another is what really matters. It's truly priceless," James insisted.

"Just seeing God put together an event like this in our little town. Seeing how He used His children to accomplish it—"

"And seeing His children co-operate—no drama in this," James interjected.

"Exactly. That's worth it all right there. We got to be used by God in a tangible way—a way we can even see ourselves. We get to see, not just know, that He loves us and treasures us to come down to our level like this." She sighed, reached for James' hand, and rode the rest of the way home happy in that wonderful feeling that comes with knowing you've been used for a purpose that has nothing to do with you.

DAY SEVENTY-FOUR

Monday, August 17, 6:42 p.m.

The Homstad family waited, each glancing at one another as if asking why Kelly sat there unspeaking. "So, I'm sure you all are wondering why I've called you here today…"

"In our living room," Dee added, smirking.

She knows it's good. Like I could hide it. "I've got lots of good news. The first is that Dr. Smith has written off so much of his personal bills that I feel guilty. It reduced our overall bill by a lot. The hospital is still more, of course, but I think he's only charging us what his malpractice is for our case or something, because it's ridiculously small."

A cheer went up from the family. Breanne held Nathan, playing games with him and seemingly ignoring their surroundings, but Kelly saw her demeanor shift from nervous to relieved. Seeing Lila ready to explode spurred her to continue the story. "One notable story. So they gave us all the checks—made out to us. And two had the same name. One was for two hundred dollars and the other was four hundred. We didn't just want to assume it wasn't a mistake, so Claire spent all day today trying to find his number."

After a second or two, Lila snapped, "And…"

Gotcha. "And what he said." Kelly swallowed hard. "He wrote out his first check and put it in the jar. During the program, his daughter leaned over and said she wanted to donate a hundred dollars of her money."

"But you said two hundred," Logan said.

"She gave cash." Kelly let those words sink in a moment before she continued. "He said he was so humbled by her generosity that he wrote another check."

"And the grand total?" Breanne sat up and brushed off her legs as Nathan scrambled away.

"Just shy of thirteen thousand—and the money is still coming in." She grinned. "Claire says that half a dozen people already asked what bank Nathan's account is at so they can go deposit money regularly."

"Praise Jesus!!!" Lila glanced around her. "Well? Geez Lois, people! Get with the program. This is a praise fest here. Get with it!"

"If it's a praise session," Kelly began with one eye on her mother. "Then let's praise the Lord for sparing Nathan's life from electrocution—"

The room cheered.

"—again."

Shock choked the voices of each person in the room, leaving a strained silence. Drew found his voice first. "What?"

"I need to borrow Mom's sewing machine pedal…"

Breanne shook her head. "Not following?"

"Well, your nephew decided to take his mother's good scissors—her *Ginghers*—and cut through the sewing machine cord… to the pedal… while it was in use."

"So a double death wish?" Dee asked.

"Double death wha—oh, first the power line and then the cord. Right."

"No, that makes it triple," Dee corrected. "First the power line, then he gave the option for either death by cutting a live power cord with metal handled scissors." She paused. "I assume he wasn't wearing rubber gloves at the moment…"

"No."

"Right. Then metal scissors plus live electrical wires equals danger. Or, if you prefer, death by Mommy who cannot handle another scare like that." Dee smiled. "Been there, done that."

Kelly shook her head, gazing at her son who now spun in awkward circles on the floor—on his bad foot, no less. "Do you think he'll make it to his fifth birthday? Right now, I'm just going for small baby steps. Just over a year. He can make it, right? One year…"

Claire Rhodes (7:02 p.m.)

I just want to offer a HUGE and heartfelt thank you for all everyone did to help with the benefit concert.
An event doesn't happen just because someone comes up with a good idea (thank you, James). It takes hours of work from many people. As you can see by the sheer number of people I tagged in this (and many more aren't even on Facebook), we had many gracious volunteers who gave and gave of time and resources.
Our performers don't get that good without much time practicing and rehearsing. You are all amazing. Thank you for using the talents God gave you. I know He was well pleased. We're already missing you tonight. Taking this week off was probably necessary, but it seems strange not to have you here with us on "our" night.
My refreshment team has to be exhausted! I don't believe they stopped moving the entire time they were there. I also know they spent much of their own money providing us with delicious sustenance.
My publicity people who spent hours driving around the loop, putting up posters and fliers (and the many churches who printed up those fliers and posters for us, saving us a bundle in printing costs)—thank you! Those who created those fliers, provided the photos, video, and that delightful scrapbook—well done. Without publicity, no one would have shown up!

The set up and cleanup crew who took time out of their day even though they had other events going on the same day. Thank you for your time.
I know I'm missing people.
ANYWAY… the reason I'm posting to you guys specifically is to let you know that your labors have not been in vain. Because of your efforts and the huge generosity of our small community, this event has already generated over $12,000. The number keeps changing as money keeps arriving. The last official tally was $12,732 but then we remembered there was another check on the way that might push us over the $13K mark. This is far and above anything I imagined. And from the pledge notes we got, money will continue to be deposited in Nathan's account on a regular basis. You've started something long-term, and God has really blessed that.
So be encouraged, rejoice, and take delight in the fact that we gave God what we had and He multiplied it. We got to be a part of HIS work.
P.S. If I've missed people, feel free to add them to this conversation.

Eli Stillman (8:02)

Missing my friends tonight too, but we'll be back jammin' next week.
Fundraiser: TRULY INCREDIBLE what God does when we do what He asks of us. When we're willing to use the talents He has given us to bless others. This reminds me of Ephesians 3:20--Now to Him who is able to do far more abundantly beyond all that we ask or think, according to the power that works within us.
God took what little we had to offer and touched it, turning it into something with SUBSTANCE. This night not only touched the Cox family but ministered renewal, hope, and strength to the entire community.
I would also like to add my own THANK YOU to all who were involved and say that I LOVE being a part of a family who SHOWS that they care, they don't just talk about it. This event was AMAZING and I walked

away FULL!

Without the work of the Rhodes family, without them opening their home to a group of wild crazies each week, we wouldn't have the space to express ourselves musically. I appreciate and LOVE the place of safety that they have provided, and I LOVE and appreciate their hearts. The Rhodes house is a home of Faith, Love, Honesty, Creativity, and I have been enriched by being able to see God's grace lived out by example.

Let the result of this event be proof that when you step out in faith GOD WILL ALWAYS MEET YOU—ALWAYS!!! You canNOT lose when God is involved. LOVE you all and thank you again for an AMAZING event.

DAY SEVENTY-SIX

Wednesday, August 19, 8:59 a.m.

Claire refreshed the page once more. Still not there. "They still haven't posted it!"

"It's probably scheduled to go live at nine. That's how most blogs work," Joy reminded her.

"True..." She punched the mouse key again. The clock flipped over to nine o'clock. The page spun. The post appeared.

Fairbury Notes & News

Wednesday, July 19th, 9:00 a.m. *(Rachel Delman-Cox)*

FUNDRAISER A ROUSING SUCCESS

"This is probably one of the most giving, generous communities around," said Claire Rhodes, the organizer of an August 15 benefit concert for Nathan Cox. Rhodes pronounced the concert an enormous success.

"They keep telling about the same stuff every time. I think

anyone reading this *has* to know how he was injured by now, don't they?" Joy asked as she read over her mother's shoulder.

"Maybe. It's probably just some rule of journalism—keep the public informed about what they already know or something." She continued reading.

Rhodes and a local group of musicians collaborated to give a concert at the Fairbury USO building with the object of raising funds to help with Nathan's medical bills. The concert played to an over-packed house with an estimated three hundred people attending.
"Altogether, the event generated over $13,000 with more on the way," said Rhodes. "People who weren't able to give that night are still asking how to donate." The staff at Bookends and Lil' Darlin's as well as Rockland Metro Credit Union are accepting donations in cash and checks for this fund, and Good Shepherd Lutheran will also accept donations on their behalf. People can make donations with a credit card at **Help Nathan & Family**.
"We well-exceeded our minimum goal of $1,500 in order to receive the one-third matching funds from Thrivent Financial," said Rhodes. "They sent the $500 as promised. Additionally, Thrivent also presented an additional check of $1000."
Rhodes said the group hopes additional donations will be able to bring in "another $2,000 making a nice round number of $15,000." She went on to say, "We appreciate the generosity of this town. When people in Fairbury hurt, the community pulls together."
"For those who want to keep up with Nathan's progress," Rhodes said, "the Help Nathan & Family page on Facebook gives updates as things change. There is also a link to his PayPal account for those who want to donate."

"Wow, Mom. That's not an article. That's a series of quotes. Cool!"

Claire read it again. *This is it. Where's the let down? I don't feel like something big ended. I just feel satisfied—that wonderful satisfaction that comes with a job well done. It's just amazing. Thanks, Lord.*

DAY SEVENTY-SEVEN

Thursday, August 20, 9:11 p.m.

Snickering at her son's words, Kelly rushed to the living room and grabbed her laptop. It wasn't much of an update, but she had to do it.

```
Jon is in there, praying with the boys before they
go to sleep. After Nathan thanked God for everything
from  grasshoppers  to  firemen,  Jon  finished  by
praying for good sleep and thanking the Lord for a
good  day.  After  Jon  closed  with  amen,  Nathan
squeezed his eyes a bit tighter as if waiting and
then they popped wide open. He stared at me and then
at Jon and said, "Daddy, you forgot to pray about my
leg!" :)
```

EPILOGUE

Saturday, August 31, 4:12 p.m.

(Kelly Cox 4:14) Today as we're putting on costumes and getting ready for the Fall Festival at First Church, Nathan said something hilarious. I still can't stop laughing when I think of it.

Nathan: Mommy, can I make a card for the little boy that got burned by the wire?
Me: Uhh… Honey, that was YOU!

Commercials… gotta be thankful for commercials or we wouldn't have programming. Dee repeated the reminder to herself as yet another commercial blasted through the speakers rather than the "America's Great Heroes" episode she hoped to see. "My grandson is on this show, you crazies! Hurry up!"

As if an answer, country superstar Chase Ashton appeared on screen, introducing the town of Manchester. A preview of Nathan choked her. "That's my boy. Wow…"

The show went first to a police foundation dedicated to helping at-risk children—keeping them off the streets and their grades high. *I'd usually find this interesting,* she insisted. *I would, but I just want to see my grandson. I'll watch it later, I promise. Just hurry up with the cutified boy.*

It didn't work, not that she expected it would. The minute hand of the clock crawled from two to the three before the singer announced that the next group they'd feature was the Manchester Firefighters' Burn Foundation. "This group of local firefighters works with the community to teach fire and scald prevention. They give folks what they need to aid in recovery, host fun, family events, and send kids to camp." He turned to face the camera. "And they visit kids in the hospital to encourage them, and that's why we're here today."

Seeing a place so familiar to her, even after just a couple of visits, added a touch of surreality to the show. She saw the singer standing outside the great double doors—doors hidden by the camera—as Ian Brenner, Nathan's favorite fireman, spoke. "There's a special kid in here we'd like to introduce you to. This boy is here after being electrocuted. He has third-degree burns."

Ashton, in a cameo interview, described his thoughts about the group. "I love what these men are doing. They're just down-to-earth guys who happen to be firemen. They volunteer their time and visit kids in the hospital, trying to lift their spirits."

Dee watched fascinated as cameramen made a large hospital room packed with people look roomy and spacious. Ian leaned over the rail of the bed and smiled at the little boy lying there. *Was he really that small? Why does he look so tiny and lost there? How did I miss that when I was there?*

"Hi, Nathan? How are you today?"

"Good…"

"This is Chase," Ian said, pointing to the large man beside him. "Can you say hi to him?"

Chase Ashton held out a hand—enormous in comparison to Nathan's tiny child-sized one—and shook hands with the boy. "Hey, how 'bout you give me some knuckles too?" Nathan hesitated and balled his hand into a fist, bumping it against the singer's hand. "Atta boy. Great to see you today."

As unofficial host, Ian made introductions. As Ashton shook Kelly's hand, she kicked baby Anna's foot in the air. "This is Anna."

The man wiggled the little foot and joked, "Not much of a talker, is she? Yeah, I don't say much when I've got my pacifier either."

Ian passed Nathan a red hat saying, "Hey, buddy. We brought you another helmet. Now you and the nurses can both have one while you're playing fireman."

Overwhelmed, Nathan just nodded and grinned, his eyes wide.

"Now, I've spent a lot of time in hospitals myself—a bit accident prone you might say—" Chuckles in the room told Dee that she'd missed an inside joke.

Note to self, look up Chase Ashton on Wikipedia.

"—does it mean for the kids to have the firemen come here like this?" A nurse or hospital representative—Dee couldn't tell which—began to speak, but Ashton stopped her. "Wait a minute. You're not from around here..."

In a heavy New Zealand accent, the woman insisted that she was a Manchester native. "It's our new accent." Ashton shook his head, but she continued. "You know, most of our patients in the burn unit aren't actually sick, but they're injured, so they need to be in hospital, so they get really bored."

"In hospital," Ashton mimicked with a wink. "You gave yourself away there. Americans say in *the* hospital."

"You win. I'm from Christchurch," she added. "The firemen coming gives the kiddies something to break up the day. They like going outside and seeing the trucks. It's a distraction from very painful procedures and long days. The highlight of their days, really."

Emotion welled up in Dee, but she stuffed it down, determined not to miss a single word of the segment. As Ashton remarked, "Can't put a price on that," she nodded.

You sure can't.

"Hey, Nathan," Ian said. "We've got the fire engine downstairs and fifteen firemen who want to see you. What do you think? Want to go down and see them?"

Nathan nodded, his eyes never leaving the enormous man towering over him.

A commercial break offered the perfect time to release pent up emotion, but Dee choked back tears and waited for the next segment. Mercifully, she only had to wait through two short commercials, one of which was a preview of the coming segment. "We're here with Ian Brenner of the Manchester Firefighters' Burn Foundation visiting three-year-old Nathan Cox," Ashton said. The camera panned back and Dee laughed to see Nathan, obviously high on drugs, bouncing his arms against the sides of the familiar red wagon. Chase Ashton pulled him along the hallway, and thanks to the miracle of video editing, exited out the front door and strolled to the fire truck.

Shiny chrome glistened in the summer sunlight. Ashton pointed out the spot-free truck to Nathan and said, "The chief had 'em wash it just for you, I'll bet."

Ian laughed and handed Nathan a real fireman's hat. "Look how heavy it is. A lot heavier than yours, huh?"

Dee jumped as someone rang the doorbell. Her popcorn—now cold—flew into the air. She punched the pause button and dragged herself from the couch. "Hell—"

"Trick-or-treat!"

How'd I forget? I mean, why else am I alone here? "Um, just a minute." She rushed for the kitchen. *Don't they know the rule? If the light is off—* As Dee raced back to the living room with a Hershey bar in hand, she saw the porch light glowing in the darkness. "Oops. Here you go."

The moment the kid hit the sidewalk, Dee snapped off the light and returned to her program. She rewound it a few seconds and sank back against the cushions. A fire horn blared as Nathan sat, fingers in his ears, and pulled a cord. The boy grinned, his eyes on Ashton. Once more, Ian encouraged him to pull it.

The focus of the program shifted, talking about the foundation's commitment to sending these burn victims to camp where they enjoyed a variety of activities, but the moment the camera panned away, Dee hardly heard another word. She sat there with tears streaming down her cheeks and lost her heart in prayerful thanksgiving for a healed grandson. *He's got so far to go, I know that, but it's ridiculous how well he's doing so far. Good ridiculous.*

As she sat there, a new idea formed, germinated, and grew at warp speed. *Maybe… just maybe...*

A laptop screen glowed in the wee hours of a nippy autumn morning. Fingers rested on the keys as Dee Homstad tried to condense a year's worth of prayers, gratitude, emotions, and awe into an opening line that might somehow do justice to the event that irrevocably changed the lives of so many. Letters formed into words and created sentences. The cursor blinked.

A pinky hit the backspace key. She sighed, sending a desperate prayer heavenward as she tried again. *Why did I ever think I could write anything, much less this?* she wondered as her mind tried to form a picture of those horrible first moments. That picture deconstructed into letters which, once again, formed words and sentences.

This time the hesitation disappeared and calm resolution followed as Dee typed once more.

Tragedy sizzles in the air, lurking beneath the streetlights...

Books by Chautona Havig

The Rockland Chronicles
Noble Pursuits
Discovering Hope
Argosy Junction
Thirty Days Hath…
Advent
31 Kisses
Not a Word
Speak Now
A Bird Died

The Aggie Series (Part of the Rockland Chronicles)
Ready or Not
For Keeps
Here We Come

Sight Unseen Series (Part of the Rockland Chronicles)
None So Blind

The Hartfield Mysteries (Part of the Rockland Chronicles)
Manuscript for Murder
Crime of Fashion
Two O'Clock Slump (Coming 2013/2014)

The Agency Files (Part of the Rockland Chronicles)
Justified Means
Mismatched
Effective Immediately (Coming 2014)

Past Forward- A Serial Novel (Part of the Rockland Chronicles)
Volume 1
Volume 2
Volume 3
Volume 4
Volume 5
Volume 6

The Journey of Dreams
Prairie
Highlands (Coming 2014)

The Heart of Warwickshire

Allerednic (A Regency Cinderella story)
Bullfinch's Methodology (coming 2014/2015)

The Annals of Wynnewood
Shadows and Secrets
Cloaked in Secrets
Beneath the Cloak

The Not-So-Fairy Tales
Princess Paisley
Everard

Made in the USA
Charleston, SC
07 December 2013